**Praise for *New York Times* bestselling author
Susan Wilson**

*A Man of His Own*

"With deft brushstrokes and an earthy delivery, Wilson develops strong characters caught together first-hand and afar through years of confrontation and frustration. And through Pax, that bond and feisty spirit is magnified in a refreshing manner that connects powerfully to the reader."     —Seattle Kennel Club

"Touching and heartfelt. The last few pages bring an unexpected ending that will call for a few tissues as readers smile through tears."     —*Best Friends* magazine

"With her latest novel, Wilson offers up a sort of *War Horse* for dog lovers."     —*Booklist*

"A Nicholas Sparks-ian romantic drama, with an 'everyone loves a dog' twist."     —*Kirkus Reviews*

*The Dog Who Danced*

"Susan Wilson dishes up another captivating story that will keep you hooked until the last page is turned."
     —*Modern Dog* magazine

"I would unhesitatingly recommend this book to dog lovers and 'non-dog' people alike."     —*BellaDog*

"Simply can't be missed."     —*Augusta Chronicle*

# TWO GOOD DOGS

## SUSAN WILSON

St. Martin's Paperbacks

This is a work of fiction. All of the characters, organizations, and events portrayed in this novel are either products of the author's imagination or are used fictitiously.

TWO GOOD DOGS

Copyright © 2017 by Susan Wilson.
Excerpt from *The Dog I Loved* copyright © 2018 by Susan Wilson.

For information address St. Martin's Press, 175 Fifth Avenue, New York, NY 10010.

Library of Congress Catalog Card Number: 2016043108

ISBN: 978-1-250-19100-7

Our books may be purchased in bulk for promotional, educational, or business use. Please contact your local bookseller or the Macmillan Corporate and Premium Sales Department at 1-800-221-7945, ext. 5442, or by e-mail at MacmillanSpecialMarkets@macmillan.com.

Printed in the United States of America

St. Martin's Press hardcover edition / March 2017
St. Martin's Griffin edition / March 2018
St. Martin's Paperbacks edition / December 2018

St. Martin's Paperbacks are published by St. Martin's Press, 175 Fifth Avenue, New York, NY 10010.

10 9 8 7 6 5 4 3 2 1

*To my husband, David, with love*

# PROLOGUE

*Human emotion is a deeply fascinating thing for me. I've studied it at length, observing how people react to certain situations or to other people; to nonhumans, to pain. To joy. Truthfully, I've seen a lot more pain than joy in the people I've studied. Based on my keen observations, I've categorized what I consider the key emotions human beings display: affection, hunger, sadness, anger. Each emotion has a range. Affection, for instance, can go from simple tolerance to pair bonding. Hunger, simply the desire for dinner, or pit-deep starvation leading to bad decisions. Sadness is sometimes just frustration, even boredom. But in its most provocative form, it is grief. Anger, though, is my specialty. I can sense the slightest beginnings of it, even before the subject realizes that a simmering, boiling, festering anger is about to erupt. Variations on these four are kind of like stew, a mix of this and that, sometimes flavorful, sometimes not. Love and anger, hunger*

*and sadness. What's interesting most to me is the lay-
ering of emotion human beings experience. Not mood,
although that's certainly an ingredient, but a spectrum
of emotion. It is my greatest pleasure to suss out the
various layers of emotion in a person, to read the un-
derlying, the core, and the surface, layers of the geology
of human experience.*

*In any case, when I met the girl, Cody, I knew right
away that she was a unique case. So I did what I always do: I gave her a good examination, taking in the
deeply personal details of her. Clues to her state of
mind. It didn't take but a moment to recognize that
she was vibrating with emotion. The unschooled, in-
experienced among us might interpret her attitude as
hostility, or anger. But, as I said, I'm an expert on anger, and this was something far more destructive. This
was bone-deep fear.*

*Not to brag, but I have a knack for making people
relax, getting them to share their thoughts and deepest
desires with me. Maybe even bare their souls to me. All
it takes is my brand of uncritical acceptance, unconditional and neutral, a safe kind of repository for secrets.
This girl needed my kind expertise.*

*So, I wagged my tail.*

# PART I

# CHAPTER 1

The tip of the fingernail file etches a groove into the laminated surface of the school desk in a less than satisfactory way. What she really needs is a knife, something on the order of the kind that her father carried, a folding pigsticker. Something with a more meaningful edge to it. But all she's got right now is this metal nail file she's taken from her mother's cosmetic bag, so she makes do.

Beneath the barrier of a cupped right hand, Cody describes the arc of haunches, a short back, then the angular thrust of a neck, the meaningful scroll of face and muzzle, curls of mane suggesting motion. Tiny forward-pointing ears. By the time she's ready to attach legs to her creation, she's forgotten to protect her work from the prying eyes of her history teacher and she's snapped out of her creative trance by the wrenching of the file out of her hand, the rasp scraping the skin of her forefinger.

"Cody Mitchell, that's defacing public property." Mrs. Lewis holds the offending manicure tool like a tiny sword, pointing it at Cody's artwork.

Cody sits back, shakes her uncombed hair out of her

face, shoves her blocky glasses up on her small nose, and folds her arms across her chest in a show of perfect fourteen-year-old defiance. "It's art."

"It's a detention and a trip to the principal."

Just another day at this stupid school. Perfect.

As she slings her backpack over her shoulder, she hears the derisive giggling, the sotto voce gibes of her classmates, not a one of whom is her friend. Her friends are all back in Holyoke, enjoying their first year of high school together, without her. She's stuck in this rural excuse for a high school.

It wasn't supposed to be this way. When her mother announced that she'd put a deposit down on an old hotel, fulfilling a longtime ambition to own her own "boutique" hotel, Cody had been as excited as anyone. She envisioned inviting the girls up for the summer, swimming in an outdoor pool, maybe even horseback riding. It would be fun.

But then everything changed.

Now it felt more like she was in hiding. She knows she should be glad to be far away from what happened that day, far enough away that maybe she's even safe, keeping her word, her exacted promise; keeping the Secret, surely safer at this distance. If he can't find them, he can't touch them. Her mother will never know.

It might have been all right, even though the LakeView Hotel did turn out to be a wreck, a giant money pit without even a pool, except that Cody is the butt of other kids' laughter, the stranger who doesn't share in their communal past. Not one friend.

Cody shoves the classroom door open, but her defiant gesture is foiled by the action of the hydraulic door closer. There's no satisfying slam. She storms down the empty hallway, her unzipped backpack thumping against her spine. The heels of her cowboy boots clatter against the scuffed linoleum of the floor, announcing her solitary presence in that hall of shame.

A figure moves out from the shadow of the girls' room. "Where you going?" The voice is curiously deep for a girl. It's a girl Cody knows because she's about the only other outsider in this school. She's a junior, but repeated failures have placed her in Cody's freshman English class. Her real name is Melanie, but she calls herself "Black Molly." To illustrate her point, Black Molly wears only black, sports a homemade haircut coaxed into something between a Mohawk and a skunk, which is saturated with shoeblack dull dye. She has oversized holes in her ears, plugged with disks. Her nails, her lips, and the tattoo on her left bicep are black. The tattoo riding her thick arm is unidentifiable; it might be a skull and crossbones or a sunflower, and probably the work of some amateur under the influence of crack. Black Molly might be thought of as a Goth, but Cody knows better. There were plenty of Goth girls in her old school, all black lipstick and eyeliner-rimmed eyes, but there's nothing romantically medieval about Black Molly's appearance. If anything, she looks like the love child of a Hell's Angel and a dominatrix. With the disposition of both. Cody's heard the kids making fun of Black Molly behind her back. No one would be stupid enough to say anything to her face. Black Molly is tough. She's the kind of kid that will think nothing of ripping your arm off and beating you with it. The jokes are best made when the girls' room door shuts behind her.

"None of your business." It's a poor riposte, but the best Cody can come up with. Black Molly may be intimidating to everyone else, but Cody holds her ground. She's already mad at the world, so why not get physical? Why not unleash the boiling anger onto this creature of the night?

"I asked you a question." Black Molly eases herself

away from the cement-block wall, which is painted a cheery pink to identify the girls' room; the rubber soles of her unlaced boots squeak against the dirty floor. She's a heavy girl, and several inches taller than Cody.

It is that fifteen-minute block in every period where the kids who wander the halls have finally settled in, where the teachers on hall duty have sneaked into the teachers' room to grab a cuppa. Where the principal, head in hands, is studying the budget and the secretaries are gossiping, their backs to the big window that overlooks the main hallway. There is no one to stop this.

"Where'd you come from?" Black Molly suddenly affects a neutral stance.

"Holyoke."

"They got that big mall there, right?"

"I guess so."

"So, why you here?"

Cody shrugs. "Dunno. My mom . . ." She lets the sentence dangle. "It's hard to explain." Cody has enough insight into this poor rural community to know that owning even a run-down hotel might seem like putting on airs.

"They don't like you." Black Molly lifts her chin in the general direction of the classrooms.

"I guess not."

"They don't like me."

Cody, who has not made eye contact, as she wouldn't with any wild animal, finally looks up from under her bangs. "Yeah. I noticed. Sucks."

Black Molly makes a chuffled noise, and it takes Cody a second to recognize it as a laugh. "They all suck. They don't like anybody who ain't like them."

"But you, you grew up here, right?"

"Yeah. But I'm different."

Now it's Cody's turn to chuckle. "You kind of like stating the obvious, don't you?"

"I'm different and I'm proud of it. I don't want to be like them, and if you're smart, neither will you."

"I don't want to be like them. I just want to go—" She cuts herself off. *Home.* There is no home, not anymore.

"Go where?"

"Back where I came from."

"Go. Run away. I've done it. Twice."

"Where'd you run to?"

"Got as far as Greenfield the first time. I got a sister there. She sent me back."

"And the second time?"

The righteous click-clack of teacher shoes and a quick warning to get where they are supposed to be. Black Molly flourishes a pass and walks back into the girls' room. Cody unslings her backpack and zips it up, shoulders it once more, and heads to the office.

The bills are fanned out on the reception desk in order of due date. I rearrange them in ascending order of amount owed, then alphabetically. It really doesn't help. Framed in the plate-glass picture window of the front office of the LakeView Hotel, I can see the Berkshire Hills, which are the chief attraction in this area. The trees, the promised cornerstone of a four-season income, aren't yet alive with the colors that should attract caravans of tourists this fall; stubbornly languishing more blue than red in the early days of autumn, awaiting some twitch in the calendar to become motivated enough to herald in true fall. The old-timers are puzzled; everyone blames global warming. Summer itself was a disappointing season of too much rain and not enough activity to tempt people northward. As we are a little too far off the beaten path to work as a convenient staging place for cultural forays to Lenox or Stockbridge, and not quite far enough up the Mohawk Trail to get the best views, all I'd had for guests at the

LakeView this summer were older hikers and a few tent campers bagging it in favor of a solid—thankfully—roof and a soft bed. Fingers crossed, the rainy summer portends a snowy winter, and skiers will help fulfill my bottom-line expectations. It goes without saying that the LakeView Hotel is just limping along, its glory days in the distant past. My own particular white elephant. Potentially, my second-biggest mistake ever.

My biggest mistake was Randy, my ex-husband. I try to think better of him now that he's met the end we all feared he would, victim of a drive-by shooting, just another small-time drug dealer who pissed someone off.

So, how does a nice middle-class girl from Agawam meet a renegade bad boy like Randy Mitchell? How else? The mall. The Holyoke Mall at Ingleside, where teens have hung out, met, cruised, and even shopped for longer than I can say. I was a high school senior, feeling flush with the heady power of having my driver's license, and my mother's grudging permission to take our car, the only one we had, since she sold my father's Lincoln after his death. My girlfriends and I were seated outside of the Orange Julius, affecting the ennui of world weariness, casting disdainful looks at the tweens giggling, arms linked, clattering by; the worn-looking matrons dragging toddlers away from the temptations of the toy store. We might have been discussing the college acceptances we were anticipating, or maybe just the latest gossip. What cheerleader was rumored to have had an abortion. Which teacher was caught working part-time at the video store.

Randy Mitchell drifted by with his posse. We feigned not noticing them. They rolled by again, blatantly checking us out. These were the boys your mother would warn you about, the ones who meant trouble, the kind of boys who were after "only one thing." We pretended that we weren't flattered, that their silent, predatory attention wasn't kind of thrilling. They were older. At least twenty. Clearly from the rough part of town. And that was a powerful attraction, being the object of an older boy's interest, a boy outside our social strata. When we didn't move away, they grew bolder and sat on a bench close by. There was a swagger to them, a fearlessness.

Randy was the first to speak, and within moments he'd cut me from the herd and he and I were having our own conversation. And then, as if I were Elizabeth Bennet's younger sister Lydia falling under the spell of the contemptible Wickham, I was smitten.

How I fell for that handsome Welsh charm, his certainty that he was invulnerable. I became Bonnie to his Clyde Barrow, without the bank robbery. Kid stuff, not sociopathic, simply rebelling against my middle-class upbringing. But I can't really blame my mother. For me, Randy was the perfect self-inflicted wound. And, despite everything, he was Cody's father.

I open up the computer, log in to my bank account, and play a round of deal or no deal with the bills at hand, balancing interest rates against relationships with the vendors I have to meet face-to-face, like the exterminator or the guy from the oil company. Bank of America will take another pound of flesh, but Berkshire Oil and Gas needs to be kept happy. I have to be able to meet the eye of the delivery guy when I bump into him in the grocery store. I dole out what I can, fiddle a little with payment dates, and log out of the Web site. It's been just six months, something I have to keep reminding myself when I think back to my original business plan, one that had breezily forecast a better cash flow, complete with college-fund contributions on a regular basis. Just for fun, I open the reservations window on the computer and stare at the empty slots, willing each one to miraculously fill. Each empty line represents an empty room. I extend out to the weekend and see two names listed. Two rooms. Two nights. Enough to pay down another of these bills.

My most current revised business plan skims along the edge of solvency; not quite insolvent—yet—there is just enough cash left over each month to keep us fed and clothed. There is no fat, no juicy bubble of impulsivity. Pizza is budgeted. Health care is at the mercy of Mass Health's sliding scale of contribution. Most important, as I continue to tell myself, I'm providing a good place for Cody, a place where she can breathe in fresh country air, and stay out of malls. Away from the influences of life in a poor city, a place to start anew. Oh, wait, maybe that's just me. Cody has never said it out loud, but it's clear from her descent from a bubbly, happy-go-lucky kid to a sullen, angry, silent, petulant, et cetera, et cetera, teenager that this move from Holyoke's mean streets to a classic New England village in the Berkshires has ruined her life.

It's a beautiful day and the rooms are done, the laundry is in the washing machine, and Cody is at school. I pull my hair back into a loose knot and go outside to the porch, pull up a rocking chair, and plant my heels on the railing. The view, even at this lower elevation, is spectacular, and it's all mine. Regrets aren't given much headspace. Buying the LakeView might be considered a little impulsive, but I still have, six months in, a deep-seated belief that if something is meant to be, it will be, so I'm not going to let the crushing worries of my middle-of-the-night wakening persuade me it's not. I will make this work no matter how hard it gets. But you know what? It's okay. It's the dream realized. It's the living embodiment of be careful of what you wish for.

"Are you staying after for a club or something?" Skye is eternally hopeful that her daughter will finally adjust to life in this backwater.

"No. I'm in detention." Cody doesn't add, *again.*

"Should I ask why?"

Cody thinks, *Yes, duh,* but says nothing more.

"Do you need a ride home?"

"I'll take the late bus."

"Okay. We'll talk when you get home."

Cody hangs up the office phone without saying good-bye. She looks at the secretary, who is minding her own business, as if Cody is no one important enough to eaves-drop on. A nonentity. Just another skinny jeans and T-shirt–wearing adolescent, braces on her teeth, backpack humped against her spine. There is a countertop that separates kids from office staff, a barricade of last defense against the uprising. On it, a ceramic jar filled with pens and pencils. With an artful swing, Cody manages to knock it off the counter with her backpack as she leaves the office. The pottery smashes against the ugly tile floor of the office with a satisfying sound of destruction; just as sat-isfying is the bellow from the secretary: "Cody Mitchell, get back in here!"

At least someone knows her name. The office door eases shut with a gentle thunk. Cody strides toward the exit, in the opposite direction from the detention room, making her heels click as loudly as she can. Black Molly stands beside the water fountain. Cody doesn't look di-rectly at her, but she gets the sense that Black Molly is smiling.

There was a time when she would have died to have been caught being destructive, mortified not to obey every rule, every directive. But that was the old Cody Mitchell. This one, the new and improved version, delights in an-archy. It feels so good. And in honor of that new power, Cody sticks her thumb out and hitches a ride. She doesn't even consider herself lucky when her Good Samaritan is a middle-aged woman on her way to North Adams. The price of the ride is a short lecture on the dangers of hitch-hiking. The woman buys her story of her mother's being home with a sick child and her needing to get to her art lesson. Which is sort of true. The art, not the mother with a sick child, unless you consider the Bates Motel as sick. And—technically—she's not taking lessons, but she is learning a great deal.

North Adams, home of Mass MoCA, has turned modern art into the last hope of a town whose industry has fled. Cody asks to be dropped off at a former factory, now an art studio complex. There are a couple of guys in there who don't seem to mind her hanging around, although she knows they think of her as more of a pet than an art groupie, but that's okay. Cody does coffee runs and cleans brushes, keeps quiet and doesn't ask stupid questions when she does speak. Kieran and Mosley, a pair of hipsters in ironic black glasses and paint-spattered skinnies; the one building installations that defy gravity and the other, Mosley, working in what he calls mixed media, which looks to Cody like anything he feels like doing. Cody just likes the smell of paint, the pungent scent of an acetylene torch.

"What up, Cody?" Kieran is standing on a three-step stool, wire cutters in one hand. "Hand me that coil of wire, would you?"

Cody finds what Kieran wants. The reel of thin copper wire is surprisingly heavy and it takes both hands to lift it up to him. He measures a length, snips it, and begins weaving it into his sculpture. Even though she has yet to discern the actual subject of this wire and felt and found-object sculpture, Cody has to admire the way Kieran seems to know exactly where he wants to attach the wire, with never a moment's hesitation, as if he has this blueprint in mind. His stuff reminds her of a bird nest she once found, filled with bits of dog hair and paper. Her own feeble attempts at creativity are more organic. Certainly less interesting.

Mosley saunters in, his blue eyes at half-mast. "Buffalo Bill, how you doin'?" His flannel shirt carries the lingering scent of his afternoon joint. Mosley suffers from some illness that allows him to use medical marijuana. He prefers his dose in the old-fashioned method, forgoing the edible for the combustible. Cody thinks that it's a little strange that the scent most reminds her of the old guy who owned the fruit stand near their old house in Holyoke. He'd sit outside all day, smoking tiny black Italian cigars that looked more like licorice than a White Owl and stank like sin.

"Hi, Mosley. I'm good. Can I help with anything?"

Today, Mosley is good for a couple of make-work tasks, and pretty soon he has Cody set up cleaning brushes and sorting them into proper coffee cans. He's older than his studio partner, and kind of looks like more of an old-school hipster, like Elvis Costello, than the trendier-looking Kieran. He sometimes slips Cody a buck or two for her help. Sometimes he doesn't. Sometimes he barely notices she's there, and other days he takes a real interest in her—talks about how he stuck to the dream, how he's going to have the best collaborative around, how he's just waiting for that right patron to discover him. Cody shakes back her lank hair and jabs a handful of brushes into a can.

"I'm going to need a ride home. That okay?"

Neither Kieran nor Mosley say anything for a moment. The LakeView is hardly on their way anywhere, a better-than-twenty-minute ride into the hinterlands. Cody holds her breath, but she doesn't look at either man, pretends an unconcern she doesn't feel. She really doesn't know what she'll do if they say no, that they can't cart her home today. In the summer, when the light persists into late evening, it's no big deal to walk the hour or so it takes to get back to the hotel, but now, well, it'll be dark in an hour and those blind curves and sidewalkless country roads are scary. Not like the well-illuminated city streets she grew up on. These Berkshire roads are treacherous and still foreign.

Worse-case scenario, call Mom. Suffer the lecture. Get a ration of shit from the old lady. Hope that she gets distracted by something and quits yelling. Even Cody knows that the tone of voice her mother uses couldn't really be called *yelling*. She kind of wishes that she would raise her voice, give Cody a proper tongue-lashing. Skye falls mostly into the world-weary, hands-up-in-surrender tone of someone afraid of really saying what she means. Cody hates it that her mother treats her like a child, like a delicate, ego-sensitive kid, not wanting to inflict bruised feelings on her by speaking her mind.

If only Skye knew just how fragile Cody really was, how vulnerable. She thinks that, six months after the fact, Cody is still upset by the death of her father, that her behavior is from grief. Randy was murdered less than a week before they moved into the LakeView. Cody's let her mother believe that she's mad only because Skye went ahead with her plans to move, as if Randy's death were of no importance. Skye offers half-felt apologies, explanations for why it had to be that way, explaining over and over that they had to stay the course and the freight train was unstoppable, the handoff from the previous owners needing to take place on the arranged day. The Closing, always spoken of with a capital letter, couldn't be put off. She doesn't say it, but Skye implies that Cody and Randy weren't all that close, that maybe some of this angst is just from being a thirteen-, now fourteen-, year-old with a sense of drama. She *is* grieving, of course. But it's for her life before the Secret took control.

It's not that. No, Cody's whole being is brittle from the Secret. The weight of fear. Of pretending. The Secret is kind of like her shadow. Like Peter Pan, who freaked out when his shadow was stolen, Cody grips her secret close, knowing that if it becomes separated from her, she'll die. It's become an entity. A physical part of her, like her stomach or her eyes. As she can suddenly be aware of her heart beating or her stomach gurgling, or her intestines cramping, she is made aware of the Secret hiding within her.

"Can you? Take me home?" Cody folds her arms across her middle. Throws Mosley a beseeching look.

"Yeah. I'll take you. But you've got to make arrangements for transportation home before you come back here again." Mosley passes her another handful of brushes.

"I will, I promise." It's a lie, but, really, what choice has she? Cody can't imagine not coming here to this studio, soaking in the atmosphere of creative juices, the adult companionship. Her peers are idiots. Pink-loving, Hello Kitty–toting, anime-fixated children. Innocents. Here she listens to the music of grown men who have evolved: Springsteen and Costello, Knopfler and Emmylou Harris. Radiohead. Pearl Jam. Old stuff, ancient history, but still surprisingly enjoyable when set as the backdrop to the work itself. Wire and found objects are defined by a sound track of classic rock and heavy metal. Swashes of color on a rough plank informed by vintage grunge.

"But I can't take you all the way. I'll drop you close, but not at the door."

"Of course." Cody rubs the sable tip of a fine brush against her cheek, smiles. Mosley's reluctance to get close to meeting her mother seems so understandable. Why would he want to get caught up in Mitchell family drama?

Or be assaulted by the well-meaning but clueless friendliness her mother has been known to thrust on unsuspect-
ing strangers; her professional friendliness.

The late bus has passed by the LakeView without stopping. I'm standing at the window, staring out to where the
road curves around the property and up into the hills. No
Cody. No surprise. The phone call from the principal,
Mrs. Zigler, also came as little surprise. An afternoon
driving around, wasting precious gas on searching for a
daughter I knew full well would make herself impossible
to find, has left me with heartburn. Not actual heartburn,
but an all too frequent emotional sensation lodged in my
chest that makes me wonder if I really could treat it with
Tums. It is the sensation of losing control of a fourteen-
year-old. A child who has grown from being a sunshiny
charmer into a sullen renegade. It goes beyond—well
beyond—ordinary adolescent hormonal acting out. Cody
simmers. She's that old-fashioned pressure cooker sitting
on a too-hot burner, the release valve rattling noisily.
Except that Cody isn't noisy. She's quiet. Very quiet.

It's closing in on dark now and I have no idea where
she is or when she will return. I've learned long ago that
repeated texts and phone calls go unanswered, like throwing pebbles into the sea. Nothing. Unlike so many of her
generation, Cody disdains the cell phone culture, and
today it's clear that she's left hers home. My one allow-
able call alerts me to the abandoned phone caught in the
tangle of sheets on Cody's bed, with its singular ringtone identifying me as the caller. I've gotten over being
miffed at the Wicked Witch theme, choosing instead to
think it funny. Too clever by half. Surrender, Dorothy!

What kid doesn't cling to her phone? It was the conso-
lation prize I bestowed upon her when we moved so far
from her friends, a way to keep in touch; a way for her to

have some freedom of movement without my abnegating parental authority. All I ask: *Just keep me informed.* Her disdainful reply: *Of what? I have no life here.*

Today, as so often, words, like those pebbles, plink beneath the surface and disappear.

# CHAPTER 2

If the weather hadn't been so rotten, Adam March would have pressed on, making his destination of North Adams and the Holiday Inn. But the rain was coming down in sheets and the visibility was almost nil. Climbing into the Berkshires and into the teeth of a thunderstorm along a winding and completely unfamiliar road had him gripping the steering wheel of his trusty Jetta and gritting his teeth in a pantomime of Man against Nature. Behind him, oblivious of the conditions, slumbered his constant companion, his pit bull, Chance.

Blurry headlights shone in his mirror, someone impatient with him, no doubt a local who knew where every switchback was on this mountain road, someone who wanted this flatlander out of his way. Ahead in the murk there glowed a white sign with LAKEVIEW HOTEL 2.5 MILES in red lettering, an arrow beneath the name, pointing to the right. He could barely read the bent road sign, identifying this as Meander Road. Another glance in the rearview mirror and those headlights were closer than ever and clearly attached to a very large truck. Impulsively, Adam signaled the turn, gunned the Jetta up the steep incline of Meander Road, and pointed the car toward the LakeView Hotel.

At the sound of the turn signal, Chance lifted his boxy head, pushed himself upright, then yawned.

"Hey, what do you say we stop now? The weather isn't improving and I'm beat." Hearing no dissension from the backseat, Adam took that as a yes.

"Sorry. We have a no pets policy." The girl behind the desk pushes her horn-rimmed glasses back up on her small nose, takes a swipe at her bangs. She looks at Chance, then at Adam. There is a scrim of regret in her wry expression.

"Look, I've been driving for hours, the weather is terrible, and I just need to stop." Adam pushes up his own spectacles. "He's a good dog. Very well behaved, in fact; he's a trained therapy dog."

"Where's his vest?"

To Adam, this girl seems a little young to be manning a hotel reception desk. "In the car. I'll get it. Will that help?"

"I'm not in charge."

"Can you please get whoever is in charge?"

The girl shrugs. "She'll be back in a minute."

Adam smiles and pats Chance on the head. "It'll be fine, old man. You bet."

Chance runs his massive spade-shaped tongue over his dewlaps, making a sloppy sucking sound. He flops down on the threadbare rug in front of the reception desk. Adam takes in the shabby collection of mismatched chairs, a small scuffed-up maple table set in front of the massive picture window overlooking the now-invisible view, a fan of tourist brochures on it. Historic Deerfield, Mass MoCA, Mount Greylock, Tanglewood. Shopping!

A tall woman with fair hair tucked up in a hasty bun pushes through the office door with a bundle of wet towels in her arms. She doesn't immediately see Adam standing near the table.

"Mom." Louder, more exasperated: "Mom."

"What is it, Cody?" The woman spots Adam. "Oh, sorry." The harried look is quickly replaced by a professional smile. "Welcome to the LakeView." She dumps the armload of wet towels behind a door. "How can we help you?"

"This guy has a dog? He wants to stay here?" The girl sounds like his daughter, Ariel, at that age, all uptalk; sentences always sounding interrogative, never declarative. Not so much petulant as insecure. His daughter, a sophomore at college, his only family now, the voice on the other end of the phone once or twice a month.

It's been three months. How is it possible that a quarter of the year has passed so quickly? Ninety days, give or take. Adam feels less like he's on a trajectory toward the rest of his life and more like he's still looking backward and wondering why Gina isn't there.

Adam March sat in the visitor chair, both hands holding the lifeless hand of his wife. He was unshaven, exhausted, too tired really even to weep. Too tired even to think. There was a meditative quality to this silence, to this thoughtlessness. The opposite, he supposed, of *mindfulness,* which was a popular buzzword flying around. To him, mindfulness was an excuse for utter selfishness. He couldn't focus on himself; his self no longer existed in the way that it had a mere hour ago, when his whole self had been lodged in battle against this robber, this thief in the night who had stolen Gina from him. Now that the battle, her battle really, not his, was over, Adam was unable to gather a single thought. Soon they would come in to ask him to let them take her away. This hospice room, this place, had become a second home to him, a comfort. What would he do without these people? Whom would he turn to now?

A weight bore down on his leg, the boxy head of his dog, Chance. "Oh, Chance, what are we going to do without her?" He wasn't even embarrassed to ask this out loud.

Chance lifted his head from Adam's leg to nudge his fingers where they still gripped Gina's. He made a sound, a soft rumbling noise in the back of his throat. He sat, looked at Adam, then raised his muzzle and howled.

The sound was what Adam would have made himself if he could. The dog's ululation was the perfect accompaniment to Adam's grief. As always, the dog, his constant companion, had said the right thing. Adam extricated his fingers from Gina's, set her hand gently on the side of the bed, straightened the bedclothes for the last time. Five days before, they had taken away all of the mechanical devices, the hiss and bip of the monitors and oxygen apparatus silenced for the first time in a hundred days. She looked nothing like the healthy, strong-willed, opinionated, loving, guiding light he'd married four years ago. This skeletal form was not how Adam wanted to remember her; he wanted to remember her as she had been. How they both had been. How she'd kept him to his better self.

He knew he should make some phone calls, but he couldn't bring himself to say the words out loud. He knew he should let the hospice workers finish their task. He knew he should take Chance out for a break. They had both been in here, in this tiny, airless room, for what seemed like years, not less than a week. It should have happened sooner; it should have taken longer. He wanted it to be over; he wanted it never to end. He went to the casement window, shoved back the curtain. It was broad

24                    SUSAN WILSON

daylight, and that surprised him. How could the sun have risen like it did any other day? He looked out over the Boston skyline. A jet etched a perfect descending arc toward Logan, filled, no doubt, with people glad of the journey's end. A safe arrival.

There was a soft tap on the door. Adam realized that it had been more than an hour since Gina was—what was the term they used? *Pronounced.* As if death were a new word that needed practicing. He'd been there, and for that he was grateful. She hadn't slipped away, as he'd feared, while he was out of the room. Every time he took Chance out to pee, Adam had rushed back to this sanctuary of waiting, anxious that she'd have passed while he was paying attention to inconsequentials, like eating a plate of eggs handed to him by one of the staff.

Adam moved away from the window and opened the door. "Come in."

The hospice nurse gave him the kind of smile that he'd been dreading, a gentle, kind smile signifying that, for the first time in his life, he was the object of pity. He, Adam March, who once was the object of disgrace, until Gina and this dog named Chance saved him from himself.

"Sir?"

Adam pulls himself out of his thoughts, walks back to the tall reception desk, puts on his best smile. "Yes, if it's at all possible, I'd really appreciate not having to go back out in that." He thumbs toward the picture window. The rain is coming down so hard now that it cascades off the porch roof, a shimmering curtain in the lights.

Chance gets to his feet, shakes himself, and opens his massive jaws in a canine simulacrum of a smile.

"That's some dog." The woman has that look on her face, the one the uninitiated most often wear at the sight of the chewed-up pit bull. Brindle-colored, one ear half gone, scars lining his muzzle, along with black crescents of scar tissue on his chest and flanks, Chance displays his past on his body.

"He's a sweetheart." Adam has had this conversation over and over.

"I'm sure he is, but we have a policy."

Adam puts one hand on Chance's smooth head, pulling the patience of the dog into himself. It's what he's learned to do when he feels the annoyance or frustration begin to swell. Touch the dog to deflate it. "Well then, can you recommend another place close by?" Adam has a good eye for desperate and he can see that this place isn't exactly turning away droves of would-be customers.

At that moment, a bolt of lightning sears across the window, followed almost immediately by the concussion of thunder, close enough that the windowpane rattles.

The innkeeper and Adam simultaneously chorus "Jesus! That was close!" and then laugh.

"Please don't make me go out in that." Adam pulls his glasses off and shoves them into his breast pocket. Smiles. Touches the dog again.

"Guess I'd be pretty mean to do something like that. Okay. You and the dog can stay, but I have to put you in the least-nice room."

"Just so long as it's grounded."

"I know, we're up high, but I'm sure you'll appreciate the view in the morning." She hands him a clipboard with a registration form attached, a blue pen. "If you would just fill that out. Sign the bottom."

Adam dips into his jacket pocket for his wallet, extracts his credit card, bends to the task of filling in the registration form while Chance patiently sits at his feet. He hands the clipboard back.

"Oh, and"—she looks at the form—"Mr. March, I'll have to charge you a fifty-dollar cleanup fee for the dog."

Adam doesn't say anything about highway robbery. In his experience, dog-friendly hotels vary from no extra charge to exorbitant fees. "No problem, Ms. . . . ?" He glances at the brass-colored name tag affixed to her white blouse. "Mitchell." Skye Mitchell. Interesting first name.

Plastic Adirondack chairs are scattered along the cement-floored porch, and the innkeeper straightens them into alignment with each numbered door as she leads Adam and Chance to the last room on the first floor. Room number 9.

She asks, "So, are you in the area for business or pleasure?"

"Business." A reluctant reentry into his working life.

The key sticks a little as she unlocks the door.

The scent of old rug and Pine-Sol waft out as the heavy door is pushed open. It's just like so many hotel rooms he's been in, two queen beds opposite the bureau with the television on it, a big flat-screen one. There is a small round table flanked by two vaguely Danish Modern chairs beneath the picture window, which is obscured by heavy drapes drawn across it. A far cry from his days of expense accounts and suites at the Ritz Carlton or the Taj. No minibar, no room service, just a little fridge and an unplugged microwave.

Skye points out the bathroom, "This might be the last room on my to-be-painted list, but the bathroom window doesn't leak. I really wouldn't have put you in here if it did." It's a tiny space, but clean and well stocked with towels and toiletries. She hands him the remote. "Continental breakfast starts at six-thirty."

Another flash of lightning, another crack of thunder, but it's clear that the storm has moved east. Adam feels a little foolish; he could certainly make North Adams easily now that the rain has let up and the visibility is better.

Chance is waiting outside, sniffing the air. Adam takes the key from Skye's hand, thanks her again. "I have a bed for him, so he won't be on one of yours."

"Good. But I'll still have to dry-clean those spreads." Then, as if she's a little taken aback by her inhospitableness, she smiles. It's a nice smile, Adam thinks, but one that she has to remember to use.

*I really like this place, I'm glad that Adam decided to stop here. First of all, there's the wonderful aroma of critters. Outside, not inside, although I'm pretty sure there was a mouse in the wall of our room. Which could be fun, but Adam always discourages me from indoor hunting. Hunting really isn't my thing, but I'll do it if the opportunity arises. Outside is the scat of all sorts of woodland creatures, most of which I have no name for. Deer, certainly. Squirrel, absolutely. Skunk. Oh yeah. Fortunately, I'm smart enough to give those buggers a wide berth. The farther away I wandered from the building, there lay odors from other rodents I've never encountered. Best of all, I got to be the first to mark the territory with my kind of scent. Not another canine has been in this area for a long time. The best I could come up with, and immediately covered, was old. Canine, yes, but possibly not dog, the idea of which gave me this excited little thrill. I shook myself.*

*Second, I like this place because Adam let me sleep on the bed. The human bed. A total crime in our own place, but for some reason, maybe forgetfulness, maybe being so tired, he didn't object when I took the second bed.*

*Third, I like this place because it is neutral. By that I mean that Adam doesn't have any association with it. There is no scent of Gina, no possessions lying around that require holding, sniffing. He had only one drink*

*before bed. He's not sitting with his head in his hands,
thinking, dwelling on her absence. I miss her, too. She
was kindness itself to me way back when I was not the
dog I've become.*

When the lady who opened the door to the room for
us came out, I was waiting for her. It's always been my
policy to befriend the people who extend hospitality to
us. I sensed that this was a near miss, this hospitality;
although the hostility I felt coming from the young one
really wasn't directed at us; and the coolness from the
woman wasn't really hostility in the proper sense, more
a tension that had nothing to do with us, and more with
the girl, who I assessed at a breath was her kin. Nonetheless, I did pick up on the more traditional anti–my
kind of inhospitable attitude; thus I waited for her on
the porch, having shaken off the rain from the tip of
my nose to the tip of my tail, which I wagged as she
came out.

She froze in place. I countered her fear with a little
dance I do, forepaws tapping, head wobbling gently from
side to side, tail whipping in my best pantomime of big
galoot. That's what Adam calls me when I do it for him,
Big Galoot, usually followed by some kind of treat. This
lady didn't have a treat, but she quickly relaxed and
timidly extended a hand, which I sniffed politely, then
licked. She didn't like that, and quickly withdrew the
hand without giving me a pat on the head, which was all
I was hoping for. That's okay. Baby steps are fine. I am
certain to win her over on the next round.

The door opened and Adam stuck his head out, saw
the two of us standing there, and said something to the
lady in their tongue language that I interpreted as conciliatory. What he had to apologize for, I can't imagine,
but in the next moment he called me in and I did as I was
told. I've been well schooled in the past few years—I am

*a certified service dog now—I hardly ever disobey, as
long as I understand what's expected of me.*

Ick. In the laundry room, I squirt a dollop of liquid soap
into my hand and scrub away the feeling of soft, wet dog
tongue. It's not that I don't like dogs; I do. At least I like
them well enough. I've just never had one. And I'm not a
big fan of dog kisses. Especially out of the mouth of such
an unattractive dog. I just hope that he doesn't have fleas,
although that seems unlikely, given his owner's well-
groomed look. Adam March hardly seems like the kind
of guy who would have a flea-bitten dog. He also doesn't
look like the type who would have a chewed-up pit bull,
but there's no figuring some people out. It's enough that
I've scored a walk-in room rate, plus surcharge for the
dog, and that will help. I won't really dry-clean that duvet. Everything here is washable in the venerable
industrial-size washer and dryer. That extra fifty bucks
will cover the overdue installment on Cody's braces. God
works in mysterious ways.

My phone jingles with my mother's ringtone, my
weekly dose of skilful interrogation. We dispense with the
formalities quickly and get down to the only subject we
both care about, Cody. Florence Lenihan should work for
the government; before I can throw up my barricades, she's
gotten me to confess that my beautiful, intelligent, perfect
child is in trouble again. I try to keep these things from my
mother, partly because I don't want her to think that any
part of my life is payback for the hell I put her through
when I rebelled against her comfortably middle-class life
and ran off with Peck's Bad Boy, the rebel without a cause,
the attractive nuisance that was Randy Mitchell.

"I still need to deal with her cutting detention. She did
the detention for defacing school property and another one
for not showing up at the original detention, but, Mom, I

don't have the feeling that she's learned any lesson at all. She's shrugged off the punishment as the price of doing business, and the question is, What *is* the business?"

"At least she's not selling dope out on the street like her father did at her age."

"He never sold it at that age." Unsaid was that he was at least seventeen before he got into the business.

"Whatever." My mother affects the lingua franca of hipness without irony. "I wish I could say send her to me, but I can't. I can't take on the responsibility."

"I could never do that. Be separated from her. As much as she aggravates me, I can't imagine life without her."

It's been only the two of us for a long time. Cody has no memory of living in a two-parent household, not that what Randy and I had could ever have been called a *household*. Ever since I threw him out before she turned two, it's all been on me. Single motherhood. A choice, a preference. Like my mother before me—in her case widowed, not divorced—I have stayed away from complicating my life with relationships. It's been a privilege, being the only parent. And, for the most part, it's been easy. Until now.

I tuck the phone between my shoulder and ear and bend to pull the sheets out of the dryer. The static snaps and shoots up my arm and I nearly drop the phone. "It's really all I have in my arsenal, so I'll tell Cody that she's grounded and she'll shrug and give me the eye roll, and happily take the grounding as yet another reason not to socialize with the kids her age."

"Still no friends?"

"None that I know of."

"She's a bright kid, a nice kid. Why can't she make friends?"

"Maybe because Cody refuses to engage, or maybe there's something about her that keeps her isolated." If she's treating me with such disdain, how is she treating others?

"So, where does Cody go when she disappears?"

Ah, yes, the very question I taunt myself with. "No-where, she says. She just walks." I snap the sheet into sub-mission, fold it, and add it to the pile of clean linen.

"Why is taking a walk a bad thing?"

"It's not the walk; it's the radio silence, the not know-ing where she is. It's the taking a walk to nowhere when she should be in detention."

"So how long will you ground her?"

"The punishment must fit the crime, so a week. And I'll assign her to clean room number nine tomorrow. We have a guy staying with us who has a dog with him, so maybe that will add to the punishment."

"A dog? Since when?"

"It was a mercy booking, and no, I'm not turning the LakeView into one of those pet-friendly places."

The sheets are folded, the pillowcases, too. I can hear the sound of my mother's grandfather clock chime six o'clock.

"Skye, you're doing a fine job. Stick to your guns and don't fall into the trap of trying to make up for what Cody thinks are your deficiencies. They aren't. They're about being a good parent."

Once in a while my mother makes me feel better.

Maybe tomorrow, after school, I'll see if Cody wants to get mani-pedis together, a little girl fun to encourage her to open up a little; take advantage of the unexpected largesse of Mr. March's arrival *avec* dog and even get pizza. I know what I'm doing, what I always do—make up for being a parent. Most of the women I know who have kids Cody's age are older, closer to fifty than I am to forty. A lot closer. The benefit of being a young mom is also a hazard. The desire to be an authority is under-mined by the equal and compelling desire to be a friend. Heck, I know women my own age who are still living at

home with their own mothers. Women still trying to figure out who they are. I've known forever who I am. Guess
that's the price you pay for being married the day after
high school graduation. A single mom at twenty-one. You
grow up fast. You simply grow up.

Cody Mitchell inserts her earbuds and scrolls through her
music until she finds the playlist based on Mosley's rec-
ommendations. In her bureau drawer, tucked into a tampon box, is a half-used joint, one that Mosley had put out
and carelessly left in the ashtray sitting on his worktable.
Cody knew he'd never miss it; in fact, she sometimes
thinks that he's leaving these treats for her on purpose.
She likes that about him. He's so cool about stuff. More
so than Kieran, who always acts all big brotherly around
her. Mosley doesn't treat her like a kid, more like a re-
spected grad student. Soon, very soon, she is going to get
up the courage to show him some of her work.
    Her old art teacher, Mrs. Dumont, really, really liked
Cody's work and made noises about her having some real
talent. But because of her academic schedule, Cody
couldn't get into the art class at her new school. Skye had
promised, on her mother's grave—which, if you think
about it, is stupid, 'cause Gramma Florence is still
kicking—that Cody would have an even better art program at the new school, and now she can't get into the
class and has had to give up her art just because her mother
got the hare-brained idea that life in this backwater would
be better. That owning a freakin' hotel was an improvement over a regular paycheck as a concierge and access
to the Ramada pool year-round. Cody has made the loss
of art class something to chew on, a plank in her campaign to keep her mother at arm's length. An injustice
that she can dwell on to the point where she actually believes it.

Well, Mosley will be an improvement over a high school art teacher, for sure. And if he liked to hold her close in a bear hug now and then, big whoop. It was him being friendly, that's all. And if the bear hug occasionally went on for an uncomfortable length of time, well, that was the price of being allowed to hang around.

"Cody? You in there?"

Cody tosses her hair back and sighs, tucks the unlit joint under her pillow. Here it comes. "Enter."

Skye is wearing that face, the one she puts on when she's about to get all parental. The one she thinks is intimidating. Her *serious* face. "We have to talk."

"I know. I won't do it again. I've served detention; don't you think it's a little late to start ragging on me?"

"First of all, drop the tone. Second of all, no, I don't. We haven't discussed where you went. You've been lucky; I've been distracted."

Cody bites back the obvious retort about how Skye is always distracted, mostly because it's not true. Because they live "over the shop," as it were, there is hardly a time when Skye isn't aware of Cody and what she is or isn't doing. Up in her grill is how Cody describes it to herself. *What are you doing, honey? Need some help with home-work? Do you want to invite someone over for a sleepover?* As if. "So, what's my sentence? Hard labor or the seg?"

"Guess it's seg. That is, you're grounded for the rest of the week, and that includes the weekend. And maybe we should be watching a little less *Orange Is the New Black*."

Cody bursts out laughing. "So how is that different from the rest of my life?" She's gratified to see the serious-parent expression dissolve.

"Oh, honey, I know it's been hard for you." Skye sits on the bed beside Cody. Now she's in for it, the heart-to-heart. She moves over. "It's hard for both of us, but you have to make an effort. You can't wait for them to come to you."

Cody knows the words to this tune pretty well. "You can't force it, Mom. And, really, I don't care. It's meaningless to me."

"I'm sorry you feel that way."

"Well, I do. And there's no amount of wishful thinking on your part that will make it different. You brought me here, and I'm suffering the consequences."

Booyah. Here comes the conciliatory hug. Cody allows herself to lean briefly into her mother's embrace. Tries not to put her head against her mother's shoulder. Just when Cody is trying to figure out how to extricate herself from her mother's embrace, Skye's cell phone rings and miraculously she's released.

Skye backs out of the room, talking in her concierge voice, and blows a freakin' kiss. Cody doesn't even pretend to catch it. Once the door clicks shut, she retrieves the joint, attaches a roach clip to it, and hunts around for the lighter she keeps squirreled away.

Mosley's stuff is good, and within a couple of minutes Cody can feel the ever-present weight of the Secret lighten. Six months, almost seven, and nothing has happened. She's kept her end of the bargain. She's keeping her end of the bargain. No one knows. Hopefully, *he* knows that she's keeping her word. The man who killed her father.

Another toke and the lightness darkens; the density of the Secret thickens. The weight in her chest feels like his hands felt, holding her against the brick wall, pressing her so that her feet didn't touch the ground.

"You will say nothing to no one." She was speechless, in shock from what she'd seen, but he shook the promise out of her; the back of her head hit the wall. "You say one word and you—and your mother—will die."

"I won't."

# CHAPTER 3

I'm staring out of the plate-glass window of the office-cum-breakfast room and wish that I could enjoy the view instead of noticing the peeling paint of the porch posts supporting the decking of the gallery above them. It's a remarkable view, with the mist rising up through the clenched fingers of the interlocking hills. Ethereal. Primeval. The mostly empty parking lot. One car. The guy with the dog. On final rounds last night, I'd expected to hear the dog bark as I walked past their open window, but it was quiet except for the very human noises of a nose being blown, a sigh.

I've put the coffee on, poured the 2 percent milk and store-brand half-and-half into pitchers, filled bowls with cut-up fruit, and cleaned the crumbs out of the industrial toaster. One guest. I put four of the six bagels back in the refrigerator, leaving out the plain and the onion. I look at the banjo clock ticking away on the wall above the reception desk. Jeepers, it's time to wake that girl up. Not since she was a little girl in pigtails has this kid been harder to get up. Every morning, it's the first battle of the day. If I'm lucky, it's the only one. If Cody is in a mood, it's only the beginning of hostilities.

The door opens and Mr. March and his dog come in.

"I know I'm a little early for the continental breakfast, but I was hoping I could prevail upon you for a cup of coffee."

I'd taken the two-cup coffeemaker out of number 9 to replace a broken unit in another guest room and never given it another thought—a rookie mistake. "Of course."

"Chance and I are early risers; we've been up since dawn. What a beautiful sunrise coming over the hills. It was spectacular, just like you said it would be, and I'm really glad that I didn't roll over when I woke at first light, but hauled myself up."

"Not as good as higher up, on the Mohawk Trail itself, but not bad." I can't seem to stop myself from being an apologist. "I mean, it's lovely here and lots of folks stop by just to take pictures."

Adam moves to the window. "So, where's the lake?"

"Lake?"

"This is called the LakeView, so I kind of assumed that, well, there's a lake."

"There used to be a view of Lake Hartnett, but the trees between us and the lake have grown up over the past century. The Conservation Commission prevents us from cutting them." The omission of that minor detail from the real estate offering was only the first of the surprises I got once the key was in my hand and my signature was on the life-altering loan docs.

I hand Adam a ceramic mug, one of a mismatched collection found in thrift shops. This one is a souvenir from Tanglewood—a place I have yet to go. "Help yourself to the breakfast. I got it started early today. It's a school day."

"How old is your daughter?" He depresses the plunger on the bold roast airpot. The coffee sputters out and he has to pump it again.

"Fourteen. Fourteen going on three."

"I know the age." He gives up on the faulty airpot and moves his mug to the airpot with the medium roast.

"So, you have kids?" I open the faulty airpot, also a thrift store find, pull out the plunger, and tap it.

"One. Fortunately, she grew up. Ariel."

"Like the mermaid?"

"No. From *The Tempest*. Spirit of air and fire."

I replace the plunger, test the pot, and a proper stream of coffee comes out. I offer him a new mug, but he shakes his head, keeps the one he has. "Did you weather the storms?"

"Mostly." Adam reaches out to the dog, who is sitting at his side. "The storms kind of kept changing." A shadow crosses his face, a tensing of his cheek muscle, which has a fine line of scar running along it. "Right, Chance?" The dog bumps his big head against Adam's knee. "Her mother and I were divorced about then. My fault entirely."

"That's hard on kids."

"It can be."

"Cody's father and I were divorced while she was a toddler. Maybe that's better. I don't know. She still resents me." I don't mention Randy's wasted life. The fact that he's dead.

"They say that what's important is unconditional love and a sense of security. I'm sure Cody knows she has both. She'll grow out of it." Adam smiles at me over the rim of his mug.

I point out the selection of fruits and cereals, where the English muffins are and the condiments. Adam March adds a little half-and-half to his mug, then stirs it slowly while looking out the window. "You're absolutely right: The view is astounding."

Adam had been rewarded for his early rising with the sight of the red-gold disk of sun as it emerged through the mist, floating up from behind the distant dark hill, less rising than simply burning through. He wished he could remember the name of the Greek god associated with the sunrise, or maybe it was Roman god, the one pulling a sun-filled chariot. Apollo? Phoenix? He wished that Gina was beside him. She would have loved the view, loved standing on that porch gazing over God's creation, and would have remembered the name of the lowercase god. He could almost feel the squeeze of her fingers through his, and he clenched his fist against the sensation. Gina's appreciation for all things Nature might have meant that he never saw meat in his own home, but he delighted in it. If she were here, she would lean her head against his chest and sigh with pleasure at the sight of so much beauty. Instead, he felt the very solid bump of a canine's thick skull against his kneecap.

The coffee is a little weak, but it will have to do for now. The homely version of a continental breakfast holds no charms for him. It's still early—his meeting doesn't start until nine-thirty—so Adam thinks that he'll go find a breakfast place in North Adams. Hopefully, someplace with outdoor seating so that Chance can enjoy himself, too.

"Find everything?" Skye is back from getting Cody up for school. She's got a newspaper under her arm and she slips it out from its plastic wrapper, hands it to Adam. It's the regional paper, out of Pittsfield, *The Berkshire Eagle*. Nonetheless, it does have a sports section, which he extracts, handing back the rest of the paper.

"Everything's great. Thanks again for taking us in last

night." He doesn't mention that he's fully aware that he was the only guest.

Skye tucks a loose strand of hair behind her ear. It immediately falls back across her cheek. Adam notices that her eyes are a nice hazel, but beneath them is the faint bruising of sleepless nights, of stress; however, she wears a crisp white shirt, a neat pair of black trousers. He imagines that she has a closet full of these garments, the uniform of a concierge, a hotelier. On her left wrist is a man's old-fashioned big-faced watch on a black leather strap.

From somewhere outside, a door slams. Moments later, the daughter bangs open the office door, comes in, grabs a plastic-wrapped bear claw, pours herself juice from the pitcher, and walks out, leaving the door open. Not a word to her mother. No acknowledgment of their guest. Chance takes advantage of the open door to trot outside. Adam sees him go, but he doesn't call him back, confident that the dog won't go far.

*I catch up with her at the side of the road. The girl has the sticky bun in her hand. The wrapper is on the ground and I sniff at it, take a lick. Not bad.*

Hey, leave that alone.

*When I look up at her, the thing sticks to my nose. She puts out a hesitant hand, then removes the plastic wrap from my face, stuffs it in her pocket.*

*I wag my tail. She still has a good chunk of the bun left. As if reading my mind, she hands it to me. I'm a gentleman; I ease it out of her hand.*

You should go back. Your master will be worried about you. *She tosses the rest of her sharp-smelling juice onto the gravel, crushes the cup in her hand.*

*Master. There's a word I'd never apply to Adam. I wag my tail again. Step closer and take an exploratory sniff.*

*Interesting combination of girlie potions, the sort I am familiar with from having had Gina in my life, and something else. Yes. I know that scent, one of my least favorites. Cigarettes. On her skin and in her backpack. In my mind, those objects will always be associated with men and bad habits. Sometimes bad men, sometimes just bad habits. Finding that scent on a girl is new for me.*

Go on. Get away. *She steps back. I keep sniffing. I'm not proud of it, but once I'm in the sniff mode, I have a hard time calling it quits. I suck in another good cell-filled breath. Yes, yes. Something else going on here. Not physical, although I'm pretty sure she's coming into that human female version of heat. My olfactory powers go deeper than mere skin, breath, and effluvia. I detect something I can only call a disease of the soul. I've encountered this in Adam, especially now.*

*I hear the labored roar of the school bus and leave off my exploration. I sit and wait while the girl mounts the steps ever so slowly, as if going to her doom. As if there is no one inside this bus she wants to see.*

*I put my nose to the air that puffs out as the doors close. Yes, absolutely. This is one unhappy girl.*

I'm cleaning up the dribs and drabs around the untouched breakfast area. Two cups of coffee and the missing bear claw that Cody substituted for the breakfast bar I'd left on the table for her are the only disturbances to the array. In my fantasy of owning a boutique hotel, I had imagined that eventually I'd have a commercial kitchen and be able to offer a full breakfast to my guests. Not a bed-and-breakfast per se, but a restaurant-quality operation that might even draw nonguests to the LakeView of a Sunday morning. Ah, well. That unrealistic notion has died an easy death. Murdered by the immediacy of other, more pertinent concerns. Like dry rot.

Shaking off that unproductive train of thought, I lock the office door and hang the little cardboard sign that says BACK IN ONE HOUR. IF YOU NEED ME, CALL . . . It has my cell number on it. Then I head to the rear of the property, where Cody and I share a tiny two-bedroom cottage, a leftover from the days when the LakeView had guest cottages as well as the main hotel, a better day, when the Mohawk Trail and environs attracted folks who would spend whole summers camped out in rustic discomfort and love it. I've got plans for the other three cabins, renovation and long-term rentals, but that plan, like the full breakfast, is a back-burner plan for now.

Predictably, Cody's room is a shambles, and I take some comfort in this suitable teenage trait. Clothes strewn on every surface; laptop closed like a clamshell, its password protecting it from the imagined invasion of prying parental eyes. The only nod to making the room her own is her *Hunger Games* poster thumbtacked to the wall, Katniss Everdeen aiming her arrow at me. Not even when she was a little girl did Cody enjoy the trappings of princesses and fairies. For her, it was Shrek and Merida, not Ariel—the mermaid, not the spirit—or whoever the princess du jour was when Cody was six. No Barbies.

I bend to pick up a discarded T-shirt, then change my mind. This is Cody's mess, and if her clothes remain on the floor instead of making it to the hamper, tough beans. A couple of days of no clean underwear might be more meaningful than a rant from me, or always finding clean, folded clothes on top of her bureau. How's that for tough love? I back out of the small room, look into my own. It's nominally better than my daughter's. At least the clothes are piled on a chair, not the floor. It's hard to be uncluttered in a bedroom the size of a box stall.

I'm just thinking that I might make myself a cup of tea, sit for a moment and read the paper, when my phone rings.

It's a local exchange, so not likely a potential guest. It's also a vaguely familiar number. I've seen it before, but I can't recall to mind who it is. I don't know that many people in town, so if it's a social call, I'll be shocked. Like Cody, I really haven't made any friends here in town. I just don't have the time.

"LakeView Hotel, Skye Mitchell speaking. How may I help you?"

"Ms. Mitchell, this is Betty Zigler." The voice is neither friendly nor hostile. Maybe a little weary. The high school principal.

So much for the tea.

It's so not fair. She wasn't the one who started it. Just goes to show you that being the odd one out, the one who isn't related to everyone else in this godforsaken town, the one who maybe knows that there's more to life than Justin Bieber, makes you vulnerable. An easy target. Showed him, though, didn't she? Good right knee right to the baby maker. That's the last time that kid will ever make fun of Cody Mitchell. He'll think twice before getting behind her in line, for sure. Whispering that nasty accusation in her ear. Just because she doesn't swoon at the sight of his fourteen-year-old swagger, doesn't giggle at his jokes and hide behind her hair at his approach like all the other freshmen girls, and some of the boys. Cody just doesn't know why he's singled her out for harassment. If she doesn't flirt or go all shy in his presence, why is Ryan so obsessed with making her life miserable? He should meet some of the guys at her old school. They'd take him down in a heartbeat and not even hang around for her to say thank you.

There is a code, nonetheless. And Cody just shrugs when Mrs. Zigler repeatedly asks her why she assaulted—her word—the junior varsity quarterback. "I don't know."

"People don't just knee other people for no reason, Cody."

"It was an accident."

"He's nearly six feet tall. Your knee in"—Mrs. Zigler pauses to find the appropriate words—"a sensitive area can't have been an accident." She comes out from behind her desk, sits in the chair beside Cody. Cody has the sense she wants to take her hand, so she quickly drops both hands into her lap, locking her fists between her knees. "Without any explanation of your behavior, I'm forced to apply the school committee–mandated penalty for inappropriate touching. Is there anything you want to say in your own defense?"

Cody gives the principal her most eloquent shrug. What good would it do to repeat the foul taunt to this woman? Didn't she want to give blow jobs to the JV team? Ryan heard she was good at it. Where the hell did he get that idea? What bitch put that bug in his ear? Cody knows that it will go worse for her if she rats. If she thinks her life is hell now, this is just the shallow end of hell compared to the shit she'll get by telling the truth. Besides, as visits to the principal's office have become something of a routine, why shouldn't Mrs. Zigler take the side of the boy whose only appearance in this office is to suck up by overachieving on some do-gooder project? Cody realizes she's a known problem child and that, in the view of the rest of the school, Ryan's you know what doesn't stink.

A tap on the closed door of the principal's office, and then the secretary shows Cody's mother in. She's wearing that same half smile that she wears whenever she has to act all motherly. Like: *Yeah, I know my kid's a problem, but what are you going to do?* On the way home, she'll start on her favorite broken record: *We have to make a living in this town. Please don't make it any more difficult.* In the next moment, she'll be all *Still like me, please!* Sorry for putting her failure on Cody, she'll suggest ice cream.

Half a year ago, Cody would have told her mother everything, let Skye sympathize with her, maybe even get all Mama Bear and go to bat for her against these stupid kids. But Cody is too afraid that any détente would jeopardize keeping the Secret. She can't weep to her mother and keep it.

"Cody, what am I going to do with you?" This time, Skye doesn't try to conciliate. She's that upset with the principal's accusation.

"Go for ice cream?"

To Cody's complete surprise, a tear trickles down her mother's pale cheek.

# CHAPTER 4

"I'm sorry, I do have a reservation. I called last night to cancel *only* last night." Adam's fist tightens around the dog's leash. "Please check again."

"Fully canceled. I'm sorry."

Adam doesn't interrogate the desk clerk as to how canceling one night has translated into canceling the whole stay that he'd booked at the Holiday Inn. He'd like to, but reason suggests that this pimply kid wasn't on the desk last night. He should have canceled the one night by computer, but Adam had thought that the best, most efficient way to adjust his plans was over the phone, speaking to a human being. How wrong he was. "Fine. Let's rebook."

The desk clerk has the distinct look of a young man about to deliver bad news. "Umm, sorry? We're full? There's a conference?" Since when did young men affect uptalking? What is this country coming to?

"Okay. So, you've probably had those rooms reserved for some time; conferences don't happen overnight. And my room, which was reserved for me for two nights, minus the one I canceled a mere twelve hours ago, is booked out from under me?"

"Umm. Yes. We have an opening on Friday night."

The fist clenching the leash flexes. Chance, wearing his red service dog vest, casts a gimlet eye upward, as if to say, *Chill out, man.* Adam practices his centering breath. Touches the dog's head. The world is made up of screw-ups, and he's learned to accept the fact that he will encounter them and that there is generally nothing he can do about it. He has all the tools he needs to conquer the anger that sometimes still takes him by surprise. The one thing he doesn't have is a hotel room for tonight. "That will hardly do."

The desk clerk shrugs. "Is there anything else I can do for you today, sir?"

Five years ago, Adam would have roared his displeasure at this clerk. He would have shaken his fist and made unrequitable demands. He would have viewed the young man as nothing more than an obstacle to his own needs. But that was before his fall, before Adam swept the streets he'd once owned—to paraphrase Coldplay. Master of the Universe, cold, calculating, epitome of the widely disparaged 1 percent, although, he wasn't quite in that economic category. Running a major company, brooking no dissent. Mistaking buying his daughter and his wife their every desire for showing love. Losing it all in a moment, caving into a long-suppressed loss. His was a life built on anger—at his father, his missing sister, and his childhood spent in foster care. It all collapsed, and Adam knows now that he's the better man for it.

Because of Chance. Because of Gina.

Back out on the street, Adam stands in the sunshine of a perfect late-September afternoon. The desk clerk gave Adam a small local tourist guide with accommodations listed. Adam almost tossed it in the trash on his way out, then thought better of it. Leaning against his car, thumbing through the booklet, he still feels pissed off. He doesn't want a B and B; he wants a hotel. He doesn't want to make chitchat over a fussy breakfast; all he ever wants is coffee and quiet. But there are only three accommodations that are pet-friendly, all of them guesthouses, so he starts calling. One is booked solid and the other two are distinctly out of his budget range.

Chance, leash dragging behind him, wanders halfway down the block.

"Hey, get back here."

Chance ambles back to Adam. The dog sits, yawns audibly, flops down on the sun-warmed pavement, beats his tail a couple of times, and closes his eyes. His red vest has slipped a little.

The service dog idea had been Gina's. Ever since Chance's brush with near death at the hands of a dogfighting ring, Adam had been reluctant to let the dog out of his sight. But it was more than that, it was only in the company of his dog that Adam felt secure, in control of himself. Gina knew that and knew how to ensure that he and the dog were never apart.

Chance and Adam had done the work, gotten the CD for obedience and the Canine Good Citizen award; had worked with a trainer to give Chance the ability not only to recognize Adam's bubbling anger but to defuse it. They took up therapy dog work in nursing homes and participated in school reading programs where little reluctant readers jockeyed for position next to Chance to get the opportunity to show off their newly acquired reading skills, as if the dog understood what they read to him. Anything to spread the joy of touching a happy dog.

The darkness receded with the light of his life, Gina, and the steadfastness of his dog, Chance.

Then Gina got sick. When they had to accept the

unacceptable, Adam felt like the darkness that had once clouded his spirit was growing back as surely as the cancer that had bloomed inside of his wife. But now the darkness has a name: grief. Three months after her passing and he still feels waves of it, prompted sometimes by no more than a song on the radio, or the sight of a woman wearing those silly Birkenstock sandals Gina loved, and it's then that the dog, Chance, proves his worth, as he is now, head-butting Adam and making that little *uhhn uhhn* noise.

Adam collects himself. "I wonder if I can sweet-talk that woman at the LakeView into letting us stay there another night?" It's just a space, a bed, a television—a room with a view. But somehow the thought of staying there again is pleasant. He can't quite put his finger on it, but going back to the LakeView feels right.

Chance shakes himself vigorously and sits in front of Adam. *Okay.*

Well, he can't spend any more time on this problem; he's only got about ten minutes before his meeting at this place, the Artists Collaborative. This is the nonprofit that his neighbor Beth encouraged—her word—him to apply to for the job of fund-raising consultant. Clearly the neighbors have decided that it's time for him to get back on track.

Adam opens the passenger door and the dog hops in. As Adam pulls away from the curb, he thoughtfully lowers the window so Chance can push his muzzle out, take in the air. He's not the kind of dog who sticks his head out of a window and barks, but he does like to suck in the passing scents, get a flavor of the scenery, let his floppy dewlaps flutter.

As they sit at a red light, waiting for pedestrians to make their slow way across the street, Chance makes this little rumbling noise in his throat—not a growl, but an alert announcing the approach of one of his own kind. In this case, it really is one of Chance's kind, a stocky pit bull on the end of a short chain leash, at the other end of which is a tough-looking customer. Except for the fact that he's clearly a teenager, he looks like he wouldn't be out of place at the Fort Street Center, the homeless shelter where Adam once performed community service and where he now serves on the board of directors. At nine-thirty on a weekday morning, the boy's obviously not in school, either truant or expelled. The baggy, low-slung jeans and the hoodie, the studied saunter as the walk light blinks in its final seconds of service, the glint of fake gold around his neck—all mark the boy as one of the tribe of Badass.

The dog wears a plastic cone around his meaty neck. Adam assumes that the cone prevents him from worrying stitches holding together wounds he probably received in a dogfight. This boy looks like one of the boys who stole Chance, stole him and dropped him in a pit with his jaw taped shut, training bait for a fighting dog. Adam's mouth goes dry with the memory of it.

Chance actually whimpers, a sound he's not in the habit of making. If Adam were given to anthropomorphizing his dog, he might think that Chance was empathizing, like a compassionate human being at the sight of someone down on his luck. More likely, it's the sight of the dreaded Elizabethan collar that has elicited the whine. It's hard not to see that, despite the e-collar, the dog seems happy enough. His rolling sailor's gait is cheerful and he looks up at his man, not with fear, but with anticipation. As if he's expecting some sort of treat. Adam signals for his turn, and Chance pulls his head back into the car. "There but for the grace of God go you, don't you know?" Adam knows he's making assumptions, showing his prejudices. Just because the kid looks like a street person, just because the dog is a pit bull type.

Chance reaches over and gives Adam a quick lick on the cheek. The boy and dog finally make their arrival on the opposite shore and Adam accelerates moments before the light turns red again.

She should hitch back down to the Artists Collaborative, get away from here. Go hang out with Mosley and Kieran and mix with cool people. Not that she knows many of the other artists in residence; most of them are only there during the day, when she's stuck here or in school.

Unfortunately, her mother's watching her like a hawk, so Cody has no idea when she'll be able to get back down to North Adams. It was bad enough when she couldn't get out from under her mother's thumb much before late afternoon, after the rooms had been cleaned and whatever togetherness plans her mother had hatched for the two of them had been decided. It's going to be far worse now that she's taken out Ryan with her knee. Her "punishment," as handed down by Mrs. Zigler, means that Skye will be picking her up every day after school, after her day is wasted in the in-school suspension room doing homework for which she's had no classroom instruction. Plus, she's grounded again, which—again—is meaningless but makes it sound like her mother is taking Mrs. Zigler seriously, doing her bit. It's the ultimate collaboration between school and home. Imprisonment by any other name. Maybe Black Molly has the right idea. Just run.

Cody smoothes the duvet over the bed, arranges the throw pillows in the pattern that Skye prefers, some variation on shit she sees in the decorating magazines. When she's feeling particularly disagreeable, Cody calls her mother "Martha," as in Martha Stewart.

Skye has glommed on to the whole New England kitsch ethic, and it turns Cody's stomach. Chintz slipcovers and fake antique quilts. Yuck. Baskets in every bathroom, holding rolled-up facecloths, toilet tissue, the cheap toiletries in tiny plastic bottles. Worse, dried weeds hanging off of grapevine wreaths on every door. Double yuck. Fortunately, there's been virtually no attempt to rehab their little cottage into anything more than a place where they retreat from the hotel, eat a late supper, and adjourn to their separate rooms, so Cody doesn't have to suffer the home decor atrocities in her own home. However, even with the mildew scrubbed off the walls and fresh paint applied, the whole place still reeks of old. Farther up the Mohawk Trail, places like this have collapsed or been chopped up into firewood. Skye's grand plan is to renovate all four of the cabins and become some kind of fake mid-century—last century—tourist attraction. She apparently has never heard of water parks or Disney World.

Room number 9 is done, no vestige left of its human or canine occupants. A blast of Febreze and the next guest will be none the wiser as to the presence of that weird-looking dog. Actually, he was cute in an ugly sort of way; a face only a mother could love. To her complete surprise, as if her thoughts have conjured him, when she opens the guest room door, the dog is sitting outside it, his chunky back end planted neatly on the center of the cocoa-fiber doormat. He sees her and that tail starts swinging from side to side as he gets up to greet her, like he's been waiting just for her. She pushes her housekeeping cart along the wide porch and the dog follows.

Chance snuffles at Cody's knees, tickling them. "Beat it." He doesn't; he trots along beside her, as if she's invited him along.

"Beat it, I said." Cody shoves the dog away, fully annoyed with his constant sniffing at her, the sense that he's trying to read her with his nose. "What is wrong with you?" The dog sits, lifts his front paw as if inviting her to shake it. "You're a jerk, you know that?" But she doesn't mean it. She's never had a dog, never had much in the way of interaction with them. The dog looks a lot like the dogs that some of the tougher street boys owned—burly, intimidating-looking creatures with names like Blaster and Killer. They'd parade their dogs up and down the streets, thick chain collars on them, short leashes held tightly, suggestive of potential violence, danger. Made the boys feel like playas. Gangstas. Most of the dogs, and not a few of the teens, were actually pussycats.

This dog is clearly pussycat, but he's a pest, blocking her progress down the length of the porch. He bows, rump in the air. Waggles his head. Looks pointedly toward the open lawn. Barks.

"I don't have anything to throw for you." Cody hunts around in the trash bag hanging from the housekeeping cart, finds an empty water bottle. "Chase this." She pitches it off the porch, and the dog bounds after it. Once the bottle is in his mouth, he crunches it over and over, evidently pleased with the annoying noise the plastic makes. "Don't leave that out there. I'll get yelled at."

As if he understands, the dog hops back up onto the porch and drops the crushed water bottle at her feet.

*I kept up my best friendly dog behavior all the way from our room, which had been doused in a foul scent in a feeble attempt to disguise our presence, to the place where my Adam was talking with the girl's mother. I was interested in what was going on, but the emanations coming from the girl overrode my desire to pay attention to Adam, and I found myself drawn to her. I kept sniffing at her exposed skin, and she kept shoving me away. I took no offense. I have been trained to recognize when Adam is about to lose his temper, to sense that vibration of dis-*

*cord and mollify it with action. Because Adam is my only concern, my only experience of deeply internal human anger, I was shocked to find the very same vibrations coming from this pipsqueak of a girl. Inside her was this absolute core of anger. The thing was, it was very undirected. There didn't seem to be any particular source of her irritation. With Adam, it's usually pretty easy to suss out where the source of the trouble is. If we are driving, it's another driver; if we are with other humans, it's usually someone's intransigence or obtuseness. I nudge Adam; he smiles, gives me a pat, and shakes himself (well, not really, but the human equivalent) into a better frame of mind. Because I couldn't pinpoint this girl's trouble spot, I could only hope that my antics would still work.*

*They did, but only mildly. A dark car pulled into the parking lot and I caught a new emanation from the girl, a frisson of fear, pungent and sudden. I felt the girl's hand on my head and I pushed myself against her. Maybe I helped because when two ladies got out of the car, the emanation of fear quickly dissipated.*

# CHAPTER 5

Adam March turned up just as I was checking in an older couple reliving their youth by visiting the places they'd been on their honeymoon fifty years before. Mr. and Mrs. Abbott had bickered their way into the office and, key in hand, were bickering their way back out. I catch the glint of amusement in Adam's eye as he stands aside to let them by. "You let me know if there's anything else I can do for you," I call to them. "Like get you dueling pistols." This last remark under my breath.

"Nothing says second honeymoon like a good squabble," Adam says as he walks up to the desk. "Ms. Mitchell, I'm here to throw myself on your continued mercy. Can we have our room back?"

I don't see the dog, so I have to ask, "You and the dog?"

"Yes." Adam glances toward the open door. "He's checking things out."

"How many nights?"

"Just tonight. I think."

I try to make a good show of studying my computer screen, scrolling down and across, as if seeing if there is anywhere I can possible squeeze him in. I even pull a frown of concern.

"And I'm happy to pay the same surcharge as I did for last night." He's beaten me to the punch. I calculate the revenue in my head and have no choice but to smile and ask for his credit card.

"Cody should have room nine all set, so I'll put you back in there."

"I look forward to another stunning sunrise."

"You should pay attention to the sunset, too. The view isn't quite as dramatic, but the sky gets very pretty. You can get a nice view from the upper porch."

"I will, thank you." He takes the key out of my hand, pauses. "This is a nice place, Ms. Mitchell, perfect for a guy like me."

"How so?"

He just shakes his head, as if he doesn't really have an answer. Smiles that nice smile. "It just is."

There isn't anyone else expected to check in on this Tuesday afternoon, so I put up my sign and lock the office door. Cody has left the housekeeping cart on the porch instead of putting it in the laundry room. She knows better. It looks terrible, this cart full of helter-skelter bottles and brooms, dirty sheets billowing out, parked bluntly in front of the stairwell door. No pride. No sense of ownership, that girl. In the next thought, I pardon Cody. She's only fourteen, after all. How responsible was I at that age?

With everything else going on in my life, I have given up meal planning in favor of something closer to "If it's Tuesday, it must be meat loaf." Tonight, it's accompanied by baked potatoes, and in deference to the idea of a well-balanced meal, I've opened up a can of corn.

Cody sits down with a thud. Contemplates the slice of meat loaf on her plate, the same meat loaf that she's eaten for years, but this time she's looking at it as if I have finally lost my mind, or that I'm trying to poison her. "I can't eat this. It's disgusting."

"You ate it last week. And the week before . . ."

"And, yeah, the week slash month slash years and years before that. But. Not. Anymore."

"And when did you decide this?"

"I've been working up to it. I'm considering becoming a vegetarian."

"Okay. So, no meat?"

"Duh. That's what a vegetarian is."

"Fish?"

"I hate fish."

"Chicken?"

Cody shrugs. "Maybe. But not every day."

"I come from a meat-and-potatoes background. We didn't do vegetarian in the Lenihan household. I don't think I know how." I say this hoping to get a smile, but, as usual, she doesn't give me an inch. I wonder for a second whether maybe the preponderance of red meat on the menu contributed in some way to my father's early death. Then I remember that he died of a brain aneurysm, faulty wiring.

"I bet there're recipes online." Cody splits her baked potato and lathers it in butter, adds a handful of shredded cheddar cheese, smooshes it all together.

"And I bet you can make them." I am not going to add specialty cooking to my task list. Uh, no. "You find them, give me the ingredients, and I'll get you the stuff, but I'm not going to cook two different meals."

"You could do it. Convert."

It's the first time in a very long time that Cody has suggested something we could do together. I should be glad. "I'll think about it. I'm guessing you aren't expecting canned corn and frozen peas as part of your diet. Vegetarians have to eat stuff like hummus and kale. Tofu."

Cody shoves her bangs out of her face, gives me the death look. "You think that I'm some baby who doesn't know what it takes to avoid meat without sacrificing nourishment?"

"Yeah." Why are we fighting about this? We should be laughing. It should be a fun thing to do, plan meals, learn how to cook with fresh food. "Are you hanging around with vegetarians?" I jokingly make the word sound like it's a cult. I want a smile. Give me something.

"No. Not exactly."

"Who are you hanging out with?" I know that this is a good parenting question, know who your kid's friends are. It gives me a little boost to think Cody really does have a peer group, even if it's vegans or vegetarians.

"Nobody you'd know."

"I'm sure I don't, but I'd still like to know their names."

"Hers. Molly."

"Why don't you have her come by some afternoon after school? I'd love to get to know your friend."

"I really don't think you would."

"Why?"

Cody doesn't answer, just shoves the untouched plate aside and goes to her room. Conversation over.

I poke at my own meat loaf. Maybe it is time to try a little harder with meals. I push the contents of my dinner plate into a plastic container, do the same for Cody's untouched dinner, search for the covers, and can come up with only one that fits. It is one of life's bigger mysteries, along with missing socks, where the tops to GladWare containers go to when they disappear.

Cody kind of regrets walking away from the dinner table. Not rejecting the meat loaf, but forgoing the baked potato, which is her favorite with cheddar cheese mashed into it. She's hungry and too stubborn to go back out and grab the potato off her plate and bring it back into this closet that her mother thinks is an adequate space. At least the dump in Holyoke had a real closet; she didn't have to hang her stuff on pegs against the wall. Well, they've got a couple of rooms occupied—that guy with the dog is back—so Skye will go hang out in the office most of the evening and Cody can get herself something to eat when her mother leaves the cottage. She pulls the remnants of Mosley's joint out of the tampon box. Lights up.

It's weird, having given up Molly to her mother, like they had more in common than the fact that Black Molly is in the in-school suspension room, too. They don't talk. No one talks in ISS; the monitor makes sure of that. But on the way to pick up lunch this afternoon, Black Molly slipped a scrap of paper into Cody's pocket, leaned close, and whispered, "Case you want some fun." Cody takes it out now. The handwriting is abysmal, like the numbers have been written by a six-year-old. She doesn't know if she should be pleased to have the attention of the only other student more despised than she is, or despondent. What the hell. She inhales a mouthful of dope, thumbs the number into her phone directory. Saves it. Exhales. She doesn't think that the fun Black Molly has in mind is going shopping together, and that thought makes her smile. Skye thinks she's trouble now, well, there's a whole world of exciting trouble out there.

Cody pulls out her sketch pad and finds a pencil that's got enough point on it to be useful. Mosley always sketches out his work on paper first, before committing the idea to whatever surface he's working on. Except about making art, he's so laid-back. Sometimes it feels like he doesn't even know she's there, but then sometimes she looks up from her sweeping and sees him watching her. He'll ask her to stop, hold the pose. He's in the "zone" and she's helping him to work through something. That's what he calls it. The zone. That's when she most likes to be there, when Mosley is in the creative zone. Cody flips to a clean page in her sketchbook. Not another horse, no. She should try to expand on her subject matter. Mosley said that. "You have to draw everything, not just what you know you can draw well." Words of wisdom, certainly.

Cody looks around the room, doesn't see anything particularly sketchworthy. She looks out the single bedroom window at the trees that form a backdrop to the property, reds and yellows and permanent piney green. Brown oak leaves stubbornly cling to twigs, and faded yellow beech leaves flutter, raining down, defeated. She's been to the top of Mount Greylock, been driven up the switchback road with its view-offering turnouts, and each wave of mountain and its trough of valley made her feel like she was at sea. Lost.

She feels claustrophobic, crowded by the relentless magnitude of the mountains, crowded by her mother. Aching with the weight of the Secret. It's not so hard to keep silent when there is no one around who knows about Randy's death, his murder. Maybe she should be grateful that they did move to this hellhole of a place; if they had remained in Holyoke, remained in the same neighborhood where everyone read the local paper and knew what had happened, where her friends were attracted by her unique status as child of the deceased, it would have been a lot harder to maintain a grip on the Secret.

Every few days, Cody checks the online version of the Springfield papers, looking for references to her father's unsolved death. Making sure that the shooter knows that she's keeping her promised silence.

Framed by the small window with the froufrou curtains wafting gently in the evening breeze is a big blazing red maple tree, its obscene color muted in the fading sunlight. She begins to work, shoves a hank of hair behind an ear. Her tree won't be pretty; she'll take liberties with its shape, and the benign maple will show its true intentions. A hanging tree. Mosley says you sometimes have to get down to ugly to make something beautiful.

The joint is reduced to an ember. She touches it to the edge of the curtain. It crumbles.

Adam thumbs off his phone after a nice, albeit brief, chat with Ariel—she's fine; he's fine—and swaps it for the remote, swings his feet up onto the bed, loosens his tie, and points the remote at the television. Chance pokes his nose over the edge of the bed, makes his little *Me, too* noise. "Come on." He pats the bed, but he really doesn't have to make a formal invitation for the dog to leap up, circle once, and snuggle his back against Adam's side. Adam finds the news. "We should go for a walk before dinner." Chance doesn't seem to care either way, although his stubby ears perk at the word *dinner.* Adam drops his arm across the dog's back, scratches gently along his ribs. In a moment, Adam gets up, opens his briefcase, and extracts a pint of Jack Daniel's. The bathroom has only plastic cups, but they'll do.

Adam takes his drink outside to the porch. Leans his elbows on the rail, studies the landscape. This time of year, the light becomes butter yellow before tarnishing into sunset. In a few minutes, he'll take Skye's advice and go upstairs to the west end of the gallery. The light here is different from that of the Cape, where he and Gina had spent a lot of time. Sunset was their favorite time to walk the beach. He wonders why they never made it up to the Berkshires, two hours and a whole landscape away. Standing, leaning, sipping, Adam is quietly glad that they didn't. Maybe that's why he is pleased to stay here again tonight. There is nothing of Gina here.

Adam finishes the drink, tosses the plastic cup into the

wastebasket. There was a time in his life when he felt the world was closing in on him in an unfair and brutal way, and Mr. Daniel's twelve-year-old product was his best friend. Now he enjoys a pre-dinner drink; later just a nightcap, a liquid reminder that, as bad as he feels now, he has regained control of himself. It was one of Chance's first influences on him, when the unwanted dog had inserted himself into Adam's life, requiring an attention that brought Adam out of his self-inflicted funk. A dog needs food and walking and a kind touch. What he gave in return was everything.

# CHAPTER 6

"So, how long did you say you've owned the place?" Adam pumps himself a cup of coffee from the airpot, looks longingly at the bear claws and chooses a banana.

"It's a little over six months." Skye empties a box of sweetened cereal into a plastic cereal dispenser, neatly flattens the cardboard. "Since the end of April."

"Work in progress?"

"You could say that." Skye blushes a little, and Adam feels like he's been inappropriate.

"It's hard. Start-ups."

"Technically, though, it's not a start-up, not if it's been in business since 1946."

"True. But, for you, I'm guessing, it's your first go?"

She opens a new cereal box. "I've been in the hospitality business for a long time, but this is another animal entirely."

"Well, it's great. Really." Adam sets the mug down, squirts a little more coffee into it.

"It's not, but thank you for saying so. It's hard keeping

up with daily stuff and then dealing with deferred maintenance issues. Deferred over a decade in some cases."

Adam's already figured out that this hotel is a one-woman shop. And it's likely that sullen kid of hers isn't much help. "I hope you have a good handyman."

Skye smiles at this. "Yeah, he's great. When he's not hunting. Or fishing. Or drunk. I've learned to do a lot myself. Except for the room you were in, I've painted all the others. I've got a punch list as long as your arm with next steps. I'm becoming conversant with plumbing, and wiring."

Chance is enjoying the open-door policy of the office and has just wandered in from his self-guided morning walk. Adam's meeting today is in the afternoon, so he's going to treat himself and the dog to a good hike in the woods, a thought that prompts him to ask Skye where the best hiking is.

She pulls out a little guidebook, points to an entry. "Folks like this one; you can see across to Mount Greylock and down into North Adams from a lookout point on it."

"Haven't you been?"

"I wish I had the time—and the freedom—to go hiking, but this place is really all-consuming."

"I guess it would be." He certainly knows about all-consuming work. "You should find some time to relax, Skye. Don't let ambition kill your joy."

"Ambition? It's survival at this point, Mr. March."

The businessman in him wants to ask her probing questions, get a sense of the scaffolding of this enterprise. The reformed workaholic keeps his mouth shut. He takes his coffee to one of the chairs by the picture window, grabs the local paper from the table. Chance flops down beside him, sighs, and is immediately in a doze.

"Does your dog like meat loaf?"

"Why, yes. Yes, he does."

"I have some in the cottage. I'd be happy to let you give it to him. Cody won't be eating it; she's become a vegetarian overnight."

"They all flirt with it, vegetarianism. Comes with a growing awareness of the world and the rampant injustices. It's something they can control." He sounds a little flippant; after all, Gina was a hardened vegetarian. It's Ariel he thinking of.

"Well, it's a waste of good meat. I mean, with it already being . . ."

"Processed?"

"Yeah. It's not so much not eating meat as repudiating me."

"As a cook?"

"As a mother. As someone breathing."

Adam laughs. "My daughter once told me that she hated the way I arch one eyebrow when I think I'm making a joke. Made her sick."

"Well, you do arch your left eyebrow."

"I've tried to control it." This is pleasant, a little repartee. It's been a while since bantering came easily. Or at all.

Mr. and Mrs. Bickering Couple arrive, not bickering just yet, but I can sense the simmering. He follows his wife as she surveys the array of bagels and cream cheese; dry cereal, packets of instant oatmeal; a hand of bananas in the fruit basket, early symptoms of over-ripeness in the tiny brown spots that have formed overnight. I feel the inadequacy of my offerings in the look on the missus's face; the resignation to further disappointment in the mister's fumbling of the stacked paper cups. I won't apologize, though. This is what I advertise as a continental breakfast, and this is what I provide. You don't like it, there's a breakfast place six miles downhill.

The dog, who has been quietly dozing beside Adam's chair, lifts his head and pulls himself to his feet, shakes and ambles over to Mr. Bickering Couple. I'm about to say something to Adam, to get him to control his dog, when suddenly Mr. BC smiles. "Hey there, fella. Good boy." The dog, Chance, whaps his tail from side to side as the man bends over him, giving the dog an experienced back scratch. "Wish we'd known you were pet-friendly, we'd have brought our girl."

"We miss her so much." This from Mrs. BC, who, like her husband, is smiling affectionately at the rather unlovely dog. "Who's a good boy?"

From his seat by the window, Adam March raises one arching eyebrow at me.

"We're not, actually. Pet-friendly. This is a special case." I throw Adam an arch look of my own. "A one-off."

"Too bad. Lots of places are going to the dogs. So to speak." Mr. BC—Mr. Abbott—gives Chance another pat. "Catering to people like us, who like to travel with their dogs."

I swallow back the obvious question: So why did they choose the LakeView if they wanted a pet-friendly vacation? It's not in my best interest to query guests about why they chose my hotel over the more upscale or more accommodating hotels farther along the Mohawk Trail. Neither do I make a remark about the way people are nuts for their dogs. Or cats, or what have you. If I allow dogs, what's next? Iguanas? "Wish I could, but I don't. More coffee?"

The Abbotts put covers on their coffees and leave. The dog wanders back to his master's side.

"He's right, you know."

"I'm not equipped."

"Sure you are. What would you have to do differently?"

"I couldn't cope with the fleas, the urine stains, the stink."

"You could designate a couple of rooms, put down tile or laminate instead of rugs. Washable bedcovers. Most people who care enough about their pets to travel with them have the flea situation under control. Clean dogs, housebroken dogs, those are the kind that get to travel. Show dogs. Therapy dogs. Service dogs."

I throw up a hand, stopping Adam in the same way I stop Cody when the girl gets on a pleading tirade. "No. I really don't want to get into any more complications. This place has enough without trying to change the program, too."

"It's not exactly like you'd be running a no-tell motel. People like me are happy paying you a premium, and I'm certainly not the only lonely traveler willing to do so to be able to keep his companion with him."

"'Lonely traveler'?"

"A figure of speech."

I think not. Although he mentioned being divorced, he's wearing a wedding band, suggesting another marriage. But he's here with his dog, telling me he's on business. The curious in me gets to wondering if he's been thrown out, along with the dog. Otherwise, wouldn't he have left his dog home with the family? Enough conjecturing about guests. "I have to go rouse Cody. Do you need anything else?"

"Go. I'm fine. And, hey, good luck." He raises that eyebrow again.

Predictably, Cody isn't ready. She always wears the same thing, so how hard can it be to pull together an outfit? Skinny jeans, layered tank tops just this side of inappropriate, a flannel shirt or a body-concealing hoodie, depending on the day. And, as always, the beat-up Justin cowboy boots that she bought at Tractor Supply. It all makes me long for a parochial school with its dependable and appropriate uniform.

With her bangs long enough to touch the heavy frames of her glasses, Sia-like, only the bottom half of Cody's face is visible. It's like Cody is hiding behind the scrim of hair and frame. She has perfect skin. A beautiful pair of hazel eyes. Tiny shell-like ears. A slender body, nearly hipless and certainly enviable. But she hides behind the hair, the glasses, the flannel shirt, and the perpetual slump of cultivated ennui.

A glance at the wall clock with its relentless second hand sweeping away the minutes. "Five minutes. Have you eaten?"

"Yes." True enough. A box of Honey Nut Cheerios sits open on the table, the milk, also open, beside it. There's a scrim of pulp on a six-ounce glass, so I know that Cody's downed some orange juice.

"Book bag? Homework?"

"I can't find my science notebook." Cody says this conversationally, as if the notebook's whereabouts is of little concern to her personally.

"Have you looked?"

I am graced with the withering look. I have once again confirmed my status as an irritation in Cody's tender life.

"Let me rephrase that. Where? Where have you looked? Did you have it in the office? I start on the litany of places lost things might be: office, bathroom, under the bed, behind the dresser.

The rumbling sound of a hill-laboring school bus puts a firecracker under both of us. "Just go. I'll find it and take it over."

"Science is first period."

"Go!"

I wander around Cody's room, looking for the missing notebook. As my cell phone chimes, I find it. The science notebook is peeking out from under the tangle of bedclothes, wide open to a drawing of a spooky-looking tree, a long braid of rope hanging from an outstretched branch. No denying the significance. "LakeView Hotel, good morning." I use my brightest voice, midweek and a new reservation!

"Sorry, wrong number."

I toss the phone down, stare at the drawing in Cody's notebook. The subject is disturbing, the hangman's noose, but the execution is pretty good, no pun intended. If this is a picture meant to show me exactly how Cody feels, I'm confused. Is Cody threatening me, or herself? Should I be worried? Maybe a visit with the school counselor is in order. In the next minute, I decide no. This is me overreacting. As Cody would certainly agree. Still, maybe an informal chat with the counselor wouldn't be a bad idea.

*Ah the scents! The sounds! The mud! I'm more of a city dog, to be sure, but this outdoor stuff is quite fun. Off leash, running after the noise of squirrels, the scent of bunny. I'm not sure I'd know what to do if I ever got close to one, but the chase is the thing. Adam is enjoying himself, too. I can tell by the way he stops along the trail and takes in a deep breath, lets it out with a soft vocalization that sounds like he's been presented with a big soup bone. Wow. I don't pretend to know what he's admiring, but it's definitely admiration. We go higher and higher and the going gets a lot more vertical. I can feel the exercise in my haunches as I have to do more pushing upward. Eventually, we come to a stopping place, and Adam sits down with a little oof of relief, pulls off one boot, shakes it out. Gina would have loved this place. We should have come. I recognize only one word in that utterance. Gina. For a while it had stopped meaning the woman we lived with and begun to mean sadness, like a different word, elongated in Adam's mouth. Like a howl. I sense that I had better make myself available for touching and go up to him. I give him a little lick on the mouth, just to let him know that I'm there. Ready.*

Adam puts his boot on and pushes himself off the bench. Come on, bud, let's head back. *I understand almost all of those words. We go back down the trail at a slightly slower pace. The woodland creatures are no longer quite so interesting.*

# CHAPTER 7

Cody sneaks aboard the school bus that will get her closer to the AC than her own Route 3 bus. This is the first day that she isn't being picked up by her mother, her first day out of ISS. Black Molly is still incarcerated, although she managed to respond to Cody's text while under the supervision of the day's ISS monitor.

*You still ISS*
*Yeah. Lucky me*
*Sucks*
*Word*

Cody keeps her head down, as if absorbed in her silent phone, pretending to belong on this route, pretending to be invisible. She makes no eye contact with anyone, especially the two girls who, along with Ryan, have conspired to make her life a living hell. Taylor and Tyler. When Cody first arrived at the high school, the lone new student in a class that's been together since kindergarten, she mistook the pair of blond, blue-eyed Amazons as twins. They dressed alike; they talked in the same lingua franca of high-pitched squeals and withering asides. That was her first error in judgment, asking a stupid question: "Are you guys, like, twins?" And that misstep opened up an avenue of abuse. With one ill-considered question, Cody was branded a cretin. "What are you? Gay?" Not meaning gay in the usual sense, or even in the traditional sense of happy. A new use for the word, meaning stupid. *Reject.* What Ryan whispered into her ear was even more heinous.

If Cody thought that the girls wouldn't notice her stowing away on their bus, she was just proving their point that she was a dumbass. She climbs down after them, keeping a safe distance, but one of them turns to look at her. "Hey, you. Girl."

Cody turns her back to them, plugs in her earbuds, and marches down the road, ignoring the taunts being tossed at her by the pair.

"Love the boots." The mean-girl drip of sarcasm. "Real shitkickers."

Cody turns up the volume. Raises one hand, offers the one-fingered wave. She doesn't think that they'll pursue her. They're not that interested.

She's got a little better than a mile to walk, all of it downhill. She'll be there in half an hour. A truck blows by her, a row of cars behind it.

Just as the road rights itself after the hairpin turn, Adam catches sight of a kid walking down the right-hand side of the road, oblivious to the danger of not facing traffic. Some idiot texting while driving could wipe her out. He shakes his head. "Kids. No sense of self-preservation." Chance opens one eye, notes that the comment is nothing he needs to worry about, and shuts it again. As he glances back in his rearview mirror, Adam is pretty sure that the kid is the one from the LakeView, Skye's daughter. What the heck is she doing this far from home? Well, Adam thinks, surely there's a reason, and, really, it's none of his business.

He's headed back to the Artists Collaborative. Even though he had deliberately not put his best foot forward, hoping to scuttle his own return to work, somehow Mosley Finch and his partners at the AC were impressed, and so he's back in the Berkshires today to present to them a précis of his fund-raising plan.

"Hey, man." Mosley claps a hand on Adam's shoulder. "Glad you could make it."

This seems like an odd thing to say to someone with whom you have made an appointment, but Adam just smiles and shakes the proffered hand, which is gritty with some substance. "I've got a couple of ideas for you, so shall we get started?"

"Sure, man."

Adam begins to think that his client here is a little high. His eyes are definitely sleepy. From his days doing community service in the kitchen of a homeless shelter, Adam is no stranger to the look of men who have indulged in illegal substances. Or to the smell. As Mosley leads him to the one room not converted into art space, Adam takes a little sniff. Oh yeah. Cannabis. Adam doesn't judge, but he does wonder if this meeting is going to be worthwhile.

"Cookie?"

"Ah, no. Thanks. Why don't I show you my proposal?" Adam props his tablet up on the old-fashioned wooden desk cluttered with the detritus of an artist's life. Brushes, torn-out pages of sketchbooks, ashtray. He fires up the device and begins his spiel.

By the time Cody gets to the AC, she's got a blister on one heel and she has to pee. It's taken her a lot longer than she thought to walk here, and it's almost four o'clock. She's a little worried that Mosley, whose office door is uncharacteristically shut, won't have time to talk with her. Not a lot of people know it, but Mosley supplements his income with bartending, and he is usually gone by four-thirty. She dashes to the industrial-chic ladies' room in the basement of the old factory building. A woman wearing an actual fox stole and a pillbox hat is standing in front of the flyblown mirror, layering bloodred lipstick on her lips. She reminds Cody of an old-time movie star. She catches Cody's eye in the mirror and smiles a foxy smile, caps the lipstick.

Cody spots the woman again upstairs, this time sitting for one of the artists; she's a model, the fox stole, hat, and red lipstick her costume. She's exotic enough that a couple of the other artists have left their work and stand behind the painter, watching her intently as she turns the model into an abstract representation on canvas, the only common thread the bright red lipstick.

Cody wanders around, visiting the other seven artists in residence today, although it's only Kieran who notices her and gives her a little wave, then drops his protective mask back over his face and fires up his torch. She feels singled out, a nice feeling. Mosley is still nowhere around. What if he's not here at all? All her efforts will be for nothing. That would totally suck. "Kieran, is Mosley here?"

"Yeah, think so." This is muffled behind the welder's mask. "In his office with that fund-raising guy."

"Okay. Do you need anything?"

"Nope. Thanks, though."

Cody finally settles down on a metal folding chair, placing it where she can keep an eye on Mosley's door and also watch some of the work taking place. On the far wall, the ancient Seth Thomas factory clock chips away at her available time. She's going to have to call her mother soon or start walking. She doesn't relish the idea of walking the miles home with a blistered heel, then thinks, given the burns and cuts she's seen these artists give themselves, there's got to be a first-aid kit around here with Band-Aids in it. She hobbles around the shared space with its cupboards and dorm-size fridge, sink splattered with the full spectrum of colors, the stained coffeemaker and the pegs of hand-thrown mugs dangling above it. At last, she opens the right drawer and finds a tube of bacitracin and a box of store-brand adhesive bandages.

Just as she is easing her boot back over her foot, Mosley's office door opens. A guy in a jacket and tie comes out first, still talking, and Mosley follows, his hand on the guy's shoulder, a smile on his face. "Great. Great. Super. Can't wait to raise lots of bucks."

"It's worth doing, and it's worth doing right." The guy throws out a hand for Mosley to shake, and suddenly Cody recognizes him: the guy with the dog. Mr. March and Chance. As if to confirm her identification, she hears a dog bark. Must be out in his car. The dog is really going at it, and Mr. March pulls away from Mosley with an apology and heads for the door. Which is when he sees her and says hello, but he keeps going.

"Hey, kid. What's up?"

"Mosley, I was wondering . . ."

"Hold that thought. Gotta go visit the little boys' room for a sec."

The minute hand clicks past four-fifteen. Maybe he's not working tonight. Maybe she has time still.

Her phone rings, the distinctive ring she's chosen for her mother, right out of *The Wizard of Oz*. Kind of obvious, but she likes it. When she doesn't answer, she gets the chirp of an incoming text: *Where are you?* All spelled out. Punctuated.

*WAF,* she responds—with a friend. She gives Skye a minute to translate.

*Home. Now.*

"So, what's on your mind, Buffalo Bill?" Mosley is back.

"Do you ever give lessons? Art lessons?"

"You mean like a teacher?"

"Yeah. No. More like a mentor."

"I have. Why? You interested?"

"Yes? I am?" Even she hears the uptalk in her voice. "I mean, I'd really love to barter some lessons for chores."

Mosley motions for Cody to sit back down on the folding chair, pulls a second one over to sit opposite. He looks like he wants to give her bad news, the way he keeps his eyes on her, the way that he gently pushes a hank of hair back away from her face. Then he pats her on the knee, and his hand stays put. "Well, here's the thing. I'm not really in a position to offer regular lessons. I'm going to be pretty stretched out with this fund-raising stuff."

Cody knows the run-up to being disappointed and she's already telling herself that it doesn't matter, that even though he's letting her down gently, it's still down. "Yeah, I was just wondering, no big deal. I mean, I can do my own thing."

Mosley's hand on her leg slides up a tiny bit. "No. Hey, wait. Maybe we could do a little barter." He is close enough that she can smell the pot on him. It's in his skin, his hair. He is looking at her with a new interest. He reaches up and pulls her glasses off her face, tucks her hair behind her ears, lifts her chin and tilts her head. Instinctively, she pulls away, pushes against the back of the chair.

"How about you give me a few hours as a life model in exchange for an equal number of hours in lessons?"

"What would I have to do?" All she hears is the word

*model;* thinks of the woman in the red lipstick and the fox fur.

"Just be yourself. That's it. No nudity, if that's what you're worried about."

"I wasn't. No. I don't care." She knows that nudity is no biggie for models. It's not like the artists are actually turned on. She'd do it.

Mosley drops his hand away from her face. "Okay, then. You give me an hour sitting for me and I'll give you an hour in lessons."

"Okay." Cody can't believe her luck; she's talked her way into art lessons with Mosley. "Cool."

"Yeah. Cool." The minute hand of the Seth Thomas hits four-thirty and Mosley pushes himself out of the chair, "Gotta run. Sorry." He pats her on the head like some kind of pet and heads back to his office.

The heavy front door clangs open and Mr. March is back in the building. "Hey, Cody?"

"Yeah?" He's got the look of a grown-up with a great idea.

"Look, I saw you walking here. Do you need a ride home?"

"Are you staying with us?

"Not this time, but it's on my way home."

"No. That's okay. Mom will come get me."

"That's silly. I'm happy to give you a ride."

"I'm okay. I want to hang around here a little longer." That should do it. It would be just too weird to take a ride from a complete stranger, even if he does have a cool dog.

Mosley bombs toward them. "Hey, man. Forget something?"

"No, I just was offering Miss Mitchell here a ride home."

"You should take him up on the offer, Cody. I have work tonight so I can't take you, and we're closing up."

"I'm good." She quickly adds, "Thanks anyway."

Unfortunately, she's up against an experienced father. "If you're creeped out by this old guy offering you a ride, that's understandable. What if we call your mother? See what she says."

"Never mind. I'll go with you." Cody swings her backpack up onto her left shoulder. She follows him out of the old factory building, dragging her feet in the hope that Mosley will change his mind.

"Chance, get in back." The moment he jumps into the backseat, Chance shoves his blocky head completely out the window and commences an uproarious barking. For the life of him, Adam can't see what it is that's getting the dog so riled. "Chance, enough. Quiet down."

Cody pulls open the front door and Chance pushes himself over the console and jumps out.

"No, Chance. Get back in." Adam is annoyed; this is so not like his dog. Then, listening as Chance finally stops the barking, he hears it, the sound of a howl, a plaintive canine expression of unhappiness. Chance wasn't challenging; he was commiserating.

Adam's human ears can't quite place the location, no doubt coming from one of the three abandoned-looking old factory houses along the opposite side of the river, remnants of the days when the company not only employed but also housed its workers. Suddenly, the yowling stops, and Adam hopes that whatever the situation was, it's been resolved. Chance doesn't flop on the backseat as is his habit, but sits upright, head cocked, anxious.

Time to go. Adam pulls his phone out of his breast pocket. "Skye? Adam March here. No, I'm just in town for the day, but I want you to know that I'm giving Cody a ride home."

The look on the kid's face is eloquent. Horrified.

Clearly, Cody's mother doesn't know that she's hanging around the AC.

Skye sounds confused. "Where did you say you saw her?"

"She's on her way home from . . ." He sees the panic in Cody's eyes. "I just happened to pass her. She's right here."

Cody keeps her eyes down. Her fingers are clenched; she makes no move to take the phone when Adam offers it.

He signs off, drops the phone into his breast pocket. "Hey, I'm not going to put a teenage girl in my car without her mother's knowledge. I'm no dope."

"Thanks for not telling her. I mean that I'm here."

"Not my business."

"Good."

"But, it if were, I'd have to wonder why you think she might object. It's hardly a den of iniquity."

Cody sits back against the seat. The dog, Chance, puts his forepaws on the console between them and pokes her with his nose. "Hey, cut that out." She pats him on his head. "No kissing."

"So, you like art?"

"Yeah, I do."

"You like the stuff at the Artists Collaborative?"

"Most of it."

"I have to admit, it kind of leaves me cold. I'm more of a Norman Rockwell kind of guy. Guess you could say that I'm old-fashioned because I like my pictures to look like pictures."

"Lots of people do. It's just that postmodern frees the artist from the restraints of viewer expectation."

"I'm guessing that's a quote."

"Mosley says that."

"Well, he's certainly a free spirit."

Cody looks like she can't decide if he's being sardonic

or admiring. He's not sure himself. At any rate, she says nothing the rest of the way home.

*The unhappy girl seems tense to me as she takes my seat. I'm happy to sit in the back, give her the priority seating even I am rarely afforded. Even though Adam keeps up a stream of tongue language, she does little more than give him back one word at a time. Words I know. Yeah. Fine. Good. I can sense Adam's growing regret that he's allowed this creature in our space. Although I have only limited experience, I find teenage girls to be mysterious, more like cats. But not any more mysterious than the howling I heard coming from across the busy river. It reverberated in my ears, grabbing my heart and making me sing out in solidarity. There was great mischief going on and I couldn't get to it. I howled my presence, my interest, my regrets. Too far to get a scent, too far to help. But I will know this dog should he ever cross my path. A dog in that kind of trouble wears it on his skin. I have been that dog.*

# CHAPTER 8

Despite the time spent in ISS, Cody has been in even more trouble at school in the past couple of weeks. Insolence, failure to do homework, refusing to participate, and skipping classes. I find myself begging her, asking, "What's wrong? What's going on?" But Cody clams up and refuses to give way by so much as one inch in her determination to be a cipher to me. "Nothing," she says. "It's nothing."

I find myself weeping in the office of the school counselor, grabbing the tissue box out of his hand and using one Kleenex after another as the crying jag goes on and on. I blubber about the hangman's noose, the silent treatment, the vegetarianism. Maybe if I had a friend, I wouldn't impose myself on this overworked school counselor, but there's no one I can babble to about my maternal fears, lance the boil of my mounting concerns. I haven't had time to waste on my own loneliness. In a former time, Cody would have been enough of a companion that I wouldn't have felt the need; now, not so much.

In his professionally gentle, concerned voice, he presses

me. "Is there any recent trauma that she's experienced? Or some big change in her life?"

I choose my words carefully. "My ex-husband, her father, passed away just before we moved here." No use going into the sordid details. Randy was the kind of father who showed up unannounced, or failed to show up when expected. "They weren't close."

As for a change in her life? Just the fact of the move here, and that's old news now. The excuse is getting a bit thin. It's time for her to accept that this is our life now, and that I'm not giving up. I say as much to the counselor. "Isn't it time for her to get over it?"

"That's why I'm asking if there may be a new situation." His eyes are tiny behind thick glasses, pinpoints of blue in a pale face; a rash of adult acne or shaving irritation cloud his rather plump cheeks. He looks like someone should scrub his face in hot water and steer him away from using harsh soap. "Sometimes if a single parent begins to date . . ."

"Oh, that's certainly not the issue." I bat at my eyes with the soggy tissue. "That ship sailed many years ago. I have never subjected Cody to boyfriends." Oh, there have been dates. Sure. But I have always put Cody first. No one is going to make Cody ever feel secondary. That was the promise I made her on the day she was born. Aching with the effort of bringing this child into the world, I was unprepared for the kind of love that broke over me like a tsunami; the seismic shift in my allegiances. I looked into my infant daughter's unfocused eyes and was lost. Maybe that was the moment I knew that I wasn't going to stay with Randy. Even before he cheated the first time— that I knew about—I looked at this helpless baby's sweet face and knew that Randy was never going to be the kind of father who put his child first, her well-being paramount.

He would never be serious about straightening out his life.

"Has Cody ever said anything about trouble with other kids?" Mr. Farrow, the counselor, takes me out of my thoughts. "I mean other than the dustup with Ryan."

I dab beneath my eyes, shake my head. "Only that she doesn't mention any of them. It's like she comes to school and there's no one here."

Mr. Farrow sits back in his slightly off-kilter desk chair. "No friends at all? Not even kids you'd prefer she not hang out with?"

At first I shake my head, then remember. "She mentioned a girl named Molly. But she's never asked to have her over and hasn't mentioned her since. I think she might have been making it up."

"Molly." Mr. Farrow rocks back in his chair. "There are a couple of Mollys in school. But none I can think of in her class. She didn't mention a last name?"

"No. Not that I can recall. Like I said, it was one reference."

"Any friends from"—he pauses, hunts down the words—"back home?"

I may be guilty of sneaking a peek at Cody's phone log, but it remains empty except for my own number, a frequent incoming call. "I don't think she has stayed in touch. You know how it is when you're that age. Life moves on."

"I have to ask this. So please don't think . . ." The rash on his cheeks grows even more distinct.

"No. As far as I can tell, no drugs."

"Sex?"

"Oh my God. No."

"It's normal, you know."

"I was eighteen when I got married, I know what adolescent hormones can provoke." I don't add that it was a

shotgun wedding. That my mother wept not tears of joy
but of sorrow at the sight of her only daughter being
walked down the short aisle to Randy Mitchell's arms.

Mr. Farrow tries a different tack. "The Internet, as you
know, has changed things. Kids aren't sophisticated, nec-
essarily, but they are worldly. Connected. Assaulted on
all sides by words and images that they can't really comprehend. Rap, hip-hop. Drugs. Violence. The list goes on,
and we're not shielded from it by virtue of being a town
of fewer than seven thousand. When I started here, teen
pregnancy was a big deal. Now, not so much. However,
eating disorders and self-mutilation crop up with astounding frequency."

"She's eating. Although she's become a vegetarian.
And she's not cutting."

"It's not always obvious."

"No. I suppose it's not."

"She gave Ryan a pretty good kick in the nuts. Did she
ever tell you what provoked it?"

Mr. Farrow's vulgarism makes me smile a little. "No."

"Is she normally more physical than verbal when she's
upset?"

"No. She can be very effective verbally."

"Look, I'll check in with her, informally, and see if
anything comes up."

I hand him the Kleenex box, which he carefully sets
back on the corner of his desk. Mr. Farrow reaches out
one soft hand, and when I take it, he pats mine with an
avuncular *There, there*. Oddly, I feel a little better. The
human touch.

I leave Mr. Farrow's office with a balled-up Kleenex still
in my hand. Cody is supposed to meet me outside the office suite, but she isn't there, as the dismissal bell hasn't

yet rung. So I hang around, pretending some interest in the bulletin board laden with out-of-date announcements: Join the Debate Club! Sign up for Chorus! Try Robotics! Big kids wander by, seniors flaunting the privilege of being seniors, I suppose. A little boy lets himself into the office suite. He looks too young to be in high school, and then I remember that this small school includes the junior high. The bell finally rings, and the doors aligned along the hallway pop open to release the hordes into the world. The din of voices is accompanied by the banging of every single locker door in a cacophonous counterpoint. As suddenly as they appeared, the students are gone to their busses or, if they are upperclassmen, to their cars. Still no sign of Cody.

Teachers begin to emerge, poking their weary faces out to see if the coast is clear. A student dressed in a short skirt and leggings, with overachiever stamped all over her worried face, runs up to one of the teachers, and I can see the resignation in the teacher's smile as she grants the student an after-school audience.

Still no Cody. I'm beginning to feel like I've been stood up. Which is ridiculous. Cody knew that I was coming today, that I would meet her here in front of the office. Just to make sure, I take a peek out of the double doors to see if Cody's outside, wondering where I am. Nope. Nobody out there. No Cody.

"Mom?"

Finally. I turn toward my daughter's voice and am struck at how sad this kid looks. For once, the usual combativeness is gone. The sullen *Wish you would get off this planet* expression is different. A trick of the light, surely, but it's the first time that I have seen Randy in Cody's face. It's there, in the cheekbones, in the way she won't meet my eyes.

"You want to talk about my meeting with Mr. Farrow?"

"Not really. Am I on punishment again?"

"No. He's just worried about . . ."

"My behavior? That it? As usual?"

"Your attitude."

"I hate it here. That's my *attitude*." Cody bears down on the word.

"It'll get better, I promise." I wrap an arm around Cody, surprised to find her suddenly a bit taller, but not surprised at the stiff resistance to my touch. My affection. Cody jerks herself away from me as if disgusted by such familiarity. A blocky-looking girl comes down the hallway, black hair like a rooster's coxcomb, eyes hidden by the excess of black mascara, black lipstick completing the ghoulish mask. She jangles as she walks, chains slapping against her meaty thighs, which are encased in what look like military paratrooper pants. She wears what used to be called engineer's boots, black, thick-soled things bearing heavy buckles at the ankles. Her appearance screams *Look at me, but don't you dare look at me,* so I pretend not to look, not to notice. Kids can be so self-destructive.

As the girl walks past us, she lifts her chin, nods at Cody, a minimalist greeting if ever there was one, which is met by a similarly vague nod from Cody. It's enough to signal that this, without doubt, must be the Molly whom Cody spoke of exactly once. Open mind, close mouth, I think to myself, and follow Cody out of the building.

Cody can feel the burn of her mother's curiosity about Black Molly. Skye doesn't miss much, and that curt greeting in the hallway after school was as blatant as a hug. Cody's kind of mad at Black Molly. What was she thinking, getting up parental interest like that? But Skye doesn't belabor the moment, thank goodness. No soppy *Oh, was that your friend?*

The nod wasn't a greeting per se, but a warning. In her backpack, in that little zipper compartment in the smallest section, wrapped in what looks like a dirty tissue, is a whole joint. A gift, Molly said. Not to be enjoyed alone, but later today, at an agreed-upon rendezvous. Black Molly told Cody that she wanted her to carry it, as it really belongs to her third-eldest brother, and if he finds it on her, he'll kill her. He may be stupid, she says, and she can easily turn his suspicions toward one of their other brothers, as they are all thieves, but why chance it. Black Molly, it seems, has a family of five brothers and one sister, the eldest, who's already a mom herself and living in Greenfield. They live a mile from the LakeView, as the crow flies, and she and Cody will meet in the state park that separates them.

Skye is quiet on the ride home. Too quiet. If she throws down some ridiculous punishment for whatever transgression Mr. Farrow has accused her of, Cody will just freak. She really doesn't want to blow off Black Molly. That would not be a good idea. Black Molly may not be the kind of girl she hung out with in Holyoke, but she's an improvement over no one at all.

An hour later, Cody says she's going for a walk, that she'll be back before dinner—in effect, throwing her mother a bone of civility. Hoping Skye doesn't ask where she's going. Or, worse, suggest she go with her, a mommy and daughter walk. Like they used to do. Back when. Back when a walk around the block, through the cemetery, ended up, somehow, always, at Dairy Queen. Back when she was a kid. There's no Dairy Queen in this town.

"Okay, be safe."

"Safe. Right. I don't think I need to worry around here in no-man's-land, do I?"

"About bears."

"Again. Right. Bears."

Black Molly is waiting for Cody close to her end of the blue flash trailhead. Neither one speaks and Cody follows Molly as she goes off the trail a few yards to a shelter made out of long branches arranged against the fork of a tree, creating a primitive lean-to-cum-tepee.

"Cool. Did you build this?"

"Yeah. I've built a few. Come in handy when you want to get away."

Black Molly sits down, looks at Cody. Raises an eyebrow, the one pierced with a safety pin. "Ahem."

"Oh, right. Here." Cody pulls out the joint. She's forgotten a lighter. "Did you bring matches or anything?"

Black Molly slides a hand into one of the multiple pockets in her pants, pulls out a matchbook. "Always prepared, like a freaking Girl Scout."

Cody respectfully waits for Molly to light up, take a drag, pass her the joint. It's different from Mosley's medical marijuana.

Molly takes the joint back. "So, what's your story?"

"Haven't got one."

"You do. We all do."

"Came from Holyoke, mother bought the Bates Motel. End of story."

"I'll tell you a secret if you'll tell me one." She passes the joint back to Cody. Smiles. Cody notices that her teeth are very crooked. Thinks that you don't see that much anymore. Should she recommend her orthodontist? He's all right, even if he does have fat fingers. She starts to laugh.

"What's so funny?"

"Fat fingers."

"Whose?"

Cody, despite the giggles, recognizes that she may have insulted Molly, whose hands are a fine match for the blockiness of her body. "My ortho."

"Your what?" Now she's laughing. "What's an ortho? Some kind of pervert?"

This sends Cody into another fit of the giggles. "Braces, teeth . . ." she manages to get out, then taps her own teeth, decorated with Dr. Odell's torture devices.

"So. That's the best you can do? That's your secret? Braces?"

Hell no. "My father was shot to death." Cody keeps laughing; it seems as though someone else has blurted this out, this weird confession, the something she's never supposed to talk about. Her Secret. She is so outside of her own body right now that it seems like all anyone had to do was ask for it and she, or this voice that comes out her own mouth, would spill it.

"Cool. I wish mine was."

Cody shrugs. She hadn't thought of Randy's death as "cool." She takes another toke, hands the spliff to Black Molly. She guesses that having a father shot dead is a distinction. It wasn't like she was one of those kids who wish their parents were dead, and what happened would have been like getting what she wished for. "I mean, I didn't, like, live with him, or, like, love him or anything. But he was my dad." She doesn't know if this is true. It just sounds true right now. It sounds like she isn't worried. And for sure it doesn't suggest that she witnessed it.

Molly speaks around the retained breath, hands the joint over. "Random shooting, or what? Line of duty?"

"Guess you could say it was random." Cody squeezes her eyes shut to help hold the inhalation in longer, so long that she disassociates herself from her THC-induced confession, the cloud in her head muffling the near-constant fear. Just to be safe, she adds, "How should I know? I wasn't there." The fact that her voice squeaks a little isn't a tell; surely it's because of the effort to hold in the smoke.

Molly gives Cody a little shove and Cody hands the joint back to her. She's feeling sapped out. Then she remembers the deal. "So, what's your secret?"

"Nothing cool like yours." Molly stubs the joint out, wraps the remainder in the tissue, slides it into her pocket. "One of my brothers likes to watch me."

"Watch you what?"

"You know."

"Say it."

"When I'm in the shower."

This strikes Cody as funny and she is launched into yet another laughing fit.

"It's not funny." But then Black Molly starts to laugh, too. "He's gross. He thinks I don't know he's there and what he's doing."

Cody finds herself flat on the ground, looking up. The light coming through the propped branches is silvery and the shimmer of beech leaves looks like fairies dancing. She should make a wish. Capture a fairy and make it grant her three wishes. No, it's not fairies who do that. It's what? Trolls. Trolls under the bridge. Her first wish would be to go back to the way it was before, when her father was a jerk, but alive, and his killer hadn't looked right at her.

"So, tell me," Black Molly says. "Why is that your secret? I'm pretty sure a shooting even in Holyoke makes the news."

"Sure, of course. It's just that no one around here knows."

"So? What's the big whoop? Wouldn't that kind of, I don't know, make you interesting?"

"I don't want to be interesting."

"Everyone wants to be interesting."

"Please don't say anything. Really." The buzz is flattening out.

Beneath the thick eyeliner, and despite the serious high,

Black Molly's eyes in her wide face are surprisingly clear, intelligent. Knowing. She scans Cody's face, smiles her crooked smile. "All right. For now."

The air is decidedly sharper this visit and it gets dark so much earlier. At least Adam is comfortable on these back-water roads now, and he finds his way to the LakeView almost without thinking. He's been up three more times since that first night. It's funny how he finds himself thinking about the Berkshires when he's back in Boston, thinking about how relaxed he is when there. It's only about a hundred miles away, but it might as well be a thousand for how remote he feels. Not one personal item to throw the switch of memory. No misplaced earring caught in the fiber of the bathroom rug, no box of herbal tea growing stale on the shelf. He can't bring himself to throw out the tea, or drink it. He doesn't know what to do with the mateless earring. He can sit in room number 9, enjoy his solitude, bear down on whatever memory he wants to, and weep if that's what he needs to do. Or just watch silly television and not think at all.

Up here, in room number 9, he can shut off his phone and not take the six phone calls a day from the cadre of well-meaning women who have taken it upon themselves to guide him through his grief, as if they have developed a schedule he needs to keep. As if solitude isn't something that he craves. Or deserves. To them, he's indulged in private grief long enough. Three months—no, four now, and he's being urged to "get back out there." He hadn't been "out there" when he met Gina. He was a shattered and very angry man serving out a community service sentence, stripped of his dignity, his family, and his shield of wealth. She took pity on him.

These women, this coven, have no idea what he needs. Certainly not a date. Certainly not a social life. He has

Chance, and that warm, solid block of dog is enough for him.

As he pulls into the driveway, Adam realizes that he looks forward as much to seeing Skye as he does to crashing into that queen-size bed. Because she has no idea of his past, recent or otherwise, she treats him like anyone else, any other guest, not someone to be pitied, or bullied back into life. She has no idea about him. All she sees is the repeat customer with a dog. The truth is, Skye isn't too keen on him coming back with the dog, but she isn't impolitic enough to say a definite no. He knows she's not remotely making enough to be able to reject his money outright, but she always waffles a bit, just for show. "You know, if I let you, I have to let everyone else."

"No, you don't. Say I'm a special case. He's a therapy dog."

"Well, is he?"

"Yes. I have issues."

"I bet you do." She smiled, just in case he thought she was being snarky.

He knew she wasn't. It was that little zinger that made him feel, briefly, normal. "Besides, aren't I proving that having a dog-friendly hotel is just as easy as any other kind?"

"No."

"I'll clean my own room."

That got a laugh. "No, no. That's Cody's job. Okay. One more time." She held up a teasing finger. "I mean it, Adam March."

That "One more time" has become their little joke.

This time, it's a little different, as he's here on a weekend for the first time. The big open-house event at the Artists Collaborative is tomorrow, Saturday night, and he's to be there to make sure that the event runs smoothly. Personally, Adam hates these glad-hand schmoozing events, but they are a necessary evil in the world of fund-raising. Friend-raising is what they are. With the Christmas holidays fast approaching, and the end of the tax year, when philanthropic impulses surge, it's high time Mosley's crew got the attention of potential donors, and made them into new friends. Friends with deep pockets. Patrons of the arts all their own.

Because it's a weekend, Adam isn't surprised to see more cars in the parking lot of the hotel than he sees on a weekday. It makes him smile, thinking that maybe things aren't nearly so dire for Skye as he's thought. Seven cars are nosed up to the concrete steps. Lights on in eight of the fifteen rooms.

"Welcome back to the LakeView, Mr. March." Skye smiles at him over the light glowing from her desk lamp. "Where's the dog?" Does he imagine it, or does she look hopeful that he's left the dog behind?

"Outside sniffing around."

"Oh. Okay."

"You were hoping?"

"Maybe."

"You know what they say, 'Love me, love my dog.'"

"They don't really say that, do they?"

"Somebody did."

"But they never said 'Love me, accommodate my dog.'"

"Sure they did."

"Ever wonder who 'they' is?"

"Are?"

"Adam. Stop. Enough."

They conduct the business of checking in quickly, the dependable rhythm of it. It's a dance they know well, and in minutes she's handed him his key. As usual, room number 9. It really is beginning to feel like home.

# CHAPTER 9

*I know the drill. I've got the whole backseat to myself, on which I am comfortably cushioned with a folded quilt that Adam has thoughtfully provided. A bowl of water is in the foot well and a yummy shinbone awaits my attention as soon as Adam gives me his command:* Stay; watch the car, *my mandate to protect this space with my life. With fresh air coming in through a lowered window, the scents of the early cold-time evening waft in, as do the sounds of the humans going past the car, the women's heels click-clicking, the men's voices. The snap of a purse clasp, a little laughter. Each time the door to the building opens up, the same two voices speak greetings. Some of the words are meaningful to me:* Hello! Welcome!

*Pretty soon the parking lot quiets down and I nose my bone in between my clever paws. I get down to a meditative grinding of the hard white surface, prodding that luscious center of marrow with my tongue. Ah, heaven.*

*I may have dozed off. Which is what I do. However, my slumber is abruptly ended at the sound of one of my kind yowling. Although I do not have a sense of time,*

*I know that I have heard this particular yowling before. Here, meaning while I was in this car. As before, I feel as though I must answer in canine solidarity. I am here. Here. I cannot see you. I cannot smell you. But I am here.*

*It translates to a furious barking. I am rewarded with a change of tone in the yowling of my unseen compatriot. His vocalization becomes more of a greeting, telling me that he, too, is here.*

*For a long time in my life, I was placed in an adversarial position regarding members of my own kind. I have long since gotten over that and have become something of a good old boy, finding myself enjoying the company of other canines. Each one has a different story, a different reality, and I no longer size them up as to how hard it would be to take them down, but how companionable they might be on a long walk or resting by the fire. The dogs that came into my life when Gina came into our lives are no longer around. Two lanky greyhounds she called Jester and Lady. I liked them, although they were a bit on the lazy side, but that may have been due more to their advanced age than to their lack of interest in wrestling. They were devoted to each other, and when Jester went, Lady soon followed. I always admired their devotion, maybe even felt a little outside of it. Not having that kind of species relationship has allowed me to devote all of my affection toward my human. My Adam.*

*The piteous howling picks up again, counterpoint to the cacophony emanating from within that solid building into which my man, my Adam, has gone.*

The string trio is playing. Adam can't quite identify the tune, but he's guessing it's something from *Phantom of the Opera*. Or *Rent*. Or maybe *Cats*. He smiles at the tall woman who has just come into the Artists Collaborative.

He picks out the wealth markers of good jewelry and Louboutins, and catches Kieran's eye. Time to mingle-mingle. The artists have worked very hard to make sure that they look like everyone's idea of an artist, short of smocks and berets, of course. Kieran wears a loose black silk shirt tucked into impossibly tight black jeans. Adam guesses that he's not worried about his future procreative chances. A pair of Doc Martens finishes the look. As for Mosley Finch, he has turned out in what might pass as a suit, if the pieces bore any relation to one another. He is sporting a tie, a wide one, hand-painted with something that looks like either split-open pomegranates or vaginas. Adam can't decide.

The women are hardly better, and at least one of them is flaunting her artistic temperament by eschewing bathing. She's wearing a flowy gown that might have been a granny nightgown from the seventies, or a bedspread. Each of the invited guests to have wandered into her work space have quickly shown great interest in the art in the next space and moved away.

A tray of plastic flutes is offered to him and he plucks a glass of Cold Duck off it, thinking that if the AC couldn't plump for real champagne and glasses, maybe their Cold Duck idea will prompt the assembly to feel sorry enough for them that wallets will be opened. Stranger fund-raising techniques have worked.

"Hi, Mr. March," the server says.

"Cody. Mosley got you working here?"

"I'm, like, doing a favor for him."

"That's nice. What's he doing for you?"

The girl blushes a little. "He gives me lessons some-times."

"So, you want to be an artist?" He's chatting up the teenage help, but his eyes are on the gathering, assessing who needs a little attention, who should be cut from the herd like a fattened calf and introduced to one of the more presentable artists.

"Yeah. I guess."

"Giving up a Saturday night to serve bad wine to a bunch of old farts is a pretty big sacrifice for your art."

Cody doesn't answer, and Adam feels a little churlish for making the comment. The kid's only, what, fourteen?

Adam places his empty flute on her tray. "I'll give you a ride home at the end, okay?"

"Yeah. Okay. Thanks." She does that little head-ducking thing adolescent girls do and moves off.

Adam spots a new couple entering the AC. There are about twenty guests now, of the hundred or so invitations sent out. All things considered, this isn't a bad return. That any of the guests will open a checkbook is doubtful. *Cultivation* is the byword. At the end, Mosley and his crew will be disappointed because they are of the mind-set that what they do and what they want will be instantly appealing to the moneyed classes. Adam sighs, wishes that he'd tossed down a second Cold Duck, and makes his way over to the new couple. It's time to start calling the steps in this eleemosynary courtship dance.

*I can't focus on my shinbone. The yowling, punctuated now and again with yaps, is stressing me out. Whoever it is seems even more upset than the last time I heard him vocalizing. There is a far more desperate message than the basic I don't like what's going on. We all get upset with our human-forced situations. I, for one, don't much enjoy the rare times when I am separated from Adam. If I can hear him, say, for instance, he's in the next room, talking with a client who has dog-fear issues, then I bear it in silence. If, on the other hand, I am locked away for no apparent reason I can fathom, I might let out a protest. Now that I'm a certified therapy dog, that scenario is rarely visited anymore. But that's just token protest. What I'm hearing, what's tearing at me, is this dog's anguish. Something is terribly wrong. If only Adam would come out, I'd convince him to let me go check on things. Go see what's going on for myself.*

*And, miraculously, someone does approach the car. The sad girl. I get to my feet and give her my best greeting, paws pumping up and down, big grin on my face, tail whipping from side to side. I rrrr and rrrr. And, also miraculously, she opens the car door. She says something in tongue language that I interpret as meaning she's doing this because* Adam *something something said something about* peeing. *I really need only a couple of comprehensible words to suss out most of what humans mean. The rest is body language. And this girl, bundled up in a puffy coat, no gloves, her breath rising to meet the stars, clearly says she is happy to be outside with me.* Leash? *But, it's too late; I'm out of the car and bounding for a narrow footbridge over the river that will take me to the sound of the yowling dog. She calls after me, and I politely pause, indicating to her that she should follow me.*

This stupid dog. Mr. March never said he might run off. He'll be so pissed that she's accidently let his dog loose. He told her, when he asked her if she'd mind giving the dog a pee break, to make sure she put the leash on. But the leash was nowhere near the dog and he's not tall, but darned strong. He pushed right past her and bolted for the footbridge. Cody finds the leash on the floor of the back-seat and charges after the dog.

The river is negative space beneath her, nearly invisible in the darkness below. The light of the three-quarter moon grazes the water only at the place where it tumbles over the dam. The water is audible in the still night as it rushes downstream toward the city. The footbridge leads over it to the street where the mill houses are, once home to long-gone factory workers. Safe yet from discovery and renovation into high-end riverfront homes, they sit either empty or illegally occupied. When she goes to the AC from school, she sometimes sees kids over there. The walls are tagged with gang symbols. Once in a while, one of the doors is open a little and a banged-up car might be parked in the yard.

She really doesn't want to chase this dog over there, not at night. But she also doesn't want to have to tell her mother's most frequent guest that she's lost his beloved dog. "Chance! Come on back, boy. Come!"

The dog pauses halfway along the footbridge. He's got this excited look on his face, like this is some kind of game.

"Please, come. Atta boy!" The pleading has no effect. He woofs softly and then continues his bolt across the span. It's almost as if he's leading her, wanting her to chase him. "Get back here!" If pleading doesn't work, maybe yelling will. Cody gets to the end of the bridge and watches as the dog crosses the dark street and runs right up to one of the empty duplexes. They are ancient, the white asbestos siding darkened with a century of mold, the windows completely without glass, the door frames splintered. Everywhere she looks, she sees the archetype of a dangerous place. Cody kneels on the bridge. "Please come back, Chance. Please!" She claps her hands together. Whistles.

Now the dog is barking furiously. Wait. No, that's not Chance. Suddenly, Cody realizes that this whole time there has been the background noise of a barking dog. Chance isn't running from her; he's running to this other dog. Oh, jeez. Cody is pretty sure that any dog in that empty house is going to be bad news. Her fingers find her phone, tucked in the pocket of her coat. There's no car outside the house, and the door is wide open. She's pretty certain no one is there. Certain enough. Hey, maybe that dog is protecting that space, or maybe he's hurt. She's watched *Pit Bulls & Parolees* enough times to know that sometimes dogs get themselves into predicaments. At any rate, Mr. March's dog is making a beeline for that open door.

"Suck it up." Cody gets to her feet, double-checks on her phone, and heads toward the open door, the leash grasped in her left hand.

"What happened to Cody?" Mosley Finch shoves his black glasses upon his short nose. "She's supposed to be cleaning up."

"My fault. I asked her go and give my dog a quick walk." Adam hopes that Cody gets an equal amount of time spent on art lessons as this guy is giving her tasks. "Besides, I'm taking her home, so I don't think she'll have time to clean up."

Mosley shakes his head. "No need. I'll take her home. I hired her for the night."

Is it Adam's imagination, or is there something about Mosley's tone of voice a titch troublesome? "No. Really, it makes no sense to keep a kid out late when I'm heading right to her place." He thinks, but doesn't add, *And I don't think you "hired" her. You're into it for a couple of art lessons.*

"Don't you worry about it." Mosley's cell phone chirps. "Hey." Mosley hands the phone to Adam. "Speak of the devil."

"Cody?"

"Mr. March. It's Cody. I need you to come."

"What happened?" Adam feels the floor sink beneath his feet with the immediate fear that something has happened to his dog. "Is Chance all right?" He quickly adds, "Are you all right?"

"He ran off, and when I caught up with him . . . Just please come. Across the river. Now, please."

Adam forgets to hand Mosley back his phone in his haste to get to Cody and Chance.

# CHAPTER 10

Everything about this scene is horrifying. The human form slumped against the wall, legs spraddled out only in the way of the dead or unconscious. The stubby dog, barking and leaping against the restraint of a short leash bolted to the opposite wall. The stink. The moonlight spotlights the scene, spilling against the drug paraphernalia, putting it center stage in this sad drama. Adam looks to the body first, some old first-aid training causing him to put a finger against the pulse point in the boy's neck. He can't tell. He's too cold and too nervous to decide if what he's touching is living or dead. He grabs the limp hand, fumbles to find the place where the pulse should be. The boy, for he can't be much older than Cody, is still as death, but his eyes are closed, which gives Adam a little hope that maybe he's just unconscious. He is the cause of the stink; the vomit cakes his mouth, and his chest is covered in it.

"Call nine one one."

"I did."

"Good girl." Adam's knees creak as he gets to his feet.

The dog has stopped barking, is making only a slight whimpering sound; he is entirely focused on them, his boxy head lowered, his ears back. His whole posture is stiff, and he is studying them with narrowed eyes.

A flicker of blue lights strobe into the small room. In a moment, a uniformed cop comes through the open door and into the room. The dog immediately growls, leaps against his chain. The police officer steps back, puts his hand on his weapon, sees that the dog is restrained, and bends to the boy, who's still lying against the wall.

Chance leaves Adam's side. Stalks toward the growling dog.

It's a perfect setup for a massive dogfight, a restrained and territory-guarding dog, one that is frightened, certainly. Another dog, a stranger, coming into that territory. Adam gives the command to back off: "Chance, leave it."

But Chance has other ideas and goes right up to the other dog; ears at neutral, tail making a slow sweep, he play bows. The other dog sniffs the offered cheek, makes his own show of submission. Sits. Does Chance look perhaps a little smug?

"Oh. All right. Good boy. Boys."

Minutes later, medical help arrives, and Adam and Cody are shouldered out of the way. Adam really hopes that this kid isn't dead. What a horrific thing for Cody to have discovered. No girl her age should be finding bodies. "Cody, why don't you and Chance head back to the AC."

She doesn't answer; she's fixed on the EMTs working with the boy. He's not dead, and Adam pats Cody on the shoulder. "You probably saved this kid's life, you know."

"It was Chance. The dog, I mean, not luck. He heard the other dog barking and knew what was going on."

"He's a clever boy, yes."

"What about the other dog? What's going to happen to him?"

"I don't know, Cody." This isn't actually true, because Adam does know what so often happens to dogs like these, not a breed, per se, but a type, pit bull. Vilified. This one is a true "red nose," his nose and his coat color almost the same shade of reddish brown. And Adam suddenly recalls seeing this dog and this boy before, at the crosswalk. "I won't let anything happen to him. I promise you that."

"You folks want to wait outside?" The police officer shoos them away from the scene.

"Sure. Do you need us anymore, or can we go? I need to get this girl home."

"I'll need a statement, but if you're in the area, you can just stop by the station tomorrow."

"Of course." Adam will spend the time calling his contacts in the pit bull rescue community. Now for the hard part. "With your permission, we'll take that dog."

"I don't think so. He'll be impounded, sir."

"He's not a useful witness. And hardly germane to the situation."

At that moment, the EMTs hike the gurney to its wheels and roll the boy out of the house. The dog sets up a pitiful wailing, balancing himself against the short chain so that his forepaws paddle in the air.

The officer touches his weapon again.

"He's upset. He's not being aggressive."

The officer looks at Chance, who has moved back to Adam's side. "That one yours?"

"Yes."

"You look too well dressed to be in a dogfight ring, but I have to ask. . . ."

Adam shakes his head, smiles. "No. Quite the opposite. I'm a rescuer." He's never defined himself that way before, and it feels kind of nice. "I work with rescues. For dogs like him."

"I'll put in a call to our ACO and he'll pick the dog up."

Cody is steps away from the frantic dog. "Mr. March, we can't leave the dog here. What if the animal-control guy doesn't show up till morning? It's freezing out."

Adam is face-to-face with the police officer. "I can't stay and I don't think you will. Let me take him for now and the ACO can pick him up from me. Or I'll drop him off at the shelter." Adam knows all too well what can happen to a dog in a shelter without an advocate, and he has no intention of making good on his promise. "Look, Officer, I'll take responsibility for the dog."

Adam can see the debate raging behind the officer's eyes, his better nature at war with his sense of protocol. "Give me a minute." He steps out of the building, presumably to call in to his commanding officer.

In the minute the officer is away, Adam steps slowly toward the dog, admonishing Cody to keep away. The dog may not look as fierce as he did when they came in, but he might snap out of panic at the touch of a stranger.

Chance is all excited, doing his happy dance, as if to say, *Look what I found!*

"Hey, fella. We're your friends." Adam takes a knee, puts out a hand. "You're okay. You're okay." Repeats those words over and over until the dog sits, and, in a dumb show of capitulation, extends a paw. Adam reaches back for the leash, which is still in Cody's hand. She gives it to him. He clips it to the dog's choke-chain collar, unfastens the clip to the chain bolted in the wall, gets to his feet. As Adam expected he would, the dog plunges toward the open door. It takes all of his strength to hold the frantic creature back. The short, compact dog is extremely strong, and Adam feels a kinship with the old-time whalers on their Nantucket sleigh rides. He plants his heels against the tug and the dog complies. He wriggles into a submissive posture, throws himself against Adam's legs, but all of his attention is pointed toward the ambulance.

*I was so excited when Adam showed up in that house. Look what I found, I said over and over. Look what I found! Adam is a smart guy; he quickly surmised the situation and took charge. I like that about him: Whenever there's a problem, he finds a solution. Whether it's to scratch the itchy spot on my back at just the right time, or bring a sad and confused dog into our lives, he's the guy you want.*

*Adam shares more words with the other man, the one who stands stiff with authority, and I can hear the tension winding up in his voice, so I do what I have been trained to do, what I love to do, and bop him in the side of his leg with my head: Hey, slow it down, bud. Adam's hand finds my ears and I absorb the anger out of him into my body. I lick his fingers. His tone sweetens, and in the next moment, we and the dog are free to go.*

*I don't mind sharing the backseat with my new friend. He's a little skeptical about getting in, but I show him how. My shinbone is on the seat, and I will admit that my being a good host does not extend to giving away this special treat, so I quickly shove it onto the floor, out of his reach. He shrugs, as if he'd no interest in it, and neatly packages himself into a curl. He has put his trust in us. In our good intentions. He is immediately asleep. I curl up, too, in such a way that our backs, of an equal length, touch.*

Mosley is standing in her way as Cody dashes into the building. His glasses are off and his eyes are at half-mast. She can smell the weed on him.

He doesn't let her pass. "What's going on?"

"Mr. March's dog found a guy OD'd in one of those houses across the river."

"Jesus. OD'd? Bad." Mosley gives her a droopy smile. "So, where's my phone?" Quick as anything, he has her forearm in his hand. "Go get it back from him."

"I just have to pee, please."

"And you didn't help clean up." He has this weird expression on his face, like he's saying one thing and meaning another. "Bad girl. You're not living up to our deal."

"I gotta go. Really. Please." Cody yanks her arm back, runs for the stairs.

In the rest room, she locks the stall door and sits, the relief in the rush of urine bringing tears to her eyes. She'd nearly wet her pants out there. She'd been anticipating that someone might challenge her as she chased the dog into the house, some creepy denizen, but she'd never expected to find what she did. In the first second, she didn't realize what the dark shape against the wall was, and then in a stomach-sickening lurch, it resolved into human form and she did.

At least, this time, it wasn't someone she knew. This time, the collapsed doll of a human being might survive. Not like her father.

Cody lingers in the rest room long enough that she's pretty sure Mosley will have wandered away. She hears Mr. March's voice calling her; he's probably wondering what the heck happened to her.

"I'm coming."

Cody pulls herself together, washes her hands, then washes them again. She's okay now. She zips up her coat and goes up the iron stairs at a trot.

# CHAPTER 11

We are sitting in the hotel's reception area and I am listening to Adam as he makes the case for letting him keep this monstrous-looking dog in his room along with his other monstrous-looking dog. He's explaining how this came about, the whys and wherefores. But what I can't quite wrap my mind around is how Cody is involved in this urban tragedy. Why was Cody there? Cody has disappeared into the cabin, a Drake's coffee cake from the breakfast-area cupboard in her hand, not a single word out of her mouth. Cody, who had said that she was baby-sitting tonight. For a teacher. She didn't need a ride either way.

I throw up a hand. "Adam, please, stop. Stop."

He pauses in his narrative long enough to let me get a word in edgewise.

"Tell me again why my daughter was there? In a crack house? With your dog?"

"I asked her to let him out of the car for a quick break."

"Where were you? Why were you—"

"In the building at the fund-raiser."

Okay, this is going to be Twenty Questions. "The fund-raiser, the one you're here for?"

"Yes. At the Artists Collaborative."

"Cody was baby-sitting tonight."

The look on his face is enough to let me know that, once again, my daughter has pulled the wool over my eyes.

"Oh, Skye. She hasn't told you, has she?"

"I guess not. Why don't you."

"Don't you think she should tell you?"

"Adam, do you really think she'll come clean with me? You once told me you had a few years of trouble with your daughter. What would you have expected from her?"

"Another lie. Probably. But I shouldn't interfere."

"You're in the middle now."

"I'm on the sidelines, but okay. All I know is that it seems pretty harmless, which makes me wonder why she's being so, well, adolescent about it. She's taking art lessons in exchange for doing errands at the Artists Collaborative. She was there tonight, passing hors d'oeuvres."

"This—art lessons—this is what she's keeping from me?" I am flummoxed, incredulous.

"I know. Kids." He holds up his hands in a classic mime of helplessness.

I can't help it, I laugh, but the laugh skims the border between amusement and frustration. "Why would she think I'd object to that?"

"Sometimes I think they rebel out of habit."

"Look, I can't throw you out tonight, so keep the dog. I have to go talk to Cody."

"Skye, maybe this is me putting my oar in, but I think that maybe you should talk about the incident before you mention the other business. She was pretty shaken up, although she was a trouper, and thought to call nine one one even before she called me."

I can hear the subtext: A child Cody's age shouldn't witness such things. And he's right. "Is the boy going to be all right?"

"I don't know. He was pretty far gone, but they had that Narcan with them, so he was making noise as they wheeled him away."

"She's going to pretend nothing happened."

"But it did."

With the two monstrous dogs following him at his heels, shoulder-to-shoulder in some kind of canine solidarity, Adam walks down the length of the porch to his door. He pauses, turns to give me a little nod, that notion of parental solidarity. I close my eyes, sigh, then lock the office door. As I approach our cabin behind the building, I can hear music blasting, Cody's phone plugged into the dock, the volume spiked loud enough to bomb through the storm windows and into the night, Florence and the Machine. What kind of a fourteen-year-old is this child? Where's the Taylor Swift? The One Direction? I trot to the door, mindful of my guests' comfort. Cody has the volume up loud enough to crack glass. The last thing I need is to have complaints from my guests. It's bad enough that I've got that damned dog here, and I live in fear of some paying customer getting knocked down or bitten, or offended by it. And, Lord help me, now there are two of them. What kind of patsy am I?

Cody sits in her room, scratching the outline of a new drawing on her sketch pad, nodding her head in time with the music blaring out of the Bose speakers attached to the wall. Mom will be in here in a minute, raging about the noise, disturbing the guests, blah, blah, blah. So predictable. Yup. There she is. Comfortingly predictable.

The music stops.

"Why didn't you tell me that you're taking art lessons?

Why in God's name wouldn't you mention something like that?" Skye stands in the bedroom doorway, arms folded across her chest.

"I don't know. Didn't think you'd care."

"Care?"

"It's no big deal."

"However, hitchhiking to North Adams, that, my darling daughter, is a big deal."

"I take the school bus."

"No, you don't. The bus doesn't go that far."

How would her mother know the school bus routes that well?

"Close enough. I walk from the last stop."

"I'll drive you from now on."

"Fine."

"So, what happened tonight?" It's like her mother has deflated, the angry mom becoming the concerned mom. It's so typical: Skye starts with righteousness and then gets all mommylike.

"Some kid overdosed on something. That dog of Mr. March's found him."

"Sounds like you found him."

"I was just trying to get the stupid dog back." The boy, on his back, the stench of vomit. Her own weak-kneed reaction at recognizing that she'd been incredibly stupid to go into that place.

Being in a place she had no business being in. The sight of her father dropping to the sidewalk. She wakes in the middle of the night with the image in her mind. She dreams of it.

"Do you want to talk about it?" Her mother always says this. It's her maternal default position.

"Not really. What's there to talk about?"

"How you feel about finding the addict."

Cody continues with her sketch. It's of a house, boarded up. "That's kind of harsh, isn't it, calling a kid an addict?"

Skye makes a little noise, that exasperated snuff she does when Cody's called her empathy into question. "So, he was really a kid, a boy?"

"Guess so." She really didn't get that close. But, yeah, young. "Maybe seventeen, eighteen."

"Cody, I'm not happy about your lying to me. But it's a good thing you were there. You probably saved his life."

"No biggie. The dog did all the work." Cody adds some shading, giving the sketched house an ominous darkness. In her sketch, in the one window she's drawn that's not boarded up, a face emerges. Square-jawed. No eyes.

As her mother closes the door behind her, Cody flops onto her pillow. She fights the tears that burn behind her squeezed-shut lids. It was so hard not to take that gentle approval, to push it away, afraid, as always, that the moment she lets her mother back in, she'll lose her.

# CHAPTER 12

*I love hanging out with this guy. He's one of those laid-back fellas that love to just laze around, maybe have a session with the chew toys, then catch a few z's. He is shy enough that, so far, he takes my every suggestion without trying to modify the plan. For instance, if I say it's time for a pee break, he's right there, following me, respectfully covering my spots. He doesn't forge out ahead, but waits for me to decide which quadrant of the backyard we should investigate first. I'm a good-enough host that I invite him to share my beds. The one in the living room is large enough for both of us to lie back-to-back, and it's nice to have the comfort of a warm spine snuggled up to mine. The one in the bedroom is a little tighter, and after a bit I toss him out. He goes willingly, finding another bed to flop into. I don't mind sharing Adam, either. Mostly because I know that I'm the chief dog. I'm the guy who accompanies him everywhere he goes, and my pal here is second chair. He's good for an Adam sandwich, me on one side, him on the other of our man while he stares at that noisy, flickering space on the wall. Adam sometimes complains that we take up all the space, but he's just joking.*

*My friend has no permanent name, so he's called by a number of things: Buddy, Pal, Bub. I get a little confused sometimes because I've been called all of those endearments at one time or another, although Adam maintains Bud exclusively for me. A distinction, I know, but one that is important to me. I want to always be his Bud. We've seen a lot together. My new friend respects that, and that's why he's such a joy. This guy, Buddy-Pal-Bub, has breached my natural reserve. It's like we were once littermates, now reunited. And, have I mentioned that he's got this great sense of humor? Really funny guy. Loves the fake crush-your-paw-in-my-mouth trick. Hilarious with a stolen towel. Oh my. We do have fun!*

The snow is forecast to begin in the afternoon, so school is dismissed early. It's expected to be a considerable storm, as it's already dumped a foot and a half in New York State and is grinding its way toward them at a slow, moisture-gathering pace. Cody, for once in concert with her otherwise-alienated fellows, is overjoyed and planning to get herself to North Adams before her mother finds out they've been dismissed. She's promised to help out with the first Open Studio at the AC, and she doesn't want her mother getting in the way of that.

The school bus will go right past the LakeView today without stopping to drop off the lone student living there. She'll be on the Route 3 bus, get off at the last stop, and then hike in the last two miles. She just knows that she'll beat the storm, at least as far as the AC. She'll get out of there before it gets really bad—even she doesn't want to be on the road at that hairpin turn in a snowstorm. She'll ask Mosley to drive her home in his Subaru, which she thinks has four-wheel drive. Skye hasn't met Mosley yet, mostly because Cody won't let her into the AC when she drops her off, and Cody always makes sure that she's standing outside when Skye comes to pick her up after her lessons. Air quote around that word: *lessons.* Sometimes the modeling takes up all the available time Mosley can give her.

Cody slips her sketchbook into her backpack, makes sure that she's got her charcoals. Mosley has moved her away from pencil. She feels like she's making progress. He's using charcoal to sketch her, too. He didn't have any chores for her on Saturday, instead setting her up in one of the little-used rooms in the basement of the building, down the hall from the bathrooms. He had a chair and a table, and first he had her sitting in the chair. Prim. Proper. Knees together like a Victorian. Then he started experimenting with her position; that's what he called it, "experimenting." Trying to find the inner Cody. "Show me your real self. Don't be a prop." He put a hand width between her jean-clad knees. Taking her glasses off, he tipped her head to the side, making her hold that position until she thought she'd never be able to straighten her neck again. He draped a handful of her hair across her left eye, calling it "à la Veronica Lake." Cody had no idea what that meant, but she didn't ask. Mosley prefers her to be quiet. She could hear the sounds of feet upstairs, the Saturday artists, those with full-time jobs who never came to the AC on weekdays, the sound of tables being moved, chairs scraping the floor. Because she wasn't wearing her glasses, Mosley blurred into a blob of dark colors, only his pale white arms showing against the dark backdrop of the wall.

It's started to snow by the time she gets off the bus. Usually, it's only the two girls who get off here, discounting the boy who follows them at a distance of five paces, and who, she happens to have finally figured out, is little brother to one of them, an eighth grader. Some days they appear not to notice her, but other afternoons they take great delight in making sure she knows that they are paying attention. Today, one of them turns around as Cody descends the bus steps.

"What are you doing?"

"How's that any of your business?"

"You spying on us?"

"Yeah. Right. Like you're interesting."

"Then why are you following us?"

Cody shifts her backpack up to her shoulders. "You wish."

"You gay or something?"

"That's original."

"You have a boy's name."

"And you don't?"

"Taylor is a girl's name. You know, like Taylor Swift."

"Right." Cody has no interest in pursuing the subject of naming conventions in the twenty-first century. Everybody's name is weird. "Gotta go."

"Not so fast." The other girl, Tyler, steps up to her. The bus has gone, leaving a black track against the new-fallen snow. It's begun to snow in earnest and Cody wants to get walking before it's too slippery. "So, you and Smelly Mellie are like BFFs now, right?"

"No." Cody and Black Molly may sit at the same lunch table on occasion, but neither one speaks. Their conversations are held elsewhere.

"Yeah you are. So, she's the bull dyke, you must be the fem."

Cody is lost. These girls are nuts.

"You know." She makes a kissy noise.

Cody actually laughs out loud. "That is so bent."

"Maybe you are, too. Bent, I mean."

Cody can see the younger brother out of the corner of

her eye. He looks uncomfortable, but not enough to put a stop to his sister, whichever one she is. He sees her looking at him and skulks off down a driveway. The two girls take one step closer to Cody. She's as tall as the other girls, but they look bigger, bulked up partly by the puffy down coats they wear, and partly because they stand on legs honed by miles of field hockey or soccer practices.

"I'm just going to ignore that." Cody does a quick about-face and strides off down the road. Not unexpectedly, she gets clocked with two snowballs. It hurts enough that she's pretty sure one of them has a rock in it. The blow brings tears to her eyes, but she doesn't turn around, just doggedly continues down the road toward town. Another snowball hits her shoulder. She keeps walking. Then another rock-filled snowball gets her right between the shoulders and she starts to run. She hates that she's crying. She hates that she's already trying to figure out how to avoid being seen with Black Molly.

Cody scrambles to keep her balance as the roadside steepens. These are the wrong boots for this weather. She's concentrating so hard on getting away as fast as she can without falling that she's oblivious to the slowing down of a car, its quiet engine inaudible against the sound of her own crying. When the nose of a black car draws parallel to her, she jumps to the side of the road, heart pounding against the idea that this is *his* black car. That her father's killer has found her.

"Cody?"

The hot tears that have gone from anger to fear don't stop when she sees that it's only Mr. March with his two dogs, and now they are infused with a sick relief. The relief squares itself against the earlier anger, and what Cody wants at this moment is to sic those two square-mouthed dogs sitting in the backseat on those girls. Show them she's not without friends. Watch those dogs rip those puffy coats to shreds, the fake down floating into the air to mix with the snowflakes.

"Hop in."

Cody takes off her glasses and wipes her eyes with the edge of her sleeve, hoping that Mr. March won't detect that she's been crying. But he's a smart guy, notices right away the melting snow on her back.

"That didn't look like playful fun."

"It wasn't."

"You want me to go back and say something?"

Cody rubs the moisture off her glasses, puts them back on. "No."

"Are you angry with them?"

"Yes."

"Will petting one of these dogs help?"

Cody feels a little smile tweak the corner of her mouth. "Maybe."

"Okay. Chance, head's up."

Chance pops his blocky head between their seats and gives Cody a smooch.

"Guaranteed to brighten your day."

"So, are you taking the dog back to his owner?"

"Oh, Cody. No. That's not an option."

It's really not an option. In Adam's opinion, this dog's been fought. That means, if he's returned to his crack-addict owner, he'll most likely be tossed into the ring again. He guesses that the boy funds his recreational habit with the dog. Adam isn't unfamiliar with the phenomenon. Poor dog. As Adam likes to think, *Not on my watch.* He should try to explain it to Cody, who has gone all sullen on him, keeping her face to the window, ignoring Chance's repeated efforts to jolly her, but he doesn't have the strength.

The snow is that fine, sizzling kind, full of water and

bound to become heavy. Adam is mentally kicking himself for having driven out here, for being foolish enough to believe that the snow would hold off until after the event and he can make it back to Boston tonight. He should just drop Cody off and turn around. Surely he won't be welcome at the LakeView with two dogs in tow. Skye isn't that hard up. Which is too bad, as he would love nothing more than to hang out here for a couple more days. His next-door neighbor, Beth, has been showing up at his place with a bottle of wine, just happening to want to try a new variety, shyly suggesting that she doesn't want to drink alone. She has become a pest.

"Are you staying with us tonight?"

"I wasn't planning on it. I was hoping to get home." He bumps up the tempo of the intermittent wiper speed. "Besides, I don't think your mother would allow two dogs again. She was kind to let me stay with both the first time, but I don't want to push my luck."

"Go ahead and push. She's not about to turn away a customer." Cody drags a finger along the breath mark she's made on the inside of the window. "A good customer."

"Thank you."

He at least had the foresight to call Mosley to make sure that he hadn't actually canceled the Open Studio. He'd called just before leaving the house, obviously waking Mosley from a deep sleep. The artist had taken a moment to come to himself, then said, "Oh, yeah." He coughed, a hacker's cough, "Yeah. Right. No. We don't cancel. People out here don't hyperventilate about a little snow."

That was the moment Adam should have just said, Fine, but I'll be staying home. But there is something in his makeup that always seems to have him challenging the weather, as if he's got some Superman complex. Here he is, acting like he doesn't care about personal safety for the sake of a bunch of artists. It's not like they're doing humanitarian aid. Adam pulls into the parking lot, which is devoid of cars except for the blue Subaru wagon that Mosley drives and an old-school black Volvo with a mosaic of bumper stickers holding it together—Kieran's car. Someone has scraped the two inches of snow off the walkway, but the lot is smooth with the heavy, wet stuff. Adam's L.L. Bean boots sink to the laces as he gets out of the car. He pops the back door open and lets the dogs out. He's got a leash on the foster dog; he's not about to trust him with canine good behavior. There's nothing to say that he won't bolt for that house the minute he's back in his old neighborhood. In fact, the dog does pause, pointing his red nose across the river, his tail at the alert, his ears perked forward.

"Uh-uh. You're with me now, Buddy."

"Is that his name?"

"Probably not. It's probably something more aggressive, like Butch or Apollo."

"I like Apollo. That's a good name. Butch is kind of, well, you know. It doesn't mean what it used to in your day." A shadow crosses her face. "It means a lesbian. A tough one." She takes the leash out of Adam's hand. "Shouldn't we try to find him, the boy?"

"I think that we should leave well enough alone."

"But we have his dog." Cody is getting worked up; she's stepped in front of him. The wet flakes dot her big glasses, obscuring her eyes.

"Cody, look, I've done a lot of this. These guys are bad with dogs. They aren't pets. They—"

"I know. I'm not stupid. I'm just saying, if someone took Chance from you because you were, like, incapacitated, wouldn't you die to know where he was?"

"I *have* been in that position." All too clearly Adam

remembers thinking that he would never see his dog again, the dog that had wormed his bulky heart into Adam's transgressive life. Yeah, sure, he remembers how it feels to be bereft. But this is different. "He might be in jail, you know."

"But what if he's not? We should ask."

"Who?"

"I don't know. His homeys?"

Adam can see how Skye is up against it with this kid. "Cody, promise me that you won't do that?"

"I can't promise. If I see some kids, I'm going to ask. Besides, around here, they're just street kids."

"With bad habits. What if they mugged you?"

"Mr. March. I lived in Holyoke. I think I know the difference between a gangbanger and a homey."

"You've lost me." Adam holds the door open. "After you."

The school bus rumbles by, the snow making it look like a giant orange pointillist painting. I've been studying up on painting styles, so I'm pretty proud of myself for thinking of the word *pointillist*. Art is fun. Something that I certainly missed out on. So lost in thought am I that it takes me a couple of minutes to realize that Cody hasn't gotten off the bus.

Cody, as usual, isn't answering her phone, but I have another arrow in my quiver and I dial the landline number for the Artists Collaborative. It's answered on the second ring by Cody, who sounds almost grown-up as she says, "Artists Collaborative, how may I help you?"

"You can help me by letting me know where you are."

A beat goes by. "Well, you found me. So, you know where I am."

"Lucky guess, and you know that I mean *before* you

disappear." I will myself to moderate my annoyance. It never does either of us any good to get Cody worked up. "How did you get there?"

"I walked. Well, actually, Mr. March saw me and gave me a ride in."

"Adam? Oh. I don't have him down—"

"He's not staying, he says. Day trip."

I push the curtain back from the picture window and stare out at the snow. "Well, you tell him he's welcome to stay. It's pretty nasty out there." The serpentine curves and descents of Route 2 can be a challenge even for locals in weather like this. I've already got a guest who's decided to stay put one more night. Snow is good business on a variety of levels. "I'm heading down to get you, Cody. No argument."

"No, don't. Mosley said he's going to take me home. You don't have to worry."

"Then he'd better get a start. I don't want you on the road."

"It's no big deal. The roads are plowed."

"Put him on."

"He's not available."

I can hear the escalating adolescent annoyance in my daughter's voice. Mom's being a stupid, dumb beeatch.

"I'm on my way."

Cody is struggling to maintain a cool maturity even as her voice pitches into an adolescent whine. "No. Please. We have work to do. It's not that bad out. You're overreacting."

"I'm sure that Mosley will understand." And if he doesn't, that's the end of this arrangement. Overreacting. Cody has never experienced the heart-in-mouth sensation of a sideways skid. I'm not about to put her safety into the hands of an adult I've never even met. One with questionable decision-making skills if he thinks it's fine to keep a fourteen-year-old girl working during a snowstorm that had the schools closing early.

The house phone rings. "Look, I've got to answer that. You tell Mosley I'll be there in twenty."

The sound of silence is supposed to inform me of how deeply aggrieved Cody is with me.

"LakeView, how may I help you?" I shudder at how exactly I mimic my daughter's greeting.

# CHAPTER 13

Despite Mosley's assertions that folks in the Berkshires don't care about a little snow, no one has shown up at the Wednesday Open Studio. Even the usual artists are missing. Kieran alone has been hard at work today on his installation. The array of carrots and celery sticks, puddled Brie, and soldiered crackers have been invaded only by the four of them, Mosley, Kieran, Adam, and the girl, who has been slipping brie and crackers to the dogs. Adam checks his watch. The only sound in the building besides Kieran's blowtorch is the sizzle of sleet banging against the enormous factory windows. A scrim of snow is stuck to them, slowly eating up the available light. It's time to go.

"Cody, do you want a ride home? I'm leaving in a minute and I can swing by the hotel and drop you off."

"I think Mosley wants me to stay." She's got a box of cling wrap in her hands. "And clean up."

Mosley has been standing by the factory door, his hangdog gaze on the nearly empty parking lot. At his name, he turns back toward Adam and Cody. "Yeah. I'll take her home."

Cody looks vindicated and, frankly, Adam is relieved. If he's going to get home in this weather, a side trip isn't going to make it any easier.

"Okay, then." Adam snaps his fingers and the dogs bound over to him. The foster dog wiggles, his head bobbing up and down so much, it's hard to find the clip on his collar. Adam swears that Chance rolls his eyes at this performance. He's certainly going to make someone a nice pet, if only he can get the dog into a proper rescue.

The temperature has dropped and the snow has been transformed from genuine flakes into tiny stinging ice needles that are blown into Adam's face as he emerges from the building. He ducks, grabbing his scarf to protect his face. The snow isn't much deeper, but the cold has turned the early wet stuff into a treacherous ice field beneath the new layer. He slips, starts to go down, and lets go of the leash to catch himself before face-planting in the snow. Chance remains by his side, licking Adam's cheek in commiseration, but the other dog takes advantage of the situation and is across the footbridge in a flash, heading right for the crack house.

"Get back here you!" Adam knows that shouting at a dog is a recipe for failure, but impulse rules over sense. "Jeez. Chance. Go get him." Adam has no reason to believe that Chance can accomplish a Lassie-quality task, but he says it anyway. "Go on. Go get him."

*I was embarrassed, as much as a dog can be embarrassed on behalf of another. The ingrate, I thought. He should be here beside Adam, as I am. I didn't quite understand Adam's command, but the two words I did understand,* go *and* get, *were enough to have me racing after my companion, with the idea—well, with no idea at all what I was expected to do. I caught up with him at the closed door of the place where we had taken him into our pack. He was putting on quite a show, I must say, what with the yapping and scratching against the door, the wild-eyed, plaintive yammering. Stop! I barked at him. Enough! I finally head-butted him to get him out of his fixed attack on the door. The snow around the perimeter was undisturbed except by us. There was no one inside or outside that place, only the rats that burrowed into the interior walls, revealed only by their minuscule squeaks and the sound of their claws scrabbling against the plaster and horsehair. It made me crave to bite their little heads off.*

*At heart, I understood what my friend was doing. This was the last place he'd seen his person; therefore, the pull to return to it was completely understandable to me. I have been separated from Adam—and returned to an old and evil use. All I could think of when that happened was getting back to him, to our life together. Fortunately for me, Adam chose my life over my death and we were never separated again. In this case, I wasn't sure if my friend's person was redeemable. He resembled more closely the youths who had misused me almost to death. I've known this phenomenon before, the sick attachment of a dog for a bad human, loyal in spite of that human's cruelty. It is one of the flaws of our species, our bad judgment.*

*I could hear Adam's voice stretched over the muffling sound of the wind, ordering us to return. The snow was obscuring him from us; even his scent was pushed away by the strengthening wind. But I knew he was there and calling. If I were deaf and nose-blind, I would know that he would stand there in the storm, wanting me by him. Adam and I have spent a great many hours establishing two things. One, that I obey him. And, two, that he expects and rewards obedience. So I snapped at the foster dog: Now!*

*The truth is, I no longer cared if the foster dog followed me. He clearly had his own desires, desires that opposed my own. I left him there, sad to see him go, but unwilling to jeopardize my covenant with my person.*

Adam leaves the Jetta running while he traipses across the footbridge to the crack house. Chance had come back, and if a dog could talk, he was pretty voluble about the other dog's stubborn failure to return. Adam hopes to sweet-talk the dog back into his possession, or, failing that, snatch the leash still attached to his collar. The dog can't get into the sealed building, so he most likely will be standing outside, incapable of figuring out what to do on his own.

But the dog isn't there. The footprints pressed into the snow lead around to the back of the house, and vanish as the wind gusts fill them. Chance sniffs around but, lacking a tracking dog's initiative, soon tires of the game and makes it clear he wants to get back into the warm car. Adam's knee hurts from his fall, and the sheer unpleasantness of being out in this storm wars with his conscience regarding the dog. The light, already muted by the storm, is fading fast and he has no idea where to begin to look for the wayward animal. "Well, Chance, this is a fine mess."

Chance shakes himself and pointedly aims his nose in the direction of the car.

"I guess we regroup and hope for the best." He can't go home now. Adam simply can't leave the dog loose like this, up against the weather and the evil things that can befall a dog like him.

Adam's first call is to the animal-control officer in the area, whose phone immediately goes to a full voice-mail box. In his experience, the local police don't respond well to 911 calls about missing dogs, so Adam lets go of that idea.

His second call is to Skye. "Skye. It's Adam. I'm at the AC and I'm throwing myself on your mercy."

"Oh. Good. Look, do you mind bringing Cody back with you? I told her I was coming, but something came up."

"I offered. She wouldn't budge, and Mosley says he'll drop her off."

"I'd rather you did."

"Does that mean you'll put me up?"

"Yes. And your dog, too." She laughs. "Or do you still have two?"

"Only one at the moment. The other dog bolted just now and I can't find him." The wipers can hardly keep up with the snow, and the windshield is outlined in a scalloped fringe of it. Adam walks around, knocking the snow off the roof and the back of the car, while Chance is burrowed into his backseat bed, enjoying the blast of warmth from the jacked-up heater. "Look, I'm going to take a quick drive around to look for that dog before I head to the hotel, so don't be worried if we're not there soon."

"Are you sure that's a good idea?"

"Probably not, but I have to try."

Adam leaves the car running with Chance in it. He calls and whistles again, claps his hands together, wishing desperately that he'd given the dog a name and stuck to it. No answer. "Oh, Gina, I've really screwed it up." It's not the first time he's spoken to her out loud, as if she's in the next seat, or the next room. "Help me get him back." Not praying, exactly. But there is a faith to his desire that his wife will hear him and provide some small miracle to prove to him that she's still there in some way.

He listens, straining his human ears to hear the sound of a dog. Nothing.

Inside the AC, there's no sign of Cody or Mosley. Kieran is wiping down his tools, shrugs when Adam asks where they are.

"I don't know. Downstairs, maybe?" He carefully sets his welding mask over a stand, giving the thing a sculptural pose. "Mose has a studio down there. Past the restrooms."

The hallway is narrow and reminds Adam of the basement of the parochial school he attended while with the last foster family of his youth. Low ceiling, painted concrete walls, cracked linoleum tiles on the floor, and lighted only by the inadequate illumination of the flickering overhead fluorescent fixtures, none of which has the full complement of tubes. He can picture the factory workers here, hanging their jackets in these metal lockers, punching time cards in the Simplex punch clock still affixed to the wall. The notice boards are filled now with outdated local information—Tomato Fest, Blue Grass Fest—but, back in the day, would likely have notified workers of union meetings or layoffs. Layoffs, strikes. A loss of a job meant a loss of a home, those ramshackle duplexes across the river standing testament to the hold a company had on its people.

Adam makes his way down the corridor, past the restrooms, the locker room, the break room. His lug-soled boots squeak against the tiles, and he's aware that he's leaving a trail of wet footprints as he works his way through the labyrinth of pipes and locked closet doors stenciled with arcane abbreviations—*Mech Room, Furn Room*—toward a spill of light at the end of the hall.

"Just lift your chin a little. No, a little to the left." Mosley takes his finger and lifts her chin with it. Steps back to assess his work, steps up and touches the drape he's had her put on toga-fashion. He fixes some flaw in the way the folds cover her shoulder. It's an accident, for sure, how the back of his hand, his knuckles, lightly graze her breast under the sheet. Of course he didn't mean to; after all, her flat little boob barely humps up the material. How's he supposed to know where it is? Still, the accidental touch sends a flush of embarrassment to her already-flushed cheeks. He's got the lamps on her and they feel like a hot summer day. Beyond the light, Mosley sits tailor-fashion on top of an old metal desk, his sketchbook in his lap. "Beautiful. Stay just like that."

"Can I see it when you're done?"

"No. This is just a sketch, a study. You know, like what we've been working on. You have to make preliminary sketches before committing an idea to a permanent medium."

"So, why can't you show it to me?"

Mosley doesn't answer, and the only sound in the room is the scritch-scritch of his charcoal against the paper. He bends over his work, his pretty mouth screwed up into a study of artistic concentration. Cody begins to relax into the pose and he snaps, "Sit up!"

A slight breeze touches her bare back, cooler air pushed into the small room by a cold, wet Adam March.

# CHAPTER 14

A wash of headlights blares through the picture window of the LakeView Hotel office. I can finally unclench my knotted fingers, relax my jaw from the tension. I have been self-flagellating with thoughts of my parental failures, administering the mental cat-o'-nine-tails in an hour of agitated worry, pretty much certain that bad judgment on my part has ended in tragedy. I should have gone to collect Cody myself, even though I'm the first one to admit that my winter driving skills are less than optimal. I should have insisted—an hour and a half ago!—that I pick up Cody from that stupid art studio and have her home here safe, if angry. It would be a small price to pay, Cody's outrage versus this certainty of disaster. Besides that, what kind of a mother lets a near stranger take responsibility for her only child? Have I fallen into the assumption that a man is a better, safer driver in a snowstorm, just because he's a man? The comforting thunk of two car doors being slammed finally calls a halt to the self-punishment. I've left nail marks in the skin of my forearms.

The office door opens to admit Adam and his dog.

Cody, no surprise, has gone to the cabin, no doubt to sulk at having been made to come home. I fix a smile on my face and square my shoulders into a proper posture for a welcoming hotelier, a woman in control of her circumstances. "Adam. Thank you for bringing Cody home."

"Sorry it took so long." He stamps a little snow off his boots.

I am too inculcated in the hospitality industry to give in to the impulse to upbraid him for putting the life of that miserable dog ahead of my daughter's and have to wait a beat before bringing myself to ask, "Did you find the dog?"

"No."

"I'm sorry. Maybe tomorrow. When the roads are clear."

"They're actually not in bad shape. The plows and sanders have it under control. The parking lot at the AC was the worst problem." Adam reaches into his jacket pocket for his wallet. "But I'm wet and cold, and looking forward to a shower. So, if you don't mind . . ."

"Right." I hand him his key. "Go warm up. I'll check you in later."

Adam hesitates at the door. "Look, it's none of my business, but . . ."

He has my attention.

Cody is in her room with the door closed, as usual. The muffled thump of a bass line filters through the space beneath the poorly hung door, the treble so low that there's no identifying the tune. I pause long enough to take off my jacket and neatly hang it up on the hook that serves as the coat closet in this made-over summer cottage. I turn up the thermostat. I pull open the refrigerator door, examine the contents, and shut it without taking anything out. All the time, I am fully aware of the thumping of my own heart, beating against the rage that is slowly elevating from the shock of Adam's story that Cody is *modeling* for this *artist,* not just doing odd jobs. All of the variations are being ticked off—anger, hurt at being lied to, exasperation at Cody's naïveté; my own failure as a trusted confidante for her—then back to fury. And, not surprisingly, being a little pissed off with Adam as the revelator.

I jerk open the freezer, pull out frozen spaghetti sauce, bang the freezer door shut, wrench open the microwave, drop in the plastic block, and slam the door. I crank the defrost dial as if it's someone's nose. Take a deep breath.

Stop. I have learned that a furious confrontation never succeeds.

Adam was as close to nonjudgmental as possible when he, with apparent and sincere reluctance, told me that he'd come upon Cody and that man in a basement room, Cody dressed only in a makeshift toga. "No improper skin showing, certainly," he said. "But I thought you should know."

What a tough place we parents put one another in. We want to know what our kids are doing, but we also don't want to be the bearer of bad news. It takes a village, indeed. I hadn't really known how to respond, and thinking back, I'm a little embarrassed to think that I might have been rude. I'd wanted more detail, but all Adam would say was, "Why don't you ask Cody?" As if that was going to make anything clearer.

"What's for dinner?" Cody has emerged. She looks impossibly cuddly in her flannel jammies, big bunny slippers on her feet. Her hair is knotted up into a waterfall of strands and she looks sleepy.

"Spaghetti. Chocolate pie for dessert."

I am rewarded with a smile. But of course Cody is hoping that I'm not in on her secret, that Adam hasn't spilled the beans. She's going to play the cheerful child.

"How was your day?" Maybe, with luck, Cody will give me something to springboard off into the line of query that will, inevitably, ruin this evening. Too bad. A snowy night, chocolate pie, and *The Voice*. Could have been a perfect mother-daughter evening.

"It was okay. We got out early." Cody wanders over to the refrigerator, pulling the door open so that I can't see her face.

"I know. I was pretty surprised when you didn't get off the bus." I fill the pasta pot with cold water. Heft it to the stove. Just an ordinary evening.

"I told you about the Open Studio. Told you that I would be there."

I know no such thing. Know for certain that Cody is making this up. Gaslighting me. "Cody. I would have been fine with you going, but you really need to start letting me know where you are. I could have given you a ride. I wasn't busy."

"You don't have to; I can get there." Empty-handed, she slams the fridge door.

"Well, I'm glad that Mr. March was there and could give you a ride home."

"Mosley would have. We weren't done."

"From what I hear, it was time."

"What do you mean?"

I bite my lip. Change tack. "It's not fair to ask someone to go out of his way when someone else is available to bring you home."

"I guess." Cody's perambulations take her to the cupboard, which she opens and contemplates with a scowl. "We took a little side trip to look for that dog."

"Mr. March said that you had no luck." I adjust the flame beneath the pasta pot.

"No. But I bet that dog found his person; I bet he's back home."

"I don't think that boy has a home, Cody. The dog is probably out on the street again."

"Don't say that." Still empty-handed, Cody closes the cupboard doors. "There's nothing to eat in this house."

"Dinner's in twenty. Have a banana."

Eye roll. Sigh. Disdain. It's such a familiar place.

I drop the pasta into the boiling water. "Crazy idea, but how about setting the table?"

The spaghetti is done, the sauce bubbling gently; the chocolate pudding is cooling. Cody has haphazardly put two plates on the table, flatware beside them, with no attempt to put them in proper alignment. A glass of water at each place. No napkins. She pulls the can of Parmesan cheese out of the fridge, plunks it down in the middle of the small table. Plunks herself down opposite me. "I don't want any sausage, and did you cook the sausage in the sauce? You know I'm not eating meat; it's gross to put the meat in the sauce if I'm not eating meat."

I struggle a moment before getting the point of her sentence. "No. I don't have any sausage or hamburger, so this really is a meatless meal. Okay?"

"Fine."

Everything is just fine. In a way, it's almost good to have something new to worry about, something to press the actual problems back a little, like today's news that my furnace is on life support.

Cody shakes Parmesan over her pasta, scrolls a lock of hair behind her ear. Without her glasses, she looks even younger than she is, if that's even possible. It would be so easy to say nothing, to avoid the confrontation sparked by Adam's parent-to-parent revelation. Certainly too young to be sitting wrapped in a bedsheet in front of a grown man. I take the can of cheese, shake it over my spaghetti, push my own hair behind my ears. No, the confrontation isn't with Cody; it's going to be with that artist, Mosley Finch. That's who needs to have his reins yanked. Cody has kept me away from the AC long enough. Tomorrow, right after the rooms are done, I'll head over the hill and give this creep a piece of my mind. If he wants to barter lessons for chores, that's fine. But no more modeling.

"Is there any more?" Cody swipes a slice of white bread along the rim of her plate.

"A little."

I'm finished, so I collect the plates and head to the sink. The little made-over cabin has no amenities; these cabins were built for old-fashioned roughing it, so no dishwasher. Which, given it's just the two of us, is no big deal. But on a night like this, when it would be great to load and go, I long for the Kenmore dishwasher I left behind in the house I sold for the down payment on this place. And for the back deck, which might not have looked out on anything more scenic than the neighboring backyards but was a place I could sit and relax and not contemplate the next disaster in the making. Sit and not have to pray that my cell phone won't go off and call me back to the front office. Which it is doing right now. Oh, for a night off.

It's one of the guests, who cannot figure out how to get the television to work.

I haul myself into my coat, shove my feet into Uggs, and throw Cody a pleading look. "Would you do up the dishes? I won't be long, and we'll have pie when I get back from solving the crisis."

Cody slides on her glasses, peers up at me. "Uh, I got homework to do."

"Have. You *have* homework."

"I *have* homework. I want to watch *The Voice,* so I want to get it done. If I do the dishes . . ."

I surrender. It's just not worth the fight.

It's stopped snowing and the wind has died down to an occasional gust. Stars sequin the growing patches of clear sky. I pause, take in a deep breath, let it out, and watch it bloom into the cold air. The handyman has cleared a path from my door to the front of the building, cleared off the upstairs gallery and then the downstairs so that the guests are safe. He's an unreliable worker, but for some reason, when Carl is faced with snow, he's a dynamo.

I knock on the second-floor guest room door, smile at the middle-aged woman standing there in her purple velour sweatsuit, as if coming out on a frigid night is my absolute pleasure. "Let's see what I can do."

The guest hands me the remote with a disgusted look. I point it at the flat screen, shoot, and the television comes on. With a quick tutorial on which buttons do what, I bid Ms. Electronically Challenged good evening.

Adam March is sitting in one of the plastic Adirondack chairs outside his room, huddled in his handsome wool overcoat. He's holding a plastic cup, and in the still air, the scent of sweet alcohol is obvious.

"Kind of chilly for sitting outside, isn't it?"

"Tell that to Chance."

"I'm sorry you didn't find that other dog."

"Yeah, me, too. Cody is hopeful that he's found his way home."

"And you don't think that's likely?"

"Maybe. The bigger question is, What's home? And how soon will he be put back in some basement, fighting for his life?"

"Sounds dire."

"It is." Adam pushes himself out of the chair, walks to the edge of the platform, and whistles.

Chance jumps to the porch from the ground, bumps his head against Adam's legs, then steps back to shake. He greets me politely, then goes back to breathing in the fresh night air. His skinny pointy-ended tail swings gently from side to side. The scars are obvious from this angle, and I suddenly realize what caused them.

"Was he in fights?"

"He was. And when he was no longer in fighting form, they used him as a bait dog." Adam's voice is even, but I can sense the lingering anger in the way his mouth grows hard. Chance returns to Adam's side, licks his fingers until they unclench, acting to dispel the simmering, and I begin to figure out what Chance's brand of therapy may be.

"But he's such a good pet. Doesn't that make them, I don't know, aggressive?"

"That's one of the myths." He runs a bare hand over the dog's blocky head. "This guy got a second chance at a new life. Who wouldn't take it and be happy?"

"Sometimes second chances don't work out."

"Sometimes, it just takes time."

I don't know if Adam is talking about the dog or my struggle with the LakeView. It really doesn't matter. It's just nice to have someone suggest that everything's gonna be all right. "I should go."

"Stay a minute."

There's a second plastic cup, and he offers it to me. My hands are cold, my nose beginning to drip, but I take it. He pours a little of the whiskey into the cup. "*Salute.*"

"*Salute.*" I haven't had a mouthful of whiskey since back in the day when Randy and I thought nothing of killing half a bottle and then jumping on his Triumph and barreling through city streets, the cacophony of the baffleless mufflers announcing our passage. Before I was of legal drinking age. I remember the burn a split second before I swallow. "Ooof."

"You get used to it."

"I know." He must think I'm some kind of *lady*. If only he knew.

We lean against the railing, elbow-to-elbow, tendrils of exhalation rising into the clear night sky. The stars in this dark corner of the mountain are freakin' spectacular, and nothing needs to be said about it.

"I could have made it home, I guess."

"The storm was moving in that direction; you'd have been driving in it all the way. You're better off here."

"Yes. I think that I am."

He offers another drop, but I decline. There's no second-string concierge to give me a night off, no other parent to give me an hour without responsibility. Of course I don't say any of that, but Adam smiles as if he hears my thoughts.

"I really love it here. The Berkshires. This place. It's a great comfort to me to have a place where I can just relax."

"You can't relax at home?" It comes out, my nosiness.

He tips his cup to his mouth. "Not anymore."

"Are you separated?" The nosiness persists into borderline rudeness.

"No." He shakes his head. "Widowed."

I wasn't expecting that. "I am so sorry."

"Everyone is." He adds some more liquid to his cup. "The thing is, it gets to me. The sympathy. I shouldn't let it, but it does."

"The soft eyes?"

Adam laughs. "Yeah, the puppy eyes, the absolute pap of greeting-card sayings posted to my Facebook page. With some, it's the fear that if they make one remark about Gina, I'll fall apart. And, the truth is, I feel like I might fall apart anyway. All by myself, without provocation."

"How long has it been?"

"Not quite half a year."

He was a new widower when he started coming to the LakeView. Still is. I figure this might be a good time to mention that my ex is also deceased. But I need no sympathy for that event; have no real common ground with a man who is in mourning. I'm sorry that Randy is dead, but he wasn't really a part of my life, hadn't been for a very long time. It would be almost a non sequitur to bring it up. "Early days."

"Not according to the various ladies who have made it their mission to get me back on my emotional feet."

"The fate of the widower. Catnip to single ladies of a certain age." What the heck, I think, and hold out my cup, measuring a pinch between my fingers.

"The thing is, when I'm here, I feel better. So much so, I'm wondering if I shouldn't just stay. At least for a little while."

"I'll give you a discount rate."

"Thank you, but I probably would find a rental someplace. Can't eat out three meals a day, your lovely continental breakfast notwithstanding."

A semi labors up the hill, raucous diesel engine hammering hard against the effort.

"If Carl would stick around long enough to get those cabins out back finished, you could rent one of those."

"Skye, that's very kind, but I'm just in the fantasizing stage." Adam throws back the last of his drink. Caps the bottle. "I don't know about you, but I'm freezing."

"And I've got a date to watch bad television with Cody."

He doesn't move to open the door. "The thing is, I feel so defeated about this dog." He pats his leg, and Chance sits beside him. "This is where I miss Gina the most. That was her name, my wife. Gina. I miss her guidance as much as anything. She was an animal advocate, but she was also blessed with a healthy dose of pragmatism. She would have put all of this into perspective; probably have counseled me that I can't possibly save them all."

I have no guidance, no possible advice, so I pat his shoulder. "You'll find him." I quickly remove my hand lest he begin to think that I'll become one of those well-meaning ladies who annoy him. "Well, thanks for the drink. And thanks for telling me about Cody, about the modeling."

"Did you talk to her about it?"

"Not exactly." I'm letting my poor parenting skills show. "I think it's this Mosley character I need to deal with."

"You're absolutely right. This isn't her doing." Adam pushes open the door to his room, letting the dog in ahead of him. "Good night."

"Good night." Maybe it's the little taste of whiskey, more likely just talking to another adult, but I feel better. Like maybe I'm handling Cody better than I think.

# CHAPTER 15

*We were now quite cozy and safe from the weather, but my thoughts kept going back to my missing friend, picturing him out there in that harsh cold. I knew that Adam was concerned as well, and that the business of driving around with the car windows down, despite the weather, was all in aid of finding him. Even the unexpected bonus of pizza for my dinner did nothing to assuage or distract me from noticing the absence. It isn't common knowledge, but we of the canine persuasion do notice absences. I sniffed around our room, teasing out vestigial remnants of his scent from that other time we were together in this room, but too much time had passed to give me any satisfaction, and certainly no answers. At the same time, I was a bit put out with him for running off like that, away from the comfort and safety of my friendship. Okay, I'll admit it: I was hurt. I don't befriend easily. Unlike wolves, or some kinds of hounds, we dogs don't pack, don't become parts of a whole, so you might even say that he was my first true canine friend, the only one I've ever*

*considered part of my family. Well, I hope he found his
man—and that their bond is as satisfying to him as mine
is with Adam.*

The dog is snoring and sporadically twitching in his sleep,
until his dreaming makes him kick out with both hind
legs, punching Adam right between the ribs. He moves
away, finding himself on the very edge of the bed, three
quarters of it given over to a sixty-pound dog. It's time to
get up anyway. Adam wants to do another drive-around
in North Adams before heading back to Boston.

Adam swings his bare legs over the edge of the bed.
Chance raises his head, flops it back on the pillow, apparently happy to let Adam shower before letting him out.
Skye has replaced the two-cup coffeemaker in room 9, so
Adam gets that started. He's got to put on the same clothes
as yesterday, and has had to use all of the hotel toiletries
Skye stocks. They're pretty little things, and he feels a little silly using the rose water–scented soaps. Any port in
a storm, he thinks, and squeezes some peachy-smelling
shampoo into his hand. He'll skip shaving, reluctant to use
the treacherous disposable shaver Skye handed him last
night. Adam would rather sport a day-old scruff than risk
slicing off bits of his chin, adding another scar to the one
on his cheek.

Chance executes a Downward Dog, then goes to the
door. The day outside is surprisingly warm, and the sunlight on the new snow is blinding. In the distance, a crow
cackles, its noisy disquisition accompanied by the music
of melting icicles. A town plow scrapes at the roadside
slush, sending a cascade of rotten snow onto the pristine
layer. Cody is at the edge of the parking lot, waiting for
the school bus. Skye will deal with Mosley, who is probably not a creep, but he is certainly lacking in judgment.
Chance is back and looking for breakfast. "Sorry, pal,

you're not getting pizza again. We'll head out in a few and grab a bite." Chance gives him a hangdog look, as if to say, *Why are you are trying to starve me*? "You'll last." Adam scratches behind the dog's ear, moves down his spine to his rump. Chance rotors his hind leg in ecstasy.

There's nothing to pack, so moments later the pair of them are ready to leave. The old fashioned door key requires that Adam check in at the office and drop the key off. Skye is in the back room, behind the reception area. Adam can see her bent over her desk, one arm akimbo, the other shuffling papers. She looks so intent that he doesn't want to disturb her, so he gently places the key on the reception desk and leaves.

After another attempt to find the dog, he will treat himself to breakfast in North Adams before pointing the Jetta toward home. Funny word that. *Home*. Home no longer feels like home, but some familiar place no longer comfortable, welcoming. Home is where my dog is, he thinks. Pats Chance, who is riding shotgun as they head out to look for the dog.

*The sun sufficiently warms the surface of the snow so that I find the scent almost immediately. Even though the tracks are covered up by the snow that has filled them, they are visible to me. I trace where my friend had repeatedly come to the boarded-up doorway of the place where we found him. I find his paw scent where he has scratched at the boards, and his urine, telling me the story of how he wouldn't give up on being let into this empty place, his canine belief that his person would eventually be there to let him in. I can taste through my nose the despair when he is forced to retreat, to shelter. I give up sniffing at the house to follow the traces, until I find him shivering beneath a bush. He is happy enough to see me, but despondent otherwise. He is stiff with cold, and labors to get to his feet to greet Adam, who has made his way through the sticky snow. He has been patiently waiting for his person to come, but it is* my *person who gently extricates him from his bushy shelter, who offers him food and warmth.*

*He is one lucky dog, this guy. Lucky for him my person is stubborn.*

The big Timex wristwatch was the first present Cody ever gave me out of her own choosing. She was about six, and my mother had taken her Christmas shopping. Cody had fixed on the watch, a man's, because she could read all the numbers. It's a reliable timepiece, and right now it's suggesting that it's time to get started on the rooms. The couple I have doing housekeeping have abandoned me for more lucrative work on the ski slopes, an annual tradition that no one bothered to mention to me when I kept them on. As with Carl, I seem to have inherited the Carrolls from the previous owner, who apparently didn't see anything wrong with the way they all carried out the business of keeping the LakeView in shape—that is, when it suits them. The Carrolls have a work ethic only marginally better than Carl's. As I was myself a veteran of the change in ownership clean-slate philosophy of firing all old staff, I bought into the concept of consistency when the previous owner made his case for keeping Carl and the Carrolls on board. Now it doesn't seem like such a smart, kind idea. Especially now that I know that they are all related. Some folks might say that's a charming small-town tradition, but the end result is impossible to deal with. I like charm along with the best of them, but this isn't charm; it's charity.

Coming out of the back office, I spot the key to room 9 on the desk. Adam has left without rebooking. I hang the key back on its hook, surprised at the little twinge of disappointment I feel; sorry to have missed his departure, to not have gotten to say good-bye.

The only other rooms to do up aren't rebooked for today, so I'm thinking that there is no time like the present to run my maternal errand. I can do the rooms later. What I intend is to gently convince Mr. Mosley Finch that he'd be wise to back off using Cody as a life model. I'll work the word *underage* into the conversation.

In ten minutes, I'm on the road, wipers beating away the backwash of the car in front of me. The day's surprising warmth has already begun to take down a bit of the winter's accumulation of snow; rivulets of snowmelt fill the ditches in a merry downhill run. It's the kind of winter day that brings with it the fleeting hope of spring, the welcome thought that all will be well.

I pull into the parking lot and only then wonder if I should have called ahead. What if this Mosley guy isn't here? What if he's too busy? Well, I'm here now, and I have enough of the Mama Bear in me that I'm not about to slink off.

Inside, the bright sunshine streams down, illuminating several workstations. There is artwork in various stages of completion. Some of it is interesting, some of it just odd. Not quite knowing where to go, I stroll down the former factory floor, taking in the atmosphere, trying to figure out why it is that Cody is so enamored of this place. The artists in residence this morning nod to me, or don't, depending on the depth of their concentration on their work. One, a scruffy but nice-looking young man, smiles at me, puts down his handful of metallic netting. "Can I help you?"

"I'm looking for Mr. Finch."

"He's in a meeting. I'm Kieran. Maybe I can help?"

"Kieran, yes. My daughter is Cody Mitchell; she's spoken of you."

"Great kid. Nice kid." Kieran gestures toward a wooden folding chair, suggesting that I might want to sit. I don't.

"Well, she can be. She's taking lessons? With Mosley?" I hear myself use the uptalk voice and tamp it down. "She does chores around here for him."

"She does stuff for all of us."

"But he's the one giving her lessons."

"Yeah. I guess."

"What kind of artist is he?"

"It's complicated; he uses several media, but I guess you could say that he's a painter." Kieran picks up the metallic cloth again. It reminds me of something a knight would wear. Chain mail. The object dangling from a beam is cruciform; perhaps it's supposed to be a person. Who knows.

"And he likes to use life models?"

The light above is so perfect that I can see the flush begin to rise in young Kieran's cheeks. "It's totally fine. Really."

"Well, I don't think so."

"Yeah, I suppose you might not. But, really, like, uh. He's fine. He's a professional."

"I'm sure he is." I turn away from Kieran and the weird half-human dangling object. A door opens, and the first thing I notice about him is that Mosley Finch wears exactly the same kind of horn-rimmed glasses that Cody has taken to wearing instead of her contacts. The second thing is that he's a lot older than I'd been led to believe. And, third, he knows exactly why I'm here.

"Mr. Finch. A word, please." I lead Mosley Finch into his own office.

The office, unlike the factory floor beyond it, is dark, no natural light filtering into the cluttered space. An industrial hanging light casts a cone of brightness over two wooden folding chairs. Finch points to one, and this time I sit, perched with a posture my mother would be proud of. Finch sits in the other, pushing himself back a little with one Frye-booted foot, as if to make a bit more space between us. Just in case I bite. Instead, I give Mosley Finch my best concierge-style smile. It's not my real one. It's friendly enough to get him started.

"Ms. Mitchell, it's been really great having Cody here. She's doing such a good job with her art, and—"

"Just tell me that you will never, under any circumstances, ask my fourteen-"—I pause so that the number sticks in his mind—"-year-old daughter to disrobe for you."

"She wasn't, um, nude. She was wrapped very modestly. Grecian. You know what I mean."

"I know that you will never do that again. Not if you want her to keep working here."

"I don't. I mean, she doesn't have to." He sits back, throws his hands into a gesture of *What's it to me.* "If you're worried about her, then we'll call it quits."

"But she loves being here."

"I know. She loves art. And, Ms. Mitchell, she's quite good at it. Maybe you want to pay for lessons instead of her working for them."

I should have known that he'd play that card. There is no margin in my budget for anything that is discretionary, like art lessons. There is barely any margin for food and gas, and certainly that's more important than art lessons. I've had to ask my mother for next month's orthodontist payment. Again. Over the phone, I got the distinct sound of her sniff, a sound I've endured all my life, the sound of exasperation. At least I couldn't see her elevated eyebrows.

Once we're on our feet, once the income is even a dollar

more than the outgo, then I'll plump for art lessons. It seems like I've been making myself that kind of promise for a very long time. "I can't."

"She's got a talent that needs to be nurtured."

"I know. And there's no way I can let her continue to barter for it by posing for you." I stand and slide the zipper of my jacket up to my chin.

"You really don't understand art, do you?"

"I understand that you are close to having me file a complaint of sexual predation on a child under the age of eighteen."

"You have no cause to go to that extreme. No proof." But the high color in Mosley's cheeks suggests he's not confident of that, certainly not confident that Cody hasn't said something to me. How is he to know that Cody would rather die than confide in her mother?

"Mr. Finch. I'm willing to let her continue to swap chores for lessons if you are."

"All right. Yeah, sure."

"But she doesn't model. And you are never alone with her."

"I can't promise that; people come and go around here."

"Yeah, you will." I tap into a reserve I'd forgotten that I own, the deeper part of me, which isn't afraid of jerks like Mosley Finch, that part of me that thrilled to rebellion. My surge of righteous maternal anger is heady stuff, even kind of pleasant for a brief invigorating second. As quickly as it rises, the feeling passes and I stalk out of Finch's office before I lose my mojo.

Outside, I have to pause long enough to still my fast-beating heart. It seems like my life is one confrontation after another. If it isn't with Cody, it's on behalf of Cody, like with this Finch guy. It's with Carl, or the Carrolls, or the sick-making amount owed on my latest credit card bill, the one that never seems to go down.

I walk over to the edge of the parking lot, where the river runs against cement walls and is channeled over a man-made dam. There are abandoned houses across the way, a rickety-looking footbridge tying the scene together. That must be the place where they found that boy, and it makes me wonder if Adam has found the dog after all. I wonder when he'll be back. If he'll be back. Poor guy. Losing a spouse is harder on a man.

I feel a sudden and desperate urge to cry, and I press the back of my glove against my mouth, but it isn't Adam's situation that's brought this on. I stifle it. I haven't got the luxury of feeling sorry for myself. I've got to find a way to make it succeed. Adam has suggested that I open the place up to the, as he puts it, dog community, and maybe I should, but in the next thought I squelch the idea as creating more work in an unequal proportion to the fact that it is still only me and, sometimes, Cody doing it. I really can't afford Carl anymore, except for plowing, and the Carrolls have done me a favor in taking off.

"I guess you get to go into people's rooms." Black Molly is pricking Cody's arm with a common pin, dabbing the bloody spots with various food colorings mixed together into a muddy black.

"Yeah. You should see some of the shit people do." She is trying hard not to wince at the pain of the homemade tattoo, or at Black Molly's questionable artistry. It's supposed to be a lightning bolt, but it looks more like a scar. "Gross, most of it." They are sitting in Molly's tiny bedroom in the double-wide trailer that she calls home. There is a pervasive odor of onions and cat urine. The mobile home, as Molly prefers to call it, has a blue plastic tarp stretched out from the side, and all of the stuff that doesn't fit inside sits under it. The tarp, which also acts as an awning over the door, bulges in the middle with snow, and a slow trickle of snowmelt drains at the lowest point.

"Ever find anything good?"

"Like?"

"You know, stuff."

"What? Like drugs?"

"Duh, yeah." Molly pricks another set of holes, dabs in the homemade ink.

"No."

"Have you ever looked?"

Cody shrugs, and Molly grasps her hand harder, holding it down on her knee. "Keep still."

"I don't think most of our guests are into drugs. I mean, a lot of them are, like, old."

"Even better. Old people need pain pills. Oxy or Percoset. Vicodan. Booze."

"Maybe. I don't have time to look around too much. Gotta scrub those toilets."

Black Molly wipes the last of the blood away, examines her work. "Why don't you see what you can find. Share it with your pal."

Cody shrugs. There's no way she's going to do that, but Black Molly doesn't need to know that. "Okay. Sure."

Black Molly is done, and she fishes a flattened box of smokes out from under her pillow, offers one to Cody, who is examining the rough image on her forearm. Cody is both appalled and exhilarated by the fact that Molly boldly lights up in her own house, doesn't even open the tiny crank-out window over her bed. Blows smoke right up to the yellowed ceiling tiles. Of course, she's never seen an adult in this place. She feels stupid, but she has to ask: "You don't get in trouble for smoking?"

Molly laughs, coughs, pulls a flake of tobacco off her

tongue. "Shit no. They don't care. Where do you think I get them?"

"I figured that you, I don't know, stole 'em."

"I do. From them."

Cody thinks this is hilarious. "I get my pot from the guy I work for, one used joint at a time."

"He gives it to you?"

"Hell no. He's got so much of it, medicinal purposes, he doesn't even miss it."

"Good to know."

Immediately, Cody realizes that she's said too much. Molly is going to expect her to share her pilfered roaches. Cody takes a drag off the cigarette, blows it out quickly. Looks at the lightning bolt inscribed in her skin.

"So, I bet it's no biggie for you to slip a tab or two out of some a-hole's bag?"

The cigarette is making Cody feel a little dizzy, not a good dizzy like pot, but a slightly nauseated dizzy. "Maybe. I don't know."

"It ain't for me, you understand? Not to use. We can make bank on all kinds of shit."

"Really?"

"Yeah. How you figure my brother has that cool Tony Hawk board? Like he's got some kind of after-school job?" Molly falls back into the unmade bed, laughs at herself.

Cody shrugs, tamps out the cigarette in the tin ashtray Molly has produced. "I'll see what I can do." It's a lie, but better to play along.

Cody isn't oblivious to what her father had been, and why he might have ended the way he did. Randy Mitchell liked the easy way, had no scruples about how he made his money. He did favors, he said; people liked him. Skye has never sugarcoated the truth about Randy to Cody, never hidden the fact that he was nothing but a small-time crook, no one to emulate; that she, Cody, has better blood in her. Skye has never said that he deserved what he got, but she's never said that she was sorry, that she felt any grief over his death, as if it had come as no surprise to her and good riddance.

But *she* didn't see it happen. Skye didn't watch as Randy went from an empty-promise deadbeat dad to simply dead. And she'll never know that Cody did. The image still has the power to make her gasp. The feel of Randy's killer's hands on her, shaking her, pushing his face into hers. Exacting a promise.

When Cody was little, maybe in first or second grade, Skye sat her down and gave her the talk. The one about how she must never keep a secret from her mother. That if someone asks her to keep a secret, her first job is to tell. "I know it sounds strange, Cody, but you must never keep a secret from me."

"Not even if Grandma is planning a surprise party for you?"

Skye had laughed and said, "Well, maybe there are some secrets."

Some secrets. Cody knows that Skye was fretting about child sexual abuse, not death threats. Her blanket rule that no one could hurt her even if they said they would simply wasn't true. The shooter's threat is the exception that proves the rule.

Cody touches the lightning bolt; it's painful and not very pretty.

# CHAPTER 16

"What's that?" I point to the black line marring the inside of Cody's forearm.

"Nothing."

"Really. Nothing?" I make a grab for Cody's arm, but I'm not quick enough.

"It's no big deal. Just a symbol."

"You're not of age to get a tattoo. Who did this? What shop?"

"No one."

"You didn't do that yourself."

"Maybe I did." Cody grins.

"You're left-handed. It's on your left arm." I'm rather pleased with my deductive reasoning.

"That's why it's not so good."

"I wish that you hadn't done that."

"It's my body."

"I'd have preferred a tongue piercing. Or an eyebrow piercing, or any other piercing. Those can heal."

"It's who I am."

"What, exactly, is it anyway?"

"A lightning bolt."

"Looks more like the letter *Z*. And it looks infected. You could have given yourself blood poisoning." Even I hear the hyperventilation.

A trip to the walk-in clinic and I am given the cold comfort that, as the artist was squeamish about penetrating deep enough and only used food coloring, the tat will fade fairly quickly. That, and a course of antibiotics just in case.

"All kids try to shock their parents. It's the natural order of things." My mother can barely hide her glee at my arrival on the shores of parental frustration.

"Look, Mom, I've read all the parenting books, blogs, and bull crap and I still can't reconcile Cody's self-destructive art project with becoming a mature human being. It's such a childish thing to do. It's one thing to rebel, another entirely to take a chance on blood poisoning."

"You did it."

"Yes, I've got a tattoo, but at least I had the common sense to go to a professional, and it meant something, something specific." And, perched on my shoulder blade as it is, it's out of sight, so I barely ever think about it. I unbutton the front of my white blouse, slide it off my shoulder, and twist to look at myself in the mirror. There it is, a five-inch artist's rendition of the old-school Triumph badge. The word itself indicative of how I felt that summer, *triumphant* as I stole Randy from his then girlfriend. Triumphant as we arrived every evening at the Three Corners Bar and Grill like some kind of visiting royalty; Randy in that slick black leather jacket, me dismounting from the bike with grace, shaking out my bleached-blond hair. Full of power.

Triumphant as I rebelled against my staid and middle-class upbringing. My reflection gives me a raised eyebrow. Maybe Cody isn't so childish. Maybe it does run in the family.

I straighten my blouse, button it all the way up. "I've got to get ready for work."

I'm going with the pet-friendly idea. I've not been talked into it, but I've done my research and really believe that being welcoming to that community Adam spoke of, his community, I'll attract a lot more travelers. Unfortunately, I also needed to ask my mother for another month's orthodontist payment. While I was at it, I mentioned the art lesson idea. This she approved of. A little culture for Cody. She'll send me a little extra.

Adam considers the number showing up on his phone. He hasn't saved it to his contacts, but it appears with such regularity that he knows who it is, Next Door Beth. Again. He's just put dinner on the table, a frozen chicken potpie he's had in the oven for half an hour. He knows that she knows that he's home; she waved to him as he got out of the car, the two dogs bursting out to make sure the front yard was safe and no trespassers were hiding behind the foundation plantings. He'd ducked into the house as quickly as he could to avoid standing in the cold, chitchatting about nothing. He knows that letting the phone go to voice mail one more time will mean she'll be over here "checking" on him. Making sure he's okay, that he's eating. That he doesn't maybe need some company. Or a pie. Beth is one of those well-meaning, generous, pie-making, lonely middle-aged women who have become habitual comforters. At least Next Door Beth hasn't propositioned him. Kimberly did that. His own fault for getting sucked into the offer of an after-work drink. He works at home.

It was pretty embarrassing for both of them. Kimberly's an attractive woman, older than Gina—than Gina was. Gina's neighborhood pal. The common thread of their friendship was the daily walk to the park. Two women in spandex, looking fine, dogs on leashes. Yakking it up all the way there and back. Kimberly is a Realtor and has that forwardness of a professional who depends on talking people into and out of things. She was very present at the beginning, when Gina was still taking walks, still thinking that this was just a difficult life stage. Less present as things got hard, reappearing only at the end, when she was helpful. She wasn't one of the friends, neighbors, and relatives who brought food, so much food that he crept out at night to dump it in the cans, collected Tupperware and GladWare and all the other wares that were left behind, raising a tower in the corner of the kitchen, a cenotaph built out of unrequited kindness. Kimberly didn't bring food; she brought booze. Poured him a drink, then left her business card on his kitchen table, two words written on the back: *Call me.*

He didn't. Chucked the card. Two weeks later and she called to "check" on him. Four months later and she came to plant her flag in his territory. He should have been clear with her. He's not ready; he's not interested. Eventually, at the worst-possible moment, he was clear as a bell. He hasn't seen or heard from her since.

"Hi, Beth." He sets the phone on the kitchen table so that he can eat as she talks. As she chatters on, being a woman who believes strongly that every quotidian task, if outlined in detail, is of interest to the listener, he takes a bite of the potpie. He's been impatient; it's only lukewarm. He throws his plate into the microwave, mumbles, "Uh-huh, yeah, right," and, at the ding, pulls it out. Now it's too hot. The dogs sit in quiet contemplation of his movements. Long velvet tongues slide along dewlaps in anticipation of leftovers.

*Oh please, please. Gimme some. Whatever it is, and it smells terrific, I want some. Lucky does too. There's plenty for all of us, right? But I want more. I get more, right? Adam, come on, stop and share with us. Me. Us. Finally, the plate is set on the floor between us. Another dog might volley for the bigger portion, but I'm a good dog. I let Lucky, as we call him now, have one half of the plate—the half, albeit, that has less gooey goodness on it, but half nonetheless. Adam keeps mumbling into the air, no words, or at least no words that have any meaning for me, but noises. Comfortable sounds, but not engaged. Kind of like when he's asleep and snores. No content, just noise. Finally a couple of words that I do know,* Okay, then. *He says that and then gets up from the table. There's a pan on the counter and he sets that down for us. I don't like the metal surface—it gives me a shruggy feeling—but I can keep my tongue from contact with it well enough to get the gooey stuff up. Lucky doesn't seem to care about the metal, and when all that I can reach is gone, he takes the pan and walks off with it. I let him, going back to the plate on the floor for one final pass.*

# PART II

# PART II

# CHAPTER 17

Her mother drops Cody off outside the orthodontist's office. Skye will be at the Big Y grocery shopping, and she reminds Cody to text her when she gets done with the orthodontist.

"Can I go get a soda or something after?"

"Yes. But stay in touch. I'm not going to be that long."

"I'll walk to the Big Y; it's only a couple of blocks."

"Just text me. . . ."

Cody walks away from the micromanaging. She yanks open the heavy glass door of the office building, runs up the stairs to Frank Odell, Orthodontics. This should just be a brace tightening, and, with luck, she'll be out in fifteen minutes and can wander the downtown area, poke into some stores. Skye always gets lost in the grocery store, especially now that she has to get creative with vegetarian meals.

It's her lucky day and Dr. Odell makes quick work of her exam and tightening, and Cody is back on the street within minutes with a slightly achy mouth and a new supply of wax. She's forgotten to give the lady behind the reception desk the check from her mother, but she's not going back. She'll "find" it later and Mom can mail it in.

Cody has ten bucks worth of tip money from cleaning rooms in her pocket and at least an hour to herself, so she makes her way across the street to a pizza place to get herself a slice and a root beer. The late March day has all the promise of spring, even though the remnants of crusty, dirt-garnished snow piles are everywhere; thin fans of meltwater trickle out from beneath the piles, making every step sloppy. Still, the air is mild, and that one empty park bench is a perfect place to people-watch and eat the double-cheese slice oozing luxurious grease into her hand.

Cody licks the grease from her fingers, balls up the waxed paper, and makes a fair shot at the nearby trash barrel. She misses and has to get up to retrieve her mis-fire. A young man comes in her direction, and she quickly goes back to her bench, claiming it as her territory. He's Hispanic, she thinks. Below his canted trucker cap, his dark hair is beautifully clipped close to his head, leaving graceful neck tattoos exposed; his slender body is dressed in sagging homeboy jeans, Joe Boxers revealed; a chain slung from wallet to belt loop slaps against his skinny shank. As he gets closer, she has a sense that she knows him, but there are no Hispanic kids in her school. He looks like a lot of the boys in her old school, but that's not what she associates him with. The sense is fleeting, a shadow of recognition quickly passing. Then it hits her.

"Hey!"

The boy doesn't respond, just keeps trudging forward, and Cody wonders if she has actually said it out loud. "Hey, you! Yo!"

He stops, considers her, and keeps moving. His eyes are hooded, sleepy-eyed, like he's just awakened.

"No. Wait."

The boy stops at the curb but doesn't turn around, and

she can see in his posture that he thinks she's teasing him, taunting him.

"I know where he is. Your dog."

"What you say, girl?"

"You're that kid, the one who overdosed."

He does turn now, gives her a glare that should be intimidating. She should run, but Cody holds her ground. "I know where your dog is. I know who has him."

"He fighting him?"

"No. He's been, um, rescued."

The boy steps toward Cody, the hooded, sleepy eyes now wide and sparking, not with curiosity or pleasure, but with anger, like he thinks she's lying. "Who are you?"

"Cody. I was there. When you . . . In the house. You almost died." She knows she's allowing him to intimidate her, but he *is* intimidating. He's tall, for one thing, and bears a gangsta swagger that isn't put on. He's the real deal. She takes one step backward, assesses the few people on the street, mostly Mass College of Liberal Arts students, wrapped up in their conversations and phones. She's hoping that they are witness and deterrent enough if this kid gets physical.

"But I didn't. Where my dog at?"

"In Boston. He's great. He's in good care."

"I want him back."

"I know you do. I would, too."

"You got a phone?"

"Yes."

"Call him. Call this guy and tell him get his ass back here and give me my dog. He has no right to him."

"He won't give him back. He thinks that you fought him."

The boy scowls, mutters, "Ain't true. *I* didn't."

"What's your name? I can't keep thinking of you as the guy in the house."

The boy folds his arms across his hollow chest, sticks out his chin. "Mingo."

"I'm Cody. And what's his name? The dog."

"He named Dawg."

"Like 'Hey, *Dawg*'?" A giggle bubbles in her throat, but she swallows it; this kid does not look amused.

"He's my dog. I want him back." He turns his face away from her. "He like my family. He's all I got." Mingo rubs a hand over the tattoo on his neck, lifts and resets his trucker hat at a cocky angle, regains his 'tude. "You gonna help me?"

"Yeah. I'll help." For the first time in a long time, something feels right.

They exchange phones, key in their respective phone numbers, and Mingo leaves her standing alone on the sidewalk. Her phone dings with a text message: *Where are you?* Mom. Probably frantic. Cody texts back: *Meet u @ BY*. Skye can cool her jets in the parking lot of the grocery store.

Back in the car, Cody's text-message alert dings again. It's a rare-enough occasion that she knows her mother is dying to know who's texting her. Cody isn't oblivious to the fact that her mother peeks at her phone. If she was the diary-keeping sort of teenager, she'd have to be totally devious about where to stash the diary; her mother's sense of personal space is, like, nonexistent. Cody knows that if her mother ever broke her laptop password, she'd freak. Beyond Internet searches for various school projects, there's a history of searches for a shooting that has become a cold case. Cody knows enough to delete her history cache, but sometimes she forgets.

*Yo kid*
*Yo*
*Tx 4 telling me abt Dawg*

*Shd let guy no?*
*No. Lt me thnk*
*K*


Cody slips her phone into her jacket pocket. Keeps the small smile on her face turned well away from her mother's sideways glance.


Chance playfully grabs his buddy's foot, then rolls onto his back. *Play with me!* The move is so like the crippling move of a fighter, yet so gentle and the submission so trusting. The other pit bull jumps to his feet and, in moments, the two dogs are play wrestling. Perfectly suited to each other.

It is one of his hard days, and the rambunctious behavior of two dogs who ought to know better does nothing to alleviate Adam's gloom. He is fetching up on their April sixth wedding anniversary—what would have been their fifth—and though he'd known that this would be hard, he hadn't known exactly how hard. Looming on the calendar like some kind of perverted red-letter day, the date pulsed its significance into his eye every time he glanced at the calendar hanging on the wall beside the phone. He took the calendar down, but the date struck him every time he opened his appointment book to jot in a new client, a dental appointment, a reminder to get the car serviced. It struck him when he looked at his phone, the calendar app's bright blue square proclaiming the passage of time in its relentless pull. A pull that minute by minute took Adam from Gina, thrusting her deeper and deeper into his past.

"Hey, guys. Knock it off." Adam straightens the coffee table, catches a lamp before it crashes. "Enough!"

The two dogs stop. Sit. Look at him as if he's maligning their good natures. Chance immediately shakes off the puppy behavior and comes to bop Adam in the chin with his head. He then presses himself into Adam's body, crouched as he is on the floor. Chance licks his man's face, tastes the upset, mutters some comfort into Adam's ear, and is rewarded with a hug.

"We need to get out of Dodge." Adam has three days clear on that calendar of his. One on either side of the one he'd like to avoid. There is no place he needs to be, and one where he'd like to be. LakeView Hotel. Not as a door-to-door salesman of fund-raising techniques, but as a vacationer. A guest with no obligation other than to admire the Berkshires and sleep in a bed that he's never shared, the dogs notwithstanding.

Kimberly called him again last night, all sweet concern and an invitation to some charity event for a cause he's not particularly interested in. Apparently, he's been forgiven, or else she's adopted a new strategy. He said yes, only because saying no would take more work.

"LakeView Hotel, Skye Mitchell."

"Skye, it's Adam." He realizes that it's the first time he's just called himself Adam when calling the Lake-View, confident that he's unique enough to Skye to need no last name. "I'm hoping I can have a room for the next couple of nights. I'd love to come up today."

"Yes, of course."

"Maybe this time I'll get to the top of Mount Greylock."

"You're out of luck there. They don't open the gate till May."

"Oh. Okay." Any further suggestion of what activities he might enjoy in the area seems silly right now. Especially because Adam mostly intends to lie in bed and watch old movies. Skye doesn't need to know that. She can suppose that he'll be doing the early spring tourist thing, not feeling sorry for himself with Humphrey Bogart.

"We'll find something for you to do. Still with two dogs?"

"Guilty."

"Then I guess room nine is all yours."

"See you in a few."

"Super."

They sign off and Adam looks at the two dogs, Chance and the dog he's ended up calling Lucky. "Want to go see Skye?"

Chance nods, shakes, and does his little two-step dance. Adam doesn't fool himself into believing the dog understands the sentence, just the word *go*.

For what he's planning, Adam doesn't need much, and he is packed and ready to leave in half an hour. He calls Next Door Beth to ask her to pick up the paper off the stoop in the morning, relieved that he gets her answering machine so he doesn't have to explain himself, sets the thermostat to fifty-five, makes sure he's got the power cords for phone and tablet, grabs a bag of dog food out of the pantry, and off they go, the two pit bulls beside themselves with the idea of a car ride.

*It's what I love best in life, along with walks, television, and dinner: a ride in the car. Especially one that takes us away from the city into the countryside. Now, I'm a city dog, born and raised, and enjoy the feel of sidewalk under my feet as much as the next guy, but the countryside has all those potent scents. Whereas my usual route brings me the fresh smells of offal and other dogs, the occasional cat, and lots of lovely food molecules drifting out of pizza joints and delis, the countryside offers me the more organic living creature smells. My kind tend toward the home-protection occupations, with nary a hunter in the bloodline, but the deeper wolfish instinct in us all makes the idea of a hunt very compelling. So when we arrived at our home away from home, I leapt out of the car and grabbed a noseful of scent. Ah!*

*My pal emerged from the car more slowly, poking his*

*head out, sniffing the air, debating whether or not he should jump down from the car and take a chance that it was safe. He's still cautious, confused a lot of the time, uneasy yet in his new circumstances. I understand how he feels; I was that way myself when I went from the cellar where I was born and fought to the streets and then to the comforts of Adam's little home. It was quite a shock for me to go from captive to independent to codependent. When your world changes so abruptly, you have to be a little guarded.*

*I barked, encouraging him, and was rewarded with his finally taking the leap. We ran side by side down the slope of the hill, the fresh scent of lake water and trees calling to our feral natures. That and the creature I knew was called* rabbit. *Having frequently snuffled up their scent in the snow and mud, I so wanted to see one.*

The dogs are bursting with spring energy, and Adam doesn't have the heart to call them back. He figures that they can't get into much trouble in the woods, if you discount the chance of encountering a skunk. They'll be back; it's too close to dinnertime for Chance to wander too far from the bag of kibble.

Skye isn't in the office when Adam arrives. He has his phone out to call her cell when Cody comes in. "Hey, Mr. March."

"Hey yourself, Cody. Can you check me in?"

"Sure." Cody goes behind the reception desk, clicks the computer's mouse a few times. Looks at him over the top of her slipping horn-rimmed glasses. "You have both dogs with you?"

"I do." He can see them out the picture window, noses firmly down to the ground.

Cody fiddles a little more with the computer, prints out his check-in form. Slides it to him along with a pen. Adam scrawls his signature, slides it back to her.

She slides the key to room 9 to him. "Can I say something?"

"Sure." Adam pockets the key. "What?"

"That dog, the one from the crack house?"

"Yes?"

"I know his name."

"Really?"

"It's Dawg. You know, like 'Hey, dawg.'" Cody's voice is a pretty good imitation of street talk. She shoves her glasses up. "I found out."

"And can I ask how you found out?"

"No. Well, I asked."

"You're making me nervous, Cody. You shouldn't be—"

"It's fine. He's an okay kid. He's just, well, he wants his dog back."

"I can't do that."

"That's what I told him. Mingo. That you wouldn't."

"Cody. Does your mother know about this?"

"Oh, jeez no. Please, Mr. March. Don't tell her; she'll freak. I saw him in town. We've texted a little. Can I tell him that Dawg is here?"

Street kid with a crack habit texting this little girl with artistic aspirations. Adam is suddenly very glad that Ariel is mostly all grown up. He doesn't think he could do it again. It was hard enough as a part-time dad; he can't imagine what it would be like to live with this attitude day after day. For one uncharacteristic moment, he thinks compassionately on Sterling, his ex-wife. "Think about it, Cody. Look at that dog." He throws a hand toward the picture window. "Look at those scars. Those are from fighting."

"He says *he* never fought him."

"And you believe him?" He knows he's being a hard-ass, but when it comes to dog fighting, Adam really doesn't care how harsh he sounds. "Cody, I can't take the chance."

"He won't. He's in some kind of program, a group home. Not jail." She's got that adolescent scowl thing going on, and he gets an insight into Skye's world.

"Hey, all checked in?" Skye appears in the doorway, the two dogs standing behind her.

"We are. Cody took good care of me." Adam winks at Cody, a tacit promise to keep their conversation to themselves, and he is rewarded by a slight smile, nothing broad enough to reveal her braces, but a smile nonetheless.

Adam swings the door to room 9 open and is met by the fresh scent of vanilla. There is something a little different about the room this time, and it takes him a moment to realize that it's finally been painted. The vanilla room freshener is barely masking the odor of latex paint. The room is brighter, and the eggshell white color instead of the formerly beige shade makes it look bigger. The carpeting is gone, replaced with something he assumes is laminate, but it looks quite like actual strip oak buffed to a shine. Two area rugs in swirls of lavender, deep purple, and pink break up the expanse of wood. Adam pushes the new, lighter drapes back, revealing the view. It feels good to be here. Unlike his home, where it is all too easy to encounter a ghost, this comfortable room on the top of a hill is simply a place to lay his head. A place to rest.

Chance butts him, grumbles. Lucky, aka Dawg, cocks his head. Rest will wait. It's time to dish out doggy dinners. And, for the record, the dog will remain Lucky.

*Dawg here cn u gt here?* Cody keeps her phone in her hand, but there is no reply.

It is a strangely mild evening for early spring in these hills. Not a breath of a breeze to chill the back of the neck, and I've only recently dared to go scarfless. My down jacket is left hanging on a hook, close enough at hand for

when the untrustworthy New England spring flirts with
turning back into winter. I finish up in the office, shutting
off all the lights except for the lamp in the window, giving the office the look of a warm and welcoming place.
At a local craft fair, I've had a hand-painted sign made
with my cell number on it, surrounded by a wreath of pink
and white primroses, and it looks sweetly professional
hanging on the hook beside the door. So much nicer than
the cardboard stuck to the storm door with a piece of tape.
As is my habit, I climb the outside stairs to the second
floor, walk along the gallery, making sure that things are
in order, then down the other set of stairs to the first floor,
where I will do the same thing before retiring to our cabin
for the night. I pause to lean over the railing. The moon
has risen and appears caught between the tops of the two
tallest pine trees. Nearly full, it casts enough light to il-
luminate the last of the snow still lingering in the frost
hollows.

Coming from below me, there is the sound of a door
opening, the scrabble of dog nails on the concrete. A
thump, another. Adam's dogs appear in the moonlight,
their tails pointing like darning needles straight out from
boxy bodies, weaving a path down the slope. I lean farther over the rail and can see Adam standing there. If I
had a water balloon, he'd be a perfect target. He sips from
a plastic cup. I head down the outer stairs.

"Good evening."

"And a lovely one it is." Adam gestures toward the
moon with the hand that holds the cup. "Could I interest
you in a glass of wine?"

This is where I'm supposed to say "Oh, gosh, no thank
you." But I don't. A glass of wine in a plastic cup sounds
kind of good. Kind of adult. Preferable to the whiskey he
usually offers.

"Why, yes. Thank you." I pull another chair next to his.

"I can only offer a mediocre red."

"Anything else would be wasted on me."

Adam goes in, comes out quickly with another cup and a bottle. "If you'd prefer, I've also got a pretty good scotch. Twelve-year-old."

"Tempting as that sounds, a little red wine is probably a better choice for me."

Adam hands me the cup, pours himself a little more. We tip our cups in salute. No one says anything for a moment, both of us just enjoying the quiet and the fresh night air. In the distance, a bark. Adam whistles.

"So you're just here on a little vacation this time?"

"Something like that." He rests the edge of the cup against his lips. "Tomorrow is, would have been, our fifth anniversary."

"Anniversaries are hard."

"I'm functioning, but some days are just harder." He shakes his head. "Sorry, didn't mean to spoil the evening with my pity party."

"Oh, Adam, you can hardly be accused of that. It's hard, I know, really hard to lose someone you love." I feel a companionable tear rise, a tear that has yet to be shed for Randy. I'm still angry with him, angry that he died the way he did. The uselessness of his life. I have to collect myself. "I might have some cheese and crackers in the office. What do you say?"

"Sounds good." Adam whistles again, and the dogs finally reappear on the porch. They are panting, clearly pleased with their exertions. They take turns pushing their way between his knees, almost causing him to spill red wine on himself. "Hey, hey, boys. That's enough." He's grinning, and I see why he keeps these animals; they are sixty pounds of distraction each.

Adam puts the dogs in his room and follows me down the length of the porch. I unlock the office door but don't flip on any other light; the lamp on the small round table in the window is enough. I duck into the back office and get the block of cheddar cheese that I nibble on during the day, grab the box of crackers and a cheese knife.

"The weather should be good for a hike tomorrow. If that's what you were thinking about doing." It's a nice topic, weather. So neutral. No wonder so many people fall back on it as a useful tool. I dated a weatherman one time. It was all he talked about, weather trivia. All I talked about was Cody and her cute little three-year-old antics. Maybe he was nervous, too. I know that I was. I sip the mediocre red. Offer the cheese knife to Adam.

"I may. We'll see what tomorrow brings." He slices off a piece of cheese, sandwiches it in between crackers.

The house phone begins to ring. I jump up to answer it, as if I've been caught malingering. It's a call from downstate; they've seen my Web site proclaiming our dog-friendly status. I book them a room for the weekend, premium rate. When I get back to the little table, Adam has poured me more wine. I almost decline, but then don't.

"Don't you ever close up shop for the night?"

"Not really. I can't afford not to be a real voice on the end of the line when there are other places staffed all night."

"Then when do you sleep?"

"I don't. Sleep is for losers."

"I bet that if you added a pet-sitting or pet-spa component, something beyond just letting people with dogs stay here, the LakeView would become a destination instead of a way station."

"Is that how you see it? A way station?"

"Not anymore." He finishes his wine.

"I should get back, Cody will be wondering where I am." That is such a stretch.

"Yeah, me, too. Those dogs will have picked out what

movie we're watching, and they always choose *Turner and Hooch*."

"That's like trying to pick out a movie with Cody. She likes the dark and disturbed and I like the romcom."

"By the way, the room looks great."

"Thanks. It was way overdue. Glad you like it." I don't mention that my credit card is pulsing with the exercise of making those rooms, his included, fresh and pet-friendly. And look at that, two nights booked for that dog couple, a little inroad in the debt. I won't charge Adam what I'm charging them. He's grandfathered in. I've even stopped charging him the "cleaning surcharge" on his dogs.

"Very homey."

"That's what I was aiming for." I am unduly pleased with the compliment.

Adam walks along the porch toward his room. The moon is high enough now to have escaped the grasp of the tall pines. The porch lights are extraneous, and he wishes that he could shut them off, but of course he can't. Safety first. His dogs are ensconced on the bed and greet him only with tail thumps. He has come without treats, without promise of adventure, and he hasn't been too long, so they don't put any energy into his welcome back. "Hey, Dawg," he whispers, and he sees that Cody is right, that is this animal's name. The dog lifts his head and cocks his ears forward at the word. "Yeah, well as long as you're with me, you're Lucky." He smiles at the unintended pun.

Adam extracts the fifth of scotch from his bag. Cracks the cap open and then realizes that he doesn't have another plastic cup. He's used up his LakeView allotment. At that moment, there's a tap at his door. The dogs sit up but don't react. A friend.

"Thought you might need another one of these." Skye

hands him a short stack of clear plastic cups, neatly secured in their sanitary wrappings. "Good night, then."

Cody hears the front door open and quickly closes the lid to her laptop. She's been surfing the Holyoke newspaper, looking for mention of her father's murder. Buried deep within the local news, a glancing mention of the case, a possible tie-in with another. No proof, no leads. Cody doesn't know if this means she's safer, or less safe. She'd love to ask her mother. *Hey, Mom, do you think if the shooter hasn't been identified by this time that maybe he's gone?* In Cody's imagination, her mother nods, and says, *Yes. There's nothing left to worry about. Everything's going to be all right. We're safe. Forever.*

"Cody?"

"Doing homework!"

The pressure of worry is knotted in her chest. Cody presses her hand against her sternum, feels the beating of her own heart, the hectic rise of panic. This has happened before. She takes a deep breath, consciously tries to slow her heartbeat down.

"Cody, dinner." Skye stands in the bedroom doorway. "Honey, what's the matter?"

"Nothing."

Skye sits on the bed, throwing an arm around Cody, squeezing her close. "Tell me."

"Don't." Cody wrenches herself away from her mother's touch, afraid that to feel it for one more second will cause her to combust. "Don't touch me." She runs to the bathroom, avoiding the hurt on her mother's face. It has to be this way.

# CHAPTER 18

Cody doesn't wonder in the least what is keeping her mother; she's just glad Skye is out of the cabin and occupied. Cody has a remnant of a joint left by Mosley in his ashtray at the AC. He'd sent her into his office on some errand and she'd seen it, snuffed out and keeping company with a much less consumed blunt. What was she to do but slip the inch of skinny joint into the pocket of her jeans? It was like Mosley had practically offered it to her. What was that word? *Tacit.* It was on her vocab sheet a couple of weeks ago. He was giving her tacit permission to take it. Why else would he be so casual about leaving his weed out? Like he did his charcoal or his brownies. Everyone at the AC borrowed from one another, materials, favors, money. Cody is pleased with her logic and digs out the box of matches she has squirreled away in the back of her closet, tucked into a sneaker, one of a pair she doesn't wear anymore. She lights up, opens her window, and leans out. Bliss. A few moments when the world goes away, the panic softens.

She should be sharing this with Black Molly, but sometimes it's nice not to share. Molly's been pushing for a chance to "help" Cody with rooms on weekends, but Cody's not keen on Skye's meeting this friend. She tells herself it's because she doesn't want to subject Molly to the interrogation Skye is bound to conduct: Where do you live? What's your dad do? Yada yada. As if anyone would want to admit they live in a trailer with five other kids, and Molly's never said what it is her dad does except hunt and drink beer.

The truth is that she's reluctant to give Molly a chance to get inside the guest rooms. Every time Molly asks if Cody's found anything, Cody tells her that she hasn't; not admitting that she hasn't actually looked, just suggesting that she hasn't found anything. Frankly, it's a scary idea, poking into other people's possessions, even though there they are, right there in full view—cosmetic bags and Dopp kits and stuff lying all over the place. Fancy creams and amber vials of pills. Cody has been tempted to spritz on a little high-end perfume, but her mother has a nose like a hound and would bust her in a nanosecond if she got a whiff of a scent neither one of them could ever own.

Cody pulls out her phone, examines it in case she might have missed Mingo's text. Maybe she was in the bathroom, or maybe eating dinner, and Mom always makes her put her phone away during dinner. Like she even gets messages from anybody. Ever. Mr. March is going to be around for only a couple of days, so if Mingo wants his dog back, he's got to get here.

Cody sucks in another mouthful of smoke, holds it, gently releases it to the night air.

The front door opens, and Cody quickly snubs out the vestigial joint, crumbles the remains, and drops them out the window, then fans the room air with her sketchbook. Takes a deep breath and decides that her mother won't detect a thing. Skye doesn't know about the pot, and she would never believe such a thing about Cody. She's a "not my kid" kind of mom. Skye is clueless, which even to Cody sounds like an unkind thing to think, so she revises her thought. The good news is that her mother is without suspicion in regards to her daughter's real life. She has no idea, and that's the way Cody wants to keep it. Keeping Skye in ignorance about the Secret has meant doing so for every other thing in her life. She has become secretive because she must. But it is lonely.

"Cody?"

"I'm doing homework."

"Why don't you do it out on the kitchen table?"

"I need privacy."

"Call me if you want help."

Such a sweet mom, so delusional. "Yeah. Okay."

The little blurp of an incoming message.

*Wht up?*
*Got ur dog*
*Where?*
*Staying here at LakeView*
*Dunno whr is*

Cody tells him where the LakeView is, but his response is slow in coming.

*Hw m I gon gt thr?*
*Hitch?*

There's no reply for a few minutes. Cody waits, ready to fire off another message, when her phone rings. She answers it before it gets to the second note of the Nokia ringtone, a sound that will surely bring her mother to the door.

"I want my dog, but there's no way I can get there."

"He's only here till Friday night."

"I don't know what to do. No way I get there; I'm like stuck. Can't hang with my homeys; got freakin' curfew. I hate this place; it's like jail but no bars. I think that I'd like jail better than this *residence*."

"Look, Mr. March is a regular here." Cody thinks for a moment. "He'll be back in, like, a couple of weeks. At least I think so. He's got an event at the AC."

"So?"

"So, maybe you could, like, get here then, and . . ."

"Okay. Text me when you know he's coming. Maybe I can figure it out, if I have more warning. I can make a plan."

"I will."

"Hey, you give Dawg a pat for me?"

"Sure." Cody flops back against her pillows, which are neatly arranged against the headboard of her bed, something she's never done, although her mother does it every morning despite complaining that she has so much to do that she doesn't have any time left over for niceties.

"Cody? You want to take a break? Have some ice cream? I've got a little of that Chunky Monkey left."

"Sure. Got any chocolate sauce?"

"No, we're out of chocolate, but there's some caramel left."

Cody emerges from her room, careful to let the door shut behind her just in case there's any hint of pot left in the air. "That's okay. I'll just have it bare." She takes the bowl of ice cream from her mother's hand, sits at the table. "Thanks. I was just thinking I needed a snack." For once, she doesn't avoid her mother's smile.

It's a lot less springlike this morning, and I shrug on a polar fleece vest when I go out to check the mailbox.

Mostly junk, ergo more recycling. A renewal notice for one of the magazines I keep for guests. I might just let that one slip. An industry magazine for me with articles that aren't really pertinent to my situation, although I like looking at the pictures of pretty hotel rooms. A letter from a real estate office. I get those and cold calls on a regular basis, as if they can sniff out a struggling business, a struggling businesswoman ready to throw in the towel. Not yet. Not yet.

The house phone rings and I set the mail down, chucking the envelope from the Realtor into the trash, and lo and behold, it's someone looking for pet-friendly accommodations in the Berkshires. Affordable, they say. And I say: Yes, we are. They ask if we know of a day care for dogs in the area; they want to see the new exhibit at the Clark. I think Adam may be right: Maybe I should offer add-ons to make this a destination. Doggy day care is an option. I could have Carl, suddenly back from wherever, do up the last cabin with whatever it takes to make it attractive and safe, put up a fence, find some ambitious dog lover who wants to lease it as a kennel with benefits. A win-win. I'd get the lease money, and that cabin would pay for itself; then I could offer a service to potential guests, increasing the number of visitors. I book the guests, promising to look into their request, by which I mean talk Cody into dog-sitting, and then go to the computer station, pull up a word-processing window, and start tapping out concepts. Maybe Adam will take a look at them for me.

Speaking of whom, I haven't seen Adam yet this morning. Well, it's a vacation, not a work visit for him, so he's probably sleeping in. I also realize that I haven't heard the dogs. Guess they know when to leave him alone. It's harder on men to be bereaved. No one to take care of them

anymore. That sounds cynical, and I edit my thought. It's
the loss of companionship. No wonder the women around
him are hounding Adam; there is something attractive
about a man bearing up under loss. And, for an older guy,
he's pretty attractive—trim, good head of hair. Whoa.
Nuff of that.

*Get up get up get up. Adam is ignoring me. Not a state of
affairs that I enjoy. Sometimes he pretends to be asleep,
but I always know when he's faking it. A truly sleeping
person breathes in a specific way. Plus, I can hear eyes
moving under eyelids. I try to get my companion to help
me awaken our sleeping door opener. He's got himself
squeezed into a corner of the room, between a chair and
the refrigerator. He looks terrified. I place my forepaws
on the edge of the bed and do something I'm not usually
inclined to do: lick Adam's face. I know. There are dogs
that make a habit of that behavior, but I've never been
one of them. However, sometimes a good lick does wonders. He stirs; I jump back. He slumbers on. If I were capable of understanding cause and effect, I might think
that the empty bottle beside the bed was the cause of my
usually early-rising human being still abed at this hour.
Nothing left to do—I go to the door and commence
scratching at it. This is a noise I know Adam detests, so
I figure that will get him on his feet. But, alas, no. I leave
a suggestion of claw marks in the wood. Not a deep
scratch, not something suggestive of panic. But, truly, it's
long since time for me to go out.*

*The other dog whimpers from his corner. Evidently,
there is something in Adam's persistent sleep that frightens him in some way, some association that I cannot
comprehend. I go over to him and clock him with my paw,
meaning, It's okay. You're safe. He sets his jaw down*

*between stubby paws and sighs, skeptical of my asser-*
*tions. I throw myself down beside him, give a big sigh*
*of my own, and settle in to wait for Adam to come to*
*himself.*

This won't do, not at all. Adam hauls himself out of bed,
glances at his phone, shudders at the hour, and then looks
to the dogs, who are sitting between the two queen beds,
side by side, like matched ponies, the look of utter disappointment clear in their exophthalmic eyes. Guess what?
The day of their anniversary didn't go away. It's still April
sixth. The thundering headache, the guilt for leaving
the dogs inside way beyond their tolerance—although
he can't spot any soiling anywhere—do nothing to supersede the hollow fact of acknowledging an important date
without the one who made it important.

"Nothing fancy. A JP and you are all I need." Gina
scrolled three strands of spaghetti around her fork. They
were sitting in one of their favorite places, an Italian restaurant in the North End owned by one of her cousins.
Adam couldn't remember which cousin, just that this
place had the best food.

"Let's at least do it someplace beautiful."

"Not the town hall? I hear it's lovely this time of year."
Gina's eyes caught his and he saw the sparkle of affection for him in them, something that he didn't take for
granted. Something that he was still a little amazed about.

"What about the Cape?" He hoped she'd see the
affection—no, too weak a word—the adoration in his own
eyes.

It wasn't an overnight *coup de foudre,* this love for this
woman. Their first few encounters were more adversarial than affectionate. But Gina found the worth in his un-

worthy soul and he found the human anchor he didn't
even know he needed.

And so they decided that a weekend visit well before
the high season was just the ticket. They found a dog-
friendly B and B, a charming lady justice of the peace,
and a beachfront setting. Chance stood as best man; Gina
carried roses. No one cried. At least not until late that
night, when Adam found himself overwhelmed with joy.
It had come about so unexpectedly. Given his past, he
never thought he'd deserve happiness again, and yet he
was happier than he had ever been. A fully forgiven man.
Gina had helped him. He lay there that night, this beautiful sleeping woman beside him, his life utterly turned
around. She almost hadn't taken him into her life, had
dismissed Adam out of hand as a bad guy, a suit with no
conscience. Chance had been the great persuader, con-
vincing Gina that Adam was a man capable of change.
Of redemption.

Adam leans over the rail, watching the dogs in their progress around the property. He hasn't got the strength to
whistle them back, nor the inclination. Let 'em be, he
thinks. They won't run away, and Skye won't care all that
much, as long as they don't poop near the front steps The
headache and the ugly taste in his mouth are no strangers. He thinks of the word *recidivist*. Shakes it off. No, this
was a onetime thing. He's no worse than a dieter falling
into the clutches of a chocolate cake. One piece, that's all
it was. He's not going back to the place he once inhab-
ited. He's standing in sweatpants and a T-shirt with something dribbled down the front. *Recidivist*. He reminds
himself of the man he was during the dark period in his
life, the one that Gina hauled him out of. She deserves
better than for him to sink back into that kind of despair.

Skye leans out of the office door, takes a look at him. "I've got fresh coffee in the office."

"I figured breakfast was over."

"I have my own supply. Come on down, if you want." She ducks back into the office.

Adam does whistle then, and is ashamed at how jubilantly his dog greets him. As if he hadn't sinned against him by making him wait so long to go out. As if he hadn't remembered that Chance, too, had a great deal to do with his recovered joy.

A soft vibration tickles his thigh—his phone. He pulls it out and reads the text message. It's from Kimberly, reminding him of the charity event on Saturday. It's a cute message, and he can just hear her voice, all coy: *We don't have to stay for the whole thing.* A wave of nausea that he doesn't think has anything to do with his overindulgence last night. He just can't wrap his mind around this reentry into dating. It is so disrespectful. It's not "getting on with his life"; it's demeaning to Gina's memory. As if the last ten months are something to forget, get over like a bad dream. Before he can think about it, he thumbs a quick *Sorry, can't join you. Something's come up. Work.* Instantly, Adam feels a wash of relief and, with it, a desire for black coffee. Chance and Dawg precede him to the office at a trot, tails swinging.

"I don't judge, but I do recognize the symptoms."

"Of an obvious loss of dignity?" Adam indicates his attire.

"Hot coffee and a greasy breakfast are the cure. I can't offer the greasy breakfast, but here you go." Skye hands him the Tanglewood mug, already filled.

She reaches into the desk drawer and produces a bottle of extra-strength acetaminophen, offers it to him.

Adam shakes out three. "Any chance you've got room for us to stay for a bit longer?"

"You're so kind to phrase it that way, but yes, of course I do." She doesn't even look at the computer.

"I'm ducking out on a date."

"And hiding out at the LakeView?"

He smiles and palms the capsules into his mouth. "I feel safe here. Like they can't find me."

"When you, um, feel better, I'd love to talk with you about an idea I've been working on."

"Would you want to join me in finding a greasy breakfast? We can talk about your idea."

Skye nods. "I could do with a little nourishment."

For once, she can't think of a single reason not to take up a casual invitation. It's late enough that her morning tasks are done, and the afternoon tasks can wait an hour. "That would be nice."

"If you don't mind riding with the hounds, hop in." Adam, freshly showered and dressed in jeans and a polo shirt, opens the passenger door for me, then brushes a little dog hair off the black seat. I get in, feel the soft touch of dog breath against the back of my neck, Chance giving me his approval. On the way to North Adams, I bounce my idea of converting one of the cottages into a dog spa, and he listens before offering some good advice. I don't bring up my delicate financial position, but he's businessman enough to figure it out. He agrees that leasing the cottage out would create a steady monthly income, and I like that he approves of my business sense. By the time we get to the restaurant, I feel like something is settled. A plan. Some forward thinking.

It's just a late breakfast, two people sitting in a sunny corner of a mom-and-pop restaurant, eggs over easy with white toast for me and a hangover-curing Sampson with everything for him, much of which Adam slips into the to-go box the server provides. But it's forty-five minutes of being off duty, of being waited on and conversed with. A second cup of coffee, a little deliberate lingering. No hard topics. Thinking that he's gotten enough of my business woes, I ask how the fund-raising campaign is going for the Artists Collaborative, which is what brought him to us in the first place.

"Well enough. Like a lot of heads of nonprofit organizations, these guys think that once they've hired a consultant, the money will pour in. They don't realize that all we do is show them how to and whom to ask for support; it's up to them to do the asking. It's hard work on their part."

"I think you are dealing with the artistic, not the realistic."

"Mosley and his crew think all it takes to raise money is parties. It takes asking for money. Nobody wants to actually do it."

"So, they're operating on a 'Build it and they will come' fantasy?"

"Something like that. Frankly, I'm looking forward to being done with the AC and getting back to working with my preferred charities."

Adam holds open my coat, and it feels like the end of a date. A breakfast date. Where is the kiss? I startle myself with the thought and by a sense of disappointment in realizing that someday soon he'll be gone, his reason for being in the Berkshires accomplished, and will have moved on to other things, other places.

The dogs are ecstatic to get the breakfast leftovers, and they make quick work of them, the pair inhaling the eggs and bacon and hash browns Adam sets down beside the car as we stand enjoying the sunshine. Chance licks his chops like a dog in a commercial while the other one keeps on scrubbing the cardboard with his tongue. Finally satisfied that nothing of flavor remains, Lucky sits next to me. I give the dog a pat on the head, think a moment about where he came from, the description Adam has given me of the abandoned house, the crackhead boy. In the strength of daylight, the scars are obvious, and I understand Adam's determination to keep this red dog safe. "He's lucky to have you."

"Thanks. I think he is, too. That's kind of why I call him that. Lucky." Adam's an old-school gentleman, and opens my door for me. "And he'll be luckier still to find a forever home."

"Nothing on that score?"

"Not so far. All the rescue organizations I work with seem to be full, so I'm fostering him till a slot opens up."

"Don't you get attached to them, fostering?"

Adam doesn't answer, shuts my door and goes around to the other side. Before he starts the car, he looks at me. "I've thought about it, keeping him. But with my travel, it really wouldn't be fair. The LakeView notwithstanding, it's hard to find accommodations for two big dogs."

"Good thing I'm a pushover."

"Yes. Yes it is."

It is a beautiful Saturday night and Adam is so happy to be enjoying it on the veranda of the LakeView Hotel, a night he might otherwise have had to spend sitting at an eight-top table, suffering through polite conversation. Adam knows that Kimberly must be pretty pissed off with his bailing on her. Maybe it would have been better to have told her the truth, that the idea of being someone's plus one was terrifying. No, not terrifying—appalling. Maybe she would have been better able to accept that reason, instead of the cowardly excuse he'd given her, that he had to be away on business, an excuse that was more like the man he used to be, who always put business before family, friends, human kindness.

Skye has inadvertently reminded him of his origins, not that his upbringing as a foster child isn't always with him. *Foster,* for Adam, is an incendiary term. He wanted to tell her that being fostered isn't a guarantee of being loved. Sometimes it seems to him that only those who foster animals are willing to do it with love, but he knows that's not fair. The short answer, the truth is, yes, he's fond of this red-nose pit bull, but he can't afford to love him. He loves Chance, and that should be enough. This dog, this Lucky, deserves a home where he'll have stability and love.

# CHAPTER 19

"My dad will give us a ride into North Adams." Black Molly leans over Cody as she does her math work sheets. "I thought we'd hang out."

Cody is hoping that the other kids in study hall aren't noticing this tête-à-tête. She hates that she's embarrassed about Molly's attention, that it signals her as even more of an outsider to have it. If Black Molly is the quintessential outlier, she, Cody, is fast becoming the second most typical by being seen as her friend. Taylor and Tyler and that wretched a-hole Ryan have stepped up their torment of her, adding innuendo and suggestive noises to their repertoire of torture, all of it implying that she and Molly are lesbians. Cody can't say for sure, but it is possible that Molly is. And that's fine. In this world, you have to be open-minded. But she hates it when they make it sound like she is, too. Still, a ride into town is a tempting thing. If she can get into town, maybe she can bump into Mingo. Even if she is seen getting into that beat-up old truck Molly's dad drives, it would be worth it. "Okay."

"See you after school." Black Molly gives Cody a play-ful shove.

Mr. Frost pulls up ten minutes after the busses have left the yard, so there are few students left to see Cody get into the cab, squeezed on either side by the double bulk of Mr. Frost and Molly. Mr. Frost doesn't insist on seat belts, and Cody is too overwhelmed to ask to get the catch for the middle lap belt out from under the bench. She just hopes that the bodies on either side of her will act like an air bag in case of emergency. Unlike her own mother, Mr. Frost doesn't ask one question about Molly's day. In fact, he is completely silent. Molly is, too. Cody thinks that this is going to be the longest ride of her life. She waits for Molly to say something, and when she doesn't, Cody asks, "So, where do you want to go?"

Molly shrugs. "McDonald's?"

McDonald's is just fine. She's got three bucks in her pocket and a cheeseburger sounds good. This vegetarian thing is getting old. A little animal protein would taste real good. Of course, Cody won't tell her mother that she's broken her vegetarian fast.

Mr. Frost pulls into the drive-through and speaks for the first time in Cody's hearing, ordering up a bagful of food. Molly swings the truck door open and she and Cody slide out. "Thank you, Mr. Frost."

He just looks at her with dull eyes. "What? Yeah. Okay." He moves the truck up in line.

As the two girls enter the building, it occurs to Cody that no one has spoken about a ride home.

Black Molly and Cody finish their sandwiches, suck down their shakes. Like good fast-food patrons, they clear their tables, dumping the trash, stacking their trays. They head across the street to the Dollar Tree. Cody is out of money, but there really isn't anything there she wants. They wander around, touching stuff, lingering in the cosmetics aisle, moving on to the card section, where Molly pulls out all the suggestive birthday cards and they laugh. It gets kind of boring after a bit, even with the only adult clerk in the place giving them the fish eye, making the loitering so much more interesting.

"Let's get out of here."

Molly ignores her, goes back to the nail polish display, which strikes Cody as weird, given Molly's less than girlie affect.

"Come on, Mol, let's go."

Molly comes back to where Cody waits by the exit. She shrugs. "Yo-kay."

They cross the street, reaching the bench where Cody had been that afternoon when she met Mingo. Molly sits next to her, shoves a hand into the pocket of her down vest. "Want one?" She offers Cody a bottle of black nail polish. She's got three in the palm of her hand.

"You steal those?"

"Course I did. You think I'd pay even a buck for this crap?" She's grinning, her crooked teeth behind the rim of black lipstick showing yellow. "What'd you take?"

"I didn't want anything. No point in taking the risk over shit like that." She hopes that she sounds derisive, not weak. "I'm gonna risk my neck, it's going to be over something worth more than a buck."

Black Molly tucks the bottles back into her vest. Sits back. "Speaking of, when are you gonna bring me something from the rooms?"

Cody has no answer for this. It's been a little while since Molly first brought up this scheme, long enough that Cody has decided that she was just kidding around. She shrugs.

"I can't believe you haven't scored at least one or two tabs of something interesting. Cough syrup, even. Shit, I get stuff out of my grandma's medicine cabinet all the time. She never knows. She doesn't miss them." Black Molly grins, swirls a finger to her temple. "She's getting loony tunes, so all she thinks is that maybe she forgot to take her pills and then took another."

"You don't worry she could, I don't know, have a bad reaction to missing her meds?"

"She's never dropped dead 'cause I take a couple of her Vicodin every time I go over. Besides, it's not like I'd take her heart medication or anything important. Just her pain meds."

"You use them?"

"I told you, it's money in the bank. I get a little collection of pills, sell them to the highest bidder."

Cody has to laugh. "I guess that makes you a drug dealer."

"I guess so. Problem is supply. That's where you come in."

Cody sees it now. She is uniquely positioned to provide Black Molly with product, and, in return, what? This kind of thing goes so far beyond her minor-league rebellion, this flirtation with real trouble, that it makes Cody a little sad. If Black Molly is going to insist, then she's going to have to give up this dubious friendship. "What do I get out of it?" Cody hopes that she sounds sufficiently skeptical that Molly won't think she's a wuss.

"A cut."

Cody picks at the skin around her thumbnail. Bites it. "I don't think so."

"What, not like father like daughter?"

"What do you mean?"

"Your dad. He was killed in a drive-by, right?"

"So?"

"Only gang members and drug dealers get shot like that."

In the paling wash of diminishing sunlight, the street-lights had come on, sodium white and ugly. Every other one flickered with a hiss. Randy was a block ahead of her, strolling, head down, hands in his jean pockets. Even though he wasn't walking fast, she had to pick up her pace to catch up with her father. She was surprised, seeing her father on a street so close to her home, a sighting as rare as a unicorn. She was going to run up and see if she could surprise him in turn. Even though Randy had visitation rights, he'd been mostly absent from her life, but that didn't mean she wasn't happy to see him when she could. He could be charming and a joker, more like a wicked older brother than a parent.

Cody was on her way home from Miranda's house, where they'd been doing homework, although mostly they'd been baking, and now she had a plastic container filled with misshapen Tollhouse cookies in her backpack. She wasn't supposed to go home this way, but it was faster than skirting around this tougher area of town, and she traveled these streets far more often than her mother would ever know. Randy was getting ahead, moving well past where she normally turned off, so she hurried her pace.

Cars rolled by, slowing for the stoplights. When the lights turned green, drivers gunned engines with a throaty suggestion of potency. A small black car with a dented right rear passenger door drifted a little out of its lane, nearly sideswiping a parked car.

Cody realized that Randy had gotten another block ahead of her. She wasn't sure if he'd turned down another street or if he was just out of sight momentarily, certain to heave into view as he crested the hill. She started to move faster. There he was, standing on the corner, maybe waiting for the walk light; or maybe he knew that she was behind him and he was waiting for her. The same small black car that she noticed before was back, like its driver had gone around the block. The passenger window was down and she saw a face, distinctive in the fading light. She thought that she knew him, and her impulse was to wave. Johnny, she remembered, that was his name. He'd been at her dad's apartment a couple of times. Never spoke to her.

The car continued rolling, moving slowly toward her father like some kind of predator. And then it pulled up to the curb where Randy was standing. Maybe this is what he was waiting for, a lift from Johnny. Cody started to run, hoping to catch up with Randy before he climbed into the car, just to say hi, see if he'd put a five-dollar bill in her hand, like he usually did. She was within a few feet, but he hadn't seen her yet.

"Randy!" Cody called to him, and he glanced her way, then motioned for her to wait a moment. Cody came to a stop a few feet from Randy, but close enough to see the charming smile on his face as he leaned toward the open passenger-side window. Suddenly, he stepped backward, almost tripping on the curb, the smile gone, replaced by an O of realization. There was a pop and then the small black car bolted away through the red light.

It wasn't like it was on television, Randy didn't sink to his knees and then fall; he dropped hard and unquestionably dead to the filthy sidewalk.

"S'up?" It's Mingo Ayala.

Cody is startled out of her thoughts. "Hey. S'up yourself."

Mingo sits down on the bench, putting himself between them. Pulls out a pack of cigarettes, recalls his manners and offers one to the two girls. Black Molly accepts; Cody shakes her head no. He gives Molly a sideways glance. "Who are you?"

Molly leans in to accept the light from his Bic. "Black Molly."

"Cool." Mingo looks at Cody. "You got my dog?"

"Yeah. I mean, he's at the hotel."

"Still ain't got no transportation. You got to get him to me here."

"I don't know if I can. Mr. March is here on vacation, not work. So he's probably not going to the Artists Collaborative. That's just across—"

"I know where it is." Mingo shoots twin streams of smoke out of his nostrils.

"You aren't back in that house, are you?"

"Not so far. Still at Front Street."

Cody notices he doesn't call it a home, or a group home or anything. Must be kind of embarrassing, being treated like some kind of orphan. She pictures a Dickensian poorhouse. "Do you go to school?"

"Yeah. Night classes. Workin' construction days."

To Cody, it sounds like Mingo actually has his life in order. Except for his dog.

Black Molly flicks the end of her cigarette with one black nail. "You interested in maybe working with us?"

"Doin' what?"

"Selling."

Mingo laughs. "Right, you two white chicks gonna supply me with what? Tylenol?"

"I'm not kidding. Cody's got access. Guest rooms at the hotel."

"Molly, I never said . . ." This ridiculous notion is getting out of hand.

Cody knows she's got a horrified look on her face, because Mingo laughs again and shakes his head. "Don't worry, little chick. I'm not sayin' I'm not interested, but I'm gonna have to pass. I don't want to fuck up my probation." He drops his butt on the sidewalk, grinds it out, then stands up, planting himself in front of Cody. "You do what you can to get Dawg into town. A-ite?"

"Yeah. I will." Cody looks up at him, shoves her bangs out of her face. "Word."

"And don't be gettin' into trouble." He nods toward Black Molly. "You, too."

Once Mingo has sauntered out of earshot, Black Molly shoves Cody with an elbow. "He thinks he's so tough. My brothers would make headcheese out of him."

"He's all right." Cody pulls her jacket tighter; it's getting chilly. She wants to ask how they're getting home, but she waits for Molly to say something.

Molly lights up another cigarette she's pulled from deep within her jacket. Blows out the smoke. With a practiced gesture, she tips the ash off the cigarette, glances over at Cody. "Call your mother. We need a ride."

"You don't want to meet my mother."

"Sure I do. What? Embarrassed?"

"Kind of."

"Of me?"

"No. Don't be stupid. Of her. She's lame-o."

"There's worse things." She takes another drag. "So, tell me. What was it like to see your dad get plugged?"

Cody doesn't answer. The smoke from Molly's cigarette is in her face.

"Come on, it's kind of cool."

"I wasn't there."

"They ever catch the guy who did it?"

"No."

Molly stubs out the cigarette. Slides her wide bottom closer to Cody. Puts a companionable arm around her shoulder. "He's still out there?"

"Yes." The panic is building; she can hear her pulse in her ears. The dry mouth taste of bile is layering her tongue.

"You worried?"

"Yes."

"Let's just hitch home."

# CHAPTER 20

I stand outside, my fists shoved into the pockets of my jeans. Why is it that every good idea goes to hell because of someone else's failings? Even to my own ears, that sounds harsh, but I'm really getting tired of Carl's failure to finish any project that he isn't interested in. Case in point, the lack of a proper run for the doggy day care that I've sunk weeks of work into and not an inconsiderable amount of money I don't actually have. I've had Carl work on the worst of the four little buildings. He's gutted it. The two bedrooms are now dog-friendly and the tiny kitchen has only a small fridge and a sink left. The tub in the bathroom has been retrofitted with a faucet that turns into a handheld shower should any dog need a bath. The floor is covered in cheap linoleum, but it looks nice even where he had to tack it down over the uneven floorboards. The doorways have new Dutch doors, so that whoever I get to lease the place can keep an eye on the dogs in residence. The next step is a big fenced-in run. Of course, now Carl has disappeared, leaving the key element of the doggy day care unfinished.

So simple, this last piece, and yet so incomplete. On the ground, where the lumberyard truck left them, are the fencing components just waiting for installation. The rented posthole digger leans against the side of the cabin, the days of rental ticking along one by one. I've been forced by finances to choose the cheapest way of building a small enclosed yard, and the least attractive. But I console myself. I'm planning on replacing it with something less utilitarian-looking than chain link just as soon as the doggy day spa begins to pay off. Which may be further away than I had hoped. The one party interested in leasing space isn't interested in leasing a property that isn't ready, even when I offered a rebate on the first month's rent. The woman said it wasn't worth it to her to have to find someone to build the run. As a sole proprietor of my own enterprise, I fully understand the sentiment. Every penny counts. In the meantime, I can't offer the service to my guests, and, with the cost of fencing sitting on my credit card like a deadweight, I'm already losing money on this proposition.

When I talked with him about this project, Adam had been very enthusiastic, assuring me that offering a pet spa to people who would rather spend money on their dog's grooming than on their own massages would put me on the map. And having a place to keep their pets safe and happy while exploring all the region has to offer will be the deciding factor for any guests who are on the fence about bringing a pet in the first place. If Carl doesn't finish this project this week, Adam's optimistic projections are going to have to be recalculated. Speaking of which, Adam is due back today—work this time, not vacation; not hiding out.

Cody comes up beside me. "You think that Carl will ever finish the run?"

"If I knew the answer to that, I might start buying lottery tickets. He's a free spirit."

Cody starts off down the slope, then turns. "What if I know somebody who might be able to do the work?"

"A friend?"

"Kind of. He's just this kid I know." Cody doesn't look directly at me when she says this, toes the dirt beneath her feet. "He works, like, for a carpenter. He's learning a trade."

"And how do you know this boy?"

"What? I make a suggestion and you give me the third degree. Sheesh. Forget it." Cody strides away.

"Wait. Come back and tell me more."

Cody pauses. Turns. "It's stupid. Forget it."

"You think he can do the work?"

"Sure. It's just that . . ."

"What?"

"He'd need a ride to get here."

"From?"

"North Adams."

"And just how do you know him? This kid from North Adams?"

"I just do. No big deal."

"Cody. Stop it. Who is he?"

"He's Mingo Ayala. He's a nice kid. He's not going to, like, break in or murder us. He just needs work."

"How do you know him if not from school?"

"I said, forget it. My whole life isn't school."

There's the clam-up. Right on schedule.

"I'll think about it."

"Mom, it would be a nice thing for us to do, giving a poor kid another chance."

"Another chance at what? Where are his parents?" Even as I throw out the questions, I know that I'm going to let Cody talk me into giving some street kid from North Adams a job. A one-off, simple, a day's worth of work for ten bucks an hour and lunch. That's the best I'll offer. That and a ride. Hey, who knows, maybe he'll prove to be a better handyman than Carl and I can let his lazy ass go. There is something to be said for Cody's better nature, this charitable urge to help someone down on his luck. We've never been churchgoers, but it is nice to think that Cody may have absorbed the basic lessons. Of course, the actual truth might be that Cody sees something of her old world, her city life, in this kid, and all this kindness may be a cure for loneliness. Near as I can figure, she still doesn't have any friends, unless you call those artists at the Collaborative friends.

"All right. I assume you have some way of contacting . . . Mingo, so ask him if he's interested in coming up on Saturday."

"And we'll get him, right?"

"Yes. We'll go pick him up and then take him home at the end of the day."

"Thanks, Mom. Thanks." Cody turns. "And, Mr. March will be here, right?"

"He's here till Sunday. Why?"

"Just asking." Cody is smiling as she heads off to do up her quota of rooms.

I head back to the office. I'll call that prospective doggy day care operator and let her know that the fencing will be up by the end of the week. Maybe saying it out loud will make it true. I know that I'm putting an awful lot of faith in a street kid. Maybe Cody met this Mingo fellow at the AC. He's probably some gifted street artist. Isn't it just like Cody to skip over the facts that would reassure me and make this out-of-the-blue request understandable.

They sit in Mosley's office, Mosley going on about the plans for the big gala, as pleased as Punch with the progress, most of the component parts having come into place already, when Adam notices the pencil sketches pinned to the corkboard wall. Most of what Mosley does leaves Adam cold, concept pieces with no rhyme or reason he can figure out. But these, these are lovely little studies, not one of them bigger than five by seven. It takes him a moment to realize whom he's looking at, but when he does, Adam feels the annoyance percolate. Cody Mitchell, her gawky, girlish figure set in various poses that make her look coy and sophisticated in one sketch, and an utter naïf in the next. Her face tilted in a three-quarter come-hither profile; another full face, eyes wide, lips pursed, hands framing her cheeks, Voguing for the observer.

Chance squeezes his big head under Adam's arm, reminding him to chill out. Maybe Mosley did these before Skye laid down the law about using Cody as a model. Yeah, that's it. Adam lets the irritation out with a breath. Pats the dog, thankful that Chance is, as always, there to push him away from the edge. Adam makes a concerted effort not to look at the sketches, but now that he's noticed them, it's impossible, and he finds himself glancing back at the array of four little portraits of a child-woman. That's what he doesn't like about them: They edge an innocent fourteen-year-old girl out of girlhood and into that dark region of female knowingness. Even if Cody were sixteen or seventeen and had come into her feminine powers, these would still be borderline prurient. Adam can't figure out why they're upsetting to him; there's no nudity per se, nothing lascivious. Nonetheless, the four sketches, to him, sexualize a child, and he digs his fingers deeper into Chance's rump, scratching the dog instead of speaking his mind. And then he wonders if there is something wrong with him, that he should see these pictures in this way.

He's got to get out of here. He interrupts Mosley's monologue. "Sounds like things are under control. I've e-mailed you the final invitation list and I think that you'd better get the invites out by the end of next week."

"Can do. I'll get some help."

"Like Cody?"

"Oh, yeah. She's always good for a little barter. Stuff a few hundred envelopes and I'll give her another lesson in the arts."

"Keep it to stuffing envelopes."

Mosley shrugs. "There's not a lot for her to do around here. She wants more lessons and her mom isn't willing to pony up. So I got to make work for her. Pain in the ass."

"Maybe she should find another teacher."

"No one around here is interested in taking on a student."

"Just you."

"Yeah. Just me." Mosley gets to his feet, drags an ashtray across his cluttered desk, then opens a drawer and pulls out an old-fashioned metal Band-Aid box. "Why do you make it sound like a flaw?"

"Guess those sketches behind you kind of make me nervous."

Chance, still on his feet, nudges Adam again, pressing his moist nose against the skin of his wrist.

Mosley makes a show of turning around to see what Adam is talking about. "Those? That's from memory. Using my imagination. It's art, man. Just art."

"Better hope her mother doesn't see how rich an imagination you have."

"This really isn't any of your business." Mosley gives Adam a conspiratorial smile. "Or, hey, you dating her, the mom? She's definitely a MILF."

"And that's none of *your* business."

Chance sits down, presses his chin against Adam's lap, hard, as if to say, *Pay attention to me.* Adam knows that he should dig his fingers into the dog's loose neck skin, soak up some of his companion's calmness. But, he doesn't. Instead, he gets to his feet. Meeting over. "Keep me posted on the guest list. I'll do more data mining on the folks who say they'll attend."

Mosley pulls a thin joint out of the Band-Aid box, snaps a match into life. "You know, Adam, maybe we're about done here."

"You've paid me for a year, and we're a couple months shy of that; but it's your call." Adam buttons the middle button of his sport coat. "The contract does stipulate that either party can call it quits. But, as you may recall, no refunds." What he is thinking is that the AC is limping along and the forfeit of a couple of grand is not a smart thing to do. What he is also thinking is that he'd be plenty happy to call it quits with this guy. It might even be worth not bothering with a negotiated refund.

And then it occurs to him: If he quits, then his Berkshire trips will be a thing of the past, and that thought makes him a bit sad. As if picking up on that brief floating sense of prenostalgia, Chance bumps his blocky head against the back of Adam's leg, whines softly.


"Girl, you out your mind?"

This wasn't the reaction Cody was expecting from Mingo.

"What do I know about buildin' a fence? I don't know how to do that."

"Can you ask your boss how?"

"My boss, he ain't gonna let me go nowhere. My RC ain't gonna let me go nowhere. Don't you get it?"

"Can my mother, like, sign you out?"

"I dunno. Maybe. But that don't mean I know how to build a fence."

"How hard can it be?"

"Plenty hard. Gotta dig holes, make it straight. They accuse me of smokin' crack, but you, girl, you high on somethin'."

She plays her trump card. "I've got Dawg. He'll be here."

There is a long-enough pause that she thinks maybe Mingo has hung up on her. "A-ite. I'll ask my RC if I can leave for the day. I'll let you know what your mom needs to do to spring me."

"Thanks, Mingo. You'll be fine."

"Doubt it. But okay."

The dog Adam calls Lucky gets to his feet, shakes from nose to tail, and moseys over to where Cody sits on the grass that borders the lake. She's dog-sitting for Mr. March and is glad of the couple of bucks he'll give her for minding the dog. She recognizes the irony: Here she is with the dog and there's Mr. March, close enough to where Mingo is to finally get the two together. Near misses. If she'd been thinking on her feet, she could have suggested that she go with Mr. March to the AC and watch the dog there. But no. She just grinned up like some kind of idiot and said, "D'uh. Sure."

The water is still too cold to put her feet in, and the ground under her bare skin is damp and cold. She hugs the dog to her. "You want to see Mingo?"

The dog licks her chin.

Nonetheless and against all odds, Cody *has* accomplished part one of her plan, to bring Mingo and the dog back together. But for the life of her, she can't quite figure out part two—how to actually give the dog back to him. Maybe Mingo can figure it out. The fact that she's managed to involve her mother in this means that she is also at the mercy of her mother. There's no way she's going to talk Skye into surrendering the dog to Mingo when Mr. March is here and so clear about that never happening. The adults will team up against the kids. Maybe it doesn't matter. Maybe it will be enough to have a short reunion, enough that Mingo will see that she's on his side, that she's his advocate. And then Cody wonders why she cares. It's not like Mingo is especially nice to her, or even grateful that she saved his life. Her grandmother would say that he's got a chip on his shoulder. It's what she used to say about Randy: "He's a little man with a big chip on his shoulder." Even at the funeral home, Florence Lenihan had trouble saying one nice thing about Randy, offering a stiff condolence to the aunt who had raised him: "Sorry for your loss."

The dog points his red nose up the slope toward the hotel. Cody follows the dog's point with her eyes, but all she can see is the east end of the building, the peak of the roof between green pines. If you could sit on the roof of the hotel, you'd be able to still see the lake. That's kind of a cool idea. Maybe she can talk Skye into having a rooftop deck built. Make this stupid, gross building into something interesting instead of an outdated box with nothing more architecturally interesting than the double porches stuck onto its face. Really, when you think about it, the place is really nothing more than a glorified motel and not even as interesting as the Bates Motel or that hotel in *The Shining*. Tyler and Taylor call it the "No-Tell Motel," followed by the usual suggestive gestures or kissy noises. Cody really wishes that they'd get some new material.

# CHAPTER 21

It's still daylight when Adam pulls into the parking lot of the LakeView after his meeting. Half a dozen cars are nosed up to the cement porch and the drapes in most of the upper-level rooms are pulled back for guests to take in the view. A few visitors are lounging on the plastic Adirondack chairs, and conversations drift down from above. It's nice to see Skye getting some traffic. Even nicer to see a couple of dogs in residence, besides his own, of course.

Cody is sitting on the edge of the porch, her skinny legs bared in Daisy Dukes, a midriff-baring crop top completing the ensemble. The early May day is all of sixty degrees, hardly warm enough for this outfit, and Adam has to stifle the paternal urge to order her back in the house to put on some clothes.

Seeing his car pull into the parking space, Cody rises, tugs a little at the frayed edge of her shorts, and comes down the steps, reminding Adam of a filly, all long legs and pretend confidence. Should he mention those sketches to Skye, or just try this time to keep his nose out of her business? *Oh, Gina, where are you when I need you?* She'd know exactly what was appropriate, would tell him that he's making too big a deal out of it; or that he should act. Adam was never a shrinking violet when it came to action. He made a career out of good, big, quick, emphatic decisions. But when his life changed, his ability to react faltered. One moment's wrongful act undermined his confidence completely.

He opens the back door and Chance hops out of the car and immediately greets Lucky, as if they have been separated for days instead of a couple of hours. The pair of them make a run around the building, heading for the cabins. Adam slips off his jacket, tosses it onto the backseat, forgetting that the seat is covered in dog hair. He takes a deep breath, and even his inadequate human nose can detect the luscious scent of frying burgers, Skye making dinner, no doubt. Another reason the dogs have scampered off to the cabins, such chowhounds.

"He was a good boy, Mr. March. We took a walk to the lake."

Adam slips a five out of his wallet, hands it to Cody.

She thanks him and slides it into her back pocket, scampers off herself.

*I missed you so much, I say to my friend Lucky. He missed me, too, but he's redolent of the exciting scents abounding in this place. Water and mud and creatures and newborn grass. And girl. He's been chumming up to that sad girl. Sometimes she's not sad. Sometimes she's kind of like my man, a little pissed off. Sometimes more than a little. With Adam, I cure that. With Cody, I don't have to, but I want to. I wriggle and act like a much younger dog, and the anger or sadness leaven. I don't know what she does about it when I'm not around. I have to say that when Lucky is with her, which is something we've been doing more over the past few visits, she is quite cheerful. Like me, Lucky has that innate sense of when to override a human's mood, supersede the negative vibes with a positive approach. Or a joke. Like threatening to chew something a little inappropriate, like a slipper or a chair leg. My favorite dodge is to grab a ball or a stick and entice Adam to play. It was one of the very first things we did together and is still my favorite. Except for my work. Since being educated in therapeutics, I love saving Adam from himself best of all. Like today. That Mosley fellow was getting under Adam's skin, as he most always does. Immediately upon sensing the disturbance, I got up from my place at Adam's feet and pushed my head underneath his elbow so that he had to stroke my head. Within seconds, the tension was gone and I was given a fabulous back scratch as a reward. All without a word, all without Mosley's even being aware that a crisis had loomed.*

*The girl, Cody, gives me a nice pat, too. And I notice that Lucky has done well keeping her company today. She seems content. Although I detect a sense of something quite deep that isn't entirely perfect. It's always there, this vibration, what I would consider nervousness if she were one of my kind. They are everywhere, the dogs who cannot relax because of some history that keeps them vigilant. Like them, she's never still.*

The veggie burgers cook too quickly on the gas grill, becoming hockey pucks the minute I take my eye off them. I start to throw them out, then see Chance come along, tail wagging, panting in the still-warm air, looking like an appetite on legs. "Here, boy. You like soy?" I break the burgers into small bits and offer one to the dog. I'm a little surprised at what a gentleman he is about picking the morsel off my hand. For the size of his satchel mouth,

you'd think he'd take my whole hand to get at the bit.
"Want another?"

The other dog, Lucky, appears, his tongue hanging
over the side of his mouth, looking more silly than fierce.
His red nose pokes at me, as if to say, *Don't forget me!*
Cody shows up, dressed now in flannel pajamas and a
nubby knit pullover.

"What did you do to my veggie burgers?"

"Overestimated cooking time. Sorry. Will you dig out
a couple more?"

Given that she's been granted her most recent wish,
getting Mingo up here, Cody does what's asked without
comment, almost smiling.

Both wriggly dogs suddenly become still, two noses
upraised, two sets of ears cocked forward, two whiplike
tails stiffened and pointing east. Then I hear the whistle,
and the dogs are gone. I lift another real hamburger off
the platter, set it beside mine on the meat-designated side
of the little grill. Two cheeseburgers is one too many.
Maybe Adam is interested in a bite to eat. After all, I've
thawed out the hamburgers and really can't waste the
meat. I've also got potato salad, store-bought at the Big
Y, sure, but decent stuff. Too much for just the two of us,
and Cody won't eat leftovers on a bet.

Cody reappears with a new veggie burger. "I nuked it,
so just let it sit for two seconds on the grill to give it a
little texture."

"Do you mind seeing if Adam wants one of these
cheeseburgers?" I say it before I can think about it, as casually as I can, as if inviting hotel guests to dinner is
normal.

There is a second of utter silence; then Cody trots off.

How beautiful my daughter really is. No sign yet of a
feminine sashay. Her dusty blond hair is skinned back into
a tight ponytail, revealing a smooth forehead, which must

be the envy of those adolescents whose skin is peppered
with acne. When Cody smiles, that rarest of flowerings,
her whole face glows with youth, and she bares a heart-
breaking resemblance to Randy.

Mr. March is sitting in the Adirondack chair, ankle crossed
over a knee. He sees her coming. Before she reaches him,
he turns his face away from her. "I saw the sketches of you.
In Mosley's office."

"What sketches?" she asks, but she knows exactly what
he's talking about.

"The little five-by-sevens hanging over his desk."

Mosley had sat there watching her as she cleaned
brushes. He'd smelled of pot, and something else, something funky. When she opened the can of turpentine, the
fumes filled the small space, masking any other scent. She
let her hair fall into her face, gave him a three-quarter profile. She knows now about three-quarter profiles, how
they make a face seem more interesting than it really is.
"I'm not modeling for him, if that's what you're saying."

"No. Not at all."

Cody doesn't believe him. Mr. March has butted into
her business before, and she thinks that he's more than
capable of doing it again. If he gives her mother any reason to worry that Mosley isn't keeping to her demands,
well, that would really suck. Cody pictures her mother
charging down to North Adams and telling Mosley off,
then making her quit for real this time. "I'm not. Modeling. He did those from memory."

"I'm sure he did." Mr. March stands up, pats his leg.
"Come on, boys. Let's go."

Cody is left on the porch, watching Mr. March and the
two dogs follow the path that she and Lucky have so recently traveled. Just who does he think he is? A father?
Her father? Some nerve. She's had one of those, although,

mostly, Randy was hardly a father. Not the kind of dad that her friends had, worrying them to death about going to the mall, what they were wearing, why it was inappropriate. Handing out ten-dollar bills so that they could buy lunch. Making the girls promise not to keep them waiting at the mall entrance when it was time to go home. Caring about them. Randy didn't even care that she never called him Dad. Or gave him a Father's Day card except that once, when he barely looked at it, like he didn't understand what it was or what it said. That he felt himself so far removed from being a father, he didn't react to the family she'd drawn on the front of the construction-paper card: mom, dad, child.

Mr. March is a nosy jerk, mentioning those sketches. Cody just hopes that he doesn't say anything to Skye. Mosley kind of makes her feel special, too, in his own way. Like she's not some kid, but a serious student of art; the way he puts his hand on her shoulder when he looks at her work, gives it a little rub in approval, or squeezes it when he has to say something critical; maybe like a dad would do.

She'll lie and tell her mother that Mr. March wasn't around. It's close enough to the truth.

          •     •     •

The veggie burgers are done and I stack them on a plate, safe from ruin. Cody hasn't come back with Adam, hasn't come back at all. The cheeseburgers will join the hockey-puck veggie burgers if I'm not careful. I don't know if Adam likes his burgers medium or well done. It doesn't matter. They're done enough for me, and it's looking like I'll be the only one eating. I set the cooked patties on the platter, go back into the cabin. Shut the door.

# CHAPTER 22

"When we get back, I want you to start with room nine first. I've got another dog family coming in."

Cody is pulling two slices of toast out of the toaster. She drops one. "What? I thought Mr. March was staying until Sunday."

"Change of plans. He's entitled." I don't mention that I was counting on that extra day to pay this Mingo kid. Adam had been contrite, explaining that an unexpected chance to meet with potential adopters for Lucky had come up, someplace halfway between here and home, so it seemed to make more sense to head back to Boston afterward.

"Is he gone already?"

"I have no idea. Probably not; it's early. He's got till eleven to check out."

"Let's go." Cody drops the toast into the trash.

"What?"

"Sooner we get Mingo, sooner you get to open that kennel."

* * *

Mingo is a long, lanky kid and his cropped black hair has lightning bolts etched into it, visible beneath the edges of his trucker hat, which is canted rakishly to one side. His sideburns are like a fine tracery, following the contours of his narrow jaw and meeting in the middle at the very apex of his chin. I signed him out of the group home, a place that reeks of adolescent boy. Mingo, however, reeks of something a bit more pleasant, an overdose of AXE. His clothes are clean, his sneakers—kicks—spotless, and it makes me wonder if he has no idea how dirty he's going to get digging holes in the thick, spring-wet topsoil. He's carrying a knapsack, and I hope that he's got a change of clothes in it.

As a practiced concierge, I chat the boy up; all the while, Cody, relegated to the backseat, leans forward against her seat belt as if she's going to put a hand over my mouth to stop me from making a fool of myself should it become necessary. I keep to the impersonal, really not wanting to know too much about how this kid ended up where he did, content enough to let us all pretend that this isn't a tad unusual. Like it's a common practice for me to pick up a strange kid with a rap sheet and take him home to do something my handyman should have done.

"I hope we weren't too early. Cody was anxious to get going." The gamma rays of annoyance are burning a hole in the back of my head and I clearly hear the huffing from the backseat. Cody had been impatient to get going and then, once at the residence, which wasn't, thank you very much, easy to find, she'd pushed to get us back in the car and on the road.

When I offer a stop at Dunkin' Donuts, you might think that I'd suggested robbing a bank along the way.

"Mom, aren't we in a hurry?"

"Enough time for a quick doughnut. What do you say, Mingo?"

"A-ite. Sound good."

Cody fumes, but she orders a glazed doughnut and an iced coffee. Mingo lingers a bit over the selection displayed on the drive-through board, settles on the same.

"You can have more than one. Why don't I get a box?"

Mingo, all Mr. Cool, flashes a very boyish smile. "That be dope."

I'm pleased with myself. *Dope.* Cool.

When we arrive back at the hotel, Mingo climbs out of the front seat, stands with his hands on his hips, for all the world like he's waiting for something. Instructions, I guess.

"The cabins are out back. Let me show you."

Cody trails along, the box of doughnuts under her arm.

"So, where he at? Why ain't he here?" Mingo and Cody stand side by side, looking at the rolls of fencing, the stack of metal posts, and the bag of dry cement material. He's exchanged his crisp kicks for a pair of heavy work boots.

"I guess he had to leave."

"So I'm here to do all this work and ain't gonna get my dog back?"

"Not today. But he'll be back. I checked the reservations; he'll be back in a couple weeks."

"So, what I'm supposed to do? Your mom got more projects for me?"

"She could. Besides, she's paying you good money."

"Good enough. This is gonna be hard." Mingo picks up the posthole digger. "I need a measuring tape and a level."

"I'll get them." Cody is relieved to have a reason to get away from Mingo, to put a little space between his disappointment and herself.

When she gets back, Mingo has marked where he will need to set posts. He doesn't speak to her, just sets to work.

In a few minutes, he removes his jacket, and she takes it without comment. She's got the tape and the level, but there's no need for them yet, not till the first hole is dug. She doesn't know if he really knows how deep to dig, but she keeps her mouth shut. Mingo's posthole digger hits rock. He spits out an expletive. "Got a shovel?"

It goes on like this for two hours. The boy works in silence, except for the occasional effort-pushed grunt. The mounds of topsoil collect; the hand-dug rocks pile up. The sun breaks through the cloud cover, and the day's warmth pushes Mingo to pull off his shirt, leaving him in a wife-beater and sagging jeans, the deep waistband of his Joe Boxers showing. His ropy arms don't seem up to the task. His sunken chest is like a much younger boy's, rather than that of a young man on the edge of a raw adulthood. The heavy scent of AXE fades against the more pungent scent of sweat. Mingo jabs the end of the posthole digger into each hole like Starbuck jabbing his harpoon into a whale. Jerks the tailings out. Sweat drizzles from under the blue trucker's cap. And he never says a word to Cody.

Like a squire, Cody holds whichever lance he isn't using—the shovel, the posthole digger—swapping one for the other as he works. Her legs are beginning to ache and she longs to sit down. Mingo keeps going. The grungy white wifebeater is soaked through, a Rorschach pattern of dark sweat wings on his back. And his angry silence does not abate. Cody is guilty of a bait and switch and she knows it. It wasn't her fault, God no. But maybe she should have let Mingo know that the dog might be gone. That Mr. March was leaving. She hasn't been fair. And then it hits her.

"You know, if you'd bailed on us today, there'd be no way I could get you back up here when Mr. March comes back. Mom wouldn't give you a second chance."

Mingo stabs the posthole digger into the last hole,

pauses to wipe the sweat from his forehead, then rests it against the handles. "Girl, I don't like being played. You played me."

"I didn't. How was I supposed to know he'd leave before you could get here? I'm not a psychic."

"Next time, come up with a better plan. One that don't involve hard labor."

"A-ite."

"Girl, you ain't black, so don't you be usin' the talk."

"Sorry." Cody hands Mingo the shovel. "And don't you be calling me *girl*."

"Yes, miss." He flashes her a grin, and Cody knows that they're past the hard part.

By noon, all of the holes are dug. As if on cue, Skye appears. "You kids hungry?"

Mingo pulls a blue bandanna out of his pocket, swipes it across his forehead, stuffs it back in his pocket. "Yes, ma'am." Mingo scoops up his discarded shirt and pulls it on.

Cody shrugs. "Guess so."

"Good. Come on into the cabin. I've got lunch ready." Skye heads back to their cabin.

"The bathroom is over there." Skye points Mingo to it, and looks to Cody to finish setting the small table. She's got a green salad and bowls of chicken and tuna salads on the counter. "How's it going?"

"Good. He's done with the digging." Cody puts plates down, jerks open the drawer to find utensils.

"I hope that he measured. Would be a shame to have to dig more."

"Don't worry, he did. Twice. Says it's better to measure twice and dig once." Figures her mom would find a way to throw shade on Mingo's abilities.

Mingo comes back into the room, wiping his hands on his jeans. Cody catches the look on her mother's face, can't quite read it, wills her not to say anything. But she does. "Did I forget to put towels in the bathroom?"

The boy doesn't answer, just shrugs and finishes drying his hands on his shirt.

"Mingo, you can use the towels."

Cody is mortified.

The kids have gone back outside to work on the fence project, leaving me to clean up. I have to say that I'm pleased with things so far. The boy seems nice enough, has enough manners to say *please* and *thank you,* something Cody failed to do. Obviously, I'm still not 100 percent happy about Cody's fascination for this street kid, but as long as he does the job he's been hired for, I'm okay with it for today. Sometimes you just have to give kids what they want in order for them to change their minds.

Unfortunately, Cody has blown off doing up the rooms, so I've spent the morning doing it all. I've got Adam's room—funny how I've begun thinking of it as his—done. I've got another dog family coming this afternoon, a couple from the Midwest with a Sheltie, which more than makes up for Adam's early departure financially. It seems like dog people need to identify their dogs by breed or breed type; it's not enough just to say they're bringing a dog. They always say they've got a dachshund, or a shih tzu rescue. *Rescue* is the key adjective, and when it's deployed, I know that these are not *owners;* these are pet *parents.* They are always surprised that someone like me, who has opened—some of—her doors to them has no animal of her own. I tell them that having a teenage daughter is animal enough. I've yet to get a laugh out of that one.

I'm just finishing up room 15 when Cody comes up to report that the one bag of cement mix isn't enough. Looks like it's back to the lumberyard. At first, I think that I'll just leave the kids here to hang out while I'm gone, but they both pile into the car before I suggest it. Evidently, a run down to North Adams with me is an attractive idea. This time, Mingo climbs into the backseat, plugs in earbuds, and looks out the window. When I have to remind him to fasten his seat belt, he bops his head in time to whatever is worming its way into his ears, but he does what I ask.

"Can you drop us off at the dollar store, Mom?"

"What do you need there?"

"We just want to look around."

"At the dollar store?"

"Ma'am, I need some stuff. Personal care." Mingo pops the left earbud back into his ear. "I don't get time to shop." Implication, what with the quasi-incarceration of a group home and an on-the-job training program.

I really don't know if I'm supposed to leave the youth on his own, and really don't know if I should trust him. That's an awful thought, but it's true. What's to keep him from bolting? Then again, no one told me I had to be watching him every minute. The resident counselor at the house just told me that he needed to be back by curfew, a reasonable nine o'clock, not that I'm going to take him back home that late. Three trips to North Adams in one day is enough, and I'm going to get him home before dark.

"How about we all go? I'm sure there are a few things I need." Offer a compromise, my best defense with Cody.

"Mom." Cody is using her reasonable voice, the one that will soon enough pitch itself into a squeal of invective. "That's not efficient. You go get the cement; we go and get the stuff he needs, and we don't spend so long that we'll lose the light and Mingo won't be able to finish the job."

"Are you sure you aren't on the debate team?" Keep the discussion light. After all, I wouldn't want to embarrass Cody in front of the boy. Again. "Okay. Okay. Against my better judgment, I'll drop you guys off and be back in twenty minutes. Be there out front."

"Got it."

"A-ite."

"Do you have money?" I ask Cody.

"Enough. It's a dollar store."

Skye drops the pair off at the entrance to the Dollar Tree, reminding them, yet again, that she'll be back in twenty, don't keep her waiting, don't make her go in and find them. She's mortifying. As soon as the car pulls out of the parking lot, Cody and Mingo make a beeline for the McDonald's across the street. As arranged by a couple of texts, there are two boys loitering outside, the giant cups of soda with the McDonald's logo giving them leave to remain on the property. They greet Mingo with all the pomp and circumstance of a returning hero. Cody has a hard time following the conversation, peppered as it is with hip-hop slang and Spanglish. She stands aside, smiles. Waits for an introduction that is clearly not going to happen. The boys are a bit older than Mingo, she thinks. Pretty close to being grown-ups. Like Mingo, they sport the rapper chic of hoodies. Precious minutes go by while the trio catch up. Cody feels more and more invisible. Finally, Mingo turns to her. "This is my man Dre, and my man Kareem. This is Cody. She's cool."

Cody feels an unaccountable sense of pleasure at the grace of Mingo's introduction. *She's cool.* Nobody's thought that of her. Ever.

"Man, it's good to see you." Dre punches Mingo in the shoulder and the pair drop into a boxing stance. Feint, laugh, feint. "You missin' some good stuff."

"I'm done with that. You know it."

"Where that dog at, man?" The guy called Kareem sucks the last few drops of soda out of his cup.

It takes a beat before Mingo replies. "He's okay. Gettin'

taken care of. You know, while I'm"—he smiles—"tied up."

"You know Russell is looking for him?" Dre shoots his crumpled cup into the trash with a three-pointer. "Not too happy with you." He laughs, puts a big hand on Mingo's shoulder, and the age difference becomes more obvious. "Best return the man's property."

"He's good where he is." Mingo shoves his hands into his pockets, twists away from Dre's grip.

"Russell says you stole him."

"It was a deal. Fair and square. I gave Russell what he wanted and he gave me the dog. End of story."

Cody is starting to get nervous. She doesn't like the way these two guys are looking at Mingo. "Hey, Mingo, we should get back. Mom'll be there in a couple of minutes and you should have bought your stuff."

She's broken the spell. Dre knocks knuckles with Mingo. "It's good to see you, man. Stay outta trouble, a-ite?"

"You, too, man." Mingo claps Kareem on the shoulder. "Keep it real, home slice."

Departing takes the same ceremonial handwork as greeting, and Cody's heart is beginning to race against the dread of blowing this whole charade by being late to meet Skye.

"Hey, look, it's Smelly Melly's BFF. What brings you here?" It's Ryan, her most consistent tormentor. Ryan's greeting is accompanied by girlish giggles. He's amusing Tyler and Taylor. The girls are dressed in their lacrosse uniforms, their hair wrestled into tight, high ponytails. "Don't you look cute in those shitkickers. Very fashion forward," Taylor—or Tyler—teases. "Bet your BFF loves you in those. Very B.U.T.C.H."

Cody can't carry off the impression that these kids

don't bother her, and she's angry at the hot flush of embarrassment that she knows has painted her face crimson. "Shut up." It's lame, but the best she can do. "Just shut up!"

Ryan makes a kissy noise and a rude gesture and is suddenly on his back. Mingo has one foot pressing firmly on his throat, and the lacrosse girls are screaming. Mingo's friends are watching, laughing, high-fiving each other. The takedown has them amused.

Mingo leans over, putting his face close to Ryan's terrified one. "You ain't much of a gentleman, are you? Why you pickin' on this kid? Ain't cool. Got it? I hear you be disrespectin' her again, you best watch your back."

"I've got witnesses; I'm going to press." At that point, it's Mingo doing the pressing, and Ryan's attempt at regaining some dignity is cut short.

"Ima lettin' you up now. You get the fuck outta here."

The girls haven't waited for Ryan. They're run-walking away as fast as they can.

Ryan is a little slow to get back to his feet, and Mingo offers a hand. After a moment's consideration, Ryan takes it.

Mingo jerks Ryan to his feet, keeps a grip on his hand, draws him close in a hostile hug. "You tell my friend here you be sorry."

"Sorry."

"Say her name."

"Cody. Sorry, Cody." Ryan yanks his hand away from Mingo's and follows the girls.

"Who the fuck is he? Why he all up in your grill?"

"Ryan. He and the Bobbsey Twins there love nothing better than to pick on me. I'm not like them, I'm not like anyone around that stupid town, and they hate me."

Mingo gently places a hand on Cody's shoulder and she thinks she's going to melt with gratitude.

# CHAPTER 23

*I was enjoying a quiet car doze along with my pal when the car stopped. Not having a proper human sense of time, I couldn't tell if we'd been on the road for hours or minutes. I didn't have the need to relieve myself and I wasn't hungry, so I think that it wasn't a long period of time since we'd left the hotel. Half a day? An hour? Even though I'd been completely asleep, I had been aware of the voices coming out of the car, and Adam speaking to them. My kind haven't evolved enough yet to discern the words that come out of cars, or the other sounds that have Adam tapping his fingers against the wheel. In this case, the words coming out of the car, just above my head as I lounged in the front seat—thank you, Lucky, for being in the back—did sound more male than female, like the female voice that Adam listens to without answering. This voice Adam had been responding to, and the only words I understood out of his mouth were the usual: Okay, good, fine. Another day. Then Adam pulled to the side of the road and shut the car off and made some noises that suggested that he wasn't certain of himself. This almost never happens. In the car, I mean.*

*Aren't we getting out? I rumbled the question and got a pat on the head. We did get out then, and Lucky and I made ourselves busy sniffing around, marking territory in this place I had never seen before, while Adam sat on a bench and watched us. Eventually, Adam stood up, called us to him, and we climbed back into the car. Where I had sensed indecision before, now I knew that Adam was focused again. After another short stop for gas and a package of those sublime beef sticks, we were headed toward the sun.*

When the potential adopters had had a sudden conflict and couldn't meet today, it just seemed more logical to go back to the LakeView than drive all the way to Boston. Adam hadn't even gotten as far as Orange when he got the cancellation from the would-be owners. Not even halfway home. And the idea of turning around appealed deeply. He dropped a quick text to Skye to see if he could get his room back, got a quick answer: Yes.

Skye is nowhere to be seen, her car gone, so while he waits, Adam takes the dogs around back to get a closer look at how this dog-run project is going. Lucky puts his nose to the ground like a tracking dog, inhaling with audible huffs; his tail is wagging, as if he's reading a good story. He keeps looking up, checking the air, then back to the ground, sniffing the ground hole by hole. Chance just goes from post to post, making his mark against each one, clearly less interested in whatever it is that has the other dog's full attention. He looks bored, yawns, and flops down on the springy grass, then rolls over and does his supine alligator imitation. Lucky circumnavigates the perimeter of the future pen, not bothering to lift his leg, just wagging his tail. He goes around once, then again.

Twice around and he begins transecting the flat area between the posts.

By Adam's reckoning, the job is half done—the hard part. All but two of the posts are up and the cement is setting, but none of the fence fabric has been attached. Adam walks around the space, thinking that it's not a bad job. The posts are straight and even in height. It's a miracle that Skye got Carl to finally start the job, but he has to wonder if the handyman will ever finish it, or will he bail on Skye because it's trout season, or pigeon season, or whatever excuse he needs to go off and leave the project where it lies. If it was his business, he'd have fired Carl a long time ago, but, he has to remind himself, it isn't his business.

Chance continues to mark territory, Lucky is still bisecting the space into quadrants, a canine surveyor of the invisible. No harm letting his boys be the first to claim rights, not that he's much inclined to have them penned up. One of the unexpected charms of coming up to the Berkshires for Adam has been the freedom that his dogs have enjoyed. Cooped up in a city town house, with leash walks to an enclosed dog park, is hardly the same as being able to run down the trail to the lake, to be natural dogs.

The dogs catch his eye; sniff fest over, they are now wrestling with each other, taking turns at being submissive. Chance pounces on Lucky, rolling him over, and plants two feet on his broad chest, mouths the other dog's muzzle. Simultaneously, they both decide that the game is over and jump to their feet, sync their nose-to-tail shakes, and bound over to where Adam stands on the front steps of the doggy day care cabin. He's an Adam sandwich, pressed left and right by the solid bodies of the two dogs. He squats to receive sloppy kisses. "Lucky, are you ready to have a forever home?" He's moderately annoyed at the cancellation by the potential adopters, but he knows that patience is key in this rescue game. Tomorrow is another day. And he gets another opportunity to be here on a beautiful spring evening with these two dogs.

Lucky doesn't reply. Chance cocks his head, as if he is thinking about the words. Adam knows that Chance is going to miss this guy, and he feels a moment of regret. But it's always what's in the dog's best interest, meaning the adoptee. Chance has his forever home and his job security. Lucky deserves the same. He's a survivor, like Chance. Deserving of a loving, safe home. And, if this doesn't work out, maybe he will just keep Lucky for himself. For Chance.

Lucky extricates himself out from under Adam's arm, puts his nose back to the ground, and, tail beating from side to side, follows some olfactory trail right to Skye's cabin door. He sits on her steps, then scratches at the screen door.

"Hey, come away from there."

Lucky looks over his shoulder at Adam but doesn't move.

"No one's home. Come." Adam guesses the dog is looking for Cody, a little surprised to think that the dog had become that attached to the girl.

Skye's car pulls into the parking space next to the cabin and three doors open up. The dog leaps off the steps and runs to the car. He's making a weird yowling noise and is fairly dancing with excitement. A young man gets out of the front passenger seat, drops to the ground, opens his arms. The dog launches himself into the boy's arms, knocking the kid's hat off in his joyful kissing, and the pair fall to the ground in an ecstasy of reunion.

Cody emerges from the backseat, Skye from the driver's. Both look at the boy and dog, and then at him. Suddenly, Cody breaks into a smile that changes her usually sullen looks into something radiant. "Mom, Mom, you didn't tell me they were coming back. This is so cool, so cool."

Skye slams her car door, the look on her face pure puzzlement.

"Don't you get it? Lucky. Dawg. He's Mingo's dog. Don't you see? See how happy they are?"

The boy gets up off the ground, where the excited dog had pinned him down, bathing his face in kisses. "He look good." He puts a hand out to Adam. "Thank you, man. For taking care of him. For bringing him back to me."

Adam doesn't take the offered hand. "I've fostered him." He can't let there be any misunderstanding. There's no way he's going to give this dog back to a kid who will put him in fights. "Look, son, he's adoptable now. He's going to a new home."

Mingo reaches for the dog's collar. "Say again?"

"What's your name, son?"

"Mingo. And I'm not your son. Ain't no one's son."

"Mingo, he can't go back with you. I was there that night, with Cody. I know what you were up to. You are in no position to keep him."

"I'm clean, healthy. You can't take him from me."

"Where do you live?"

Mingo goes quiet. Keeps his hand on the dog's collar.

"He's in a group home, in North Adams. He's here to build that fence." Skye has stepped up, puts her hand on Mingo's shoulder. He promptly shrugs it off. "Somehow, and I don't know how, he and Cody have become friends." Skye shoots Cody a look. "And I'm guessing that this friendship has something to do with that dog. Which suggests that Cody has been less than forthcoming about the fact that Mingo here is the boy she found in the crack house that night last fall."

"Mom. Don't." Cody has stopped smiling and is now radiant with embarrassment.

"Yes, he was. Cody found him half dead. This dog was chained to the wall." Adam feels Chance bump up against him, drive his head up under Adam's fist. "I'm very glad to hear that he's gotten some help, no doubt sentenced to it, but that doesn't change the fact that he's an unsuitable owner. That he probably used this dog to pay for those drugs. In the pit."

"I may have done a lot of things, but never that. And the things I did, they're my business."

"Mingo, he's got scars. Recent scars. You've fought him, haven't you? That's how you earned your money."

Mingo pulls himself up to stand tall. "He was fought, yeah. But I took him. I paid for him." He looks into Adam's eyes. "I saved him. I got him stitched up and I got him neutered."

The one thing Adam is certain about fighting dogs is that the boys who pit them don't get them neutered. It's the masculine ethos carried out by a type of dog that only wants to please. But Adam won't be defeated. He didn't succeed in business by backing away. He's always prided himself on recognizing liars. "Mingo, be reasonable. We found you nearly dead in a crack house. I know that you're in recovery, and that's commendable, but your history would suggest that this dog is better off—"

"Man, ain't you ever done something you regretted? Something you had to work past?"

*Regrets? Oh, yes. One moment's loss of control and a whole life goes spinning away.* It takes Adam a moment to collect himself. "Of course I have. But do you regret fighting this dog?"

"What more do I have to say to you? I never fought Dawg. I saved him from—" He stops. "Someone."

"Could that 'someone' take him back?"

"I'll never let him." The boy's hand is on the dog's head, and the dog is looking up at him with the same kind of attachment Chance shows to Adam. It's uncanny how even the worst owner can evoke this canine passion.

"He won't, Mr. March. I know he won't." Cody steps up to stand beside Mingo and swipes off her glasses. "Dawg is like his—"

"Don't say it, girl. What I said, that was between us."

Adam gathers himself. "That doesn't change the fact that you certainly aren't allowed to have dogs where you live."

Mingo scowls, nods his head. "Yeah, but . . ."

"Don't you want him to have a stable home? A forever home?"

Mingo, who has met Adam's eyes throughout the conversation, suddenly drops his head, pets the dog, his long, tapered fingers finding purchase in the dog's loose neck skin. He makes a derisive sound. "Forever home? What the fuck is that?"

And then Adam gets it. He and Mingo have a lot more in common than would expect. He, too, knows about not having a family of his own. Of being insecure. Of being a ward of the state. He's trying to talk the boy into giving a dog that which he will never have for himself, a home. He doesn't know where to go with his argument.

"Mr. March, I have an idea." Cody's head comes up only to Mingo's shoulder, but her look is that of a tough chick with flyaway blond hair. A determined little chick.

"Cody, this really isn't our business." Skye looks like she wants to reach for Cody, pull her away from the boy, but she keeps her hands fixed tight to her hips.

Adam wonders for a moment what she thinks of him. Does she think he's a bully now? Is he showing her a side of himself that he's struggled so hard to keep under control?

"It *is* our business, Mom. It is. What if we keep Dawg here? Mingo can come up and visit with him, and—"

"Cody, really." Skye looks panicked, and Adam certainly understands why she might be.

"Say yes. Please. Don't you always say you want to do the fair thing?" Cody doesn't sound like a petulant teenager; she sounds like a negotiator. "This is fair."

Mingo sucks at his lower lip, not looking at Cody, not looking at Adam. Then he does. "I'm down wi' that. Till I get out. No longer than that."

Skye throws Adam a look, pleading for some adult help. He doesn't envy Skye. After all, he's been there before, helpless in front of a persuasive and fired-up adolescent, and it's a scary place, even for a former Master of the Universe. He is greatly relieved when Skye falls back on the only thing she can do to defuse the situation.

"I'll think about it."

Score one for Mom.

"How long is that going to take? Mr. March is going to take Dawg away tomorrow."

"Tomorrow. I'll let you know tomorrow, before he leaves. Okay, Adam?"

"That's fine, but remember that I've got potential adopters out there. We're meeting tomorrow night. To introduce Lucky to them."

"His name is Dawg. Don't rob him of that, too." Mingo lets go of the dog's skin. "Come on, boy. You be with me for now." Mingo walks back to the car and pulls out the bag of dry cement, the dog following, his nose fairly buttoned to the boy's leg. "Meantime, I keep workin' on the fence." He gives Adam a deathly look. "It's good money."

Skye manages a weak smile. "Thank you, Mingo."

Skye and Adam stand side by side as the kids go back to working on the dog run. Skye shrugs. "Shit, Adam. What do I do now?"

"I guess you think about it." Adam has never liked compromise, but he has learned how to accept it. "At least you'll get that run done."

Chance has trotted off after the trio, and the two dogs flop down on the grass to watch Cody and Mingo unroll the chain link for the fence. After a minute, it's clear that Cody isn't quite strong enough for the task, so Adam joins the workforce. No one says anything as the dog yard is assembled.

*Humans can be so clueless. To me, it was clear that Dawg, for that's how he thought of himself, had picked up on the scent of his boy. I had, too; it was potent. I had no interest in it, so I let him inhale the clues as they appeared until, lo and behold, the physical boy himself appeared. The reunion made me think of my reunion with Adam after that dark time. I was in no condition to leap up and kiss his face, so I had to satisfy myself and show him that I was glad to see him by simply placing my tongue on his cheek. What shocked me, as much as I am ever shocked, is my man's hostility toward the dog's boy. Adam is an interesting example of the duality of humanness. He can appear to the casual eye to be acting in one way—for instance, friendly—and then, to the trained observer, appear quivering with the opposite feeling, such as anger or frustration. In this case, Adam's inside and outside were unusually in sync; he really distrusted this boy. I tried very hard to let him know that the boy, Mingo, is okay. Because humans depend so much on their sight, they fail to use their other senses. I could feel Mingo's grief; Adam could not. I could smell his fear; Adam could not. All he saw was a boy who resembled the boys who once controlled me. All I saw was a boy my best canine friend adored. Those of us who have been in the ring were as gladiators, doing what we'd been trained to do. It didn't mean that we were slavish adorers of those who put us in that position; not in the same way we become adorers of those who take us out of combat, retool our spirits into trust and the ability to love. Dawg, my friend Lucky, had no need for rehabilitation. He already had a good boy.*

*I was pleased when everyone stood down and Dawg was allowed to be with his boy. Adam had nothing to say in tongue language while they worked together, at least not words I recognized—*Hand me, *and* Pull tighter—*but I did recognize the moment Adam decided that he could leave Dawg and the boy and the unhappy girl alone and we went to get dinner. He said something to Skye, words again I didn't quite understand, but figured out.* It's your decision, but I have to advise against it. *And her answer:* It is. *He touched her shoulder with the kind of touch he sometimes gives me.*

# CHAPTER 24

"We're going to take the dog down to the lake before we have to take Mingo home." Cody makes this a statement, not a question, and is out the office door before her mother can register an objection. She really needs to have a few minutes with Mingo alone. She needs to talk to him about what happened today at McDonald's. She needs to thank him. Besides, she knows that he wants a last few minutes with the dog, because it may be the last time he ever sees him. And if that's the case, it's likely the last time she'll see Mingo. It may be that she's done Mingo no favors by getting him back together with his dog if he's just going to be denied access to him after all. She really can't read the cards on this one. Mr. March is clearly not in favor of the idea, and her mother isn't giving a clue as to how persuadable she is. Usually, Skye tips her hand with a softening of expression, that defeated look she gets when Cody gets her way. This time, it's different: Skye is remote, having kept busy in the office all the while the three of them worked on the dog run.

An hour ago, Mr. March left to get dinner, leaving

Cody and Mingo to finish up the job. He'd called his dog to follow him, quietly letting Dawg stay with Mingo. Dawg didn't even notice when Mr. March left with Chance. He'd had his eyes on Mingo the whole time, as if afraid that if he looked away, his boy would disappear again.

"Want to head down to the lake for a bit? Take Dawg for a walk?"

"I ain't got a leash."

"He's fine without one around here."

"A-ite."

They head down the slope, the dog running ahead of them to clear away any squirrels showing bad judgment. The lake is a flat nickel color in the early-evening light, its depths darkening to pewter in the center. A faint breeze tickles soft pine branches into movement. Pulling off their shoes, Cody and Mingo walk around the edges, letting their toes sink into the lush leaf mold fringing the lake. Although the water is still too cold for swimming, the shallow places are warm. Dawg plants his legs up to his belly and laps at the water, at one with his feral side.

"Hey, umm, you know, like, thanks." Cody doesn't look at Mingo. Picks up a rock, tosses it into the water.

"Your mom hired me."

"No. I mean about today, at McDonald's. Those kids."

"S'okay. Felt kind of good."

"Yeah, but what if, like, the cops had been around and you'd gotten in more trouble?"

"I'd deal with it." He rolls his shoulders back, puffs his chest a little. "You sometimes just gotta do right."

Cody shoves her glasses up her nose, hopes he doesn't see the flush rising to her cheeks. She's touched by this rough boy's words, but more than that, she wonders what it would feel like to give up the Secret, to *do right,* as Mingo puts it, to finger the man who killed her father.

She's got to keep the Secret. She *is* doing right—by protecting her mother and herself with her silence.

Mingo flings a handful of little stones into the still lake, scattering a covey of ducks. "Ain't right. Him takin' Dawg. It's like he be stealin' from me, right in front of my face. Disrespectin' me."

"I know. I'm sorry. I really thought that he'd see that the dog should be with you. But, Mingo, really. What would happen if you took the dog? Where would you keep him? Isn't he better off—"

"No. What kinda man you think I am, lettin' him get away with it? He ain't gonna *think about it;* he gonna give my dog away."

"I won't let that happen."

"What you gonna do about it?" Mingo straightens up, gives her a look that makes her take a step back, out of the water, to the safety of shore.

Cody can see the anger in him, the heartbreak. She knows so little about how he ended up where he is, but however it happened, it's made him tough. He was so gallant, knocking Ryan down, defending her; and now he's intimidating her, he's scary. Suddenly, he's one of those dudes you'd see coming and cross the street to avoid. Bigger somehow, dangerous. "I don't know."

"I do." Mingo whistles and Dawg splashes over to him. "You comin' wi' me, boy." Mingo grabs his sneakers off the bank and slips them on over wet feet. He unhooks the chain attached to his belt loop, unclips it from his wallet, then attaches the short chain to the dog's collar. He straightens up and looks at her. His face is a degree less hostile. "Cody, look. Thanks for tryin'. I know you meant to be helpful." He slings his backpack over one shoulder, flips the hood of his sweatshirt up.

"What are you doing?"

"What I shoulda done long time ago. Beatin' it." Boy

and dog walk away, following the trail that will lead to the parking lot of the state park.

"You can't! Mom will kill me! You're going to be in such trouble!"

Mingo doesn't turn around, doesn't react to her at all, and she realizes that trouble isn't anything he is afraid of. He is unfettered by the fear of punishment. She's a bit envious. Cody knows she's going to be the one to have to face her mother, who is going to go ballistic. To say nothing of Mr. March. Despite the good intentions, she's going to be the one in big trouble.

The sun is down, and in the fading light, the boy and the dog are barely visible. It is only the quick glitter of the reflective trim on his crisp white sneakers that alerts me to the boy and dog on the side of the road, walking with their backs to traffic. I pull up beside Mingo, scroll down the window. I really have no hope that he'll get in the car, and fully expect that he'll book it and disappear into the night; but he does get in beside me, holding the chunky dog in his lap.

"Seat belt."

Mingo manages to buckle the strap despite the bulk of the dog in his lap.

"Thank you, Mingo."

"A-ite."

"I'm taking you back, you know. I took a chance on you, at Cody's insistence, against my better judgment. And if you hadn't gotten into this car, I would be on the phone to the police, and I don't think that you would be happy with that."

"I want my dog."

"I understand that, Mingo. I really do. But you can't run away and blow off all the good that you've done—

learning a trade, getting sober—just for the dog. If he were a human, would he want that?"

"No." He says it exactly as Cody says it when she's been on the losing end of an argument. The *no* of adolescent capitulation.

My purse is between us, lodged in the console. I reach in and pull out five twenty-dollar bills. "Besides, you didn't get paid." I hold out the money.

"Dawg, you get in back." The dog seems to understand and hops into the backseat. Mingo takes the cash. Folding it, he slips it into his pocket. "Thank you."

"A hundred bucks is a lot of money to walk away from."

"Yeah." He nods. "Word."

"Word up." I catch the suggestion of a smile on the boy's face. "Cody hates it when I use slang; she thinks I'm trying to be hip and I'm not acting my age."

"Lotsa grown folks are hip. You never too old to be hip." He glances away, then back. "Not sayin' that you're old. You cool."

I take that as high praise indeed.

Mingo pulls out his phone and a set of earbuds.

I feel a little excluded, a little bit shut out. I know I should try to engage him, not let him get away with shielding himself with thuggish bumped-up base. Then I recognize the maternal reaction; it feels exactly as it does with Cody half of the time. An audio wall of music shutting out any chance of a meaningful conversation. I plunge in. "Who's your favorite artist?"

Mingo shrugs. "Old-school, mostly. Fifty Cent, Dr. Dre. Not much into Kanye. Like Jay Z."

I nod, as if I'm familiar with these rappers' work and the relative merits of each. I give myself props for at least knowing who they are. "What about female artists?"

Mingo thinks for a moment. "I'm okay with Nicki

Minaj. Missy Elliott, she's good." He doesn't move to put the earbud back. "Actually, I'm good with Alicia Keys. She does something for me."

"Me, too." I point to the glove compartment. "You might find one of her CDs in there."

The kid pulls out the four or five jewel boxes I've tossed in the glove compartment along with my secret stash of Radiohead, Sting, and Johnny Cash. He finds the Alicia Keys disc and plugs it into the slot. Mingo Ayala sits beside me, his long fingers tapping out a rhythm against his knees, bobbing his head in time with the music. I don't know anything about him, or why Cody has taken up his cause. Maybe it's a genetic predisposition to being attracted to misfits. This boy is enough like Randy that I worry that a version of the old adage—like mother, like daughter—is being played out here in front of me. He's handsome, a bit charming, a drug addict, and probably a thief. And, if Adam is right, he's a Michael Vick in training.

I won't be like my mother. I won't object to Cody's friendship with this kid. I won't be like my mother, whose dislike for Randy effectively threw me into his arms. Cody is such a contrarian that the more I like Mingo, the quicker she's likely to abandon her advocacy of him, a sad thought that makes me wonder why every interaction with Cody has to be strategized. Nothing is ever simple.

# CHAPTER 25

Cody is too freaked-out to even think about contacting Mingo. Her mother blew out of here like she had a zombie on her tail, not even asking where Cody thought Mingo might have gone. A friend would warn him that her mother was on his trail, but maybe she wasn't his friend. Maybe he wasn't hers, despite the fact he'd defended her in front of Ryan and the mean girls. Maybe that was just a thug wanting to give a white boy a whuppin'.

She's in the office, like a good employee, standing ready to help the itinerant traveler who might wander into the LakeView. They get them, mostly single men. Her mom calls them the "lost souls," traveling alone, not on vacation, but on jobs that keep them moving from town to town, from motel to motel. Kind of like Mr. March.

Cody doesn't like being in here alone at night, doesn't like opening the door to strangers, to men. She wouldn't open the office door if a square-jawed man climbed out of a black car. No, she wouldn't. The only reason Cody has stationed herself in the office tonight is so she can see when Mr. March returns. She really doesn't want him to know that Mingo took the dog, but she doesn't see any way out of it. The dog is gone. Ergo, as her science teacher likes to say, *ergo* Mingo must have him. If she thought her mother had gone ballistic, she can't wait to see what Mr. March does.

From the front window, Cody can watch the approach of headlights coming up the hill, and with each one, her heart beats a little harder. All keep going, bending around the curve, red taillights dipping out of sight. Her heart recovers. And there's another. Is that him? Or Mom? It's been an hour. Long enough, if she's found Mingo, to get to North Adams and back, but not long enough if she's had to drive around trying to find him, which, oddly, reminds Cody of the snowy night she and Mr. March went around looking for the dog. It's a truck; Cody can hear the downshifting to get it up the hill. She flops into a chair. Scrapes her hair into a fresh ponytail. Looks at her nails, two of them shattered by her day's work as assistant fence builder. There's a car coming. She goes to the window and, sure enough, this set of headlights angles up the drive and comes to rest right in front of her, in easy proximity to the outside stairs that flank the office. She steps back into the room, hoping that Mr. March hasn't spotted her. She should bolt the door, make it look like no one's here. That they're asleep in their cabin, inviolable. Bad news can wait.

Feet going up the stairs, two sets in arrhythmic clumping, the sound of a stumble, a giggle. Cody peeks out the window, realizes that it's not Mr. March's car out there. It's a blue Toyota. It's the newlywed couple in room 14. Old newlyweds—in their forties, maybe. Both overweight and yet can't keep their hands off each other.

The sound of her own phone going off startles Cody away from the window. She peeks at the number and then smiles. It's not her mother; it's Mosley.

"Hey, missed seeing you today. Thought you were coming down."

"I had stuff to do. I'll be there next week." The truth is, Cody had forgotten that Mosley asked her to come help set up a mini-exhibit. The whole Mingo thing had pushed it right out of her mind. She can hear him take a long drag, and waits into the silence for him to speak.

"So, tell me, you been helping yourself to my stash?" His voice is pitched upward with the effort of holding in the toke.

Cody feels the scarlet of guilt prickle her face. "No. Why would you think that?"

"Cuz I do." Mosley laughs, inhales again. "This shit is for medicinal purposes only. You know that."

"I didn't take it."

"Right, and I'm the king of England."

She doesn't have an answer, or a ready fabrication. She had no idea that he'd ever miss the roaches. Plural. She thought that providing Black Molly with a little dope would placate her, a suggestion of agreement without committing to Molly's moneymaking idea. She was stupid and now Cody just knows that Mosley's going to tell her to never come back. "I'm sorry?" It comes out like a little kid's forced apology.

"I should tell your mother."

"Are you going to?"

There's another moment of concentrated silence. "Tell you what. I won't if you'll let me keep drawing you. Model for me again. We don't have to tell your mother about that, either."

This seems a reasonable request; after all, he's been sketching her despite his coerced promise to Skye not to. Sketching her while she putters around, no harm in continuing to do that. Seems a small forfeit for a potentially disastrous bargain. "Okay. Fine. I won't tell."

"If I won't, huh? Ha. Okay. When can we get together?"

There is something in that phrase "get together" that seems off. "When I come for my lesson on Friday?"

"No, no. You've been a bad girl. I want to sketch you sooner than that."

"I guess I could come after school on Monday."

"I'll pick you up after school."

"I don't think you can do that. There're rules about who can pick us up. You could pick me up at the last bus stop. That's at the intersection of Route Two and Canterbury Road."

"I'll pick you up there. Monday. What time?"

"Two-thirty."

"I'll be there."

"Okay."

"And Cody?"

"Yeah?"

"I'll give you a little weed of your own. No more taking mine."

"I'm sorry. I really am."

"I'd have been tempted, too. Not to worry." Mosley's gone, and Cody is left to wonder if she's gotten away with something or if she's being played.

The wash of headlights into the big picture window announces another car, and this time it is Mr. March. Cody watches as he climbs out of the vehicle. His dog, Chance, hops out of the backseat, immediately starts sniffing around, probably looking for his missing companion. As is Mr. March. Cody keeps herself out of sight, hoping that he'll just go to his room, not worry about Dawg. But, of course he doesn't. He tries the doorknob of the office, which by now she's locked. She knows that he's got two choices: go around back and see if anyone is home in the cabin, or dial Skye's number. Either way, he's going to find out that the dog is gone, and it might be better coming from her own mouth than from her mother's; that way, she can spin the story her own way.

Cody dashes to the door, flips the lock, and opens up to call out to Mr. March. "Mom's taking Mingo back to his residence." At least she hopes that's what's happened.

"Where's the dog?"

Cody raises her chin, smiles, lies. "With them. But it's okay."

"Yeah, that's fine." Mr. March steps back onto the porch. "Look, I know I sound like a hard-ass, not letting the kid keep his dog, but you know that I'm right. I have to look out for the dog's best interest. Mingo probably loves his dog. I understand that, but even if he isn't fighting the dog, he's certainly in no position to care for him. Don't you agree?"

"Sort of." She hears that tone adults take with kids, that *reasonable* tone.

"Cody. If your mother agrees to foster the dog so Mingo can see him occasionally, I have no problem with that. Although I hate losing the opportunity, I'll let the potential adopters know that circumstances have changed, at least for a little while."

Cody gives him an authentic smile, which quickly turns into a frown. There's no way Skye is going to agree to keep the dog for a boy she has no attachment to, and God knows, there's no compelling reason for her mother to even care about Mingo. "I don't think she will. She's not into stuff like that. She says she's got enough on her plate without taking on a dog."

"He's a pretty easy dog." Mr. March smiles at her, shrugs. "But I certainly get it. When Chance was foisted on me, I balked, I tried like anything to get rid of him. You see how that turned out."

Cody nods. She pulls the elastic out of her hair, letting it fall in a sheaf across her face, hiding her smile. Maybe this will work out. Then she remembers that her mother is out looking for Mingo, not driving him home like she told Mr. March, and that the dog is with him, and not on their way back to the halfway house. The minute Adam figures that out, no one wins.

It's altogether too close to the nine o'clock curfew when I pull into the parking lot of Mingo's residence. A post light illuminates the path to the door. We all get out of the car, the humans and the dog, who wags his tail, sniffs the beaten-down grass alongside the cement walkway, pees like a gelding, then regroups with the people. Mingo has his hood up, obscuring his face from me, hiding the expression of grief I know must be there. He must say goodbye to his dog now. I turn my back, giving him some semblance of privacy. I have no experience of this, of attachment to an animal, but the boy's obvious affection for the dog is enough to spark a little sympathy from my cold, cold heart.

"I got no choice, Dawg. I got to stay. You got to go. You be good. A-ite?"

I turn slightly and see the boy on his knees, his face pressed into the neck of the dog. I can't stand it. "Mingo, okay, okay, I'll keep him. You can come and do some more work for me next Saturday. I'll pick you up at nine."

Mingo gets to his feet. Walks over to stand in front of me. He's taller by half a head, and he no longer smells of cheap cologne, but honest sweat. He pushes his hood off his head, extends a hand. "Thank you. You won't regret it."

"I might, but that's for me to worry about."

"Ma'am?"

"Yes?"

"You cool. I'll work hard for you."

My turn is here, up the less spectacular mountain, the road less traveled. I'm anxious to get home, to open my cabin door, and if Cody is still awake, maybe we can talk a little bit about what changes will need to be made in order to keep this dog, however temporarily. This is not a permanent state of affairs, and Cody and I need to come to some agreement as to how long the dog will stay with us and next steps. Nonetheless, for at least a little while, I've made almost everyone happy. I allow myself to bask for a moment in the anticipation of winning Cody's approval, such a rare occurrence lately. In the morning, I'll knock on Adam's door and let him know of my decision. I'm a little less sure about his reaction, given his concerns.

The dog, riding shotgun, pushes himself up into a sitting position, gives me a sideways glance. He's so heavy that I've had to buckle the seat belt behind him to keep the alarm from sounding. He snuffs, and his tongue slips over his red nose. He makes a sighing noise, as if he's been thinking about his situation and is reconciling himself to it.

I pat the dog on the head. "You get to stay with us for a little while. You'll like it. It's okay, fella, you'll see Mingo again soon."

Dawg, or Lucky—take your pick—lifts one paw to set it on my arm, for all the world like he's thanking me. Adam credits Chance with an almost humanlike comprehension, and who knows, maybe he's right. This sure feels like Dawg understands what I'm trying to tell him and, as Mingo might say, he's down with it.

To my complete surprise, Cody and Adam are sitting together on the porch. Chance is stretched out between the Adirondack chairs. He's the first to rise, lumbering over to greet Dawg as he hops down from the front seat. I step up onto the porch, sling my purse down.

"All right, my friends. The dog stays here."

"Mom! You're the best!"

"Are you sure?" This from Adam.

"No. But, as you say, Cody, it's the right thing to do."

*The people are giving off a nice, friendly, happy vibe, even the unhappy girl, Cody, although Adam's happy is muted. Dawg is not quite as cheerful as he was, and I know that this is because his boy, Mingo, is absent again. But I can smell the boy's touch on him, so I decide that maybe this is a temporary absence and that Dawg won't be lonely for him much longer. In the meantime, I offer myself and my affection to tide him over.*

*Soon enough we bid good night to one another and Adam, accompanied by me and our friend, unlocks the door to the place I have come to think of as my little home. Adam flops on the bed and I join him, pressing my nose against the sweet skin of his neck, making him laugh. He gives me that halfhearted order to stop, but I don't until he sits up. The other dog watches us from the safety of the space between the chair and fridge. Sudden movement still frightens him. Loud voices frighten him. No one saw it but me when the humans were having their discussion, laden with one or two tongue-language words I knew—dog and no and please—but filled more with the language of upset. With each succeeding increase in decibel, he shrank closer and closer to his boy. I noticed, too, that he didn't greet Adam with the enthusiasm he deserves when Dawg came back tonight. He's respectful, but clearly he's not taking my word for it that Adam is his friend. We need to fix that. Tomorrow.*

# CHAPTER 26

*I couldn't believe it when Adam drove off, leaving my friend behind. I got it that Dawg was attached to the girl, and that his boy, although absent, was still in the picture. I just couldn't understand why we didn't take Dawg with us anyway. That's what we'd been doing since that night when we found him and I became his best friend. Best canine friend. I have to qualify that, because part of our job is to be a friend to our human companions, and they to us. It's a wonderful dynamic for most of us. Oh, yes, of course I know of dogs whose lives are proscribed, kept at arm's length from their humans. Attached to chains that allow only a few feet of movement, forgotten, unloved. My heart cries out for them when we see them. Sometimes Adam, with me close by to prevent his anger from blooming, will knock on a door and have what he calls a* conversation *with the home owner. Sometimes we even go meet the disheartened dog, who will often display the reason he (as they are most often males) was remanded to life on the end of chain. Fierce but meaningless barking, or jumping up and planting heavy paws against Adam's chest. He'll calm them. I'll calm them. And sometimes, they go with us.*

*Dawg should have gone with us. I fear that he will spend most of his time in the pen that they built, not a cage, exactly, certainly not a chain, but not a home. I worried myself into squeezing my head over the edge of the half-lowered car window, barking like some undisciplined cur, calling to Lucky to keep the faith. We'll be back!*

*I had no reason to believe we wouldn't come back to this place, although every time we left, I never knew if that was true. Hopefully, his boy—Mingo—would be back to take him on a walk, scratch his belly, let him sleep on the couch. That was what was most important, so when the edge of the window came up under my chin and I had to pull my head back, I cast Adam a sidelong glance. He reached over and squeezed the back of my neck, said something that I interpreted as a promise that we would be back.*

The problem is, she needs to get home so that she can take Dawg out for a walk. It's great that Skye has granted a reprieve of sorts by allowing Dawg to stay with them, but it's not like she's going to be the one walking him; she's just letting him use the new dog run, but that's not enough. One of the stipulations hammered out on Saturday was that Cody would be completely responsible for the dog's well-being and care. That means feeding, walking, and, yuck, cleaning up after him in the dog run. When she agreed to meet Mosley after school, Cody hadn't had Dawg's presence in the mix. In between classes, when students are allowed to use their phones, Cody calls the AC, but no one is answering, and because no one ever takes responsibility for erasing old messages, the answering machine is coming up full. That was one of the things she'd heard Mr. March mention to Mosley and Kieran: that if they wanted to be accessible to potential donors, they had to straighten up their act. Not quite in those terms, but she understood what he was saying. Be less free-spirited and more businesslike.

The precious minutes of passing time tick by; the flood of students in the hallway thins out to a trickle. She'll be late again, get written up yet again. She hits Mosley's cell phone number. It rings, but he doesn't answer; he probably can't hear over the sound of Kieran's blowtorch. Before she can tap in a text message, the bell rings. She's officially late. Maybe she'll get detention. Maybe that wouldn't be a bad thing, a viable excuse for blowing Mosley off.

"You're late." Tyler, alone, blocks Cody's path. "Waiting on someone? Your lesbo BFF?"

"You're heinous. Why do you keep picking on me? What did I ever do to you?"

Tyler shrugs, flips a lock of hair. Cody realizes that, without an audience, a Greek chorus, Tyler has lost momentum. Without backup singers, she's just a mean girl all out on her own. There's nothing she can do. Tyler is a head taller, and with her lacrosse physique, at least fifteen pounds heavier, but Cody stretches to her maximum and steps close to Tyler. "Get out of my way." The other girl allows herself a moment to make it look like she won't, but then she steps away, giving Cody only just enough room to squeeze by.

Cody pushes past her, making sure that she doesn't look like she's running away, that she isn't intimidated. She makes for her classroom, hoping that the hard beating of her heart isn't audible. It might help if she knew why these jocks were so down on her, what she had ever done to make them turn on her. But in high school, as in life, sometimes things are just inexplicable. You just have to accept the circumstances and move on. When Mr. Ronkowsky in science class doesn't ask for a pass, or send her to the office, she's grateful.

Once, when they were driving up Interstate 91 near the Holyoke Mall, a car had crossed into their lane, nearly hitting them. Cody was just old enough to be sitting in the front seat at that time, and the nearness of that encounter made her cry. Skye had reached out and taken her hand. "It's okay. It was a miss. That's what counts."

Cody's face slowly loses the flush from the encounter with Tyler. Her heart rate lowers, and it finally occurs to her that she didn't back down. That her near miss with Tyler was just that, a miss. She casually leans back in her chair, slips her phone out, and, one eye on Mr. Ronkowsky, making sure he's still facing the whiteboard, types a quick text to Mosley—*Sorry, can't make it today*—then slides the phone out of sight. Almost immediately, her phone vibrates.

"Miss Mitchell, can you tell me what is the periodic chart symbol for carbon?" Mr. Ronkowsky must have eyes in the back of his head. He's nailing her for not paying attention. As if cued by some unseen director, the class laughs, as if none of them had ever been caught not paying attention.

The first chance she has to look at Mosley's text is on the way to lunch. Lunch, the all-time worst part of her day, when her isolation is out there for all to see. This is a really small school, and there is only one lunch period, when every student in the high school congregates to eat in the "all purpose" room. They slide plastic trays along the rail, picking and choosing from the offerings—pizza slices, soggy salads, premade sandwiches—most of which will end up in the big garbage cans. Cody brings her own lunch, buys a milk. As she waits in line to pay for the milk, she checks the text. It's a two word text: *No excuses*

There is an open seat in front of Black Molly, and two
on either side of her, as well. She glances up from her
lunch to look at Cody with an expression that is more
command than invitation. Cody really doesn't want to sit
with her, but there actually isn't any other choice. It's not
like anyone else will ever invite Cody to sit with them,
and besides, just plain sitting down near an established
group is nuts.

Cody has danced around Molly's crazy drug-stealing
idea, but she's running out of excuses. If Cody thought
that Black Molly would get tired of trying to talk her into
stealing drugs, she's wrong. The half-teasing insistence
has lately become more like pressure. And along with it,
really weird questions, nosy ones all about Randy. Cody
wonders if she's got some kind of sixth sense, some instinct about Cody's Secret. In her worst moments, she
wonders if on that day when Molly's superb pot loosened
her tongue, she actually did spill her Secret, said more
than she remembers, confessed to being a witness.

"Cody, you want to have lunch with me?" It's Mr. Farrow, the counselor. He's got a tray loaded with salad, a
water bottle, and two slices of the pizza that tastes like
machine oil. "We can have a chat."

For once, Cody doesn't even try to come up with an
excuse. "Uh, I guess." This is one of those things that separates her from everyone else, this attention from the
school counselor. Someone might as well stick a sign on
her back, DWEEB, or DORK. Or, worse, *mental case*. Poor
Mr. Farrow thinks that it helps, to have "individual attention." Ha. He likes to try to get her to talk about her problems, so she accommodates him with stuff she makes
up—stuff that has little to no bearing on what her life is
really like. She doesn't talk about being bullied. She's not
going to do that, because it's one thing to be a target; it's
another to be a rat. Besides, who's kidding whom? Tyler

and Taylor and Ryan and all their ilk are the popular kids, the ones who may not be smart enough to be valedictorian but are athletic enough to be courted by colleges, thereby making this Podunk high school a blip on the radar of the NCAA. Her woeful tale of being called names wouldn't be enough to cause Mrs. Zigler or Mr. Farrow to do anything about it. So she talks about how unfair curfews are, or how the homework is stressing her out. Sometimes he slips in a question about her mother. The first time he asked "How's your mom?" she got kind of creeped out, but then she realized that what the counselor really wanted to know was how things were between them. Another question she dare not answer. It is becoming second nature now, to hold her mother at arm's length. It's the only way, the only way to keep the Secret.

Mr. Farrow keeps his door open as they sit at the little table he has in the center of his office. "So, Cody, how are things going?" He gives her that sincere look, like he really cares.

"Good."

"What's new?"

For once, she has something to offer. "We got a dog."

"That's great."

The conversation circles around what kind of dog, where they got him. "We're kind of watching him for a friend."

"Dogs are great. I have two. Cairn terriers. They run my life." Mr. Farrow's face changes a little, and Cody can see that thinking about his dogs makes him happy. Makes him normal. "A pit bull, huh? Aren't they kind of, I don't know, aggressive?"

"Not this guy." Cody feels a genuine smile erupt. "He's like mush. We have a guy who stays with us, at the hotel. Mr. March. He's got a pit bull, too, Chance, who's his therapy dog."

"What kind of therapy?"

"Dunno. He wears a red vest and goes with Mr. March everywhere."

They talk a little about the kinds of work therapy dogs can do, and before you know it, lunch is over and she has just enough time to drop off her tray and then call Mosley.

"Thanks, Mr. Farrow."

"My pleasure, Cody. Pat that dog for me."

Released from her informal chat with Mr. Farrow, Cody pulls her phone out of her back pocket and presses the contact for Mosley. She intends to tell him she can't make it, tell him the truth. He'll be okay with it. She just knows that he's going to be fine about it.

"Mosley Finch."

"Mosley, this is Cody."

"Hey, what's up? You aren't going to bail on me, are you?"

"Ummm. Maybe?"

"Hey, sweetheart. A deal's a deal."

"Yeah, but . . ."

"If *ifs* and *buts* were cookies and nuts, we'd all have a merry Christmas." Mosley laughs and then coughs. "I've organized my day all around your being available. It wasn't easy."

Cody knows Mosley's routine well enough that she is skeptical about that. "My mom needs me home right after school."

"Does she also need to find out you're filching joints from me? That would put an end to your time at the AC pretty quick, wouldn't it?"

She has an art project that she's been working on for several weeks at the AC, one that she's really enjoyed do-ing, and one where Mosley has been unusually helpful by showing her how not to be afraid to use different media, how to make something out of nothing. It's almost done, a collage of found objects like feathers and stones and one of those rubber bracelets identifying the wearer as a supporter of some popular disease. She'd hate to leave it behind. "Don't say anything. I'll figure it out."

"You're an accomplished liar; of course you can. I'll be at the bus stop—well, a few feet away—by two-thirty."

"Okay." Cody taps the call dead. Pushes the message function and texts her mother: *Got detention no big deal late for class home on the late bus.* As an afterthought, she sends a second text—*I'll walk Dawg when I get home love*—and fires it off before she can redact the word *love*.

An accomplished liar.

The bus ride is blissfully uneventful, as Tyler and her sidekick Taylor are at lacrosse practice and the younger brother—she still isn't sure whom he belongs to—sits quietly, ignoring her. The bus empties out in drips of twos and threes, grinding to a stop at every crossroad. Finally it's just Cody and the boy. They stand up at the same time; he's ahead of her but then steps aside to let her get off the bus first. He gives her a slight smile, impossible not to notice and give him one of her own. She marches to where Mosley's familiar car waits, pulled off like its driver is taking a phone call.

"Hey." It's the boy, jogging to catch up with her.

"Yeah?" Cody feels herself stiffen into readiness. If he's going to pick on her, she's going to paste him one. He's at least six inches shorter, but stocky.

"Umm, don't mind them. They're bitches."

"I know they are. And I don't. I don't let them get to me." She won't let anyone think that they do, ever.

"Good. They're just going to be fat middle-aged housewives in a few years."

Cody bursts out laughing. "Which one is your sister?"

"Taylor." He says it like the name tastes bad.

An ally. Who'da thunk it? "What's your name?"

"Devin."

"Thank you, Devin."

The boy slouches away, kicks at a stone in the road, then breaks into a trot. Cody watches him till he reaches his house and disappears.

The Subaru is backing up toward her. She waves him to a stop, pulls open the passenger door, throws her backpack into the backseat, and climbs in. The car smells of turpentine. Mosley smells of turpentine. The skin of his forearms glistens where he's cleaned off paint.

"That your boyfriend?"

"No. He's a year younger than me." Cody pulls her seat belt into position.

"Wow, a whole year." Without signaling, Mosley one-hands his car back into the roadway. "You'd be a cradle robber, wouldn't you?"

"He's not my boyfriend." Cody pulls the too-tight belt away from herself. "I don't have a boyfriend."

"Why not? Pretty girl like you? You should be beating them off with a stick."

"I'm not. Pretty. Or beating anyone off with anything." She blushes at the double entendre. She prays that Mosley doesn't laugh.

Mosley's right hand grasps the back of her neck, gives her a little squeeze, and then he gently slides the hair off her cheek and behind her ear. "I'm an artist; I know beauty when I see it. Sometimes it's just there, under the skin, waiting to emerge."

His fingers continue to stroke back her hair. It is an oddly comforting and equally disturbing gesture. She can't tell if she likes it or if it's going to make her cry.

"Sometimes you have to get close to your subject to see what lies beneath."

Cody nods. Notices that they have already passed the Artists Collaborative. Mosley takes his hand away from her neck, signals for a left-hand turn, and takes the car up an incline that winds through woods to a parking lot and a state park building. It's the little park, site of some old quarrying business long defunct, famous for its marble bridge and the rushing stream water. If Cody had lived in the area when she was in elementary school, she would have been brought here by her teachers. By the time the local kids got to high school, that field trip was old news.

The parking lot is empty, the park—seasonal from Memorial Day to Columbus Day—is technically closed, but that doesn't stop Mosley from stopping. "Hop out."

"Why are we here?"

"You've heard of plein air?"

"I think so."

"It's a fancy way of saying painting outdoors, in the natural light. I want to paint you here."

The light is indeed beautiful as the sun arcs overhead, making its slow springtime descent into the west, limning the sweet new leaves on the trees, shadowing the flow of the river down into the glacial sculpture of the marble walls below. Mosley hands her a box of paints, and expects her to follow him, past the historical signage explaining the history of the place, along the groomed trail, over the little river, to a small open grassy area, marshy underfoot. Mosley sets up his easel, opens the box of paints, all of which look brand-new. He plucks a sheaf of brushes, all sizes. He points at the waterfall throwing itself over the marble dam. "Over there. The sun is perfect."

Cody feels awkward, unsure of what to do. Stand? Sit?

Mosley sets the brushes down, walks over. "Like this." He presses her down until she's flat on her back, then takes her limbs and positions them carefully, as if she's a mannequin, a doll. One hand is angled back beneath her head, the other reaching away from the waterfall. Instinctively, she pulls her knees up, knocking them together, but Mosley isn't happy with that and instead fixes the angle so that her bony hip is perpendicular to the wall. Finally, he tilts her head so that the sun is in her eyes, making her squint. He pulls off her glasses, folds them, and puts them in his breast pocket.

"Think elf. Think water sprite."

"I think this position is pretty uncomfortable. This stone is hard."

"Okay. Let's try something else."

It takes several attempts, refinements on her recumbent pose, but finally Mosley is satisfied. With the sun in her eyes, she can't see his face, and he says nothing as he works. She could almost fall asleep, but the stone is digging into her hip and it hurts where her hand cradles her head against the rock. Mosley abruptly stops and, releasing her from the pose, calls her over. "We need another location." He hands her back her glasses.

They walk down the steep steps built into the walls, going from view stand to view stand, up and down along the ravine pocked with spectacular kettle holes, curvaceous marble walls molded by water and by man's use. The air is alive with the wind generated from the plunging water, and Cody's hair flutters in the breeze. She feels Mosley hold it back as she leans over the fence to admire the spectacle. He puts an arm on either side of her, fingers gripping the fence, his body behind her, not touching. She feels his breath against her ear as he whispers into it against the roar of the water and the acoustic boom off the walls. "Let's try right here."

Is it her imagination or does he linger a bit, holding her pinioned against the fence, like an adult version of London Bridge Is Falling Down. The air down here is cooler than in the parking lot, and a chill scurries down the length of her back. She looks from the height into the roiling water and shudders back a desire to drop into it. "I should be getting home. The late bus gets to my house by four. If I don't show up, Mom will have a fit."

"Call her. Tell her you've got a school project. Something important to do. Chess Club?"

"I don't know." It's so weird to have a grown-up suggesting she do something she might happily do of her own accord. "I have the dog to walk. If I don't do that, she'll send him away."

Mosley steps back, picks up his equipment, and marches away for all the world like a pissed-off boyfriend. Not that she's ever had one of those, but she watches how the few actual real and true couples behave toward one another. The girls are always testing the boys with jealousy and demands.

"I could be a tiny bit late. She might not notice for a while. Can you get me back by four-thirty?"

He doesn't answer the question. "Just let me sketch you. Crouch down, link your fingers into the fence . . . no, just your left hand."

She does what he commands. A strand of hair catches against the fence, trapping her there.

# PART III

PART III

# CHAPTER 27

With the phone tucked close to my ear, I'm scrambling to make up the three rooms left from this morning's check-out in time for the three families checking in, and talking with my mother at the same time. "The doggy day care is finally open and suddenly the LakeView is operating at two-thirds capacity, which is one-third more than my best-ever occupancy over the past year." I know I sound like an infomercial, but by now I can actually do a proper comparison.

"That's good, Skye. I'm glad to hear it." She sounds almost sincere.

"Obviously, part of it is the spectacular June weather, and part is certainly the ability to offer doggy parents an option that will allow them to visit not-so-dog-friendly attractions in the area."

"Doggy parents? You've swallowed the Kool-Aid, haven't you?"

"Maybe." My phone chirps with an incoming call. "Sorry, I've got to go."

"Are you still doing all this by yourself?"

"It's only a few days before school ends, and then Cody can help." If I hate the idea of making my kid into a chambermaid, the fact is that she's old enough, and diligent enough, to do the work. After all, loads of fifteen-year-olds do this kind of work in the summer at resorts. It won't kill her, and it will mean that the money not spent on hiring help will go toward improvements and not just making the mortgage payment.

"How is she?"

"Fine." It's what I always say.

"Good. Have her call sometime, will you?"

"I will."

Whoever was calling is gone. No message.

I push my housekeeping trolley down the gallery to the last room. The key sticks a little, so I pull out a can of WD-40, spritz some into the keyhole and on the key, which then clicks into place like magic. I love little fixes, finding them satisfying in a way that coping with big fixes isn't. Sometimes, when I can't sleep, I think about all the little things that need attention, think about what I can do to make them work. Better than counting sheep is thinking about these minor but manageable tasks; far better than thinking about the big ones, the impossible repairs that can't be fixed with a screwdriver or a can of WD-40. I am Shawn Colvin's Sunny, come home to make a few small repairs. Inside the room, I strip the beds. Then snap duvets over the beds, slam the side of my hand under the pillow to tuck the duvets close. Arrange the decorative pillows to my satisfaction.

Lucky/Dawg impulsively hops onto the freshly made bed. I shouldn't have left the door open, but I like to air the rooms out.

"Get down from there." I shoo him off the bed. The

dog obeys, but it's clear he's got mischief in his mind. He play bows, woofs. "What's your problem?" But he's irresistible in his own way. "Where's your ball?" As if he really understands, the dog dashes out of the room, thundering down the stairs. I don't think that we even have a ball. I wouldn't say so out loud, but I've kind of grown attached to the mutt. I haven't told Cody, but when I break for lunch, I've been taking the dog down to the lake for a walk. He's a good excuse to get away from the building. It's actually quite pretty down there. And he's a nice companion. Always keeps me in sight.

I face the small bathroom, wet towels everywhere, every hotel-size bottle of shampoo or conditioner opened and half used. The tiny flat bars of face soap and bath soap lie open, glued to the edge of the sink and tub. I pull on rubber gloves. "Blaghh." It's after two-thirty and no Cody. As usual. I give the bathroom a scrub, then plug in the vacuum and run it around the room; a quick touch with a dust rag and that's done. As yucky as a used hotel room can be, there is something so satisfactory about bringing it back to order. Conquering disorder with a can of Scrubbing Bubbles and an industrial vacuum.

Dawg is running back up the stairs. He meets me as I pull shut the door to room 12. His tail is madly swinging and his amber eyes are on me. I can see the faded yellow of an old tennis ball lodged in his big mouth. With a dull thud, Dawg drops it at my feet. Wherever this ball came from, it's a dead ball. It hits the deck with a mushy thunk.

"You're smarter than you look." I retrieve the rather moist object, contemplate pitching it over the second-story porch rail, then worry that the impulsive dog will jump over to get it. He's patting his boxer's feet on the deck, his delight in the game making me smile. "Okay. Here you go." Falling back on my junior high school softball skills, I wind up, snapping the ball down the length of the gallery, where it nearly smacks Adam March in the head.

There is a large portfolio on the counter in Mosley's office. Inside of it is the series of plein air paintings he's done of her over the past couple of weeks. Cody flips it open, leafs through the eight-and-a-half-by-eleven deckled-edge pages. No matter what she was wearing as he posed her in a variety of sylvan settings—jeans and T-shirts, shorts and tank tops—the images are of Cody as a sylph or a fairy. Wings she never wore are attached to her back; butterflies she never saw alight on her fingertips. She looks like one of those garden statues that were so popular in the Victorian age, or those grim baby angels in old cemeteries. She's seen photographs of them, and knows about the works of Charles Dodgson, who she also knows is the guy who liked photographing little girls and wrote that book about Alice. Lewis Carroll, that was his pen name. They talked about him in English class.

What Cody likes about these little watercolors is that they make her look pretty. They're flattering in a way that her mirror is not. She's fifteen now, and finally beginning to develop hips and a bust. It's like some switch has been flipped; and, glory hallelujah, her braces are coming off next week. She's begun to wear her contacts again. She wakes in the morning with the feeling that some internal combustion engine deep within is ready to be thrown into drive. Anticipatory. Ready. Mosley has captured some of this. Maybe that's what the wings represent.

Hearing the main door scrape open, Cody closes the portfolio, ducks out of Mosley's office. She's not supposed to see the unfinished paintings, although he's promised to show the finished ones to her in time for the July gala. Part of the event will be an art show featuring the best work of the AC's artists. Their work will be displayed in the lobby of the downtown hotel where the fancy dinner and dancing will be held in the ballroom, followed by an auction of those pieces. It's going to be a big deal and she knows that everyone at the Artists Collaborative is banking on its being their breakthrough fund-raising event, something that will put a spotlight on the AC as an organization worthy of attention in a town already flooded with artistic endeavors. Mr. March calls it "branding."

She's hoping to get to go, to help out. Maybe she can help set up. Take tickets. Something, anything, not to be left out of the fun.

Cody slips into the space that Mosley and Kieran have designated for her use. It's a tiny space, eked out of one of the larger work spaces, which was recently abandoned by a sculptor who moved out to Los Angeles to work for a game developer. It's little, but it's a place to keep her things, someplace where she doesn't have to put anything away if she doesn't feel like it. There, under the hanging industrial light, she's got her materials and the half-finished art project, which is beginning to take form.

Mosley waited for her after school yesterday, this time meeting her close to the school itself, telling her that he wanted to visit another pretty place close by. It seems like the whole countryside is filled with these places, some under the state park system, some just local, and Mosley knows them all. Tannery Falls was the place du jour, and on a weekday it was, in Mosley's words, "sublimely deserted." They hiked down the railroad-tie steps, which led down to where the stream pooled beneath the tall, narrow waterfall. The falls made a nice backdrop as he sat her down on a flat rock, arranged her just so.

"Don't move. Just like that." And so Cody sat, arms wrapped around her knees, head tilted as if taking the water right in the face, eyes closed. The sun beaming through the tall trees felt nice on her face. In books, it's always called a "companionable silence," and that's what she was thinking, neither she nor Mosley saying a word as he worked.

From above, laughter, a girl's squealing giggle, more flirtatious than amused. Cody's eyes flew open. She knew that giggle. Knew the heavier laughter that accompanied it. Ryan and one of the mean girls. The girls' voices are so alike, she couldn't possibly discern who was who, Tyler or Taylor. One of them, alone with Ryan. Cody scrambled to her feet, ignoring Mosley's scowl. Being found out here, modeling, sitting in this dumb pose for an artist, would further encourage the taunting, adding to her reputation as a weirdo. God help her, but this would be fuel for another year of torture. Except that there was no escape. The trail led down, and the trail led up, and there was no other way to go. Then Mosley heard the intrusion. Slowly, he gathered up his things, folded the easel, wiped his brush with a rag, set everything carefully into the paint box. Without a word to her, he started up the trail.

Cody slipped on her boots, brushed off her backside. The switchback nature of the trail gave her a few minutes before they'd see her. Cody heard Mosley speak to the pair, as any stranger might acknowledge someone on a walking trail: a brief "How you doin'." She was on her own, and it was up to her whether or not they tied her presence in this secluded place with that man. Cody bolted for a thick stand of trees, pressed herself against the trunk of the widest, and hoped that Tyler (or Taylor) and Ryan wouldn't see her hiding there like some freak.

From her vantage point, peeking between the close-growing oaks, Cody could see that it was Tyler, not her bestie, going solo with everybody's favorite crush, Ryan. From around her tree trunk blind, Cody watched as the pair jumped to the flat rock in the brook where she'd just been posing. And then she got an A-1 surprise as the pair lip-locked. Oooh, this was good. This was power. She knew for certain that Ryan had asked Taylor to be his date for the upcoming Spring Fling dance, effectively choosing Taylor as his girlfriend. Everyone was talking about it, even if they weren't talking to *her* about it. The benefit of being an outsider is that no one knows you're there. And Tyler and Ryan didn't know she was there right now, feasting on the sight of the two of them betraying Taylor; Tyler's descent into being the "other woman" and Ryan's elevation into becoming a true a-hole. She can't wait to tell Black Molly.

It was like watching a smarmy video, Ryan easing Tyler down to the hard surface of the rock, sliding his hand down her shirt until she lifted it over her head, tossing it away. It fell into the stream, but they were in such thrall to their passion that neither one noticed and the shirt drifted to a bend in the brook, a mere two feet from where Cody was hiding. It was too good to pass up. Cody, figuring that the couple were sufficiently distracted, reached for the shirt with a long stick, snagging it. It was a pretty little T-shirt, pale pink, made out of that soft slinky stuff, probably expensive. Cody squeezed out the water and stuffed it into her waistband. Finders keepers, she thought, and then decided that it was a far better thing to discover than to be discovered when Tyler went hunting for her missing shirt, so she boldly walked out from behind the tree, stood on the very edge of the stream, and made sure that Tyler and Ryan looked up from their make-out session to see her standing there. "Hey, guys. S'up? Taylor know you're here?"

And with that, she ran up the trail, heart pounding.

Tyler's T-shirt actually fits her very well. She's wearing it under her zip-front Old Navy sweatshirt. Cody thought about using it as a brush rag, but she's never owned a Banana Republic T-shirt before, and certainly never a pink shirt, but she likes it. Besides, today, in school, wearing it gave her this little frisson of excitement. She's got something on Ryan and Tyler, and if they noticed the pink cotton showing above where she's lowered her zipper, they must have been gagging with the fear she'd reveal their nasty little secret to Taylor.

"Hello, Cody." It's Mr. March, his dog beside him.

"Hi." She's reserved with Mr. March, but she swoops down to wrap her arms around Chance's neck. He smells like a mixture of outdoors and indoors, which is an odd thought but seems to define it, the smell of a dog. Not unpleasant, but nothing you'd want Yankee Candle to manufacture for a scented candle. She hopes that Mr. March won't ask about Dawg, ask if she's keeping up her end of the bargain, because even she knows that she's not doing such a good job. It's hard to have the will to take a walk after she gets back from a long, hard day at school, and a session with Mosley or doing AC chores; and then there's the fact that she wants to work on her art, and she can't do that if she's outside walking a dog or picking up poop.

But, of course, he does ask.

"Lucky working out okay for you?" Clearly he's sticking to the name he prefers for the dog.

"Oh, yeah. Great. He's great." Cody can see by the look in his eyes that Adam March is onto her. Face it, he's probably gotten an earful from her mother. "I mean, I get him out in the mornings, real early. He likes that."

"It's hard, isn't it? Having the responsibility?" Mr. March pats his leg and Chance pulls away from her embrace.

She stands upright, digs her hands into the kangaroo pocket of her sweatshirt. "Yeah. But it's still worth it."

"Yes, I think that maybe it is." He gives her a smile, a

real one, and strokes Chance's head. "I should let you get back to work. Do you want a ride home when I leave? I'll only be half an hour, maybe less."

Cody nods. "Yeah, that would be great." That would mean not having to walk all the way home, or, worse, call her mother and admit that she's gone to the AC after school instead of going home as she was supposed to, to walk Dawg and help with the rooms like she's expected to do. She just can't explain why she would rather take the heat from her mother than miss an opportunity to be here in this big brick building, a place no one expects her to be. No Molly, no Ryan and Taylor. No shooter. "Okay, see you in about half an hour." Adam and the dog go into Mosley's office. The door shuts.

Cody looks at her unfinished collage with a critical eye. It sucks. It's not at all what she had in mind when she started it. She pulls out her sketchbook, looks at the rendering she'd done there of what was supposed to be her first three-dimensional piece of art. It was meant to be something that the viewer would have to assign an interpretation to instead of her making it comprehensible to the beholder. She wanted it to be one of those things people would stand in front of, like they did Kieran's work, stroking their chins and making up stories, like they knew what he meant by the wire and gauze and stick sculpture. What she's got here is a mishmash of junk stuck to a board.

Maybe it's being around all these real artists, like their talent and their industry and their karma are clouding her own. When she's home, or in school fooling around on the back of her math paper, her drawings seem alive, real, full of potential. But the minute she tries to do something here, it's pure shit. Mosley is always saying stuff like "Try this," or "Try that." "Don't do this," or "Don't do that." Rarely does he say "Nice," or "Good job." He tells her that she's not ready for postmodern. She should perfect her skills first. "You have to be like a figure skater, learn the figures before you start doing double axles." Frankly, it's disheartening. Back in Holyoke, the art teacher had praised her to the moon. Mosley laughed when she told him that, which kind of hurt because it felt like she was baring her soul to him, admitting to praise. "You're pretty good for a kid, yeah. But let's not get ahead of ourselves because some failed artist told you that you had talent."

The little watercolors of Cody as sylph seem to her to be as representational as her stuff, the wings and butterflies notwithstanding. They're not like the work Mosley has shown to the world, so she wonders why he says he'll display them at the gala. Maybe he's just bullshitting her. Or—and this makes her laugh a little—he'll turn her into some weird conceptual thing that no one will associate with the little watercolors.

Cody slowly begins to pull off the glued-on objects— broken glass, stones, feathers, that rubber bracelet. The things that won't come off easily she attacks with the edge of a putty knife. She throws all the stuff away, each bit clinking in its own particular way into the unlined metal wastebasket. Denuded of the objects, it's just a piece of plank. A piece of wood now scarred with the residue of Elmer's glue. A little kid's art project, macaroni on cardboard. Just about as interesting. Maybe not even as interesting, because you'd expect more from a fifteen-year-old.

Dumping the stripped board into a bin of scraps, Cody grabs her sketchbook and tears out the rendering. Rips it into fours, then sixteenths. She's deluding herself. She doesn't have any talent. What the heck made her think that she could do anything better than draw pretty horses?

Cody finds a piece of charcoal and tucks her sketch pad under her arm, then heads out the door to sketch the mill race and wait for Mr. March. She sits on the stone wall, sketchbook on her knee. She makes a few exploratory lines, trying to capture the power of the falling water, but soon gives up. She pulls out her phone, checks to see if Black Molly has texted back. She's got a little weed to give her, a quiet present from Mosley that will keep Molly happy, get her off Cody's back about the other thing. Cody knows that she's on thin ice with her only friend. Once school is out, there'll be no excuse that Skye has done all the rooms, that she's had no chance or plausible reason to go into them. She'll be chief chambermaid, and Molly knows it.

Weird, there's a friend request from Ryan. Maybe not so weird. He probably wants to make sure she's not posting anything about what she saw yesterday. A little surge of power ripples through her gut. She accepts his request.

# CHAPTER 28

*It was so good to see my friend again. I don't know how long it had been since we drove away that morning without him. I also don't know why humans stick to the fiction that dogs don't understand the passage of time. Sure, we're not fixated on the clock, every day broken up into equal parts. We know time by habits. Breakfast time. Walk time. Playtime. Sleep time which comes in several blocks. Maybe the best one of all, dinnertime. Snuggle time. We like to keep to a schedule as much as any of our human counterparts, but ours is dictated by our carnality. Hunger. The need to relieve ourselves. Sleep. Most of my kind, at least the ones utterly domesticated, don't have the sex urge anymore. I once did. I remember it, so sometimes I behave in a fashion more suited to an intact male, but that's just hubris.*

*Anyway, my point is that I was glad to see Dawg and demonstrated my joy with knocking him to the floor and play-biting his feet and neck. I might have picked a better spot than right under the humans' feet, but I was in the moment—as dogs are—and not sorry even when*

*Adam made me move out of the way. Dawg and I banged down the stairs and out onto the meager lawn, which is quickly interrupted by the gravel parking lot. The people came down after us, and even in my enthusiasm for play, I could hear their voices chattering in that comfortable way that humans have when they reacquaint with one another. I'd seen humans reacquaint more demonstrably, with close physical contact, but these two preferred the verbal greets. Sometimes I am verbal, too, but Adam always discourages my barking.*

*Sadly, our reunion was brief, only long enough to go mark some territory together, and then Adam had me back in the car and we drove away, once again leaving my friend to stand and watch us go. I kept my chin on the backseat, facing where we'd been, not where we were going. I saw Dawg sit beside the woman, Skye, lean his head against her knee, just like I do to Adam when he needs me to be his guide.*

*As usual, we arrived at the place I think of as Adam's work. Frankly, the smell of the place bothered me, and instead of being happy to be Adam's constant companion, I was grumpy about it. But there was Cody, and I was happy to see her, sniff out what she'd been doing, see if her girl mood was any better. I got a good whiff of female disquiet. Although that's something I was beginning to realize is just Cody's natural state of being, she seemed particularly agitated today. That aside, she is a very fine admirer of my attributes and gave me a good huggin'.*

*Alas, I was duty-bound to follow Adam into that office with the one human in this place I really didn't care for. It wasn't anything Mosley ever said or did, and I accepted his unenthusiastic hello with grace; it was more that he was just not my sort. I don't think he was Adam's sort, either. There is a vibration that anyone as sensitive as I am can detect when two humans face each other*

*without honesty. I don't mean lying or cheating or steal-
ing kind of dishonesty. I mean the sort of dishonesty of
intention. Adam and Mosley were pretending to like each
other. Pretending is a sort of dishonesty. At least it is in my
world. One time, Adam and I stood in a group of others
and watched two men talking to each other. Their
speech became more and more tense, until they started
shouting at each other. Suddenly, they actually started
poking sticks at each other. But, as hostile as the tone
was, and the obvious aggression, there was no sense of
true dislike. In fact, I got the very real impression that
the two men doing this were quite fond of each other.
Weird. Weirder still was that when the battle was over,
with one man clearly the victor because he then addressed
all these witnesses with a long tongue-language valedic-
tory speech, all of us who had witnessed this open-air aggression clapped their hands together, I wagged my tail,
and the man on the ground jumped to his feet, smiling
and hugging his combatant. Pretending goes both ways,
I guess.*

*Fortunately, Adam and Mosley only sat for a little
while, not even long enough for a decent snooze. Adam
scraped his chair back; I leapt to my feet. I shook myself
while they shook hands, a tradition among human males
that I have finally figured out is similar to our nose-to-
nether routine. Hands are important to people, not so
much hindquarters. With more false cheer, Mosley walked
us to the door, closing it behind us with a thump.*

*I spotted Cody perched on the flat wall that separates
the parking lot from the river. She was sitting with her
knees up and her chin resting on them, the picture of deep
contemplation. She turned and smiled at us as we ap-
proached, and I gave her my best tail-wagging greeting,
making like we hadn't just seen each other. I was truly
overjoyed when she got into my seat in the car. Being a*

*gentleman, I had almost offered it to her even before Adam ordered me into the backseat. Cody in the car meant that we were going back to the place where I slept well. Where my pal Lucky was waiting for us.*

Adam casts about for chitchat, keeping the subject of Lucky, aka Dawg, out of bounds. He's talked with Skye, who's been honest with him about Cody's very normal falling off of enthusiasm for the quotidian responsibilities associated with dog ownership. Being the kid's mother, Skye is pretty sanguine about it. It's exactly as she expected, so there you go. The good news is that she's actually pleased with Mingo's work. Maybe not exactly a win-win, but certainly a nice draw. The next best topic is art. The art lessons.

"Fine. I'm learning that I don't know anything."

So much for thinking that this was a safe subject.

Cody adds, "Mosley says that even great artists have to practice."

"So this kid carrying a violin case meets an old man carrying a cello case. The kids asks him, 'How do you get to Carnegie Hall?'"

Cody flashes him a derisive look, followed by a sigh of weltschmerz. "Practice. Practice. Practice."

"You've heard that joke before."

"Everyone has."

"And they said that vaudeville was dead."

Cody is intent on her phone, thumbing, scrolling, and sweeping, using fine motor skills he imagines that she does in her sleep. Maybe Adam doesn't need to engage her in conversation, since she's already having one.

"Oh." Cody puts her phone down. Then picks it up and studies it. Puts it down.

The look on her face is stricken, and his paternal urge is to see if there's anything he can do to relieve her distress.

He's no one to this kid, just a convenient ride home, and Adam knows better than to ask what's wrong. What bit of news or gossip flashed on the tiny screen of that infernal instrument has caused her to go pale? Out of the corner of his eye, he can see the quiver in her lips, the glint of moisture in her eye. And that's enough to prompt him. "Cody, is everything okay? Did something happen?"

She nods, then shakes her head. Doesn't look at him. Turns her face to the passenger window. Adam keeps both hands on the steering wheel, fighting against that ingrained fatherly gesture of patting her on the shoulder. This girl is so fragile, he's certain that even an avuncular touch would set her off.

Fortunately for both of them, Chance is on the case. He pokes his head over the console and licks Cody on the cheek. She wraps her arm over his neck and buries her face into the skin of his neck. Adam allows himself a sigh and speeds up to make the crest of the hill. They'll be at the LakeView in moments. Skye will sort this out. Even though Adam tells himself this, his fatherly impulses take over. "You okay?"

Cody pushes Chance away, back into the rear seat. "Yeah. It's just stupid stuff."

"Stupid enough to upset you?"

"There's these kids." Cody leaves it at that. *These kids.*

It doesn't take a child psychologist to figure out whatever it was "these kids" said, it was upsetting to *this* kid.

"Jerks?"

"Big-time." A little smile. "Bigger than the word *jerk.*"

Encouraged, Adam pushes it. "Assholes?"

Cody nods and gives him a crooked smile. "It's so trite. The jock and the cheerleaders. Scuse me, this season they're lacrosse players."

"Cody, this may sound like old-guy talk, but there have been jocks and cheerleaders since high school was invented. And they love nothing better than to make the world think that their you know what doesn't stink."

"It's not like that. Not exactly. They want the world to think that I stink."

A generation ago, no one would have given serious worry to a kid being teased. Not so nowadays, and Adam's paternal antennae go up. "Are they bullying you?"

Cody puts the phone facedown on her lap. "No."

"Does your mother know?"

Cody throws him a look of utter panic. "I can deal. It's fine."

"You don't have to. If they're bullying—"

"They're not. It's just stupid stuff. It's fine." Cody shakes her head. "Please, Mr. March. Don't say anything. She'll just get all freaked-out and overreact over nothing. It's what she does."

Funny, the woman Adam knows doesn't seem like the overreacting type, but what does he know? She comes across to him as pretty well grounded and pragmatic. Kids have such harsh opinions of their parents. Adam knows from bitter experience that some parents deserve it, but somehow he can't imagine that Skye is nearly the ogre her daughter portrays her to be.

"You know, Cody, it seems like you're always asking me to keep things from your mother."

The girl nods, shoves her glasses back up on her nose, and gives him a rueful smile. "She's a helicopter mom. What can I say?"

Those sketches on the wall, all aboveboard, all theoretically done from casual observation as the girl sweeps the floor. All with just the faintest suggestion of sensuality.

*You should just kill yourself. Save the world from ugly.*

She should never have accepted Ryan's friend request. This posting already has sixteen reposts, and they haven't even gotten home yet. She checks her other social media accounts, and every one of them bears the marks of a campaign to wither her.

Chance plants his feet on the console. His shoulders are too wide to allow much more than his head to squeeze over, but this he does and snuffles at her cheek again. His dewlaps tickle. Mr. March usually orders the dog to back off, but this time he doesn't, and she's grateful to have the dog's blocky head between them. Every little notification on her account that someone has liked or commented on Ryan's outrageous posting is a slap, and it is getting harder and harder to hold back the tears. Neither can she simply put the phone down. It's watching her own demise; her inexorable slide into the oblivion of total ostracism.

> *Liar and a thief.*
> *We don't like you.*
> *Lesbo. Dyke.*
> *We don't want you here.*
> *Your stink spoils our class.*
> *Go back to wherever you came from.*
> *Die, bitch.*
> *Commit suicide. Do us all a favor. Don't be a coward. Do it.*

"Block whoever it is." Mr. March has his eyes on the road, and the dog is between them, but still, somehow he's figured it out. "You don't have to put up with that."

"But if I do that, I won't know what they're saying."

"They'll stop saying it if they don't get a rise out of you."

"You don't understand."

"If I had a nickel for every time my kid said that to me . . ."

Mr. March pulls into the parking lot, and she's out of the car almost before he stops it. Cody stalks away, then remembers that her backpack is in the backseat, so has to stalk back, yank open the door, and retrieve it.

"Cody Mitchell, where have you been? You know that I needed you here this afternoon." And there she is, the she-devil herself. "You went to the AC?"

"Yeah, what of it? I did. I don't want to be your slave here, your minion." Cody bolts for the cabin, Dawg close on her heels.

"Cody, darling, I need you now. Right here. Now. We still have two rooms to do and guests arriving any minute." It wouldn't do to show anger in front of guests, so Skye's voice is a strange concoction of level tone and hissing, the righteous maternal outrage packaged in a pretty box.

If she slams the door hard enough, she won't hear her mother's restrained beckoning. Cody knows that she's her mother's daughter when she refrains from slamming the cabin door, but once inside, she takes it out on the bathroom door, slamming it shut behind her, and when it bounces open, slamming it again, over and over, until the dog barks at her to stop this loud and unpleasant game. He needs a walk. Cody comes out of the bathroom. "Let's go."

Dawg tap-dances in front of her, blocking her path to the hook where his leash hangs, getting underfoot as she swaps out her cowboy boots for sneakers. Cody feels like she's running against the clock. Skye will burst in any second now, and if she's still inside, she's going to get yelled at for sure. It's not that she can't take the dressing-down—that's easy enough, meaningless enough—but

Cody's nerves are frayed and she's more afraid that she'll say something that will start a conversation she has no intention of having with her mother. Or that she'll start to cry.

More than anything in the world, she wants her mother to hold her, to lie and tell her that this will all go away someday. That she'll outlast them. But one loving touch and she'll lose everything.

     •    •    •

Randy dropped to the ground gracelessly. The sound of his head striking the cement was like a ripe fruit splitting open, sickening, but Cody had no time to think about it. She was close enough, so gleefully running to catch up with him, that she could smell the urine he released. The black car was gone. She was alone on the sidewalk. There was a moment's complete cessation of breath and sight and hearing; she was fixed in Lucite, boxed in by what she had seen, the suddenness of it, the extraordinarily fine line between life and death.

Cody's backpack thumped against her spine as she ran not the way she had come, but down the first cross street, not blind to her destination, home and the safety of her closet, but with intention. Down this street, get between the school on one side and the factory on the other, dash up the alley between three-decker houses, left and then right, over the hill and down the jogging path that wends its way through the cemetery. Her only thought was to get home, where she should have been, not here on this street to witness what she had.

A black car. It slowed, moved off. Cody didn't know if it was the same one. Cars all looked so alike. She made the alley, where hopscotch patterns were scribbled on the bumpy surface, a safe place for little girls to play out of the traffic. Her head was down; every oxygen-denied

breath burned the back of her throat. The open end of the
alley was mere steps away. And then it was blocked, the
black car facing her, the passenger door opening.

Giant. Black glasses obscured his eyes. Lantern-jawed,
like a cartoon character. Distinctive. He strode toward her.
Johnny Mervin. Her dad's friend. His killer.

The lantern-jawed man swept Cody up by the straps of
her backpack, slamming her against the brick wall, his
breath stinking of chaw and garlic. "You say one word and
you die."

"I won't."

"I know who you are. I know where you live. You
speak of this, you die." He leaned his face even closer.
"And your mother dies, too."

"I didn't see anything."

"That's your truth from now on."

He slammed her against the wall one more time for
good measure.

"Hey, we gotta go." The driver leaned out the window
of the black car. Sirens split the air.

Johnny dropped Cody and she landed hard on her
backside. He bent from the waist, leaning so that his lips
were at her ear. "I'll find you, wherever you go, for the
rest of your life."

Before she could scramble to her feet, they were gone.

Cody can't control the constant fear of a lantern-jawed
man in dark glasses waiting for her. She can't take the
chance of breaking down in front of Skye. She can't risk
their lives.

"Cody? Are you in there?" It's Skye, and she's bearing
down on the cabin.

They never use the back door, and the door sticks so

much that Cody has to wrap both hands around the knob and brace one foot against the jamb to be able to pull hard enough to get it open.

"Cody, I need to talk to you."

After all the years of being stuck, it finally gives. Cody kicks open the screen door with its spiderwebbed mesh, the dog right behind her.

# CHAPTER 29

It feels as if I've been bucked off a bull. My bones ache, I'm so tired after turning over all these rooms by myself, and now I've got Cody's drama to deal with. I swing the wide-open back door shut, making a mental note to bring the can of WD-40 back from the next trip to the hotel. Well, let the kid settle down, get over her mad, and then we can hash out a regular schedule of chores. Cody knows darn well that she's got responsibilities. And the dog is just the top of the list right now.

Cody's backpack is where she dropped it, in the middle of the hallway to the two tiny bedrooms. Her sketch pad sticks out, almost like an invitation to take a look. Cody is so coy about her work, rarely, if ever, openly sharing it with me. On occasion, she leaves a sketch out, like an afterthought, or something she meant to toss away. I've learned not to compliment the work too effusively, because Cody invariably shuts me down, which isn't a kind of false modesty; she is her own harshest critic. And yet Cody persists in trying, and I have to admire that.

I lift the eight-and-a-half-by-eleven pad out of the mouth of the backpack. Every page but three have been ripped out. On the first remaining page, a head study of Lucky—Dawg—and Cody has definitely captured his impish personality. On the second, a rather pretty charcoal drawing of the mill race behind the Artists Collaborative building. The last page is blank. Impulsively, I fish around in the bottom of the backpack for a pencil or pen. Finding only a broken piece of charcoal, I draw my own sketch, two stick figures, obviously mother and child, and scrawl "I Love You" in a deliberately childish hand, adding a big heart to frame it all.

A tap at the door. "Skye?"

"Come on in, Adam."

"You've got a couple in the office. I tried your phone, but it didn't ring through."

I pull my phone out of my pocket. "Dead. I forgot to plug it in last night, and I was hoping that the battery would last till I was in the office this afternoon, but then with all the rooms to do, I never got there."

"Well, they're here and waiting. I've been entertaining them with my local knowledge of trails and art museums."

"You're hired." It's meant as a joke, but just saying it makes me wistful. It would be so nice to have a fully functioning partner in this endeavor instead of a contentious adolescent and an MIA caretaker.

"Thanks, but I've got a job."

"You wouldn't want to trade helping worthy causes for twenty-four/seven worrying if the guests are safe and happy or if there are any guests at all?"

"You make it sound so tempting." Adam leaves me at the office door; he and Chance head to their usual room, the first-floor room 9. The nicer room, the dog-ready room upstairs, is booked for the couple with their poodle, who are waiting for me in the office, and I'm grateful for that. Grateful to Adam for being persistent.

Mingo Ayala is standing outside his residence. He's got his hood up, his hands deep in the pockets of his saggy jeans. He flings his backpack into the backseat and slides into the passenger seat. "Good morning, Ms. Mitchell. Nice day, ain't it?"

"Lovely. You seem cheerful."

"I am. It's a special day."

"How so?"

"I'm eighteen years old today."

"Well then, happy birthday." He seems a lot older than eighteen to me; his swagger gives him a certain faux maturity. This kid's never been a little boy.

"Thing is, I'm what they call 'emancipated' now and I'm clearing out of this place. Time served."

"Where will you go?"

"Don't know. Don't care. Still got probation, so I can't go far. But, I don't have to live in a house with sixteen other at-risk youth." He puts finger quotes around the "at-risk youth."

"How far can you go?"

"Got to stay in the county, or in the state. Something like that. In the country, but I ain't got no passport, so I don't think I'll be doing much leaving the country. 'Less I join up. Might do that. Think that the army would take me?"

"I don't know. Maybe. Would you really want to do that?"

"No. Not really. I like the construction work. Look like I got mad skills with a hammer."

"I know you do. And I appreciate the work you've done for me." I signal and pull into the Dunkin' Donuts parking lot. It's become our habit, but as it's Mingo's birthday, I feel like I should do something more, but nothing much comes to mind other than treating him to pizza after work.

"It's a-ite. You keeping Dawg for me, so I'm obliged."

"So, are you willing to keep working for me? I mean now that you're emancipated? Now that you might find a place to live where you could keep him?" Best not to mention this conversation to Adam, the fact that I'm opening the door to Mingo's taking Dawg away.

He doesn't answer right away. The hood obscures his face, and I hate that. It's like he shelters himself from the world underneath his Champion tent. Protects himself from my middle-ish-class, white, do-gooder self. The thought is so sudden that I break into a sweat. Is that how he sees me? That, to me, he's just a charity case?

As I pull out onto the street, he pushes the hood back. "I would. I'd like that a lot." For the first time, I notice that his eyes are green, framed by sooty lashes. The shy smile that he gives me is genuine, unpracticed. He doesn't smile much, this kid. This young adult. What kind of a life has he had?

"Mingo, this may just be the Coffee Coolatta talking, but I could really use a lot more of your help."

Mingo takes a long swallow of his iced coffee. "I dunno. It's . . ."

"I've got a cabin I want to rehab before the first week of July. It wouldn't be just cleaning rooms; it would still be construction. Would you want to come on full-time? You'd get a room out of it, plus an hourly wage. More than minimum. Not a lot more, but with a free room, it's a living wage."

He does that thing with his mouth, sucking in his lower lip, revealing the shadow of the cute little boy he might once have been. Under the tildes of his black brows, he looks at me with distrust. "Why would you do this for me?" There is a rosy tint to his usually sallow cheeks.

"I need the help, Mingo. You're a hard worker."

He says nothing. He turns his face away and flips up his hood.

Has no one ever praised him? Does he think I'm bullshitting him? Teasing him?

"Think about it. You don't have to answer now."

I maneuver around the traffic that's building up on this Saturday morning, both hands on the wheel, my drink secured between my knees.

Mingo takes another gulp of his coffee, rubs a moist hand on his jeans. "I'd keep it clean."

"I know you would."

"I'd keep clean." He pushes his hood down. "Know what I'm sayin'?"

"I do."

"A-ite. Probably some paperwork you gotta do, but, yeah, all right." Grinning, he leans over to switch on the radio, finds his station, and we drive home, our heads boppin' to the beatz.

As I drive home, I can't help but notice that it takes a former street kid to make me feel like an acceptable parent.

To say that Cody was surprised speechless at her mother's offering Mingo the Carrolls' job and attic room would have been an understatement. Who knew her mother could be so crazy? But for once, Cody thinks that's a good thing. "Great. Thanks, Mom. I know it'll work out." It felt so odd, this effortless compliment, but it was painful to watch the pleased look on her mother's face bloom, as if she'd just told some little kid "Good job." "So I guess you won't need me as much."

"I'll need you just as much. He's going to concentrate on the cabins for the first few weeks."

"That's so not fair." What a relief it is to wipe that pleased look off her mother's face, replacing it with her more usual one of battle weariness. It would be so easy to fall into a comfortable moment, allow a chink in this wall she's built, into which would pour disaster.

"You and Mingo will do the rooms together, and after that you can go to the AC or whatever it is you want to do. Mornings, less than half a day. Not a sacrifice."

"I hate cleaning rooms. People are so gross."

Skye waves off Cody's complaint. "So do I, but it's part of the deal."

"What deal? Your deal, not mine."

"Our deal. Our living. Yours and mine. Something of our own."

Cody really doesn't want to engage in this useless and all too familiar argument. Her mother can get really worked up about her fantasy of one for all and all for one. She veered off. "What does Mr. March think about it? Bet he'll be pissed off."

"I don't know. I haven't told him."

Because the dog will be back with Mingo, she'll miss having him with her at night. More than she could have imagined, having the bulk of the sixty-pound pit bull beside her in bed had afforded her a whole string of restful nights. No one would dare touch her. Dawg was keeping her safe.

I love this time of night, when all the guests are settled into their rooms, when I can take a lungful of this pristine mountain air and let it out in a cleansing breath. One door opens. It's Adam, letting his dog out for last call. He sees me standing there, waves. I've got to tell him of my decision to bring Mingo on full-time, how I've impulsively given the kid a place to live, this street kid, this unknown quantity.

"Hey, got a minute?" I keep my voice low, knowing that even a whisper can penetrate the quiet of a sleeping hotel, gesture toward the closed office door, unlock it.

He's a moment, waiting for the dog to do his thing. Then: "What's up?"

"I've invited—no, better word, *hired*—Mingo full-time."

"What brought that on?"

"He's eighteen now. He used a word . . ."

"Emancipated." Adam strokes Chance's head. "An adult in the eyes of the system."

"Yes. That's it. Anyway, I've really got to find a replacement for the Carrolls, and he's a good worker. He'll do housekeeping and help me get another cottage into shape."

Adam doesn't say anything at first, then leaves off petting the dog, who flops to the floor with a sigh. "Are you sure about this? Have you thought it through?"

"That's really not your concern. With all due respect."

"No. You're right. I just don't want to see things get worse instead of better."

"You mean worse than having to rely on Carl? Worse than running this place and doing all the housekeeping, too?"

"You're not worried?"

"Of course I am. Worried that next week we won't have enough bookings to pay the electric bill. Worried about the damp patch on the ceiling of room eleven. Worried that the washing machine won't make it through the season." Worried about Cody. I don't say how worried I am. That her behavior toward me is getting worse, not better. That she treats me like I'm the enemy. That my touch is painful, my concern, my being her mother, is intolerable. When I try to give her a good-night kiss, she turns her cheek so far away that all I can reach is an ear, and then she pulls away, as if I've burned her.

Chance pushes himself into a sitting position and throws a look at Adam, then at me. He's taking the temperature of the room. Analyzing the rising tension to see if there's anything he should do about it.

"I mean about his history. Mingo."

"No. Yes." I point at him. "Aren't you the one who helps organizations that give people down on their luck second chances?"

"Yeah." He sighs. "Yes. And I've been the recipient of second chances. But, Skye, with a kid like this, you have to be prepared for backsliding. It's not a smooth transition."

"I'll take my chances."

As if he thinks I've spoken his name, Chance gives me a look, sits up, waits to see if I have something in mind, then stretches his front legs out until he's back on the rug, sphinxlike. He lowers his head onto his paws, blinks, closes his eyes.

"Do you still think he fought that dog?"

"I don't know. Someone did. Maybe not him, but that's not to say I trust that Mingo won't ever fight that dog. If his circumstances change."

"You mean if he goes back on drugs."

"Yeah. Or falls in with his former crew."

"Then I guess I'd better keep him busy here."

Adam shifts, pats his knee. His dog is immediately there beside him. "You're a good woman. You remind me of someone."

I don't have to ask whom he means.

# CHAPTER 30

It's the last day of school and Cody waits at the edge of the parking lot for the yellow school bus that will carry her to her place of torment for the last time this horrible year. The texting and social media posts have been relentlessly mean, but she's gotten immune to them and to the perpetual poking, teasing insults and remorseless harrying. She never lets them see her looking upset, even when she is sitting right in front of them as they invent more and more ways to insult, offend, and demean her. Their fast-moving thumbs constantly sending evil messages to her on devices hidden beneath notepads and in sweatshirt pockets, right in front of teachers. How they trust her not to show anyone what they've sent is proof that Cody Mitchell is the perfect target for their animus. She's invisible. She's no one.

Its being the last day of school, a half day, things are fluid—teachers returning final papers, chatting and jokey, music blasting out of computer speakers in every other room, the air fairly bursting with the promise of summer. The seniors are gone; the juniors are standing tall with their elevation to seniors. Freshmen are no longer the little kids they were when they walked through those doors for the first time, frightened and shy, now sophomores armed with experience. Sophomores are fledged into juniors, at the midway point in their high school careers, and will return in the fall with all the rank and privilege of upperclassmen.

Taylor and Ryan come down the hallway hand in hand. They look like everyone's idea of a high school couple, the beautiful people. The chosen ones. Her blond hair is loose, swinging with every turn of her head as she, with queenly serenity, greets classmates right and left. Ryan is hand-slapping and shoulder-butting his classmates, firing at them with a pointed finger, king of the little world he inhabits.

Cody is cleaning out her locker, stuffing her backpack with the detritus of the year from hell that is high school. Lost homework, scraps of sketches. A sock, a shirt. The gym shorts she refused to wear. There's the book she thought she lost, the one she had to pay for, jammed way in the back, wedged in such a way that she has to kneel on the floor to reach it.

The blow shoves her right into the locker, the sharp edges scraping at the tender skin of her arms. She bangs her head trying to back out, and feels herself pushed back in, someone's foot against her rear end. Laughter rackets off the metal interior of the locker. Cody kicks as she wriggles free, hoping to prevent a third shove. The laughter sounds like a jet plane taking off, louder and louder, until Cody just wants to put her hands over her ears and crawl deeper into the locker, shut the door after herself, and die.

A pipsqueak voice pipes up. "Knock it off, Ryan. That's not cool."

She backs out of the locker, successfully this time, and

turns to face her assailant. Ryan and his squeeze, Taylor. Facing them down, that kid, the brother, Devin.

Taylor punches the kid in the arm, a sisterly gesture of sovereignty. "What? You got a crush on Miss B.J. here?" Her laughter is not queenly at all, more crow than crowned head.

"Yeah, no accounting for taste. Tay, you'd better coach him; unless . . ." Ryan strokes his chin contemplatively. "Dev, are you, perhaps, looking for a little head? Or is the hand more your speed?"

Devin doesn't come up to Ryan's chin. He's a couple of inches shorter than his sister. He's a kid, with a half day left as an eighth grader. A rising freshman who hasn't transitioned into a proper teenager. Cody holds her breath. She should slam her locker door shut, stalk off, forget this last round of insult and injury. Except she doesn't have to. "So, Taylor, how do you feel about your boyfriend cheating on you with your best friend? Kind of sucks, doesn't it?"

"Fuck you." Ryan leans toward her, braces one arm on either side of her, trapping Cody against the locker.

"No, I think that Ryan is fucking Tyler. Why don't you ask him what they were doing out at Tannery Falls. Just the two of them."

"Shut up, you bitch."

His face is close now; she can smell the Altoid on his breath. She doesn't flinch. She's got the whip hand now. "Don't touch me." Cody shakes the hair out of her eyes. "Don't you ever touch me."

Taylor steps up, grabs Ryan by an arm but doesn't pull it away from where he braces it against the red locker. "What does she mean? What were you and Tyler doing at the falls?"

"Nothing. It's not important. She's a liar and a—"

"Tell her, why don't you? Clear your conscience." Cody

smiles into Ryan's face. His ears are red, the skin of his throat.

"Ryan. What about you and Tyler?" Taylor's voice has gone all Minnie Mouse.

"Nothing. I swear. She's crazy." He shouts the words into Cody's face.

"Go ahead, Ryan, tell her the truth." Cody gives him an encouraging nod. It feels good. "Tell her. Ask her why Tyler hasn't been wearing that little pink T-shirt from Banana Republic lately."

"There's nothing to tell, you whack job. You're crazy. Taylor, she's crazy."

What's crazy, Cody thinks, is how afraid he is of Taylor.

Taylor lets go of Ryan's arm. Flips her hair back over her shoulder, affects her best look of boredom. "Yeah. She's nuts. Mental case. Loony tunes. Let's go."

Cody watches them, arm in arm, continue their regal progress down the long freshman hall. "Yeah, but I planted some doubt, didn't I?"

Devin shoulders his backpack, gives Cody a half-hearted smile, and follows.

Carl doesn't seem the least bit concerned that this Hispanic kid with the tattooed neck, further embellished by clunky fake gold chains, is being asked to do most of the chores that he had been given over the winter and somehow never found the time to accomplish. Carl's "So what?" attitude is actually a relief. I hate confrontation, and really didn't want to have to tell Carl that he was fired. This half measure is just fine. Mingo needs some guidance for the part of the rehab work that isn't just demo, and Carl is a pretty good teacher, showing the boy how to properly cut the Sheetrock, how to mud it to cover the seams. Mingo, for his part, seems to enjoy the tutelage. I can't afford two handymen, however, so it's also a relief when Carl decides that the trout are calling and vanishes once again into the wild. If things work out with Mingo, Carl will have quite the surprise the next time he returns to pick up a few bucks between disappearances.

The little cabin is coming along nicely. Standing in the open doorway, I watch Mingo roll paint over the Sheetrock, pleased with the color I've chosen for the room, not quite white, not quite yellow. By taking down the non-load-bearing wall between the living space and the tiny kitchen, the whole effect is one of airiness and space. Pristine. The old sprung couch and dubious wicker chairs are gone, replaced by a faux Arts and Crafts–style set. Once the trim painting is done—a complementary buttercup yellow—I'll hang Roman shades, replacing the dusty, musty curtains that fairly disintegrated in my hands as I pulled them down. The other half of the cabin is an en suite bedroom. Unlike the two-bedroom cabin, this cottage was never meant for families, but for honeymooners. Unfortunately, I don't have the resources to make the bathroom into anything more interesting than a clean, bright, and functioning facility—no Jacuzzi, no high-pressure multiple showerheads, just a step up from the showerheads in the other rooms.

I've invested in several inexpensive souvenir photographs and put them in cheap frames, and I hold one of the framed photographs against the newly painted wall. I'm disappointed. It seems small, lost, against the creamy expanse. Well, I can't use these here. And the budget— funny word that one, as if I've been thoughtful about the expense—is blown.

I had hoped to be able to offer Adam this cabin for his most recent trip, even though he isn't staying long and the cabin is meant for long stays, a week or more. It felt like a nice thing to do, give my most loyal guest a treat, but the place isn't ready for inspection, so no guests till the building inspector grants the certificate of occupancy.

*My friend and I met up during our before-bed outing. His boy and my man stood chatting quietly as Dawg and I made sure that the perimeters were safe. I confess that my attention was not entirely on the task at hand; rather, the voices, quiet but intense, had caught my ear, and I kept closer to the pair than I might normally have done. Just in case I was needed. I shouldn't have worried. My compatriot, although seemingly distracted by the night scents, moved himself closer to the humans as well, leading me to believe that he, too, caught the whiff of discord.*

*The voices grew marginally louder, then dropped back quickly, as though the humans understood that they were venturing close to making a ruckus like some dogs do, invariably inciting more ruckus from other dogs who get excited by the noise. I don't mean to suggest that they were snapping and snarling. It was more like a little fear aggression on the one hand, and dominance on the other.*

Adam sees Mingo standing slouched against the side of the building. In the moonlight, his hood gives him the outline of a monk. His dog bounds over, wriggling in pleasure at seeing Adam, greeting him as an old and dear friend. Lucky and Chance give each other a good going-over before getting down to business.

"Hey, Mr. March." The kid pushes himself away from the wall, pushes the hood back. "S'up?"

"Hello, Mingo." He has no answer for the "S'up?"

When Skye told him of her decision to hire Mingo as the new handyman-cum-housekeeper, Adam was mostly able to bite his tongue, forbidding himself to expound at length on why this might not be a good idea. This is no innocent youth suffering under unfortunate circumstances; this is a crackhead who may have even fought his dog to feed his habit. A kid on probation. How was she ever going to trust him in people's rooms? Adam could see that Skye expected him to say something about it. She had that hooded eye, tensed jaw of a woman ready to do battle, ready to defend her decision—bad or otherwise—and her right to have made it. Which is why he finally responded with the only civil remark he could come up with: "It's your decision."

"Yes, it is. He'll be fine. He just needs a chance."

And right then he was ashamed. It was as if there were an overlay of his past and present. It wasn't Skye's voice he heard; it was Gina's.

"Mr. March, I'm guessin' that you probably ain't on board with me bein' here, but I gotta tell you that I'm good. Like I told Ms. Mitchell, I'm clean, and I'm going to stay that way."

"I'm sure you will." He can't keep the flatness out of his voice, his skepticism.

"I owe her. She the first person in however long to treat me like a human being."

A bullfrog croaks with a tympanic thump. Adam listens for the reply, and there it is, answered in kind from a distance.

"She's a good person. But, Mingo, it takes your making a decision you can stick to. Change comes from the inside."

"I changed. I did. I have. You helped, too. You pulled me out of that place and found my dog. Took care of him. I owe you, too."

"You don't owe me. And I'll be honest: I still don't think Lucky's best place is with you."

"It is if that place is here." Mingo flips the hood back over his head. "And his name is Dawg."

Suddenly, Adam realizes that the dogs are close by, back from their saunter down the hill, their eyes fixed upon their two men, Chance's on him, Dawg's on Mingo. Tails wag.

"I'll make a deal with you. If things fall apart, you give me the dog. Dawg. You won't have to worry about him."

"I ain't makin' that kind of deal with you. You make it sound like I'm a fuckup. Maybe I was. But now I'm not. I've already told my boys not to look for me. I'm done with that life. I'm stayin' here as long as Ms. Mitchell wants me to be here. My dog with me." Mingo faces Adam. He's a little shorter, lots more wiry. One hand is tucked into the kangaroo pouch of his sweatshirt and the other is in a fist by his side. Adam takes an involuntary step back.

Dawg nuzzles his way into Mingo's fist, and the hand opens up to grasp the dog's moist muzzle. The tail begins to whip from side to side. The dog pats his feet against the dry grass, dancing in joy at his person's touch. The dog loves this boy. It really all comes down to second chances. Giving them, and getting them. Adam needs to remember that.

Gina knew what he had done, knew what he was capable of, and still she gave him the opportunity to prove himself to her. She taught him how to ask for forgiveness.

"Mingo, I'm sorry. You're right. This is your transcendent opportunity and I'm raining on it."

"I like that. Transcendent opportunity. Sweet."

The hand comes out of the pocket, and Mingo teaches Adam how to execute a proper homeboy handshake.

*But then, as humans are known for doing, they stopped talking and touched hands. Immediately the air around them cleared and both smiled, not in fear-aggression fashion, but more like gently wagging tails. All is well.*

*Dawg and I gave each other a quick sniff and simultaneously decided to reconnoiter the farther edge of the property. Our people watched us disappear into the darkness.*

# CHAPTER 31

Cody and Black Molly sit on the rump-sprung couch in the double-wide trailer. The old-fashioned boxy television is on, but the only channel they can pull in using the dish is a news station. They have a green bottle of beer stuck between the couch cushions and are taking turns sipping from it. This isn't the first time Molly's stolen beer from her father; it's usually a can of Bud Light that she says he'll never miss out of the case he keeps under the trailer. Cody doesn't particularly like the taste, something between warm, flat soda and sour water, but she's always ready to prove she's got game. She takes little sips of the Heffenreffer while Molly slugs back the lion's share, which is fine with Cody.

It's really not important what's on television, and they start getting silly as the beer, their second stolen from the case beneath the trailer, goes down. It's hot out and the trailer's air conditioning, if it ever had any, is off. The beer doesn't taste good and it's tepid, but with each sip, their hilarity expands.

Black Molly sits back, snaps her Bic lighter, and blows

a stream of smoke into the air. She offers the cigarette to Cody, but she refuses. "I'm quitting."

This strikes Molly as hysterical. "You're such a wuss."

"Better a wuss than sucking oxygen through a straw in your neck."

In answer, Molly shoots a stream of smoke right into Cody's face.

"Cut it out. I'll stink like smoke and my mother will—"

"Aww, baby girl is afraid of her mother."

"Am not." Cody grabs the bottle, takes a healthy swig. "Beer and smoke. I'll get a wicked good lecture. Can't wait." Something on the television screen catches her eye. "Hey, turn that up."

By some quirk of the dish, the local news that they are watching isn't local to the Berkshires, but to Springfield. It feels like home, briefly, to see the familiar faces of the two anchors, like people she used to know. But it is what they are saying that grabs Cody's attention.

". . . sought in connection to an unsolved drive-by shooting last year, reportedly gang-related . . ."

It isn't just the words; it's the photograph.

"It's not him."

"It's not who?" Black Molly stubs out the cigarette, her attention entirely on Cody. "Who?"

"That guy. It's the driver. Not the shooter."

"And you know this how?"

And Cody suddenly realizes the extent of her mistake. "I just . . . Umm, I don't."

"You *were* there, weren't you?" Molly pulls the bottle out of Cody's hand, wraps an arm around Cody's neck. Shakes her. "Hey, I'm your pal, your bestie. You can tell me anything."

Cody looks into Black Molly's eyes. Behind the thick mascara and wide swath of eyeliner, they are a surprising blue. For once, they aren't hard. Floating in a beer haze, Cody feels herself surrendering. "Yes. I saw my father on the street and I was following him, hoping maybe he'd give me a couple of bucks."

"So, it's pretty traumatic, but why didn't you just go to the police?"

"Because he said he'd kill me and my mother if I did. The guy. The shooter."

"You talked to him?"

"He chased me."

"That is way cool, like being in a movie."

"No. It wasn't. I was terrified; I almost peed myself."

Molly reaches over and pats Cody's cheek. "That's a pretty big secret." And suddenly, her eyes are no longer sympathetic, but calculating. "So, your mom really doesn't know that you saw your dad shot?"

"I told you. I can't tell her. The guy said he'd kill me and her if I said anything."

"Yeah, but you moved here; he's not going to go looking for you."

Cody shoves her hair behind her ears. "He said he would."

"He was just trying to scare you."

"You don't know. You weren't there. He meant it." Cody grabs the beer bottle, takes a swig. It tastes just like the bile in her throat when she thinks of his breath in her face, his hands on her.

Molly leans forward, her thick neck sinking between her rounded shoulders, the dark circlets of eyeliner not quite obscuring the glint of mordant curiosity. "And you don't want your mom to ever know."

The beer leaves a sour aftertaste in her mouth and Cody swallows, hoping to move it off her palate. "She can't. Ever."

"So, except for me, no one knows that you saw your father gunned down."

"No. How could they?"

"Not even Mr. Farrow?"

Cody reaches for the bottle, lets her hair slide down across her cheek so that her eyes aren't visible. No one can know. Especially a counselor. How can she explain this to Molly? If you get other people involved, word will get back to the authorities, and if word gets back to the authorities, the shooter will come looking for her. For Skye. Cody shakes her head. "No one can know. Please don't say anything to anyone. Promise me?" She sniffs back against the pressure of tears. "It's life and death, Molly. No lie."

Black Molly smiles, her crooked teeth framed by black lipstick, giving her a jack-o'-lantern look. "Then find me some dope."

The nausea boils up and Cody barely makes it to the toilet.

•     •     •

Skye was willing to let Cody stay home, to not attend the funeral, but Cody didn't want to be left alone, so she made a fuss about doing the right thing, saying she was old enough to go, yada yada. Skye seemed proud of her, of Cody's mature handling of this tragedy. Skye had no idea. And Cody was going to keep it that way.

The cavernous Roman Catholic church would have looked half empty anyway, but only a few pews were occupied, and the ushers actually tried to get people to move to the front, to fill in the long benches so that it didn't look quite so obvious that Randy was unmourned.

The frontmost pew held only Randy's aunt, who had raised him, and her next-door neighbor, there as emotional support for her. Behind them, his three boys. Her half brothers. "Mom?" Skye looked at Cody, nodded. Cody slipped out of their pew and went to sit with her younger brothers. They looked foreign to her, almost strangers, as they were dressed in button-down shirts and clip-on ties. Their mothers had combed their hair, sent them in with clean hands. Like Skye, their mothers were dispersed amid the thin crowd, none acknowledging the presence of another. The "baby mamas," Cody knew Skye called them, nominally superior only because, of all the women Randy had fathered children with, she was the only one who had been married to him, even if only at the last moment and only briefly.

For the first time in a week, Cody felt safe. Truly in a sanctuary. As the coffin was wheeled out by the funeral home's attendants and they all got to their feet, respectful eyes following the coffin, she saw him. And he looked at her with a wolfish smile. The message was clear: *Are you keeping your secret?* She glanced away, then looked back. Johnny was directly behind her mother and he made just the slightest motion with his square chin toward Skye, then discretely drew a finger along his throat in a gesture that might have been mistaken for a botched sign of the cross, but to Cody, the meaning was clear. She nodded. The Secret would remain between them. It had to.

Time to go do another room. The people in room 7 are leaving today and Cody hopes that they'll remember to leave a tip; not everyone does. The first time Mingo went into a room to clean it after a checkout, he brought the money he'd found lying on the nightstand into the office, handing it to Skye. "Looks like they forgot this." It was so painfully obvious that he thought it was a trick, a trap to catch him backsliding. Skye folded his fingers over the proffered cash. "It's yours, Mingo. It's a tip. For good service. You and Cody split the tips."

Mingo is already in room 7, vigorously vacuuming, and

doesn't hear her approach. Dawg does, though, and he comes along the porch to bump himself against her bare legs. He's panting, and she takes that as his doggy communication—*Hello, how are you? I'm glad to see you*—rather than the fact that the day has grown warm. Dawg is a red-brown block of *Happy to see you.* She kneels, presses her face against the dog's skull, breathes in his not entirely unpleasant odor of dog skin and fur. He reaches around and gives her a lick on the arm.

"You okay?" Mingo leans out of the doorway. He's wearing his wifebeater and low-slung jeans. A dust cloth sticks out of his pocket.

"Yeah. Fine." Cody sucks in a deep breath, keeps her face away from him, wishing that she had on a shirt with sleeves so that she could discretely wipe away the moisture building up in her eyes. It was a bad night last night. It wasn't just the dreams that haunted her; it was the relentless back-and-forth of her mind, a constant debate as to whether, if the driver was known, that meant that she was safe, or if they were in more danger. Despite the hours spent online last night, trying to get as much information as she could, coming up with very little more than the television news had offered, there wasn't enough to still her fears. There was no mention of a second man. Just that the driver was sought in connection to the shooting. A person of interest. He wasn't in custody, so surely Johnny wasn't, either.

Worse, now Molly has stepped up her game, pressuring Cody about stealing the drugs with not-so-veiled threats to tell Skye the Secret.

"You don't look fine. I mean, hey, you *fine,* but you look upset."

Mingo has succeeded in making her laugh. She shakes her head. "Well, maybe not so fine, but thanks. It's a long story." Dawg works himself up under Cody's elbow, vying for her renewed attention. She gives it to him, then gets to her feet. "I'll get started on the bathroom."

As she moves past him, Mingo touches her shoulder. "I don't mind long stories. I got a long one myself. Give it up, girl."

She falls back on the usual, a complaint about her mother. "She's just such a pain."

"Cody, why are you so up in your mom's grill?"

"I told you: She's a pain."

"You know what I'd give my left arm for?"

"What?"

"A fuckin' mother. Someone who worried where I was, someone who cared about me." Mingo's mouth hardens, and he reminds her of the first time she saw him. "You know where my mother at?"

Cody doesn't answer.

"Freakin' jail. Want to know why?"

"Ummm, maybe?"

"Bunch of reasons. Biggest one is that she tried to kill me. Me and my brother. So strung out by drugs and not being able to feed us, she thought killing us was a good idea. We were babies."

Cody takes an involuntary step back, then stops. "I'm so sorry, Mingo. That's awful."

"Yeah. It is. But you know what? She's where she belongs, and right now, I'm where I belong and ain't nobody gonna disrespect your mother to me. I owe her."

Cody nods; unfamiliar with being chastened, she has nothing to say. And then she asks, "What happened to your brother?"

"He's dead, Cody. She managed to kill him."

Cody swallows hard, reaches tentatively to touch Mingo's exposed shoulder, the one with two initials tattooed on it. "Those his?"

"Yeah. Stand for Ricardo Ayala. We called him 'Rico.' He was four."

Mingo leans his forearms on the windowsill, looks out over the back of the hotel, down on the cabins, over to where the one doggy day care guest is taking in the sunshine. "We done in here? I got one more room to do."

"Yeah. I'm good."

"Okay. A-ite."

"Mingo?"

He doesn't look at her.

"Can I ask you something? And not get you mad?"

"Depends."

"Why did you do drugs, I mean, if your mother . . ."

"Was a crack whore? I don't know. I guess the apple doesn't fall far from the tree."

If she provides Molly with drugs, isn't she just like her own father? A small-time drug dealer, someone whose life was a complete waste.

"But you're better? You're doing all right?"

Mingo smiles at her, a sad smile. "Girl, we got work to do."

"What did I tell you about calling me *girl*?"

"Okay, *woman*. Get back to work."

"That's better."

Mingo goes out to grab new sheets and towels. Cody starts on the sink, catches sight of herself in the mirror. Mingo said she was *fine*. She pushes her bangs aside, cocks her head. Smiles at her image. She's still surprised to see the braces gone, the whiteness of her teeth making them look too big to her, like Chiclets. *Fine*.

# CHAPTER 32

"Listen, I'll be up a few days before the gala. So I'll book five days all together."

"It's two days shy of a full week." Skye taps her upper lip with a forefinger. "You know, by the time you come back, that little cabin will be available for a long-term rental if you want to consider staying for a bit longer. Call it a summer vacation. A little R and R."

"I have a board meeting that week, back in Boston." Adam shakes his head, truly regretful. "I wish I could."

As he pulls out onto Meander Road, Adam feels Chance breathing down his neck. "Ready to go home?" The dog makes no reply. Adam rolls down the back window, and the dog, uncharacteristically, sticks his head out and barks. There's Mingo, on his knees, pulling weeds, Dawg lazing beside him. Adam slows the car down, sticks out his arm, and waves to the boy. Mingo waves back.

What if he did blow off his meetings? Give himself a whole week to relax. A summer vacation. Time spent in a little cabin nestled in a nice scenic crook of a mountain, plenty of time to decompress, to walk the dog, to read something besides the paper, to contemplate the next move. Maybe even see if there are any fish in that little lake. Go for a swim. Explore the little towns and byways of Western Mass. Head up to Vermont. Spend a little more time with Skye. Whoa, where'd that idea come from?

Chance pulls his head in, sits, then flops on the backseat. A great sigh issues out of him, sounding not of contentment, but disappointment.

What exactly is he heading back for? Solitary reheated dinners? Unwelcome pity invitations? Unwanted advances from middle-aged women? But he has responsibilities, important work to be done. Tasks unfinished. Suddenly, Adam is reminded of his former self. The one who proudly never took time off; who sent his wife and daughter to their Vineyard summer house with unfulfilled promises to join them on the weekend. The man who sat at the head of the boardroom table on a Friday night negotiating some power move instead of seeing his only daughter off to her first dance. A man so intense that he finally exploded.

Losing everything had given him a new chance at finding a balance. Gina made no bones about reminding Adam, when he was on the verge of backsliding, that he was a new man. And here he is, blowing off an opportunity to relax, and, let's be honest, be with someone whose company he does enjoy. She's not Gina. She's no substitute for Gina. But Skye has become something he's lacked for a long time. A friend.

Adam fires up the Bluetooth, tells Siri to call the LakeView Hotel.

"Skye, any chance that cabin is available for the month of July?"

Skye doesn't even hesitate. "Yes."

"Book me in."

Black Molly is sitting in one of the folding lawn chairs staged around a cold fire pit filled with scraps of unburned paper and cigarette butts. The sound of a soap opera blares from the open door, playing to an empty room. No one is there. Molly's parents are nowhere to be seen; both the pickup truck and her mother's ancient Cutlass are gone. Molly's siblings are out in the woods riding a borrowed four-wheeler. The baritone whine of the ATV's motor comes and goes as the boys circle the lake on walking paths not meant for all-terrain vehicles.

Molly tosses her smoked-to-the-filter butt into the pit, sits back. "You want a beer?"

"No."

"Got something for me?"

"I want you to stop harassing me."

"I want you to do what I ask. A little somepin' somepin' for Black Molly. A handful. Nothing more."

"I can't."

"Sure you can. We've been over this. You're just being a mama's girl."

"I'm not going to steal."

"Guess I ain't got no choice then, do I?"

"No one will believe you."

"Sure about that?"

Cody isn't. Cody isn't sure about anything. She has stopped searching online for information about the hunt for the driver. She just can't do it anymore. "I told you: No one will believe you."

"Bet your mother will."

"No, I don't think she will. She won't believe you over me."

"Sure she will. I'm your best friend. Don't friends tell

each other everything? Don't they watch each other's backs? Don't they keep their bargains?"

Walking down the road away from Molly's trailer, Cody has to wonder if she's just traded one kind of unhappiness for another. The unhappiness of no friends for the unhappiness of a treacherous one.

"Skye, I don't know if you've heard, but I thought you should know that there's been a break in Randy's case. They've identified the driver of the car." My mother tells me this in the same tone of voice she might use to let me know that the price of boiled ham has gone down—good news, but hardly earth-shattering.

"I didn't. Who is he?"

"I can't remember what they said. Something Polish, or maybe Russian." In other words, not Irish. Like us. Or like those Randy ran with.

"So, he's a fugitive?"

"Oh, no. Not anymore. He's dead. Shot execution style."

I know that anything my mother might tell me will be corrupted by having come through the sieve of her perceptions, so I thank her for the news and then hop onto my computer.

*Stanislaus Prezwieski, a suspect in the slaying of small-time drug dealer Randy Mitchell, was found dead in his car, a black Honda Civic, a single shot to the back of the head. Forensics are testing to see if the weapon used in Prezwieski's murder is the same as that used in Mitchell's.*

There isn't much more, the excitement of an execution à la Whitey Bulger is quickly subsumed by more interesting tragedies of the week. A final mention shows up in the Saturday edition. Yes, the same gun was used. So my ex-husband's killer is out there. The obvious conclusion to draw is that the police were getting close, having Prezwieski on their radar, and he, the shooter, eliminated the problem. As far as I knew from the minimal police investigation, Prezwieski was the only witness to tie him to the crime.

I wonder if I should tell Cody.

Preparing to leave town for a month is mostly about canceling things—the paper, a long-scheduled physical, a bath for Chance at the groomer's. Maybe by now the new dog spa lady has shown up and he can get her to do the honors. It's a good thing Adam has never been an indoor plant kind of guy. The two dish gardens he received as condolence gifts he's already managed to kill off. The neglected perennial garden out back is weed-choked and will have to fend for itself—as usual. All of that was under Gina's purview. The irises were just coming up when she went into the hospital for the last time; the daffodils in full glory when she said no to more treatment, the tulips voluptuous on their stalks. The night after the funeral, a sudden cold wind had come up and with it a heavy rain that beat down the summer blooms, flattening them into the ground. Adam stood at the kitchen window that next morning and saw the destruction, the waste of all that effort to break through the soil, to emerge into the light, to spread forth leaves and give birth to such transitory blooms. He'd forgotten to look at them. Forgotten to take a picture and show it to Gina in those last days before she faded into her own transition.

This year the daffs and the tulips emerged again and he cut them all and placed them on her grave. Now the summer flowers of another year are up. Peonies and lilies. The hydrangeas in various shades of blue. He'll take some to the cemetery before he goes west.

Chance is there, leaning his weight against Adam's leg.

The dog sighs, as if he, too, is thinking of Gina. How is that possible? Adam kneels and wraps his arms around the dog. "You are such a good boy."

The dog doesn't disagree.

*There is something different about this departure. I'm used to the efficiency of our travels. I can tell the difference between a quick car ride and a trip. A trip means a bag. A bag that goes into the back of the car. This is clearly a trip, but there are more things put in the back of the car. I can also tell the difference between clothes that Adam wears for work and those he wears for not work. Of course, I don't really see anything we do as work, which is his word, but when he wears the leash thing around his neck, he's quieter. When he pulls on those heavy boots, we get to explore the outdoors. Today he's pulled out both. I'm beginning to catch on. But there's something else different about this time. Adam is bustling around the house, whistling, but not a* Come here *whistle. He's opened the fridge and thrown out all the potential goodies inside. Travesty! Oh no, I whine. He hands me some meat. A leftover slice of cheese. At last we leave the house, Adam following me as I lead him to the car.*

"Hello, Adam." It's Next Door Beth.

He really doesn't want to be rude, but he wants to get to the LakeView before dark, and it's already taken him more time than he thought to get ready. "I'm kind of in a hurry, Beth. Sorry."

"So, how are you *doing*?" She has that sympathetic expression on her face, and he's a little puzzled as to why she's giving him that look right now; she hasn't asked that question in exactly that way for some months. "I know, it's a hard time, isn't it?"

For a nanosecond, he doesn't know what she means.

And then he does. He's holding the bunch of flowers he intends for Gina's grave, telegraphing his very private intention, a quick visit to tell Gina he's going away for a while.

And then it hits him: It'll have been a year at the end of this week. A lifetime and a moment. The "almost a year" he's been saying has come to its terminus. Tomorrow he pushes into the second year without Gina.

Beth takes a small step toward him. "Would you like to come in for coffee?"

Chance turns around and stalks back to Adam, pushes aside the bouquet dangling from his hand. Bops Adam on the knee as if to say, *Come on, we need to go.* Adam declines Beth's invitation. "Thanks, no. I've got to get on the road. Look, I'll be away for a bit."

"Anything I can do?"

"Beth." Adam walks over to where she stands on her side of the driveway, takes her hand. "It would be great if you would stop asking me that."

*I like that lady, but I can tell that there is something about her that brings out the stress in Adam. He stiffens up, kind of like a dog meeting a rival. No, that's not it exactly. Maybe we dogs don't have an equivalent. She says* Gina *fairly often, and each time she does, I feel Adam's heartbeat alter. His pulse changes. This time, he hurried me along to the car, as if I had to be encouraged to move quickly. In a few minutes, I could sense that he had calmed down. His hand squeezed the skin of my neck gently.* It's okay, boy. She doesn't mean any harm. *I wasn't sure of the entire meaning of his words, but the slowing of his pulse told me that he was back to normal. I counted it as good that his recovery period was so short. There were times when it took him days to get through one of these stress times. As soon as I recognized that we were traveling west, I felt myself relax, too.*

# CHAPTER 33

Cody has four rooms to do. Mingo thinks that it's more efficient if they do all the rooms together, but she's discouraged him from joining her, telling him that she thinks that doing them separately gets them done faster.

"What ev." He grabs what he needs from the one housekeeping cart that the business owns, then heads downstairs to do up room 4.

Cody unlocks room 11. It's late enough in the morning that the guests, an older couple from Michigan with a dachshund named Slinky, have headed out to see some scenery. They are tidy people, here for three nights. No clothes are draped over chairs; the remote is where it belongs. No dirty glasses on the nightstand. The used towels have been hung up, the universal signal that no change of towels is necessary. Ecology-minded tourists. Yippee. Less to deal with.

All of their various and sundry toiletries are neatly arranged on the bathroom shelf. All of their medications, his on the left, hers on the right, nothing more interesting than all too common Lipitor. A blue vial sits in the center of the shelf. Apparently, Slinky has back problems. Tramadol. Pain medication.

It isn't even in a child-safe vial. Cody pops the top off, extracts two of the pills and carefully sets the blue vial back between the human meds. She slides the pills into her hip pocket, where they mingle with the rest of this morning's finds: a Vicodin, an Ambien, and a pair of Demerol tablets. The vial of Percocet she found in room 15 had only two left, so she put it back. No one will miss one dose if the bottle contains enough pills, but there's no way that a guest wouldn't miss one out of two left in his prescription.

Cody finishes up the room, unplugs the vacuum, wheels the cart to the next room. One more to go.

Unlike the people with the dachshund, this single guest is a slob. Clothes, towels, empty beer bottles, half-empty soda cans strewn on every surface. A pizza box with two slices left in it sits on the floor between the double beds, one of which looks like the occupant had been fighting with the blankets; every pillow, decorative or otherwise, is on the floor and the covers are all twisted up. Cody starts at the perimeter, leaving the bed till last. She hates picking up a stranger's clothes, but she does, draping them over the back of the chair. She tosses the nasty pizza into the trash bag, the cans and bottles into the recycling bag. She's sticky and feels disgusting. Her mother has talked about getting uniforms for her, something she says will make her look more professional as she does her work. Cody's fought the idea, but today, in this mess, she wonders if a uniform wouldn't be a good idea. Something she could strip off and save her own clothes from contamination.

The bathroom is as bad as she's expected. Whoever this guy is, he's got lousy aim. Rubber gloves on. She's going to ask for a raise. Not just a raise, pay. This bullshit about it being her unpaid job because it's their living and she's got to pull her weight has got to stop. Doesn't she deserve at least some pay? Having her mother buy her whatever she needs isn't even the same as getting an allowance; not to say getting actual pay for work. She ought to take it up with the Democrats. Never mind raising minimum wage, how about simply getting a wage? This is nothing better than slave labor.

Cody finishes up the bathroom. Nothing more interesting in there than toothpaste and a razor filled with hair. Done, she finally approaches the bed, half-expecting to find something really nasty. She pulls the coverlet off the storm-tossed bed, then yanks on the top sheet to pull it off. Something flies through the air, lands at her feet, its contents spilling out. Like she's playing jacks, Cody scoops up the majority of the pills with one hand, then hunts around the beige carpet between the beds for any that may have gotten farther afield. There's the vial. She reads the label. She's got sixteen little tabs of diphenoxylate in her hand. She doesn't exactly know what it is, but anything with the middle syllable of *oxy* has to be good.

"Cody."

At the sound of Mingo's voice, she nearly jumps out of her skin.

"You done yet?" He leans into the doorway.

She slips the pills into her pocket. "Not quite. This guy's a slob."

" 'Kay. I'm done. Catch you later."

She must have some kind of weird expression on her face, because he pauses, gives her a look, like he's about to ask her something, then just walks away.

Cody drops the amber vial to the floor, kicks it so that it rolls beneath the edge of the coverlet on the other bed, the one not slept in. Like any cheap hotel bed, these are on platforms, with fake headboards nailed to the wall, no underbed. She runs the vacuum between the beds, back and forth, back and forth, sucking up every hair and fleck of lint. She does a really good job, and if these carpets had a deeper pile, she would be leaving a track, but they don't.

This is a one-off. This will be the only time she provides what Black Molly is demanding. She's told her that it's just this once. Just to keep the Secret safe.

I am standing outside as Adam and Chance pull up into the parking lot, and I wonder if it looks like I've been waiting for him. Obviously, I haven't been. Not exactly. If I'm looking more forward to his arrival than that of any other guest, it's probably because it gives me something more pleasant to think about than the increasing truculence of my daughter. I look forward to a pleasant exchange, something more substantial than the monosyllabic conversation I have with my only family. A grown-up back-and-forth. Adam and I know each other well enough by this time to actually talk about more than the weather.

Here's Adam. I come down off the porch and greet him like a friend. Chance sits and waves one paw in the air, wanting his special greeting, too. Not satisfied with simply shaking hands, as it were, he starts to lick the back of my hand, working his flat, wide tongue up my arm until I pull it away. He stares at me with these bulgy eyes, his face a little like Winston Churchill's with the weight of the country on his shoulders. I stand up, shoulders back. Adam puts both hands on my shoulders. "Check me in later. Let's go get lunch."

We head into what passes for a town center for this town, a crossroads really, but the variety store there has a pretty good natural-foods bar and we can sit at one of the little wrought-iron tables on the wide front porch to eat our sandwiches, and the dog can sit with us.

"So what's going on?" Adam picks the sprouts off his sandwich. "You look a little down."

"The usual."

"Bookings?"

"No. Actually, that's improving. Bills all got paid this month."

"Miss Cody not behaving herself?"

"It's not misbehaving; it's more attitude. *More* attitude."

As usual, Cody ate her breakfast without comment, and I fussed with last night's dishes, two women in a kitchen with nothing to say to each other.

"I don't know, Adam. She looks unhappy and she has looked this way for so long that I almost don't notice. I know that she's been unhappy at school, but it's summer, and surely she can put a bad school year behind her. She's unhappy with me, and there's nothing I can do about that. I want to believe that all children, on some level, hold their parents in contempt, but this seems less an adolescent attitude than something deeper. More troubling. Something from which she may not recover." I take up one half of my sandwich. "I gave my mother hell, so perhaps this is just karmic payback. I cringe to think that maybe Cody is just carrying out some kind of genetic predisposition toward making a mother's life pure hell."

I pray, agnostic that I am, that Cody doesn't ruin her life in the way that I did just for the sake of defying me. No. That's not quite true. My association with Randy was wrong and misguided and dangerous, but I have Cody, and I wouldn't have her if I hadn't fallen for him. My life wasn't ruined; it was changed.

"I'm sure you've asked her. And probably gotten the cold shoulder, but keep asking."

"She used to tell me everything, Adam. Almost too much. And, then one night . . ." I can't go on. It's too painful. How in the aftermath of Randy's death, my daughter slammed the door on our relationship. I haven't told Adam anything of who Randy was. How he died. How can I start now?

"And then one night she turned into an adolescent. It's the oldest fairy tale in the book." Adam puts his half of sandwich down. Pats my hand. My own sandwich is untouched.

"I wish that's all it was. She has physically alienated herself from me. We used to sit on the couch and share a bowl of popcorn; now she sits apart, as if she would be contaminated by getting too close to me." I yank a paper napkin out of the holder, blow my nose, but I'm not embarrassed. This is a guy who had his own battles with his daughter. "But maybe you're right. You've been through it. Maybe it's just extreme adolescence in her case."

"Skye, Ariel hated me because I did something heinous, not imaginary heinous, but actual. It cost me everything, including her. It took a very long time to normalize relations, and, sometimes, it's still obvious that I ruined her life."

"I can't believe that of you."

Adam doesn't say anything for a moment, shifts his eyes away as if looking at something distant. Chance stands up, plants his boxy jaw on Adam's leg. I watch as Adam visibly relaxes. "The point is, I deserved her anger, and I knew it."

I wonder if he's suggesting that I look deeper into myself, but I don't have to. "I know in my heart that Cody's transformation has to have something to do with Randy's death.

"That night, after Randy's funeral, I'd wanted to do something cozy, to purge away how we'd spent our day. All day Cody had been dry-eyed, even at the graveside. Even I had shed some tears of grief, of regret for his sad ending. So I suggested a night of movies and ice cream sundaes, dressed appropriately in our jammies, our go-to happy place. She and I made the sundaes, flipped through Netflix, found something to watch, and planted ourselves on the couch, where she cuddled up to me. At some point, I felt her shaking, and squeezed her gently, whispering to let the tears come, that they were a good thing. I told her, 'I love you.'

"She said, 'Don't touch me.' In the next moment, she was gone, off the couch and behind her closed door, where she still is."

"Maybe it's latent grief."

"She never, ever, speaks of Randy. It's like he never existed for her."

"How did he die? Maybe she's afraid she'll die the same way. Kids fear heredity."

Would it be better if my ex had died of cancer, or in a car accident? Would it be easier to have this conversation? Adam is so willing to listen. Living up here, so far from my old friends, there hasn't been anyone I've been able to talk to in so long. So I tell him. "He was gunned down. Randy was a small-time criminal. A drug dealer who pissed someone off." Adam has the grace to say nothing, just quietly takes my hands.

Four little cottages, spaced fifteen feet apart, close, but not too close. The first occupied by Skye and Cody. The second is still in its tumbledown state, green moss growing thickly on its ancient roof, porch posts tilted. The fourth is the doggy day care/spa, empty right now; all the dog people have taken their dogs with them on their Berkshire drives. The third cottage is situated between the tumbledown one and the dog spa. New screens protect freshly washed windows, sparkling in the afternoon sun. The porch boasts hanging baskets of geraniums, bright red against the blue door. It looks like a fairy cottage, a welcoming hideout for a man sorely needing refreshment.

Skye unlocks the front door, which opens silently on greased hinges. The screen door slams behind them. It's beautiful, bright, and sunny, and equipped with a small kitchen behind a peninsula counter topped with butcher block and complete with two bar stools for early-morning sitting and admiring the view of the hills outside the window. He has four blessed weeks to enjoy this little place with its sketchy Wi-Fi and ever-evolving cast of characters.

Skye points out the few pots and pans she's supplied, where the dish towels are. "We'll do linen changes twice a week."

"Skye. Stop. Stop being an innkeeper for a minute. Sit down."

They sit on the couch, but clearly she's not comfortable relinquishing her role now that they are back on the property. He asks if she wants a cup of tea.

"Oh, no. Thank you."

"Actually, I don't think I brought any. But if I had, I'd make you a cup."

*The humans are settling down, so I mosey over to the couch, sniff at both of them, and then settle myself on the rug at their feet. I stretch out, exhausted after our long journey, more exhausted by the emanations of powerful emotion I've had to cope with since we got here. Not Adam's, but Skye's. She's quivering with emotion—fear, anger, and that peculiar one humans alone can claim, frustration. Sadness. She's kind of like some of the dogs I knew when I was much younger. Always expecting a challenge. Unable to accept consoling. A little like Adam was when we first paired up. I yawn, close my eyes, then open them. This is a bit unusual. Adam is doing the con-*

*soling. Skye has let him put his arms around her. He looks
at me over the curve of her shoulder and raises one eyebrow. Their voices do not lull me into peace. I keep my
eyes closed, but my ears are wide open as Skye uses co-
pious tongue language and Adam uses words that I know,
his soothing ones that he speaks whenever I am confused
or, rarely, afraid.* Okay. It's okay. Everything's okay.

"Really. I should get back to work." Skye gently shifts
away from him. "Sorry to have dumped all that on you."

She has been so open with him that the only thing he
can do is be honest with her. Friendship cannot survive
without revealing the key elements of a life. It is no longer enough that she knows about Gina, or about his work
with human and animal nonprofits. Or that he depends on
Chance for some unspecified therapy. She needs to know
that he's a bit like Mingo, an abandoned child; a foster
child for whom anger became a defining attribute. An anger that elevated him into power, an anger than brought
him low. "Skye, I should tell you something."

She listens without a word. When he finishes his story,
she looks him in the eye. "Gina was right. You're not that
man anymore."

# CHAPTER 34

"Nice haul." Black Molly nods her approval at the collection of drugs that Cody has laid out for her. As if she is a jeweler, sans loupe, she picks each one up to examine it closely. "Any idea which is which?"

Cody sorts the pills into groups. "Antidepressants, opioids, amphetamines, over-the-counter stuff." She's pleased with herself, remembering which pill is from what classification just on looks. Maybe she should think about pharmacology as a career path. Maybe she's a natural.

"Okay. Let's get busy." Molly pulls out her ancient iPhone, scrolls her contacts. "I hear Ryan wants to join the wrestling team. He's gonna need to slim down for that." Molly slides two amphetamine capsules into a plastic bag. "That skanky girl, what's her name? She's interested in anything we've got she can grind and smoke."

So it goes for half an hour, Black Molly dropping coded texts, setting up a round of rendezvous sites. Keeping each client, as she refers to them, separate. "I charge on a sliding scale," she says. "No sense in anybody knowing what I charge anyone else."

Cody just wants to leave the goods behind. She wants no part of getting face-to-face with any of those kids. "I gotta go."

"You did good today, Cody. Keep it up."

"I told you. This is it. I'm not doing it again."

Black Molly flashes her yellow snaggletoothed smile, but there is no humor in her black-ringed eyes. "Did I mention that the guy you say was the driver was shot dead?"

"Shut up."

"Saw it on TV. Execution style. Wonder who did it?" For a girl who comes across as kind of dim, Black Molly has a certain clever wit. "So, tell me again, why won't you tell your mother that you know who did it?"

"Because he'll kill us. Both of us."

"Not if you put him in jail."

"I can't take that chance. Please, Molly. Don't say anything."

"Then you know what to do."

"And you promise you'll never speak to my mother?"

"Deal."

The guest in room 12 is waiting for me in the office when I come back from Adam's cabin.

"I need to talk to you about something." The guest is a guy from upstate New York on his way to Boston. Arnold Simonson. He looks distressed and a little angry.

"Of course. Come sit." I gesture toward the pair of chairs at the picture window. The hills are magnificent in their summer dress, every shade of green from lime to blue-green, a flash of white from the occasional birch tree breaking up the solid wall of vegetation. I know that beneath that canopy lie narrow country roads, threading their way up and around the mountains, leading to cabins and homes and overlooks. I wish I was on one of them now as Mr. Simonson informs me that his pain medication is missing.

"I had a full vial last night, and this morning it's empty."

"And you're suggesting that . . . ?"

"The kid, that Spanish one, did he clean my room?"

I don't know the answer to that. I've left it to Cody and Mingo to work out who does which room. I don't want to hear this; I don't want to have my faith in Mingo destroyed. I've come to like him. But I've let my guard down. He's reverted to type. At least that's the obvious answer to Mr. Simonson's missing medication. All this "I'm clean" crap. The crack addict doth protest too much.

"I'll look into it. Is there anything I can do to help you get another prescription?" Making a useless offer is about the best I can do. My hands are shaking. I want to bring Mingo in and shake him until his teeth come loose. Slick boy. I've been Eddie Haskelled.

"No. But I think a refund might be in order."

My business hackles come up. What if this guy is bullshitting me? How do I know he ever even had a vial of painkillers? Is this some kind of shakedown? Some variation on the "fly in my soup" dodge? I don't think so, Mr. Simonson. I wasn't born yesterday. I almost make the accusation. But I don't. I am, after all, in the hospitality business. Besides, the way this guy gets up out of his chair, it's pretty obvious he's in serious back pain. And then I remember: He's on his way to Boston to see a specialist; that's what he'd said coming in. "Can't wait to get this surgery over with."

I refund his night's stay. Wish Mr. Simonson good health.

Outside, a dog barks, a happy, playful bark. I stand at the door. The late afternoon is hot, but there's a breeze, a suggestion of rain. It's been dry; maybe a shower wouldn't be a bad thing and wouldn't mean that another rainy summer is inevitable, like the one last year that started my first year of running the LakeView on such a bad footing. If I have to fire Mingo, it'll be just Cody and me again. With the recent uptick in activity, we'll need to replace him quickly. Maybe this Molly friend of Cody's is interested in a summer job.

I hate this. I hate being made a fool; I hate losing faith in someone. I hate that I buy into Mr. Simonson's suggestion of Mingo's guilt. But, what's that expression? If it walks like a duck, talks like a duck, et cetera. In other words, if you take a reformed drug addict and, as Adam worried when I hired Mingo, give him carte blanche in guest rooms, that might prove to be not such a good idea.

Live and learn.

The dog comes loping toward me, Mingo's dog. Dawg. Fit and happy and friendly. He comes to a halt at the bottom of the stairs and casts his doggy gaze upon me as if he's been looking for me, as if he's looking for something from me. I go down the steps, sit, and take his somewhat juicy dewlaps in my hand. "What am I going to do?" He has no answer, just gives his head a shake, little ears flapping, then burrows beneath my arm almost to his shoulders, sucking up the hug.

I know that Mingo will be looking for him, and as I have always believed that there is no time like the present to deal with unpleasantness, I sit and wait with Dawg for his soon-to-be fired master. And there he is. Baggy jeans and wifebeater T-shirt. I really need to do something about uniforms. For once, he's not wearing his trucker's hat, cocked sideways or otherwise. He's bareheaded, and it makes him look younger, more boy than the man the state says he is. "Hey Ms. M. My dog being a pest?"

"No." Oh God, my heart is breaking. I gather myself, my employer self. "We need to talk. Come in."

The dog starts to follow, mostly because he knows that

there is now a jar of dog "cookies" on my desk. His tail starts up in anticipation, going from a slow swing to an accelerando of crisp beats. It strikes various objects on his way into the office, the chair, the side of the reception desk, the doorjamb. He seems not to notice, his focus entirely on the object of his expectation. A gentleman, Mingo allows me to go into the office first, and then I point him toward the guest chair. I close the door.

I tell him what Mr. Simonson said. I watch as his cheeks flood with pink. His mouth hardens and the muscles in his neck pulse. His green eyes don't meet mine. He keeps them on the dog, who sits between his knees. He strokes the dog, says nothing. Doesn't protest, doesn't explain, doesn't tell me that I'm wrong. He doesn't say a word. Very slowly, his shoulders sag. He leans forward and kisses the dog on his head. Then stands up and meets my eye. "I don't suppose there's anything I can say that will convince you that this isn't true? That I would never do something like that." Mingo knows the system. Knows that kids like him don't get too many second chances and that if I can believe this of him, then this second chance is finished.

"Probably not."

He considers my words. The defeat shows only in the way he sucks in his lower lip. "A-ite. I thank you for giving me a chance, Ms. M."

Only a deposed king could have left my office with as much dignity. I close the door behind him and sink into my chair. What will become of him?

Adam has opened a nice bottle of wine, made himself a better-than-average dinner of scallops and rice. The dog, supine on the couch, is snoring, peaceful, his front paws folded delicately over his broad chest. Outside, the last of the long evening light has faded to blue-black and he can hear those bullfrogs ramping up their evening conversation.

"Chance, move over."

The dog rolls from back to side, stretches, and gives Adam about a quarter of a couch cushion. It's enough. Although there's a Red Sox game on, Adam doesn't really feel like disturbing the quiet, contemplative atmosphere of his new sanctuary with commentary, so he doesn't touch the remote. Skye has done a lovely job with this cottage. Of course, Mingo had a lot to do with the quality of the paint job, and the way the apartment-size appliances are so well boxed in. Kid maybe has some potential. Good for Skye, bringing him on.

Chance suddenly rolls off the couch to the floor, gives himself a great shake, and then heads to the door. The front door is open, letting in the fresh evening air. No need for air conditioners this high in the hills; nature has it figured out. The dog pushes against the old-fashioned wood-frame screen door and lets himself out. Adam, taking advantage of the dog's departure, swings his feet up onto the couch. Sips his wine. Considers how much he wishes that he and Gina had found this place a long time ago. She would have loved the cottage, the fact that Skye has turned the LakeView into a welcoming place for people like them, dog people. Tonight, the thought of Gina doesn't pinch his heart the way it usually does. It's less pining than most thoughts, more mild; one thought in a stream that will always have Gina's spirit at its source.

The gala looms over his weekend. Ticket sales have been respectable, and the artists themselves have been bustling with last-minute preparations for hanging their show. His tuxedo is hanging in the small closet in the bedroom, safe in the dry cleaner's plastic bag. His shoes are polished. Gina would have reminded him to bring black socks. She would have helped him tie his bow tie. She would have overseen the final dog hair removal after he recklessly sat on the couch. She would have gone with him. They would have deconstructed the evening on the way home, laughing at the foibles of human nature on display, all the poseurs in their dress-up clothes. She'd have helped him put into perspective the successes and failures of the event.

Chance is back in the cabin, having figured out how to paw the screen door open. He climbs up onto the couch, rests his head in Adam's lap. Adam fingers the dog's ears, the whole one and the chopped. "Wish you could come with me."

The chopped ear wriggles at the word *come*.

"Want to be my date?"

*Date*. An inflammatory word. Poor Kimberly. Poor Next Door Beth.

The dog throws a deep sigh. Picks up his head and listens to the voices just audible to Adam. Skye's and Cody's.

"You did what?" Cody can't believe this. Her mother has freakin' fired Mingo. "I can't believe you would do that. Why? He's been doing a great job, even with the shitty jobs that you make us do."

Skye pats the couch, as if Cody is some kind of dog that needs to be invited up. Nonetheless, Cody sits.

"He stole Mr. Simonson's medications. And I have no idea if he's been doing this all along."

The heat of realization climbs up her cheeks, and Cody breaks into what she knows is called a "flop sweat." Embarrassment, guilt, horror. Oh Jesus. This is her fault. The next thought is even more oppressive; evidently, he didn't rat her out. He took the fall. Unless he tried to throw her under the bus and her mother, always her champion, refused to believe him. That seems the most likely, but she has to find out. "How do you know? What proof is there?"

"Mr. Simonson said that his vial of pills, pain pills, was gone. What else can have happened?"

There it is, the chance to make it right by Mingo. The chance to utilize her own escape plan, that she didn't see a vial, but there was something crunchy under the rollers of the vacuum. Did Mr. Simonson look under the bed skirt? A beat goes by, a second. Another and it's too late. "I just don't think Mingo would do that. He's happy here."

Skye takes Cody's hand in hers, pats it. If she's surprised that Cody doesn't pull away, she keeps it hidden. "It hurts, I know. I really feel terrible about this, but I have to put my guests first. You know that."

Cody pulls her hand away, gets up, and stands in front of her mother. Again she thinks that she can finesse this mistake, and again the devil on her shoulder reminds her that one little slip and she's the one under suspicion. She's the one who will suffer the consequences. She's the one who will trigger a disaster if Molly's name comes into this. "Where will he go?"

"I don't know. I'm giving him a couple of days to sort it out, but he won't be cleaning rooms again. That's going to be you and me for a bit."

"Okay." Cody's mind is racing; she barely notes Skye's words.

"Do you think that friend of yours, Molly, might want a job?"

"No."

She's done with Black Molly. Somehow, someway, Cody has to put a stop to this blackmail.

Mingo is in his room, stuffing a backpack with the few things that he owns. A couple of shirts, socks, a jacket.

The other pair of jeans. The crisp kicks that he wears when he's not working.

"Can I come in?"

He looks at her with hooded eyes, contemptuous, but doesn't say no. He keeps stuffing the backpack.

"Where will you go?"

"What you care? Just outta here. Gone. Back where I belong, on the streets with my boys."

"I'm so sorry." She's afraid to say more, afraid that to say anything else is to admit that she understands his sacrifice. A sacrifice she doesn't deserve. Another secret to keep.

"What does that mean to me?"

"I'll keep talking to her; I'll try to get her to change her mind."

"Don't bother. Once you fuck up, you're fucked-up forever in most people's eyes."

"I know I can talk her out of it."

"Don't you see, girl? It's spoiled. It's done. Let it go."

Mingo shoulders the backpack, flips up the hood of his sweatshirt. "Get outta my way."

"Don't go. She said you can stay a couple of days more."

"Ain't stayin' where I ain't welcome."

"What about the terms of your probation?"

"Don't see how that's your concern."

"It is. I'm the one—" Cody stops.

"Yeah. I know. You stay away from that girl, that fat Goth bitch. This is your *transformative* moment, Cody. Your 'Get out of jail free' card. Don't screw it up." Mingo pauses, places a hand on Cody's cheek. "You gotta get over yourself, girl. You'll be fine. I'll be fine."

As Mingo storms down the back stairs, her tears flow, like no other tears she's ever shed in her life. No longer the tears of a selfish child, but the full-blown tears of one who finally understands how destructive she's become.

# CHAPTER 35

*I'd left Adam sitting on the couch, holding an object in front of his face and touching it gently every few minutes. I think it's called a book, but don't quote me. Anyway, now it was time for some outdoor fun. Ever since we moved into the little house, we've been having lots of outside fun. I can't wait to see what Adam has in store today. Yesterday, or maybe the day before that, we drove into the sky, then got out of the car and hiked back down. We were pretty tired and slept hard that night. Best part was that before we got back to the little house, Adam went into a restaurant and brought back a whole hamburger just for me.*

*I have to work hard to get Adam's attention, pressing my jaw down on his knee, whining, climbing up beside him, resting my muzzle over his shoulder. But once he puts the book down, he's all about making me happy. "Go for a walk?" Sweetest tongue language ever. Except maybe* Want some?

It is a spectacular afternoon, made even more special by the fact that he has nothing on his agenda except getting the dog out for a good hike. Later, he'll leave Chance with Mingo and head down to Mass MoCA, a cultural destination he's been meaning to visit since he started coming to this area. Mosley and the crew always speak of it in hushed tones, the Everest of their artistic ambitions. First he's got to return this book to the little lending library set up in the office.

Skye is leaning against the porch rail when Adam comes around the corner. She has this look on her face, inscrutable. It takes some of the natural kindness out of it, leaving a harder beauty. "I suppose you heard that I fired Mingo."

"I had not. What happened?"

Skye doesn't answer.

Adam wishes that he could be shocked at Skye's canning Mingo, but he knows all too well that the recidivism rate for kids like Mingo is pretty sad. He's sadder for Skye, who had placed such faith in her nice-lady instincts. It's tough to be wrong about someone. It makes you second-guess yourself on lots of other choices. Unfortunately, it means that not only is Mingo gone but so is Lucky, and that is worrisome for him. With no job, no housing, it's not a good situation.

She looks so stressed that he finally has to say something. "You all right?"

"No."

Adam climbs the steps to the porch, takes Skye by the elbow. "You want to talk about it?"

She glances down at his hand on her elbow. "There's nothing I can tell you. It's what you might have expected."

Apparently, yesterday's openness has become today's stone wall. "Skye?"

Nothing. She looks at him with those stress-bruised eyes and he thinks she's never looked relaxed, or seemed like she takes any enjoyment in this place, in her accomplishments.

"Hang in there." Adam touches her arm again. Moves closer, puts his arm around her. "These things happen." He's surprised at his own disappointment in Mingo. It keeps him from suggesting even a hint of "told you so." He takes no joy in being right. At the same time, he feels a bit like a sucker. Even he'd begun to believe in the boy.

This time, she doesn't pull away; neither does she seem to notice. She's staring out over the parking lot; her head is shaking slightly, as if she's having an argument with herself. "I'm really tired, of this. Of every day being a battle."

There's really nothing he can say. He can't thrust some platitude on her and not come across as a pathetic old fart.

"Sorry." She extricates herself from his arm. "Unlucky for you. You're around so much that you end up seeing the Mitchells, warts and all."

"I think that's a good thing."

Chance has done his reconnoitering of the area and is back up on the steps with them. He presses his head against Adam, then moves to Skye's side, does the same thing with her. "Chance, don't be a pest." Adam pats his leg and the dog returns to his side.

"He's not a pest. He's a good boy." Skye calls the dog back, gives him some love, which gets her a smile from Adam, one tick away from an "I told you so" smile. He's been waiting for Skye's Road to Damascus moment.

"Look, this may be late notice, and maybe borderline, but would you consider going with me to the gala?"

"A date?"

"If you want it to be. Otherwise, look at it as a nice free dinner and a night away from your responsibilities here."

Skye folds her arms across her midriff in the classic

body language of uncertainty. He's surprised himself with the suggestion, and is equally surprised at his building disappointment; surely she will find some kind of reason not to take him up on his invitation. Then Skye drops her arms to her sides. Nods. "I'd like that."

Instead of heading out for the day's planned hike, Adam drives toward North Adams. Turns out that he actually has forgotten to bring black socks. Chance is riding shotgun, his muzzle resting on the half-open passenger window. Adam reaches over and grabs a handful of neck skin. The feel of the dog's soft skin in his fingers is good and Adam wishes that Skye had such a comfort. While in town, he'll keep an eye out for Mingo. If the kid is back in trouble, Adam wants to recover the dog.

*I'm gonna tell* Every time the text message alert dings, it's the same. *Im tellin yr mom today* Every fifteen minutes, the same message, the same threat. *I know what you saw*

The threat of it, of Molly revealing the Secret because Cody hasn't brought her anything more, keeps Cody staring at her bedroom ceiling. And the guilt over what happened to Mingo vies with the ever-present fear of Johnny coming to make sure there is no living witness left to Randy's death. A stew of worry keeps her wide awake. She wishes that Mosley had given her some pot yesterday, but he's getting cheap with the freebies. And he's been too busy to work with her, as student or as model. He told her as much the other day: "Got all I need for now. I'm just doing the finishing touches now. I don't need you for that."

She's rolling over and then over again, pounding her pillow with such violence that Cody hears her mother get up to come see what's wrong.

"Cody. What *is* the problem?"

If Skye had stood at the door and suggested that a little warm milk might help, she would have just yelled at her mother to get out. But Skye doesn't. Uninvited, she sits on the bed and does that thing that mothers for centuries, since the dawn of time, have done. She strokes Cody's hair back from her face and presses her lips against her daughter's forehead, as if what ails Cody is determinable by temperature. "What's wrong, sweetheart?"

It's different this time. Skye's voice holds an unlimited reservoir of maternal love; despite the months of emotional separation, it says, *No matter what, I'm your mother.* In those three words, "What's wrong, sweetheart?," Skye has offered her unconditional love, and all Cody wants is to fall into that safe maternal place.

"Mingo didn't steal those pills."

Skye sighs. "Then who did?"

This is the ultimate example of her mother's blindness. A woman who makes no bones about the illegal mischief she once got into has this ginormous blind spot where her pot-smoking, beer-drinking daughter is concerned. Cody is so undeserving of this trust that she can't hold it in any longer. "I did."

If she thought that telling the truth would be like lancing a boil, the relief utter and complete, she is mistaken. The guilt, the grief, and the fear are still there. But halved. Shared. She waits for Skye's reaction, half-hoping that her mother will do like she used to do when Cody's worst infraction was breaking something and then lying about it. Her mother would always say that no harm would come if she spoke the truth. Upon coming clean, punishment for the breakage would be forgotten and, generally, a reward for truthfulness would be given. The shards swept up and thrown away.

Skye moves her body away from Cody's in a subtle retreat; the hand stroking her hair drops. "Say that again."

And then it hits Cody that confessing this theft opens

up a whole new raft of problems. Her mother is going to want to know what she was doing with the purloined pills. Was she taking them? Selling them? Thanks to Randy, Skye has more than a passing acquaintance with drug culture.

Skye reaches across Cody and turns on the light. "What did you say?"

"I stole them. I gave them to Black Molly."

"What did you say?" This hollowed-out repetition frightens Cody.

Cody considers lying, but she finds herself unable to come up with the energy. "She . . . she made me." Cody prays that Skye doesn't ask her *how* Black Molly was blackmailing her.

"No one makes you steal." In place of the comfort and understanding, Skye is stiff with anger. "I don't know what I'm more upset about, Cody. The fact that you stole the pills or that you let me believe that Mingo—your friend, the kid you begged me to take a chance on—did it." Skye gets off the bed and begins to pace around the tiny room, kicking discarded clothes out of her way as she does. "I don't know what to do about this."

"Please, don't do anything. Except, maybe, hire him back."

Skye stops her pacing, stares at her daughter. "You do realize that you've committed a crime?"

"Yeah. I guess."

Skye's face in the soft lamplight looks pinched, drawn. "I guess the apple doesn't fall far from the tree."

It's what Mingo said about himself.

"You are your father's daughter."

# CHAPTER 36

Cody sits in the office, a pile of paperwork in front of her, a wastebasket nearly full beside her. She's to sort through things, file what she should, toss the rest. She has no phone. Mom has taken it away from her, and the relief is astounding. Without the phone, and its near-constant texts from Molly, she's safe. In a weird way, it's like she's not being punished. Not only is she free from the onslaught of texts but she's forbidden to enter the rooms. This is clearly a twisted idea of Skye's, but if she thinks that not trusting Cody in the rooms is a penalty, an illustration of her deep disappointment, Skye is sorely mistaken. A little filing is a fine substitute for cleaning toilets.

Being forbidden the AC, that's a little harsher. She's no longer afraid of Mosley's ratting her out—what more can he do than her own confession has done to further destroy her relationship with her mother? Stole some pot? Ha! Who cares? She's filched actual drugs. Pot is no biggie. She can just hear her mother laugh. It's more that she's actually made some progress in the past few weeks, and even Kieran has complimented her on her work. She's got some momentum going, and being denied access to her art space is painful. Besides, the AC is the only place where she can put everything aside and just focus on something pleasurable.

But what truly hurts the most is being given the silent treatment by her mother, being treated with the kind of hostility that she herself has dealt her mother for more than a year. It should make things easier. If they don't speak, then there will be no accidental revelations. But it still hurts. It's the first time in her life that Skye hasn't been there for her.

Cody has the bills sorted into paid and unpaid, then alphabetized, arranged by date and ready for filing. She slices her finger on a file folder. The blood oozes, streaking the top of the folder, where the stain quickly turns brownish. She should make a new folder, but Cody kind of likes the idea that she's bled over this make-work job.

She hears the sound of the housekeeping cart being wheeled by. Skye tending to the rooms. For the first time in their ownership of this white elephant, they are at 90 percent capacity. One room unoccupied. No help.

"Mom?"

Skye glances back at Cody. Doesn't speak.

"I'll help you."

Skye doesn't answer.

I'm alone in the office when a rather nice-looking man comes through the open door. I'm a sucker for type. Like Randy, this guy is dark-haired and dark-eyed. He's got a jaw like an old-fashioned Hollywood star, a Kirk Douglas or Cary Grant. A dimple square in the center of his chin. I give him my best hello and he asks if there's any chance I have an open room. One more room. I can't believe that I'll be at full capacity with the click of the mouse. Two nights. Sweet.

He fills out the registration form, slides it back to me. Tom Blair. An address in Rhode Island. He's left the auto information blank.

"Just fill out the line for your car."

"Can't think of the tag number. It's a rental."

"Don't worry about it. Just the state is fine, and make and color, if you don't mind."

Rhode Island, Chevy and silver.

I ask for his credit card.

"Do you take cash?"

"Of course." This is a bit unusual, but money is money. "I'll have to ask for it up front, but cash is fine." Registration complete, I do what I always do: take him to his room, show him the layout, see if he has any questions, and then hand him the key. I like to chat up my new guests, get a sense of their interests in case they need some restaurant or sightseeing suggestions, so I ask, "Are you here for work or pleasure?"

Tom Blair pauses, a tiny hint of a smile at the corner of his mouth. "Both."

Chance lounges at Adam's feet, eyes closed, but his ears twitch, keeping tabs on the comings and goings of those walking through the postage stamp–size park. Adam sips at his take-out coffee, picks chunks of crumbling apple muffin from the white paper bag in his lap. They've just hiked a good couple of miles up Mount Greylock and he's due a reward. His shins are screaming from the effort of climbing up, and then down, the trail. Chance suddenly sits up, makes a throaty little grumble, which quickly becomes his excited greeting voice.

"Mr. March?" It's Mingo, Dawg beside him, wagging his whole body.

"Mingo. It's good to see you. Sit down." Adam moves over on the bench to give the boy space. He tries to appear sanguine, betray nothing of his anxiety about finding this kid who has miraculously appeared when least expected. "How've you been?"

"You heard?"

"I did." Adam offers Mingo the bag with the muffin in it. "Where are you now?"

"I'm okay. Doing day labor. Pays better."

"That's good." Adam runs a hand down Dawg's bumpy spine. "Can I ask where you're living?"

"I'm bunkin' in with one of the guys. It's all right. But—" He stops.

"But what?"

"You said you'd take Dawg if, you know, if things changed."

"I did and I will." Adam can't believe his luck. Patience has won out.

"Can I tell you something?"

"Of course."

"It's about how I got him. I need to tell you that, 'cause it's why I got to give him to you for safekeepin'."

If the kid wants to use the word *safekeeping* to make himself accept the wisdom of this act, then so be it.

"Guy name Russell had him. Trainin' him up, road work and chains and such. Dawg was one of four Russell got. Youngest, and biggest. First time Russell fought him, he won big. Lotta money. Dawg already lookin' like a champ."

It's what Adam has suspected, but expecting this doesn't make the truth of it any easier to hear.

"I knew Russell a little, like people do, seen him around and knew he was into dogs. My boys and I ran into Russell one night and he invited us to see his dogs at work. Now, Mr. March, despite what you think about me, I don't hold with dog fightin'. Not one bit. I've done a lot of bad things in my life, but I never looked highly on dog fightin'. But I was with my crew, so I went along.

"First time I saw Dawg, he'd just finished his fight. This one he lost, and he looked terrible, bleedin' and limpin'. Russell was mad as hell. Dog's all beat-up and he's cowerin' at Russell's feet, wantin' help, but what I saw was that Russell was gonna punish him. The dog, Dawg, looked at me. My heart, Mr. March, my heart died right there. He looked at me to save him. I told Russell I'd buy him off a him. Right then an' there, the whole wad of cash I had that I was gonna use, well, for other stuff. I stuck it in his hand. Russell so mad, he said, 'Take him.' Pocketed my money.

"Thing is, Russell wants him back. Says I stole him."

Adam crumples the paper bag, twists it. In some ways, this is Chance's story, too. Brutality and hope. "I'll keep him safe for you."


"Where did you find Mingo?" Skye is seated in the freshly vacuumed front seat of Adam's Jetta. She's wearing a silky teal-and-blue cocktail dress she says she hasn't worn since attending a cousin's wedding three or four years ago.

"He found me." Adam has Dawg hanging out with Chance in the cottage. He fills Skye in on how this all came about.

"Adam, I have to tell you something. I shouldn't have fired him."

"Don't beat yourself up about it. There are only so many chances a kid gets."

"No. You don't understand. He didn't do it. I reacted with prejudice and without any proof, and I was wrong."

Adam looks over at her, puzzled. "Then who did it?"

Skye reminds him of Cody, always staring out the window when she doesn't want to answer a question.

"Oh." He gets it. "That's pretty serious."

"I thought you should know. I didn't want to keep you in the dark, being that you've been a part of this."

"I appreciate that. What are you going to do?" Such a loaded question.

No answer.

"Can I say something?"

Skye nods. Pulls her gaze away from the window and looks at him.

"Why did she take the pills? To get high?"

"To sell. Her friend, Melanie Frost, the one who calls herself 'Black Molly,' convinced her to steal them so they can sell them."

"Enterprising."

"Like her father. It's like she's turning into him. And you know how it ended for him."

Adam takes Skye's hand. "Don't. She's maybe mixed up, but I don't think she's a criminal."

"But there's the rub. She is a criminal. She's a thief. How do I deal with that?"

They've arrived at the Holiday Inn, where the gala is being held. Adam slides the car into a space in the garage and shuts it off. "What did Molly say to convince Cody to do this? I can't believe she'd do it on her own."

"I don't know. She won't tell me."

"Is Cody maybe the victim here?"

"Adam, it would be so easy to make that assumption, to be, as usual, the parent who sees no wrong in her kid's behavior. The one who always blames others. I can't keep doing that. This is serious."

Because of the full house, Skye has ordered Cody to spend the evening in the office. She's given strict orders that she's to be the smiling face of the LakeView Hotel tonight. There was her mother all dressed up, her sandy hair swept into a proper updo, bare legs above the strappy sandals Cody has never seen before. A stranger, a glimmer of the person she might have been had her life been easier. But she wasn't smiling, wasn't looking the least bit like she was going to go have fun.

After all her begging and pleading to be allowed to attend, Cody had the ultimate humiliation of having to tell Mosley that she couldn't help out after all. Not with hanging the show, not with ticket taking, not with being the coat-check girl. Grounded with a capital G, and she can't tell him why.

So here she is, alone. Hoping that none of the guests will need her. Without her phone, she doesn't even have the distraction of playing games. She's supposed to be doing her summer reading, *True Grit,* but she can't concentrate on Mattie Ross's life right now. Her own is just as crazy, without having a Rooster Cogburn to help.

Cody pulls a couple of sheets of copy paper out of the drawer and finds a number 2 pencil. She sharpens it and begins to sketch. Maybe Skye won't let her continue with lessons, but she's not going to stop drawing.

The long evening light lingers over the hills, backlighting them, an areole of rose-gold light defining their shapes for a few minutes until the darkness overwhelms the shapes. It is so quiet that she can hear the peepers, the white noise of crickets. The rush of a car speeding up and over the hill. The sound of the pencil against the paper. Her own breath.

The food was okay, and the free wine mediocre, but it was lovely being waited on and to sit at an eight-top table with six strangers and talk about inconsequentials and art, to pretend I knew anything about what's trending and postpostmodern art. Adam was showing his style as a professional mingler, and I was growing a little bored with the

incessant live auction of pieces of art that were out of both
my intellectual league and my budget. I wouldn't hang
any of this stuff on the walls of my hotel. The crowd was
polite, and one by one the pieces sold.

"Having a good time?"

It's Mosley, standing over the woman opposite me. At
first, I think he's speaking to her, but then I realize he's
speaking to me.

"Yes, thank you. I hope that you've raised a lot of
money."

"Me, too." He comes around and sits in Adam's empty
seat. "I'm sorry Cody couldn't be here tonight. She's
earned a little fun."

My impulse is to say *Not really*, but I don't. "She had
to work for me. Family business."

"Of course." He gets to his feet. "You know, she is
coming along with her work. Has she shown you anything?"

"No."

"She should. For a youngster, I see some potential. I
hope that you'll let her keep on with lessons."

After her revelations, I'm not ready to give Cody anything. The damage she's done, despite Adam's kind suggestion that it might not have been her doing, is still too
fresh, too painful to think about. "For the time being,
she's not going to be able to take lessons. We'll see what
happens in the fall."

The auctioneer announces the next lot, an original
Mosley Finch triptych, oil on canvas. To be polite, I fix
my attention on it. Our table is comfortably close to the
auctioneer, so it's easy to see the painting. At first, I am
actually impressed; it's a pretty thing, very ethereal, its
composition clear in its meaning, not abstract in any way,
more like those lush Victorian paintings of children. And

then I realize that I'm looking at three versions of my fifteen-year-old daughter. With wings.

The auctioneer mistakes my gasp for an opening bid.

Adam sees the look on Skye's face. Sees what she's looking at. That bastard Mosley. The little sketches on his wall have evolved into this three-paneled exploitation of a kid. What Adam had seen in the prototypes, the subtle borderline between child and woman, has been expanded, and he feels himself blush in anger, never a good thing for him, particularly on a night when his dog, his calming agent, isn't at hand.

"Who'll give me a thousand?" The auctioneer is a semiprofessional and is obviously getting near to the end of his stamina. His tie is loosened. "Opening bid. Come on, people, this is an original Mosley Finch. Do I hear five hundred?"

Mosley stands nearby, a goofy smile on his face, expectant. He's of the generation that received participation awards and thought that everything it did was perfect. He can't imagine that no one wants this piece of . . .

Adam waits, watches, and when the starting bid comes in at an even hundred, he raises his hand.

It's over in less than two minutes. Adam buys the triptych of Cody Mitchell for $135. Worth every penny to get it out of the sight of this crowd. He'll offer an X-Acto knife to Skye, see if she wants to cut it up.

The triptych sits on an easel at the back of the room. The overhead lights have been turned up as the crowd departs, some of them clutching their acquisitions close, others just scrambling to get to the parking garage and out before anyone else. Adam joins me, a half bottle of wine in one hand, two glasses in the other.

"Honestly, what do you think?"

He hands me a glass. "Objectively, it's quite lovely."

I stare at the three images of my daughter. The fairy wings, the suggestion of the primeval and dark woods. Looking closer, I see that there is actually a theme here, a progression. From the first image to the third, it is a story of transition. A girl growing up.

"It reminds me of who she was not so very long ago." It breaks my heart that all the lightness Mosley Finch has depicted in Cody is gone. How did he ever see it?

# CHAPTER 37

*Since Adam never specifically told us to stay, I see no problem with Dawg and me heading outside when the screen door just happens to bounce open with the nudge of my nose. It's a perfect night and I can hear the scurry of woodland creatures beckoning us to the chase. We hit on the scent of something I've always wanted to pursue and off we go, avoiding the man-made trail with its human scent obscuring the mammal, pushing ourselves through the underbrush, the sound of our passage no doubt alerting our prey to our presence, but the sheer joy of pursuit is really our goal. We head away from the confinement of our cottage, our place. Away from our better natures. We revert to our wild side, if just for this moment. Being civilized is wonderful, but sometimes it feels good just to be an animal.*

It's almost ten o'clock. Skye told Cody that she can go back to the cottage at ten, as long as things are quiet. There have been a couple of problems. The couple in room 3 accidentally locked themselves out. Another call was from the lady with the Cairn terrier, wondering if it's safe to walk around in the dark. Cody assured her that there were no bears this close to the hotel, and that the motion-sensitive lights on the front of the building would come on to frighten off anything else. Other than that, Cody hasn't seen anyone. She reaches for the CLOSED sign.

Outside, there is just the sound of peepers and crickets, the whisk of car tires climbing the hill. A million billion stars speckle the sky without casting light on this as-yet-moonless and soft night. Skye forgot to leave a light on in the cottage. Only Adam's cabin is illuminated, the soft glow of a table lamp warming the interior beyond the screen door. There are no motion-sensitive lights on the back of the building, so Cody's left to pick her way carefully in the dark.

It is so quiet that she hears his breath moments before she feels his hand around her mouth.

Johnny Mervin shoves a wad of something into Cody's mouth and manages to one-hand a strip of duct tape across it even as Cody struggles, twisting and ramming her sneaker-shod heels against his shins. He's silent, and in the dark it's like she's being assaulted by a phantom, except that she can smell his overpowering cologne. No phantom ever stank of cheap aftershave. She tries to slither out of his grasp, dropping to the grass in an effort to wriggle free, but Johnny is twice her size and has no intention of letting his prey get loose. He picks her up, hikes her a short distance from the cottage to where he's got his car. He forces her facedown into the backseat, shuts the door with a gentle push, disturbing no one in the hotel with the slam of a car door.

He hasn't bound her hands, so Cody reaches for the door latch.

"Childproof. Don't bother." Johnny climbs into the driver's seat. "It's a short ride."

Cody tries the door anyway. It won't open. She pulls the tape off her face, spits out the gag. "Please, I never told. Why are you doing this?"

"Things changed. Sorry. Got to tidy up some loose ends, and that's you." He's driving slowly, well within the speed limit, around the unpredictable curves of the mountain road. A car approaches from the other direction. Cody pounds on the window, but the car doesn't slow. She's invisible in the dark. Inaudible.

She sits back against the seat. Curiously, she's not crying, or even breathing hard. It's as if a switch has been turned off in her brain, the one that has dictated that she agonize about this very moment, the anxiety that has controlled her dreams, and her waking nightmare of Johnny Mervin's threat. She has lived for more than a year in fear of this very moment. She's used it all up. She's not afraid. She's angry.

Johnny suddenly flips off the headlights and makes a hard left turn. Cody knows where they are, in the parking lot of Lake Hartnett State Park. Within walking distance of the LakeView. Within walking distance of Black Molly's trailer. She waits as Johnny gets out of the car and comes around to let her out of the backseat. "Let's go for a walk." She doesn't move, and he reaches in to grab her, yanking her out of the car and into his arms. The momentum ensures that the sharpened number 2 pencil she's pulled out of her pocket digs deep into Johnny Mervin's face.

*I hear an animal in pain but quickly forget about it as Dawg and I latch onto a new scent. This one I know is rodent, and within the realm of capture. Not far away, I can smell the water of the lake where Adam has tried to convince me that immersion is a good thing. Sorry, not my cup of tea, but I'm happy to wade in, inspect for tiny*

*fish. Snap at them. Dawg pauses, making me stop short
in my tracks. He cocks his head and gives the air a listen. I follow suit. We are definitely not alone in these
woods. The sounds travel; others are hunting, breaking
through the brush, ducking the low-hanging branches.
Panting. The faintest of breezes carries a new scent.
Human.*

She runs, cursing the sound of her footfalls against the
summer-dry leaf detritus and rocks. She might as well be
leaving a trail of bread crumbs by making this much
noise. Cody stops, touches her face where she's been
sliced by brambles. It is so dark, so impenetrable, but only
for a little while longer. Already the moonrise over the
mountains is easing the darkness. Cody needs to find a
hiding place, someplace that even if the moon lightens the
scene, she'll be hidden from Johnny. Cody leans against
the trunk of a pine tree, listening for him even as he's listening for her. It catches her eye; the sharp, bright light
of his phone's flashlight app is a miniature beacon. She
has to keep moving. He's making as much noise as she
is, but he has no reason to remain quiet. Every few minutes, he actually calls to her, as if expecting she'll give
up this game of tag and submit to him. Cody slows to a
crawl, begins to work her way through the mountain lau-
rel and sweetbriar, carefully moving foliage out of her
way, treading gently on the leaf fall. Either her eyes have
fully adjusted to the darkness or the late moon is taking
some of the depth out of it. In either case, she can discern
the darker weight of the bigger trees, and goes from one
to the other, depending on that pinpoint of flashlight to
keep herself oriented. As long as it's behind her, she's safe.

"Come on, Cody. You should just give it up. Come to
me." Johnny Mervin's voice is sweet, seductive, a lover's
cajoling voice.

Another tree, and another. The pinpoint of light is higher than she is, and Cody realizes that she's descending the hillside, that she's worked her way to Black Molly's side of the hill. The half-moon has risen, and although its light is muted, nothing like the strong light of the full moon, Cody can see not just the darker shapes of the tree, but also the intermediary branches and the lichen-covered humps of boulders strewn by the volatile upheaval of ancient geology. Suddenly, she knows where in this forest she is.

It blends in with the brambles and deadfall of storm-wrecked trees—the fairy house, the shelter Molly built, where they came so often to share their contraband. You have to know that it's there to see it. Cody crawls under the hodgepodge of beech and pine branches, tucks her knees to her chest, and prays that Johnny doesn't recognize the shelter as anything other than a pile of branches. Not a bolt-hole. She looks up, and through the porous roof of Molly's play fort she can see the pinpoint of light as Johnny descends the slope. She hears a mutter of cursing as he stumbles, slips a little. The flashlight's bright spot reminds her of that tool the optician uses to examine her eyes. Cody closes her eyes, afraid that they will reflect his light like an animal's.

"Cody. Cody. You come to me, or your mother dies first."

Her mother. She's got to get back and warn Skye. There's no more hiding this secret.

It's much later than I intended when we get back home. In the backseat is the triptych, safe, not damaged, although Adam had suggested that I could take a box cutter to it if I felt I wanted to. He's given it to me. A present, he says, for kindness and going with him to the event. I'm out of practice, and have no witty reply. I don't even pretend to refuse the gift. I tell him maybe I'll hang it on that blank wall in his cottage.

He walks me to my cottage, which is totally dark. Cody has forgotten to turn on the porch light, or maybe deliberately chosen not to. He waits to see if she's also locked the door against me, but it's open. I flip on the light. "Well, thank you." I mean for the evening away from here, for listening to my sorry story about Cody's transgression against Mingo, for buying the painting.

Adam leans in and kisses me. Touches my face. Bids me good night.

"Wait. Would you like to come in?" It's not all that late. Then I worry that I've become one of those women he's here avoiding. "I can offer coffee."

Adam smiles, nods. "Let me go let the boys out. Why don't you come to my place. We can have a nightcap."

"Okay, and at the risk of sounding like a bad B movie, I am going to get out of this outfit and into something way more comfortable. And check on Cody."

Except that Cody isn't there. And neither are the dogs.

*Dawg and I both freeze in mid-step. We're dogs, so we don't look at each other to corroborate our impressions. We both know what that whistle means.* Back here. *Judging from the faintness of the sound, we've gotten a bit farther afield than we've ever done before. But the lure of night life has been intoxicating to us. We've run to ground moles and voles and even a mouse or two. Dawg came closest to achieving capture, but the truth is, neither one of us actually would know what to do with a mouse in the mouth.*

*Game's up. The whistling continues, and I know that my stellar reputation for obedience is in jeopardy. Dawg is scratching, his hind leg going at it and his chin in the air, his jowls stretched back in a weird show of ecstasy.*

*I'll give him a moment; then we head home. I put my nose to the air, suck in a snootful of luscious night air. And that's when my ears pick up on another sound, and my hackles go up.*

"I'm losing my patience, little girl. Show yourself, or you'll be an orphan." As if to illustrate his point, Johnny casts one last sweep of his flashlight, coming within twenty feet of Cody's hiding place. He turns around and starts up the hill, pauses. "Don't think I won't find you wherever they put you. An orphanage, maybe a foster home? Your grandmother's? Whatever, no matter to me. I found you before and I'll find you again. In the meantime, bye-bye Mommy."

Cody can't hold back the involuntary sob, and he hears it. Johnny grabs fistfuls of branches, tearing away the hiding place, reaching in and grabbing Cody by the arm. He slaps her, twists her arms around, clutching both wrists in his one hand, wrenching her to her feet. "I'm done here." He pulls his gun out of its holster, frog-marches Cody a few feet, then presses on her wrists until she drops to her knees.

Cody screams. And screams. Terror deafens her even to the sound of her own voice pleading for her life. She feels the muzzle of the gun press against the back of her neck right in the place her mother used to call her "sweet spot," and would then kiss it. *Mommy* will be her last word.

*I had never before set teeth to human, but I had no hesitation in doing so and doing it with the same ferocity I once used in the pit, in the time before I knew peace. Dawg was beside me, doing the same. We knew the right places to subdue, the right places to make this a win that would take this opponent out of the pit forever. I could hear the girl's screaming, encouraging us, inciting us to further leave our marks on this singularly dangerous human being. There was also screaming coming from him, the tongue language clear:* Get them off me! *As I bit deeper and deeper into his forearm, Dawg stood on his chest, threatening, but not quite ready to go in for the kill. Behind us, the girl, Cody, wept, and even over the pungent scent of blood, I could smell the agony of her fear. At that moment, I understood Adam much better. The anger and rage that he struggled so to keep, with my help, under control; I suddenly understood what anger is. I had never been angry at my canine opponents all those years ago in the fight ring, but this time I felt a rage that reddened my vision. This stinking man would hurt this girl of whom I had grown fond. I would not have it. Dawg pushed his face into the face of the man on the ground, and I knew that he, my dear companion, felt exactly as I did.*

Johnny's phone, the flashlight app still on, is on the ground, well out of his reach, as is the gun. Cody watches as the dogs keep him from moving, from escaping. In fact, he is very still, but she can see the life in his eyes, the fear that these dogs, arriving out of nowhere, will tear him limb from limb.

Cody picks up both the gun and the phone. Holding the weapon's muzzle down, she speaks to the dogs. "Don't let him up. Good dogs." She thumbs 911 into the phone.

# EPILOGUE

I feel the weight of another human body. Cody has climbed into my bed, pressing herself up against me as if she were a much smaller child. I roll over to wrap an arm over her, brush her hair away from her face. I feel the moisture under my fingers. "It's all right; it's over."

What Cody has been enduring is beyond belief. The ultimate in a parent's inventory of things to fear for her child. Made to keep a secret so heinous that it nearly destroyed our relationship. A secret that nearly cost her her life.

"Mommy?"

I love hearing that babyish name once more. "What, honey?"

"I don't feel relieved. I still feel like I have to lie."

"That will pass. By tomorrow even. It's like you've been wearing a cast, and now that it's gone, you still feel it."

"What if he gets out on bail?"

"He won't." I don't know that for sure; a good defense lawyer can come up with anything, so it is possible, but for now, Johnny Mervin—my guest Tom Blair—will cool his heels in jail.

She snuggles into me and I nearly weep with the joy of it.

Mingo isn't easy to spot because he blends in with the other workers, yellow hard hat, reflective vest, protective glasses. He's ripping the plywood off the windows of the boarded-up house where he once almost died.

Adam lets Chance and Dawg out of the car, and Dawg runs over to greet his boy with a full body wag. Adam sits in the Jetta for a minute, taking in the scene, gathering himself.

Mingo lifts his face from his dog's lapping tongue and nods in Adam's direction. Adam climbs out of the car, walks toward the boy.

Mingo puts out a hand. "Mr. March, what brings you here?" He tugs Adam into a homeboy hug, a gesture that gives Adam an unexpected sense of connection, of acceptance.

"Skye needs to talk to you."

"Ain't got nothing to say to her."

"No. She's got something to say to you."

Skye gets out of the Jetta. It's clear that she's nervous about this meeting, and that she's struggling to get the words of her apology out. In the end, she simply takes Mingo by the hand and says, "Come back."

Cody's phone tings with an incoming text. Molly. Her usual threat. *Im telling*

And that's when it finally hits Cody—she's truly free.

She texts back: *Go ahead Here's her number Maybe I'll be doing the telling*

The silence is sweet.

\* \* \*

*I took in a great breath of human. It was a smorgasbord of human emotion, and the four people didn't seem to mind my extensive examination of them. I tested for the usual symptoms of unrest and, happily, found none. Except hunger. They were worshiping at the grill, and the lovely scent of meat and cheese upheld the other scents, framing them in a happy cloud. The people laughed. I love that sound, and if I had one wish for canines, it would be that we, too, could make that sound. Instead, I whip my tail from side to side, and grin. Dawg is doing much the same, and both of us know that life is good, very good, when our people are happy. When they tell us that we're good boys. Such good dogs.*

# ACKNOWLEDGMENTS

If it takes a village to raise a child, it certainly takes an army to get a book published. Bottomless gratitude to Annelise Robey and Andrea Cirillo, who continue to believe in my work. And to the rest of the Jane Rotrosen Agency staff, who work tirelessly on behalf of so many writers, thank you for all you do. A particular shout-out to Don W. Cleary and Don Cleary, Christina Prestia, Julianne Tinare, Michael Conroy, Peggy Boulos Smith, Liz Van Buren, and, always, Jane Rotrosen Berkey, who has advocated for the bully breeds for years.

Thank you to the good folks at St. Martin's Press, namely, Joan Higgins, Sara Goodman, Chris Holder, John Murphy, Kerry Nordling, Sally Richardson, Anne Marie Tallberg, Stephanie Davie, and Lisa Davis. Thank you Young Lim, for the wonderful cover.

Especial gratitude to Caitlin Dareff, who rides herd so much.

I am indebted to the incomparable Carol Edwards, who keeps me from misplacing my modifiers. Even as I write this, I worry about comma placement. Thanks also to the tireless players at Macmillan, for keeping the voices in my head accessible to other ears: Brant Janeway, Samantha Beerman, Mary Beth Roche, and Robert Allen.

And to my dear Jennifer Enderlin. What words can express how deeply grateful I am to have you in my life?

The LakeView Hotel is a creation of my imagination, but the inspiration for it is the Whitcomb Summit Retreat in Florida, Massachusetts. Thank you, Jim Pedro, for sharing some of your story with me.

Read on for an excerpt from
Susan Wilson's THE DOG I LOVED—
coming soon in hardcover from
St. Martin's Press!

# ROSIE

The judge gaveled her verdict and gray flooded my vision, as if a Technicolor world had reversed itself into black and white. The gray shrouded me as I was led from the courtroom into a holding cell. I don't remember anything beyond being in that cell until the van that took me to Mid-State Women's Correctional Facility drove through the high gates that would be my perimeter for however many years I would be incarcerated. I had been sentenced to twenty years. At my age, then just turned twenty-five, it might as well have been life. The grayness that encompassed my vision was abetted by the grayscale of my environment, walls, floors, bars, even the stainless steel tables and tan chairs in the dining hall; the bland beige food. The high windows, cross-hatched with wire, showed only the hazy dirty white of sky. The only dash of color that broke through my clouded vision that first day was the bright red tie that Warden Hinckley wore against a dingy white shirt.

I was marched, hands and feet shackled—as if I was a

danger to anyone—into the building, processed in every way as humiliating as possible, and then meekly followed my inmate guide to the cinderblock and steel space that would be my new home. A set of bunk beds, a seat-less toilet/sink combination. Two tiny three-drawer bureaus. My cellmate—sorry, *roommate*, as in some arcane nod to civility our cells were always referred to as our *rooms*— wasn't there but evidence of her presence was dense in that tiny space. Crayon drawings taped to the walls, a single photograph of a curly-haired child. A pervasive odor. I sat on the edge of the lower bunk, and waited.

If my vision had become monochromatic, my hearing had gone dull. The silence of submersion. That's what it felt like, being underwater. This time my submersion might have been giving in to drowning.

The gray cloud that enveloped me darkened perceptibly. My roommate had arrived. Treena Bellaqua was a big woman, tattooed like a Fiji fisherman, and fifteen years my senior. "Don't talk to me, don't look at me and don't put your stuff anywhere near mine and we'll get along." I'd had bad roommates before, and I should have tried to muster some spine in order to claim what should be mine, but that might prove to be futile and, frankly, dangerous. Instinctively, I didn't look her in the eyes. I presented no challenge. The fact was, I wasn't up to any sort of challenge, I could hardly breathe, much less go toe to toe with Treena. All I wanted was the quiet oblivion of elusive sleep.

"Get offa my bed. You got the top."

"I'm sorry. I didn't know."

"That's your one and I repeat, one, pass. Next time, I won't be so nice."

Self preservation is involuntary, even in one so distraught by circumstances that the only imaginable release is self-destruction. I meekly climbed up onto what would be my only oasis in a metal and cement jungle.

It wasn't a predestined trajectory. I was the good girl, the smart one, the hope of my parents, the only girl and the youngest of six. I had the exquisite Communion dress, the tap dance lessons, the pink, pink, pink of my tiny bedroom, my bike, my dresses. My mother indulged herself in creating out of my rough clay the girl child beloved of big Irish families. Innocent; devoted. Loyal.

No, I wasn't the Collins destined for a life of crime. Bobby was the one in our family voted most likely to end up in Walpole. He, too, bucked our expectations and thumbed his nose at his past. Instead of ending up behind bars, he ended up with an MBA. I started off with a Seven Sisters education, and found myself on this very gray day being escorted into Mid-State Women's Correctional Facility, convicted of murdering my fiancé—well, technically I was convicted of *voluntary manslaughter*, but when you're sentenced to twenty years, why quibble about legal nomenclature? I was behind bars.

Charles Montgomery Foster came into my life in a somewhat old fashioned way, given the ubiquitous on-line dating scene that most of my friends liked. I was a recent college graduate marking time before my first 'real' job with a minimum wage gig as a barista. Charles was one of the Hugo Boss-suited people who came down from the glass towers of their downtown Boston office buildings to grab a macchiato skim no froth soy milk caramel drizzle. He looked like he might have been in finance, or a lawyer; there is no distinction in the uniform of suit jackets and slightly loosened Vineyard Vines ties. What Charles looked like to me was the kind of man who might be interested in hiring a very well educated, unskilled but enthusiastic to learn, young woman desirous of a high income career path. He looked, in other words, like someone *with* a high income. My Bunker Hill slice of Charlestown might not have been considered a sophisticated neighborhood, more Dennis Lehane's mean streets than Charlestown Navy Yard penthouses overlooking Boston Harbor, but I knew good threads when I saw them, and good manners. And a really nice haircut. Charles was in real estate development, which I soon learned meant being among those whose main interest in the poor side of town was to urban renew it until the locals were forced out.

I never intended to fall in love with Charles. I only wanted a job, a good one. One that would help me keep up with the student loans that sucked my barista paycheck dry and left me living back with my parents and my paraplegic brother Teddy. Teddy was thirteen years old when he got in the way of a bullet meant for someone else. I was eleven and suffered a quick demotion from highly favored child to appendix. The rest of his brothers treated him like he was not just handicapped, but emotionally fragile. While they would beat on each other and say truly horrible things, with Teddy, they were reserved. Not so much me. And Teddy loved me for it. For treating him like he was just like the others, rude, smelly, dirty-mouthed and bossy. Teddy hated Charles on sight.

Charles—never Charlie, or Chuck, or Chick as anyone named Charles would have been called in my neighborhood—hadn't actually become a Hugo Boss wearing corporate type through hard work and an upward trajectory. He was a lifelong rich kid. When they speak of being born with a silver spoon in his mouth, Charles was just such a one. It's a pretty common story. The inherited wealth coming down through generations of really smart money manager types, the original wad having been earned on the exploitation of workers. In Charles's case, his family wealth came from oil. Not crude, but whale oil. His whale ship owning ancestor was smart enough to get out of the business before it became last century's technology, moving right along to textiles, and then, when that industry began to fail, the early-20th century version of Charles Montgomery Foster turned to armaments. Given the never-ending need for the materiel of war, the family has been capitalizing on the world's propensity for conflict ever since. Of course, Charles never spoke of it, preferring to let most people believe his money came from the more pacific growth industry of real estate development.

Throughout that summer I began to anticipate Charles's daily arrival, to notice that he was beginning to flirt back, our banter becoming a well practiced foreplay to a better acquaintance. I started keeping a second white shirt just in case the first became stained. Even early on, I recognized a fastidiousness in Charles who always accepted his frothy drink with a napkin in his hand. Coming from a big messy family I thought him ever so sophisticated *Refined*. That was the word.

If I thought that being in prison was going to be a little bit like being in a women's college, I wasn't entirely wrong. Estrogen-stoked drama. The sameness was a cadre of women all vying for sink time. Getting our periods simultaneously. Mooning over the pretty boy—or girl—celebrity of the moment.

In college there were LUGs. Lesbians until graduation. I quickly discovered that in prison there are LURs. Lesbians until release. There were some real love affairs going on, and if one partner was released, there was real heartbreak. The divide between the incarcerated and the free is of Grand Canyon proportions. The released did not come back to visit the left behind; they were not allowed to come back—even if they had wanted to.

Another key difference was the range of ages among the incarcerated. Where college had at best a prodigy of fifteen and a thirty-year-old mom attending on a special returned-to-college scholarship, here my peers ranged from nineteen to seventy-five. Pubescence to senility and every life stage in between.

The differences showed in other ways. Where my classmates in college demonstrated their superiority to my origins in fashion and in high culture-referenced witticisms, my fellow inmates at Mid-State flaunted their bad-ass-ness in demonstrations of power. Influence. Intimidation. I thought I was as unlike them as I had been unlike my classmates. But, in college, all I wanted was to be *like* my classmates, to blend in.

In college, I was Target to their Bergdorf. In prison I was Target to their St. Vincent DePaul charity shops. In college I was a quick study and by my second year no one would ever know that I hadn't actually skied Aspen. I presented myself as just as sophisticated as they were by wearing thrift store chic. I started a trend. In prison, we all wore cheap jeans and Keds.

I thought that as I had acquired the right table manners and used impeccable grammar, I would easily fit into Charles's world. I had moved beyond my respectable if rough around the edges upbringing. If my neutral accent slipped now and again into east Boston, Charles would let me know. I thought I was passing. Except that Charles's mother, Cecily Foster, sniffed out my humble beginnings like a bloodhound sniffs out a fugitive. More than a misplaced 'r', it was my name. Mary Rose Collins. Rosie. The Mary is after my maternal grandmother, herself named in honor of the Virgin. The Rose is after my dad's eccentric aunt Rosalie who left home to pursue stardom and ended up portraying an Irish maid on a radio soap opera before she tragically died. Mrs. Foster, neé Burgess, was one generation from English aristocracy, or so she would have you believe, and we all know how the mid-century English viewed the Irish. Good for servants, not so much for family.

In prison, I was once again the odd one out. I wasn't raped by an 'uncle' or been a drug mule for a boyfriend. Or impregnated at fourteen. I wasn't there because of strict mandatory sentencing for possessing a few too many ounces of pot. My blue collar origins stood me in no good stead in this mix of rural poor, urban poor, underserved, undereducated and overwhelmed women. And my venture into the upper class world, however horribly it had turned out, only made me less adaptable. Besides, I was only one of maybe seven white women in the prison. I stood out. If you were white, you had to do something truly heinous to get put in this maximum security penitentiary; white women with slightly lesser crimes were sent elsewhere to serve out their terms. The fact that I had killed my fiancé didn't even give me enough cred to get a little bit of respect among women who had tortured rivals, shot or stabbed boyfriends. Women whose craving for drugs was ceaseless and their moods volatile.

Oh, yes. Cecily Foster had made damned sure that I was thoroughly punished. I was never offered a plea bargain that at worst might have put me in a minimum security correctional facility; at Mid-State there were no white-collar criminals; no accidental felons.

Money and influence. Cecily Foster wielded them as if they were the tools of some craft known only to the upper reaches of society. Charles was her only child. Even before the accident, Cecily hated me, the cheap harpy who'd dragged her boy down into associating with the common.

I, of course, had neither money nor influence. The valuables I might have hocked to afford a real attorney—including my massive engagement ring—were declared not my property at all; the heirloom ring and everything else of Charles's estate went to his only living relative, his mother. Every avenue toward relief was blocked to me by Cecily's seemingly limitless reach into the bastions of law and society.

I picture her still, sitting in her Long Island living room overlooking the sea while I sat in a cheap motel room and stared at a cheesy seascape. Her manicured fingers working the phone, making a call or two, a plaintive injured tone; a promise of support for a judge's favorite charity, anonymous, of course.

I was poorly defended and that failure led to the worst of the charges that might have been brought against me, voluntary manslaughter, a crime of passion. In all of this, I have never denied that I caused the fatal accident, but I have never said that I wanted it to happen. It was an *involuntary* act. An accident. I should never have stood trial. I should never have been defended by a public defender stooped under a case overload exacerbated by her screwed up personal life. But my almost mother-in-law was the one who really managed my conviction. What public defender, even one without the challenges Wendy Delorusso had, could stand up under the assault of one of Connecticut's best prosecuting attorneys? Cecily Foster made damned sure that I was punished for the death of her only child, her son Charles. As if having caused his death wasn't punishment enough. As much as I truly hated him, truly felt so aggrieved at what he had done, I was sorry about what had happened. Even if I had been exonerated instead of incarcerated, I had to live with the knowledge that I had killed someone.

One Saturday afternoon in the late fall Charles Foster arrived at my coffee bar dressed down, no suit, just a pair of Diesel jeans and a North Face jacket zipped up. He was wearing boots, those good heavy Timberlands. Without a tie, and with a woolen cap pulled on over his expensive haircut, Charles looked years younger, less unobtainable.

For years now I have looked back at that day, playing the game where you say to yourself, "if only . . ." If only I hadn't agreed to fill in for a co-worker, this wasn't my regular shift, I was never at the coffee bar on Saturdays. If only I hadn't taken that not-quite-earned break. If only I hadn't worked up the nerve to stand beside Charles, intent on his Blackberry, and set the last chocolate chip cookie in the case down in front of him. "On the house."

The months of banter, the flirtation, even at this point a few inside jokes, I was emboldened to push past the barista slash customer definition of our association. I sat down opposite him. "Would you ever want to go get a drink?"

Charles pulled his attention away from his BlackBerry. His eyes were an oceanic gray, surrounded by spiky dark lashes. He paused long enough for me to worry I'd overstepped myself. Then, "Yeah. I would."

If only Charles Montgomery Foster hadn't decided to grab a hot drink before driving to New Hampshire to ski, he might still be alive.

When you are in prison, all you want is for time to pass quickly. You want the hours to fly by, the days, weeks and months to slip away. Every day passing is a day closer to release. Of course, they don't fly by. Boredom lengthens the days; you live with a routine that seems designed to slow time down. When you are a child, days are elongated, school lasts forever, Christmas will never come. Everyone knows that as you grow up, those days shorten, weeks are fleeting, one season falls into the next with astounding rapidity. Try living in a prison. If you want to slow time down, that's your place. I had my jobs, six months in the prison laundry, a stint as a janitor, another in the kitchen serving up heavy starchy meals. I had a place at the white women's table three meals a day. I stood in lines. I circled the exercise yard working off those meals. I flattened myself to the ground during lockdown. In the outside world you know what day of the week it is by your to do list or your agenda or your favorite television programs. In prison, it didn't really matter what day of the week it was. Or month. Or year.

Time was measured out in paroles and release dates. My first cellmate, Treena, fulfilled her sentence and vanished. A new inmate replaced her, and I claimed the lower bunk and warned her off trespassing into my territory. A week later she managed to hang herself in the shower room. The next inmate to bunk with me was a repeat offender and I was scared back onto the top bunk.

The one day that had some variation in it for me was Sunday. Out of a deep seated need to feel normal, I attended the non-denominational service in the chapel. And then I stood in line for a turn at the rank of phones. Even though I knew that it was no longer true, I pictured my mother, still in her church dress, apron tied over it, getting Sunday dinner into the oven. I pictured her in our kitchen, an imagined summer sun warming the pale yellow linoleum, even if it was actually snowing outside, the wet snow against the windows further obscuring any natural light where I stood in my fluorescent world. I just wanted to hear her voice, to ask after everyone. And, every Sunday, the phone went unanswered.